THROUGH KESTREL'S EYES

~ EARTH'S PENDULUM ~

~ BOOK II ~

YVONNE HERTZBERGER

Cover Design by Neil Jackson

Set in Times New Roman

ISBN 978-0-9878260-2-2

Website ~ www.yvonnehertzberger.com

Twitter ~ YHERTZBE

THROUGH KESTREL'S EYES

~ EARTH'S PENDULUM ~

~ BOOK II ~

YVONNE HERTZBERGER

For Brooke + Michael
Happy reading!

ACKNOWLEDGEMENTS

To all those who read and loved *Back From Chaos* and encouraged me, no demanded that I write and publish this sequel, I want to express my heartfelt thanks. You all help me to believe in myself and in my writing. A special mention to Dana and Betty, tied for 'number one fan'.

To Mark, who agrees that writing is 'real work' even though it adds little to the budget.

To Wendy Reis, editor and now friend. I could ask for none better in either capacity.

To my readers and friends, too numerous to name, who gave me such wonderful feedback. You made this a better book.

~ LIST OF CHARACTERS ~

Merlost: (MER-lost) Lord of Lieth, in the hands of traitors
Rellnost: (RELL-nost) His heir, age ten
Wartin: (WAR-tin) His son, age seven
Leyla: (LAY-luh) His daughter, age four
Garneth: (GAR-neth) Ouster of Merlost
Morna: (MOR-nuh) Maid at inn
Bern, Griel and Morler: Guards
Baylin: Advisor to Garneth
Senth: Advisor to Garneth

GHARN
Corrin/Lord Dugal: (CORE-in, DU-gul) Deposed lord of Gharn, age
twenty
Larn: His trusted man, age twenty-one
Farsh: His trusted man, age nineteen
Merrist: (MARE-ist) His trusted man, age sixteen
Vernia: (VURR-nee-uh) Maid
Burrist: (BURR-ist) Older man, will be advisor to Dugal
Biel: (BEEL) Dugal's man
Sherroll: (SHARE-ull) Traitor
Seltan: (SELL-tun) Traitor
Kerran: (KARE-un) Guard, loyal to Dugal
Sella: (SELL-uh) Maid

BARGIA
Gaelen: (GAY-lun) Lord of Bargia
Marja: (MAR-yuh) His lady
Lionn: (LEE-un) His heir
Sennia: (Senn-ee-uh) Their daughter
Liannis: (lee-ANN-iss) Seer
Klast/Hurst (klast/hurst): Liannis' father and Gaelen's most trusted
man
Brensa: (BREN-suh) Liannis' mother
Kira; (KEE-ruh) Kestrel, familiar of Liannis
Cloud: Liannis horse, familiar of Liannis
Janest: (JANN-est) Gaelen's eldest advisor
Brest: (Brest) Council member

Grolsh: (grOlsh) Council member
Kamdeth: (KAM-deth) Advisor and council member

PROLOGUE

Eleven year old Liannis sat on the sod roof of her parents' cottage in her night-shift, stroking No-tail's soft fur, and gazing into the night sky. She loved to sit here to think, but chose to do so only after she was sure her parents slept soundly below. They did not approve, fearing she might fall off and be injured. Liannis knew better. At times like this, No-tail, their small cat, usually followed her and took advantage of the warm nest made by the hammock of her skirt as she sat cross-legged.

As a small child, Liannis had spent many happy days at court playing with Lionn, Lord Gaelen's son, Sennia, his sister, and Borless, the son of Lady Marja's maid. But as she grew older, the press of her growing inner gifts made it harder to be among so many people. The impressions of their emotions pressed on her spirit and threatened to overwhelm her. Like Liethis, seer to the court of Bargia, she preferred the isolation of her home outside the city.

At first Lord Gaelen and Lady Marja had been reluctant to have their son and heir come to the cottage to visit with her here, fearing for his safety away from the guards. But Liannis knew he would come to no harm. She told them, with full confidence that nothing would happen to him as long as he was with her. Earth had told her so.

Gaelen had relented only upon assurance from Liethis, official seer of Bargia, that Liannis' sight was true. From that time on, under the watchful eyes of Liannis' parents, the three children had visited with her often. They had occasionally accompanied her in her night vigils on the roof.

Liannis had not returned to court again after her eighth summer. The press of impressions there caused her too much pain.

Tonight, Liannis kept her vigil alone. She considered what her future would hold. When she reached her twelfth birthday, she understood she would start spending the winter months with Liethis as her apprentice.

Liethis had already explained to Lord Gaelen and her parents that Liannis would grow into a much more powerful seer than she was. Liannis' gifts of truth-reading and her ability to mind-speak birds and animals already outshone her own and had not yet grown into their full strength. But the girl needed other skills that would help her use her gifts to their full potential; how to dampen the press that would drive her mad otherwise, how to deal with persons of influence diplomatically and how to handle unwelcome questions from those whose problems were too small for Earth to be concerned with.

Liannis did not look forward to leaving her peaceful home but she understood its necessity. Already, she found it hard to control the barrage that assaulted her senses, and this would only increase. But at least the summers would still be spent here at home.

Liannis smiled, as she sensed her father reach for her mother and lay his sleeping arm across her waist. Earth had given her special parents. She knew they would never have another child. Seers were always only daughters. Earth never burdened a seer with siblings, as they matured too quickly and felt the emotions of those around them too keenly, to thrive in larger families. They needed a serene environment in which their gifts could grow without constraint.

She dreamily pulled a blade of grass from the sod to chew. Then, stroking No-tail one last time, she smiled to herself, content, climbed down and went to her bed in the loft.

FUGITIVE

I felt no pain now; not the weariness from my headlong flight, not the burning of the pain in my fingers, nor the bone deep chill in my limbs. The cold brought peace and the desire to sleep. If this was what Earth wished for me, I resigned myself. This sleep would be my last.

As if from far away I became aware of the sound of voices. Almost unconscious, I had not the strength to move and so could not indicate to them that I lived. Truth be told, I knew I hovered near death. Perhaps Earth had no further need of me and would allow me to sink back into her eternal embrace. Is that what I wanted, to be free from my duties to Earth, released from my gifts? I had not had a choice in receiving them.

Perhaps rescue would be no more than a wishful dream. But no, this was real. I had been found. The voices above me penetrated dimly through the foggy haze of my awareness.

"Ho, what is this?" I heard one mumble as he stumbled over my cocoon of branches, leaves and snow, and his boot uncovered a patch of my red cloak. With my seer's sight I sensed him scrabble the remaining cover of snow, leaves and branches away with his hands.

"Farsh! Merrist! Over here!"

"Hey, watch out! That branch almost took my eye out," one complained as he emerged out of the trees to stand behind the one who had discovered me.

"Not so loud!" cautioned the other as he joined his companions. "Do you want to be heard? Corrin will not thank you if we are taken."

"What have you there? A woman? Is she dead? What is a woman doing in the snow here?"

My discoverer stopped trying to tug me out of my burrow, put me back down and checked. "She breathes, barely. Help me get her to the cabin, or she may yet die."

"I do not know if that is a good idea. She will learn our location. Corrin will be furious! Best to let her stay where she is."

"What? That is murder! Have you no honour, Farsh? Corrin may not be pleased but he would not expect us to let her die." I could hear eagerness in my finder's voice. "Merrist, run ahead and stoke up the fire. Put the blankets close to heat them. We need to warm her up if she is to live, though I fear it may be too late already." He grunted with effort to lift my lax form from its cocoon. "Come on, Farsh, give me a hand!"

11

Farsh bent to help, grumbling half-heartedly, "I like this not, Larn." Then, curiosity overcoming reluctance, he added, "How came she here, do you think?"

"Mayhap she will tell us when she wakes. Get ahead and put a kettle on. She will need hot tea when she does...if she does."

I sensed the excitement their find brought the one called Larn. This mystery called to his imagination. His thoughts came through clearly. She is no peasant. I can tell even through the dirt that she is young. And her clothes are fine, so she had not been poor. What tale might she tell? What brought her to this outpost, hidden deep in the woods? Whose side is she on? The questions tumbled over one another in his mind.

I experienced, with my sight, what Larn thought and felt as he carried me, my ability heightened by contact. His awareness became mine. I hope Lord Dugal is not too angry. What a find! Three moons in this cabin and nothing happens. And now a woman finds us...no, we found her. Surely a woman can pose no threat.

I caught the smell of wood smoke as Larn followed his nose. Through his eyes I beheld the small, rough cabin that served as safe house for his young lord. Soon I could sense the glow from the hearth fire seeping out from behind the oiled leather that covered the small window. The door opened, and I saw Merrist limned by the light of the fire.

"I cleared the bed. You can lay her down there." Merrist closed the door tightly as we entered, then pressed close behind, as my rescuer carefully lay me on a straw mattress.

"We best see she does not get away," Farsh worried, standing behind the other two. But in him, too, I could tell that concern had overcome reticence, and I knew he hovered behind the others.

"We need to undress her and get the warm blankets on her." Two opposing needs warred in the young man's mind. She needs to be warmed up but she might not take kindly to three strange men seeing her without clothes on. Finally, need overcame decorum, and he began to tug at my cloak.

"Her clothes are all wet. Help me get them off." I sensed the exact instant his eyes fell on my left hand. He looked up at his friends, all of his previous eagerness replaced by shock. "Oh, dear Earth, she has been tortured! Look!" He held up my hand for the others to see.

I knew what they had discovered. The two outside fingers of my left hand each ended in a pulpy red mass, stark against the icy white of the rest of my hand. My nails had been torn off in an unsuccessful bid to get me to divulge the whereabouts of Lord Merlost's wife and children.

I felt Larn shudder, and sensed him imagining the pain in his own fingers. He looked at his friends and I knew he saw the same horror mirrored in their eyes.

A low moan, unbidden, escaped my lips. I could not hold it in. At that same moment I understood death would not claim me today.

The men's conversation reached me clearly now, with normal hearing. I felt the warmth of the cabin begin to insinuate itself into my body. It awakened my conscious mind, much against my will, while it increased my pain.

"Help me get her undressed. Hurry. Get a blanket around her before she wakes. She will be frightened enough, without waking to strange men undressing her."

I caught an image from him, imagining my reaction if I came to while being mauled by three ruffians.

Mercifully, I managed to feign unconsciousness until after they had replaced the heated blanket three more times. Gradually, as the warmth brought heat to my blood, I began to shake, unable to control myself, an effect of the cold beginning to leave my body. Even then, I did not allow them to see signs of my waking.

Without warning, and completely beyond my tight efforts at control, I lifted my injured hand away from my body and moaned again. I forced it slowly back to the bed as if it had never happened. I knew, then, I would have to let them see that I was awake.

All three jumped back from the sound, eyes wide with shock.

"It must have been the heat," Merrist offered. "I have had frostbite. When the flesh warms, the pain is almost unbearable." His voice hushed in empathy. "It will happen again I think. What can we do for her?"

Before the others could respond, the door flew open, banging hard against the inner wall.

CORRIN

"What goes here!? Why is the fire so stoked that I can smell the smoke across the river? Are you mad?! Your orders were to stay hidden. We will be found out..."

From his air of authority I deduced this must be Corrin. As his eyes fell on my lax form on the bed, I sensed his rebuke transform into surprise. He banged the door shut and demanded, "Explain. Why is a strange woman in our safe house? What could possess you to endanger our safety so? Larn, I left you in charge. This better be good."

"We could do no less. She would have died if we had not brought her here! And she has been tortured."

"Tortured!? What do you mean? Why would a woman be tortured?"

Larn reached under the blanket and, with great care, pulled out my mangled hand. When I moaned again, unable to hold it in, he quickly put it back and withdrew.

Larn hastened to fill in the rest of the tale. "...so you understand, we could not let her die. Besides, she may have valuable information."

Farsh piped up. I sensed he must be very young, as I heard his voice crack. It had not fully changed yet. "I told them at first that we should leave her but now I agree that we need to question her. And to let her die out there would be murder... You would not have us do that...would you?"

Corrin sounded exasperated. "Certainly not. But you do see what danger this places us in?" I watched through Larn's eyes as Corrin sank onto the lone wooden chair next to the rough raised plank that served for a table. After a moment of silence during which I could tell the others waited for him to speak, he asked, "Anything to eat here?" Merrist hurried to fill a bowl with stew from the copper kettle over the hearth fire.

"If I am ever to attain my birthright I need to stay alive. This house is safe only so long as no one knows of its existence...or ours."

When I moved slightly, causing a plank beneath me to creak, I could sense four pairs of eyes turn toward the bed and fix on me, four breaths held, waiting to see if I would waken. Merrist rose once more to replace my blanket with a warmed one.

When I settled down again, I saw Corrin give the bed a searching look. Unaware that I followed it all in my mind, he jerked his head in the direction of the table, indicating to the others to gather around on the three stools that made up the remaining seating in the cabin. He sent another cautious look toward the bed, and bent his head toward the others.

Keeping his voice low, I heard him say, "She is no mere peasant who has lost her way. We need to find out how she came here, who tortured her, what she knows that they tortured her to find out...and if she gave them what they wanted. We do not even know where she came from, whether she is of Lieth or Gharn...or Bargia for that matter. She must be kept here until we find out if she poses a danger to us, and who she serves...or served. I trust this not. Yet, I do not think she is known at court here in Gharn, else I would remember her."

The three youths regarded him solemnly, waiting for him to continue. Corrin caught Merrist stealing a glance at the bed, then looking back quickly, and almost laughed. "Merrist, you will never make a good spy. Your face hides nothing. Ever the one for the ladies, hm, no matter if they may be trusted?"

Merrist blushed with embarrassment and he took a sudden interest in the table.

Now Corrin did laugh. "Friend Merrist, of your loyalty I have no doubt. But you cannot look at a pretty face without becoming the gallant... What shall we do with our guest, do you think, until we decide if she poses a threat to us? And may you be trusted to keep her safe without letting her escape, if I take Farsh and Larn scouting with me? What say you, Merrist?"

Merrist's eyes met Corrin's, embarrassment replaced by earnestness. "Of course, I would consider it an honour to guard her."

LIANNIS

Almost five years had passed since I pondered my future on the sod roof of my parent's cottage, five long winters learning all I could from Liethis, four blissful summers at home. But that last winter Liethis fell ill, wasting with the coughing sickness. She told me that I must learn all I could as quickly as possible, that by spring she would no longer be there to teach me. I stayed well beyond the last thaws, nursing my beloved mentor until, as the first blossoms opened on the apple trees, Liethis coughed her last and fled back into Earth's embrace.

I was left to mourn her with my training still incomplete and without having earned the privilege, or the protection, of wearing seer's whites. Part of me wished to be released to lead a normal life, with a man and children of my own. I had never spoken this aloud, fearing I would seem ungrateful for the gifts and honour bestowed upon me. Another wondered if I had failed in my studies, if I had disappointed Earth and she no longer wished to use me as her seer.

Other than my parents, Lord Gaelen, Lady Marja and my three childhood friends no one knew that I was a seer, or how exceptionally powerful my gifts were. That anonymity had proved to be a boon. When the summons from Earth had come, I could follow it and go to Lieth with my identity undisclosed. The letter of introduction from Lord Gaelen had secured me a position in Lord Merlost's court as nurse to his three children. There I would keep my senses open to find out what I could about the unrest rumoured to exist there.

After two brief moons there, during which time my senses seemed less acute and painful, I learned that I must get Lady Nairin and the children out of Lieth to safety. I helped them find asylum in Bargia when Lord Merlost had been taken by his ousters. Upon my return to Lieth to learn what I could of Lord Merlost's fate, those same traitors captured and tortured me in the belief that I knew the family's whereabouts.

Now, as the warmth of the blankets slowly brought me back to wake-fulness, Earth sent me a warning. My gift must still remain secret. So, in spite of the excruciating pain in my fingers, I suppressed the urge to cry out as I came to full awareness. Instead, I forced myself to remain still and listen. I needed to know where I was, and why these four were in hiding in this remote cabin. After my escape from my captors in Lieth I had run blindly and had no idea where I had ended up. Which demesne was this? Who was in charge here? Who were they allied to? What should I tell them?

True seers avoid telling lies. Deception causes us painful headaches. It is an abuse of our gift. But now, I knew, it might be necessary.

The growing heat made my fingers feel like someone was pressing red hot coals to them, and the best I could do to hold back my cry was to turn it into a long moan. I would tell them as much of the truth as I could, I decided, and try to leave the crucial parts unsaid.

When I opened my eyes, four pairs met mine. In them, I could read their thoughts as plainly as if they had shouted them aloud; eager, inquisitive Larn, cautious Farsh, Merrist, so full of concern, and Corrin...the leader and a lord...worried about what to do with me and how my presence would affect his future. But I could detect no cruelty in any of them, nor any intent to harm me. I remained safe for now.

NOW WHAT?

By the time Corrin left with Farsh I had almost stopped shivering. Knowing that my clothing would, by now, have dried by the fire, I looked at Merrist. "Please hand me my things, so I may get dressed. And turn your back until I am ready."

Merrist quickly complied checking to make sure my gown was actually dry before handing it to me. "We could wait outside...to give you privacy." He shifted from foot to foot, looking decidedly uncomfortable. Larn rolled his eyes at me as if to indicate that Merrist was touched in the head. In other circumstances it would have made me laugh.

"No, it is cold out. Turn away until I tell you I am finished and that will not be necessary." I arose painfully, the blanket clutched around me with my good hand and almost smiled as both men turned abruptly away.

I dressed one handed, with agonizing care, trying not to bump my fingers. To avoid the blackness of dying flesh that would make amputation necessary, I knew they would have to be cleaned...a prospect that filled me with dread. To do this I would need to soak them in salted water. I quailed at the thought, aware how much it would increase my pain. But it must be done. I tried to lace my bodice, but could not manage it with only one hand. What to do? I studied the two. Larn seemed the least flappable.

"Larn, can you assist me with my gown? I fear I am unable to tie it with only one hand."

"Certainly, Lady." He turned, a look of surprise coming over his face. "You know our names?"

Merrist resolutely kept his back to me.

"Yes, I heard you speaking...before...uh, Merrist, my fingers need bathing. Do you have salt?"

"Yes, Lady." He still did not turn.

"If you would give me a large bowl of very warm water, please, and the salt."

He hastened to do my bidding, still keeping his eyes averted.

It did not occur to either of them not to obey me. Later, I knew, they would wonder at that, that they had not thought to question my authority.

My bodice laced, Larn drew away, and I eased myself back onto the bed. Still chilled, I re-wrapped myself in the blanket. The effort left me exhausted. I wished I could just lie down and sleep but knew I had to stay awake long enough to tend to my fingers... Oh, Earth, why have you chosen such a weak and untried vessel? I am not ready for this. But at Merrist's approach I pushed thoughts of self-doubt firmly aside.

Merrist set the wooden bowl, and a small clay pot from which he had removed the stopper, beside me on the bed and gave me a troubled look. I sensed that he, too, could imagine what this would cost me.

"Do you need help, Lady?"

Shaking my head I reached for the salt and added half of it to the water. I stared at the bowl for a long moment, trying to gather the courage to force my fingers into the water. Then I looked at the two. "This is necessary if I am to keep my fingers. If my courage fails, hold me down and keep my hand in the water for at least half a span. Do you understand?"

Merrist looked grey and unsteady.

Larn nodded. "We will, Lady." He gave Merrist an admonishing elbow in the ribs.

Merrist took a sudden interest in the ground, embarrassed, then squared his shoulders and raised his eyes to me, grim determination behind his fear. "We will, Lady. You may rely on us."

"I am no lady. You may call me Liannis."

I looked once more at the bowl, took a deep breath, squeezed my eyes shut, clenched my teeth and plunged my hand into the bowl. This time I could not block my scream. The pain almost eclipsed what I had felt during my torture. I sagged back onto the bed in a half faint.

Larn spoke to Merrist. "Good, she will not fight us, now." He reached for my hand which had fallen from the bowl. "Hold her, in case she wakes. And do not go soft on me."

Merrist hurried to obey.

Some part of my awareness remained, and I heard as though through a fog. When Larn placed my hand back into the water, a long moan escaped me. I felt Merrist increase his grip on my shoulders with trembling hands, and heard him whisper, "Oh Earth."

Larn kept his hand firmly around my wrist.

Slowly, oh so slowly, the pain began to subside. Not wishing to answer questions, I kept my eyes closed and my body limp long past when I needed to. I could sense the salt drawing the poisonous pus, in spider thin threads, from my festering fingers and out into the water. My fingers would heal, though I knew I would need to go through this again, on the morrow.

When I had soaked long enough I opened my eyes. "Enough. Larn, have you clean linen to wrap my hand in?" When he shook his head, I told him, "Reach under my skirt and tear a strip from my under-shift. It will have to do. I fear I cannot do it myself."

Larn hesitated, but at an affirmative nod from me he bent to lift the skirt of my gown. Merrist removed the bowl.

"Merrist, where am I, what demesne it this? I fled without keeping track of the direction."

"Gharn, Lady."

"Say nothing," Larn barked at the same time.

Merrist blushed at his oversight.

I pretended not to notice. "I must have crossed the border from Lieth, then. Good." I managed a smile. "Your Lord Dugal has nothing to fear from me. I know that is who Corrin must be. I have heard that Lord Dennist has been killed and his son is missing. Yes, I see from your faces that I must be right. There is much unrest in both Gharn and Lieth. Earth will suffer for this imbalance, I fear. Such events are hard for her to bear." I shook my head, saddened, as I took the strip of linen from Larn and began to wrap my fingers with my good hand. When I finished I held my hand out so Larn could tie the ends, to keep the wrapping in place. He grasped my intention immediately. Then I sank back onto the bed, pulled the blanket firmly around myself and fell into a deep, healing sleep.

CORRIN

The demesne of Gharn lay just north of Lieth and east of Bargia. Their peoples had traded peacefully with each other, with Catania to the northwest, and the other surrounding demesnes for almost a generation, ever since the Red Fever had ravaged all the demesnes on the One Isle and made war untenable.

"Three moons ago," Corrin explained, "my father was killed by traitors. Three of his loyal advisors have also died in unusual ways and I suspect they were murdered as well. A maid warned me just in time for me to escape with my hide intact."

Here Corrin stopped and I detected a blush. Though I did not seek out his thought I could not help but sense that this maid had warmed Corrin's bed a time or two.

"The remaining three advisors, traitors all, now control Gharn," Corrin spat out, his tone murderous.

He went on to tell me that at twenty-one he had been trained well, but since his father remained hale, Corrin had not expected to ascend to power for many years.

He and Larn, his best friend and ally, had stumbled upon this abandoned cabin near the border with Lieth and had affected the necessary repairs that made it habitable as a safe house.

Now, with winter almost over, Corrin grew anxious to further his campaign. My appearance put a wrinkle in his plans. "So you understand that I cannot let you go. The risk is too great, and why I have taken a false name."

He wanted to know why I had been tortured and if that information might be valuable to him and his cause. "You must tell me what you know. It is essential that I be aware of anything that could affect my campaign."

When I remained adamant about protecting my secret he shook his head in frustration, turned abruptly on his heel and strode to the door. "I need to take a walk. We will speak of this again. No, Farsh, I need to go alone."

I sensed he wanted to believe my assurances that my mission had nothing to do with Gharn but he remained uncertain. He had been so badly betrayed that trust no longer came automatically.

I watched him leave and took a moment to study his three friends. Larn seemed capable, a young man of about nineteen, of average height but broad shouldered and well muscled. He moved with the assurance of a trained soldier and wore his sword with ease, as though it were a natural appendage.

Farsh appeared far less confident. I had been correct. Though he already stood half a head taller than Larn, he looked thin enough that I suspected he had not yet grown to his full height and the lack of facial hair told me he had not yet reached maturity. I estimated his age to be fifteen. He clearly looked to Larn for leadership and wore a permanent worried expression.

Merrist appeared to be between the others in age. His voice had not quite settled into its adult timbre. His upper lip showed the shadow of down but it would be another year before he would need to shave on a regular basis. He stood as tall as Larn but had the rangy build of a youth who still had a year or two before he filled out and developed the muscling of a man.

I could not help but think that if Corrin looked to these three to launch his campaign it would be long before he could accomplish anything that would threaten his usurpers. Yet their loyalty was true and I felt sympathy for their cause.

QUESTIONS

I woke once more to the aroma of fresh rabbit sizzling on a spit. Even before I opened my eyes I sensed that Corrin had returned and that he had a head full of more questions for me. I think he had hopes that he would get more information out of me but what I had already told him would have to satisfy him. I knew that if I had to lie I would suffer a headache.

He had not seen me waken, so I observed him as he sat deep in thought, elbows on the table, chin resting on one palm, a deep frown creasing his brow.

As soon as I sat up, he noticed the movement and pierced me with his gaze. I did not give him time to speak. "Something smells wonderful. I have not eaten for two days. And is that tea I see on the brazier?"

"Larn, get her some food and tea." Corrin immediately turned back to me, looking annoyed and determined to get his answers. "My men tell me you came across from Lieth. I am sure you understand that I must know who you are, what brought you here, and why you were tortured. Did you tell them what they wanted to know?"

I caught a whisper of warning from Earth in my mind and sighed inwardly knowing I would likely suffer a headache before Corrin let it drop. "Lord Dugal, I do understand your need for an explanation. Again, I will tell what I may. Please understand there is much I cannot reveal. Lives depend on my secret. As for your last question, no, they did not get what they wanted from me. My name is Liannis. I am of Bargia, but have spent the last moons in Lieth until traitors, enemies of Lord Merlost, captured him in a coup. I was employed in the castle as a nurse to his children so his spies had reason to believe I could tell them where they had gone into hiding."

"How came you here?" Corrin's frown had deepened at my assertion that I would not tell all.

"After they tortured me they put me in a cell and posted a very young guard to see that I did not escape. I convinced the lad that I did not have the information they sought. He took pity on me, and leaving my cloak by the unlocked door, created a diversion which allowed me to escape. I hope to Earth they did not realize he had let it happen, and that the poor lad does not now suffer a fate worse than mine.

"When I could run no more I covered myself with branches and must have fallen asleep. You know the rest. There is really no more I can tell you. I can assure you, however, that I am no threat to you or to your campaign...nor is the secret I carry of value to you."

"I cannot rely on assurances. Until I am convinced, you must remain my guest, here in this cabin. I cannot risk letting you go, or anyone seeing you."

"Then, perhaps Earth conspires in my favour. It seems I have stumbled upon the safest hiding place in all of the demesnes, though I do regret that my presence causes you difficulty."

Corrin ran his hand through his hair in exasperation, his thoughts, almost a refrain, plain for me to read...a woman in the way, one with a secret that could prove dangerous, the last thing he needed now. He shook his head. "Indeed. For the moment I must be satisfied with your tale, since I am averse to torture. But we will speak more of this. There is much you hold back, much more I need to understand...and you must address me as Corrin."

"As you wish, Corrin. but I will not betray those who have entrusted me with their lives. Nothing will persuade me...nor anyone."

"Then we are at an impasse."

"For now," I agreed mildly, and bent back to my bowl.

Corrin scowled, thwarted.

When I had eaten my stew and had several mugs of tea to replenish me I returned to the bed. My sleep was not to be the dreamless repose I hoped for. Earth had other ideas.

NAIRIN

I dreamed. The images came so clear I knew it for a true seeing. I travelled in my spirit-body and became an unseen presence in a chamber.

* * *

"Mama, when can we go home? I miss my pony, and my toys...and I miss Papa. I do not like it here." Young Leyla fretted petulantly and tugged at her mother's skirts.

Nairin sighed as she hugged her four year old daughter close, and met the same question in the eyes of seven year old Wartin, her second son.

"Is Papa all right, Mama?" Wartin piped up. "And Rellnost...why is he not with us? When can we see him again?"

"I wish I could tell you, sweetings. I truly do not know. But I am sure they miss us as well." She sighed again. "For now we must learn patience and ask Earth to protect them. I miss your father and brother, too, but it is not safe for us all to be together right now."

Nairin, Lady of Lieth, looked at the door of their well appointed chambers. While she could open it if she wished, she knew that it led only to the tiny courtyard that allowed them some fresh air.

My scout had brought them here, was it only two eight days ago? They were guests of Lord Gaelen of Bargia now, but they might as well be prisoners, for all the freedom they had. Gaelen took a great risk in harbouring Nairin and the children. I had sent them here under cover of darkness, placed in a covered carriage I had procured at the border. Nairin's only sureties had been the small copper ring and scroll of introduction I had given her. I had paid the driver his normal fee and given him only their destination, with the promise that his fare would be doubled once they had been safely delivered. Nairin had not understood where the gold had come from and had been suspicious of my motives as a result. But she had gone along with my plan because the alternatives looked even less hopeful.

"Leyla, where is your needlework. You must practice your stitches. Papa will be so proud when he sees how neat they are." The children had little to keep boredom at bay. I could see the effort it cost Nairin to maintain patience. "Wartin, bring the sand bowl. Make sure it is damp. I will add some new symbols for you to practice. Good. See, this is the sign for Lieth, our home. That is where Papa is. Copy it and ask Earth to keep

him safe there."

* * *

When Merlost, then heir of Lieth, had returned from a mission in Catania, seventeen years ago, he had found Lieth ravaged by the Red Fever, his father, Lord Rellnost dead of it, and his father's advisors at a loss as to how to act without his orders. Merlost, too, had been poorly prepared to rule. More accustomed to taking orders than giving them, he had proven an ineffectual leader who tried to please everyone. Now Nairin and their children suffered the consequences of his ineptitude.

It had taken all my powers of persuasion to convince Nairin to let Rellnost be separated from her and her two younger children. I had had to nudge her hard with my gift of persuasion to help her see the sense of my plan. Rellnost, eldest and heir, had come with me to my parents' cottage, where my father, Klast, could guard him and also see to his education in weapons, history and strategy. I had been captured on my return to Lieth, when I had tried to slip back unnoticed. My absence had been noted and my role as nurse to the children brought me under suspicion.

So, they were safe. Abruptly I found myself torn from that dream into the next.

RELLNOST

I was home, in my parents cottage at the edge of the forest outside Bargia City. I tried to speak to my mother but she was unaware of my dream presence. So I watched and listened, able to read their thoughts much more clearly than if I were awake.

Rellnost looked at my mother mending a tear in my father's breeches by the fire, and narrowed his eyes.

"I do not like it here. As heir of Lieth I demand to go home. I want my horse, my friends and I do not like the food. You do not wait on me as you ought. If my father were here he would flog you for disobeying me." Rellnost scowled at my mother and waited to see her reaction.

She looked up from her needlework and mildly lifted one eyebrow. "My, what a show of temper. Such unbecoming behaviour for an heir apparent when guesting in the home of an ally." I smiled to myself. Mama had always known how to defuse such shows of temper.

Rellnost blushed. His temper had been for bravado only, but pride kept him from backing down. "But there is nothing to do here. I miss my mates, my own chamber." Then, realizing he sounded childish he decided to bluff it out by raising his voice again. "This is a poor safe house. Only a peasant can live here. I deserve better."

"And that is precisely why no one will think to look for you here. If you wish to become a good lord, you need to learn how all your people live, and to respect the things they do that make all that luxury you say you deserve, possible."

Rellnost's lip began to tremble, and he took a deep breath to upbraid Brensa further so that he would not cry, but she pre-empted him, her face softening, her needlework lax in her lap.

"Rellnost, I know you find it boring here and that you miss your family and are worried about them. That is much for even an heir such as you to bear. You have acted bravely since coming here two eightdays ago. Come, let us go to the shed and feed the cow and chickens. Then, if Klast returns early, he may spend some time in weapons practice with you before dark. Did you know that he was Lord Gaelen's strategy and weapons master? If you ask him politely, he may be willing to give you lessons in strategy as well." Mama's face broke into a mischievous smile. "Perhaps he may even have some treats for us on his return."

Rellnost thought a moment. "But I have no sword. Mine was left behind."

Mama's eyes danced. "True. Perhaps you might ask Klast to show you how to make a wooden one, just for practice. Have you not seen the soldiers in your father's army practicing with wooden swords?" She rose and Rellnost followed her out to the shed wondering why Mama seemed so cheerful, as if she knew something she had not told him. He decided to wait and see, his anger blown over for now.

* * *

I had taken Rellnost to my parent's cabin, knowing it was the safest place he could possibly be. My aging father had recently retired from active service as the head of Lord Gaelen's personal guard, though Lord Gaelen still relied heavily on his advice. The isolation of our cabin had only been one factor in my decision. I knew there was no one more qualified to make sure young Rellnost stayed alive and well. And my father could continue the important parts of the heir of Lieth's education. His knowledge of strategy, history and weapons remained unmatched. My mother, Brensa, who had received a good education as a ladies' maid at court in Catania, could see to Rellnost's reading, writing and ciphering lessons.

I woke back in the cabin with a jolt. This was not my home and my mother was not with me. A wave of loneliness washed over me. Though I knew it would use up much of my energy, and give me a headache to boot, I sought my mother again with my waking sight.

IN GHARN

I smiled as I found my mother's aura, a calm blue. It had not always been so. I remembered the years when it had been shot with red and orange, the colours of fear and anxiety. Over time those had faded, the result of my father's patient love and care.

His aura, too, had lost its angry black splotches, and his red streaks had become less prominent over the years they had spent together.

I sent my senses to search him out but I could not find him at home. Ah, there...in Bargia city. His purplish blue pulsed evenly, letting me know that he saw no danger. If he had gone into the city for supplies I knew he would bring back the sweets my mother had mentioned to Rellnost in my dream. Those treats had always delighted me as a girl. I wondered if Rellnost would appreciate them as I had.

Reluctantly, I let the connection go. Now, comforted by my brief touch with my parents, I sought out Lord Merlost. When I finally located his aura it was murky and dim. His deep green had faded almost to grey, and it wore an overlay of red.

Just as I was about to let the connection break I saw his red bloom brighter for an instant, then the connection broke. My spirit sank. I could not deny what I had seen. Merlost was dead. Lieth had a new lord. Whether Rellnost would ever claim his birthright remained hidden to me. Earth did not always know or show me what the future held.

I stretched, saddened, my search over. I saw Merrist nod on his chair, unable to stay alert with nothing to do but see that I did not leave. If I wished, I could escape and be on my way. But for now, I had no better place to go, and Merrist had been kind to me. I had no wish to bring Corrin's ire down on his head.

With a jolt, I felt my mind pulled elsewhere.

* * *

In my vision I stood before Lord Gaelen, Corrin by my side. Corrin gestured to include Larn, standing just behind him, Merrist, Farsh and myself. Gaelen looked at me and I nodded as if in agreement.

* * *

When my vision cleared I opened my eyes to see Merrist peering with a stunned, frightened expression into my face.

"Are you all right? You were sitting very erect and I could not wake you."

"Thank you Merrist. I must have been having a bad dream. I am quite well. But some camomile tea would be welcome. Shall I make some for us both?" I rose, took the kettle from the hearth with my good hand and set it on the table, then I took down the little clay pot that held the dried yellow flowers I needed for the tea. The small ritual gave me time to regain my composure. Earth's sending had left me with a headache, and I wanted to think about what it meant before I spoke with Merrist again.

Merrist reached up to the single shelf to take down two of the chipped clay mugs. "That will be fine. Here are the cups."

As I poured I asked, "When is Corrin expected back, do you think?"

"Oh, before dark, unless he is delayed."

"I understand the campaign is going well."

Merrist looked embarrassed. "I am not at liberty to say. Perhaps it would be best to ask him yourself, when he arrives."

"Of course, I shall." I managed a smile for Merrist. I knew he was completely enthralled with me. Had I wanted to, I believed I could ask anything of him and he would do it. I could even have him allow me to "escape" if I pressed him. I suspected Corrin knew it, too, but he seemed to have come to the conclusion that I posed no threat, so had said nothing and continued to have Merrist "guard" me. Gentle Merrist, only sixteen, without a nasty bone in his young body. Life had not yet shown him its darker side, to test his mettle and his trust. That would come, as it does for all men and women. But his heart was loyal and he served Corrin with an awe found only in the innocent. It warmed me to him and it saddened me to think it would not last much longer. War would turn the boy into a man.

Corrin burst through the door just before dusk, accompanied by both Larn and Farsh. I immediately filled five bowls with stew from the kettle always kept bubbling in the hearth, and set them on the table. With no extra stool available for me, an empty wine cask had become my perch when all four men were present.

Corrin kept silent throughout the meal, a brooding crease between his brows, unusual for him. From time to time he glanced in my direction. Finally, he broke his silence.

"I must travel to Bargia. The snows have gone and the trails are passable now. I need Gaelen's support if I am to win this campaign. We leave tomorrow at dawn. But," he looked at me, "I cannot decide what to do about you. I am loath to simply let you go. You still have information that may be useful to me." He narrowed his eyes. "Is there any more you are willing to tell?"

"No, though I have told you all that can be of value to you. The rest does not concern you." The import of my vision had just struck me. "Corrin, I must go with you. I am acquainted with Lord Gaelen and can help convince him to listen to you. I believe your claim is a good one and I know him to be a fair and reasonable man."

Corrin's eyes widened in surprise then narrowed again. "How do you know him? What makes you think he will listen to a maid such as yourself? You said you came from Lieth, not Bargia."

I smiled, doing my best to look confident, not to let the urgency I felt show. Somehow I had to convince Corrin to take me along, though I still did not understand why. At the very least, once there, I could see my parents and check on Rellnost's progress. I also needed to let Gaelen know that Merlost was dead. That would be news his enemies would be at pains to keep secret until they felt more secure in the success of their coup.

"I am not what I seem. I spent the early years of my life in Bargia. Lord Gaelen's son Lionn considers me a friend."

"Impossible," sputtered Corrin, growing more suspicious.

I interrupted him before he could say something he would not be able to back down from. "Lord Dugal." I used his true name to jolt him out of his train of thought. "My father is the head of Lord Gaelen's personal guard and his valued friend. I played with Lionn as a child. I wanted to travel, so when I turned fifteen I went to Lieth, where, based on references from Lord Gaelen and Lady Marja, I obtained a position in Lord Merlost's household." I waited for that to sink in. It was more than I really wished to reveal. I hoped it would be enough.

Corrin studied me silently for several moments.

"I find that hard to believe. However, if there is any chance that there is truth in what you say, it might prove useful. If not, I will find you out when we get there. But see to it that you do not slow us down." He scowled, "And do not use that name again."

"You will find me an accomplished rider. Just provide me with a horse. I need no more than your men. Besides, if I cook it will leave your men free for other duties."

Corrin snorted his disbelief. "We shall see."

While Larn went to find me a mount, the rest of them spent the evening packing travel fare and blankets for sleeping, and checking tack and weapons. Corrin took out a set of ankle chains stored in the horse shed, and for a moment I thought he might hobble me. But then he threw

31

them back with a shudder and shake of his head. I allowed myself a small sigh of relief.

TO BARGIA

In good weather and by a well travelled route the journey usually takes four days. But the season conspired against us. Freezing drizzle prevented the paths from drying, making the footing difficult for the horses. Since we rode in secret we avoided the main route. We travelled under cover of the forest when we could, and by night when we could not. Corrin deemed fires out of the question, either for reasons of safety or because we could not light the wet wood.

So the group that presented itself at the gate at Bargia city six days later was cold, wet, hungry and bedraggled. Fortunately our appearance masked our identities, and we were able to enter unremarked by all but the two guards at the gate. These saw no reason the question us. But when Corrin requested admittance at the castle gate he was unable to convince the guards there that he needed to speak with Gaelen. When he became angry and insistent, the guards threatened to put the men in the dungeon to cool off.

Things looked like they were getting out of hand so I stepped forward. I took the small copper ring that I always carried out of the pouch at my waist and handed it to the head guard. My father had loaned me his as Nairin still had mine. We each carried one to use whenever we wanted Gaelen to know we needed him. Keeping my voice low and calm I said, "Please give this to Lord Gaelen. He will know what it means. We will await his reply."

The guard did as I asked without hesitation, the result of my mind push. I expected that later he might wonder how I had persuaded him so easily. But Gaelen responded quickly with an order to escort all of us to his council chamber and to have food and drink brought there for us.

Corrin looked at me askance, and not a little irked, at the ease with which I had accomplished what he had been unable to do.

By the time our escort admitted us to the council chamber a blazing fire burned in the hearth to warm us. Gaelen, already seated in the cushioned chair at the head of the great table, rose as we entered.

"Welcome, sirs. Please be seated." He took no obvious notice of me, but I sensed his warm regard. "Please refresh yourselves with food and ale. You must be hungry from your journey."

Lionn, his heir, sat to his right, now old enough at seventeen to be admitted to council. He sent me a small smile and a wink. I returned it with slight nod of my own, not wanting our guests to know the depth of our relationship yet.

The others did not even notice the tall older man standing in the shadows in the corner closest to Gaelen, but my heart leapt at the sight of my father, looking strong and well. He gave me the briefest of nods and it was all I could do not to jump up and embrace him. But I kept silent, my hands folded demurely in my lap, as I had learned to do. There would be time for that later.

The maid who brought the refreshments poured wine for everyone and stood back, waiting.

Gaelen looked at her, and smiling, said, "We will have no further need of you. You may return to your duties."

She dipped a brief curtsy and left. Gaelen rose, barred the door behind her and returned to his chair but remained standing. Seeing that we had all helped ourselves to food, he addressed Corrin.

"I do not know, sir, who you are or why you have come to seek audience with me, but I know Liannis would not send me this if it were not important." He held up the ring for everyone to see and walked around to hand it to me. Then he went back to resume his seat.

I tucked it safely back into my pouch.

Corrin looked at me again, clearly wondering how I could have such influence over the lord of Bargia.

Gaelen gave him no time to ask questions. "Sir, please tell us what has brought you here."

Corrin rose. "Lord Gaelen, I thank you for receiving me. I am Lord Dugal of Gharn. I have come to ask for your assistance." He hesitated, and seeing that Gaelen did not question this, continued in a rush. "You must have heard, my lord, that my birthright has been taken from me by traitors over three moons ago. What you may not know is that they poisoned my father, and killed two of his loyal advisors even before that. I barely escaped with my own life, thanks to a warning received just in time. The three remaining advisors to my father, traitors all, are strengthening their positions as we speak. If they manage to crown a new lord, of their choosing and under their control, it will be unlikely I will ever regain my rightful place." Corrin hesitated, looking uncomfortable. "Lord Gaelen, I realize that Gharn has had a policy to remain independent. My father and his before him were loath to form alliances with our neighbours. We have managed to remain neutral for three generations. Now, I must place myself at your mercy, with no right to request it, and beg for assistance to take back my rightful place."

When he paused to take a deep breath Gaelen interjected.

"I sympathize with your situation, Lord Dugal. But Bargia also faces possible problems from Lieth. That rule is also under siege, and I expect a similar request from that quarter. Lord Merlost is imprisoned there and his family fled to safe-houses, or so we have been led to believe. There are rumours that he has been assassinated. My spies are seeking confirmation of this. If I am to present your request to my council I must be prepared to convince them with good arguments. We have lived in peace for over seventeen years now. Both I and they will be reluctant to prepare for battle on two flanks." Gaelen's eyes narrowed as he regarded Corrin. "Tell me, what will Bargia gain if we decide to support you? And what may we expect from those who have taken over Gharn if we decide in their favour?"

Corrin sputtered, unable to control his anger. "But it is my right! They are traitors! They cannot be trusted!"

"I suspect that is likely," Gaelen demurred. "But what assurances can you give me that you may be trusted? And what can you offer me in return, if we decide to support your claim?" When Corrin made to interject, Gaelen held up his hand to forestall him. "I will attribute your outburst to your youth, Lord Dugal, but if you are to rule you will need to learn to rein in your temper. I must set my support behind those most likely to keep faith with Bargia. Convince me that you are that one."

I took it all in with both outer and inner senses. I knew that my father, too, would be asked to recount his observations when the meeting ended. But I did not need to rely on my inner sight to see that Gaelen felt far more sympathetic than he let on. He was testing Corrin's mettle to see just how volatile he might be.

Gaelen had come into his position as lord at much the same age as Corrin was now, after his father had been killed in Catania the year before I was born, so he understood the challenges Corrin faced.

Corrin took the rebuke and thought carefully before responding. When he did, he kept his voice carefully modulated and earnest.

"My lord, I give you my oath that Gharn, and I, Dugal, as its rightful lord, will pledge alliance with Bargia and support any campaigns you undertake. I see the need for allies now, and if I regain my rule it will be one of the first changes I make as lord."

Gaelen gave him a small formal bow in acknowledgement. "Lord Dugal, I do not foresee the need to attack any of our neighbours at present, though the lord of Lieth may need similar support from us that you request. Nor do I have any reason to suspect mutiny from within. Since both Gharn and Lieth have problems of their own, I do not expect attack from them, either. Our hold on Catania is secure, the people content with our rule there. Our ties to Franken, our allies to the south are strengthened by trade." Gaelen let it hang waiting to see Corrin's reaction.

Corrin sat back into his seat perplexed, his hands falling into his lap from where he had leaned them on the table when he had sat down. He clearly had not expected this. It did not take my gift to read his confusion. What was Gaelen asking of him? What could he offer that would convince him?

Gaelen let him stew for a moment then relented. "Lord Dugal. If we manage to help you regain your title as Lord of Gharn, will you pledge your men to join us in support of our other allies should they ask it of us? Will you ally with us in future, when we support the valid campaigns of those allies, even if that means that your own position may be weakened by loss of troops, and even if you do not see direct gain for Gharn? In other words, can Bargia rely on your support, even if it does not have immediate benefit for Gharn?"

Corrin's eyes widened in understanding. He sat up straighter, thought a moment and answered formally, "My Lord Gaelen, when I have resumed my rightful place, I swear to you that Gharn will offer whatever assistance it may to Bargia. I pledge our forces to your need, whatever that may be. I hope we may rely on the same from you, should it ever be required in the future. May we always be allies, each to the other."

Gaelen smiled his approval with a small nod.

They all spent the next spans going over, in detail, the events that had led to the coup in Gharn and the ways in which Corrin hoped Bargia might be able to assist him. When the conference ended, Gaelen asked, "And what of Liannis? Do you regard her as a hostage or prisoner, or is she free to go?"

Corrin blushed. "My Lord, we had no idea she is such a friend to your court. I regret that this made it necessary to keep her as our guest. I trust she will tell you she was well treated while in our care."

Gaelen grinned at Corrin's discomfiture. "As do I, Lord Dugal." Sobering again, he added, "Please understand that Bargia has enjoyed many years of peace. My council will not be easily convinced to your proposal. I will consult with them over the next few days. Please accept our hospitality until we meet again at that time. You will have my answer then." He rose, indicating the meeting over. All the others rose as one, Corrin and his men bowing deeply.

At a nod from Gaelen, my father opened the door, and while Gaelen saw the party out, strode over to me and engulfed me in a great hug. "Ah, daughter, it is wonderful to see you. You will have time to visit your mother?"

"Yes, Papa. Among others." I included Gaelen as well, as he remained inside and closed the door again. "I have much to tell you both."

My father noticed my fingers when I winced in his grip, and his face went ashen. "Liannis, what has been done to you?" His voice filled with barely suppressed fury and his expression became dangerous. "This is not how one treats a seer! Who has done this!? They must be made to pay for this. It is one thing to torture a spy like myself, but I will not have my only child, and a seer yet, treated so."

"I will recover, Papa. And they do not know I am a seer. I do not wear the whites. Earth has her own wisdom." I reached up a hand and wiped away the tear that had found its way onto my father's cheek. "Do not weep for me, Papa. I knew what I went to, and those I sought to protect are still safe...but I wonder if you could prepare Mama. She will take it hard and I wish to spare her the shock." I could sense my father's pain as acutely as if it were my own and knew my mother's anguish would be even greater. And I also knew I would not be able to block the intense emotion that would come from her.

"Please, Papa, I can bear this pain much more easily than hers."

He merely nodded, unable to speak lest he lose control, and held me close again, before forcing himself apart.

Gaelen interjected. "Let us hear what you have to tell us, Liannis. I can tell you that Nairin and the children are safe, but," Gaelen smiled, "I am sure you already know that. And the sooner we get through this the sooner you can go home and away from the din of court. I know how difficult it is for you to be here." As an afterthought, he added, "You do know that Liethis' old chambers are always available to you when you come to court? No one else uses them."

"Thank you, my lord. I expect there will come a time when I shall need them. For now I am still able to go home, something which I am most eager to do." I smiled at my father to reassure him. "But first I will need to assure Nairin of Rellnost's safety... and inform her of her husband's death."

"It is certain, then, that he is dead?"

"Yes, my lord. I saw the moment of his death though not the method, though the suddenness makes me think it was murder. But Earth has not shown me where that may lead, or what we must do now." I filled the two men in on all that I knew with regards to the situation in Lieth. Much of it they had already heard.

37

"Then Lieth has a new lord. This makes it even more critical that Rellnost receive the proper training, if a regency can be set up for him. We will need to do what we can to insure that those who speak for him may be trusted, and that his education continues on the correct course. Liannis, will you see if Nairin will speak with us on this?"

"I will, my lord."

Gaelen changed the subject. "And when may we see you don your seer's whites? It will give greater strength to our cause if we are seen to have a true seer behind our decisions."

I shook my head. "Earth has not shown me when that may be, my lord. When the time comes, I am sure I will be given a sign. Until then, it seems I have other work to do. Now I must visit Nairin to assure her of Rellnost's safety. I will sound her out on the regency, my lord."

"And what of young Lord Dugal? What can you tell us of him? Has Earth given you any signs regarding himself or Gharn?"

"Only that we would meet here with you, nothing more. But I can vouch for his character. He is passionate, but may be reasoned with. He has worked very hard to gather support for his campaign but has not resorted to wild promises or unsavoury methods. Nor is he a cruel man. In time, as age tempers his passions, he can become a just leader. I believe we may trust his word. He did not take his oath of alliance with Bargia lightly. But it is his word only. Time can change the good intentions of any man. We must rely on Earth to guide us."

Gaelen quirked an eyebrow in question at my father. "Klast?"

"I concur, my lord. He meant what he said. Only time will show if that may change."

"So now we are called to support two causes, neither of which has a certain outcome and both of which will require many armed men. I do not think we can fight both at once." Gaelen sighed, passing his hand over his eyes and pinched the bridge of his nose. The familiar gesture warmed me. Then he straightened and gave me a wry smile. "I could really use some guidance from Earth. Which cause do I support first?"

I smiled back shaking my head. "I am afraid I know no more than you, my lord."

"Ah well, then." He rose. "You have had a difficult journey and want to go home to see your mother. Please tell her she is missed at court. My Lady Marja especially, misses Brensa, since the secrecy around Rellnost's arrival prevents their visiting each other."

"I will tell her. I am certain she feels the same. But now I must visit Lady Nairin before I go home. She will need to hear what has transpired."

"I will accompany you. Brensa would never forgive me if I arrived without you."

"No Papa. Go and prepare her."

"Then when may we expect you, daughter? Or do you wish me to return for you?"

I understood the anxiety around my safety that had prompted his offer. "I would have liked that very much. But I need to speak with Nairin in private. You need not concern yourself over my safety. The danger to me is passed for now."

"I see, very well." He opened the door with obvious reluctance and we two followed Gaelen out. "My lord...?"

Gaelen anticipated him. "Go home, my friend. Your duty lies there tonight. But I will need you present at the meeting of the council tomorrow afternoon." He hesitated. "Perhaps you would meet with me in private over the midday meal. I would like to hear what you think."

"As you wish, my lord."

I already strode away toward the walled stone house where I knew Nairin and the children stayed.

My father called after me. "When may we expect you?"

"Before the moon reaches the tops of the trees, Papa." I turned and saw him nod, a worried expression still on his face. In his mind I am still a little girl.

12

NAIRIN

As I walked the streets of Bargia city I struggled to block the waves of emotions and impressions that pressed upon me. Like all seers, I preferred the quiet of the countryside. There, away from other people, I could relax. Here it was all I could do not to put my hands to my temples and try to squeeze out the noise. It would not help, I knew, but the temptation never quite went away.

I tried to distract myself with the familiar sights of Bargia city. At this time of year, before the heat of summer, the stench of the gutters remained quiescent. The branches on the few trees that dotted the streets and peeked over courtyard walls blushed with the promise of green. Tufts of old grass showed new green spears in between the brown of last year's growth. Here and there tiny bluebells opened their first blossoms, a welcome touch of colour, harbinger of spring.

I looked up and met the mind of a small kestrel, out of place in the city. The small falcons usually kept to the forests and adjacent fields where mice and other prey were plentiful. *What are you doing here, my little friend? This is a bleak place for one such as you.*

The kestrel circled above me. *I am for you. See what I see.*

I wondered what she meant. Kestrels were loners, hunters. But I raised my eyes and saw the city laid out under me. And here, so high above, the noise in my mind abated a little. *Thank you, little one.* I sent a sense of gratitude into the bird's mind and felt an answer vaguely like a smile. When I reached the safe-house I checked around from above to make sure no one saw me enter then dropped back into my own vision. The kestrel flew off and settled on a nearby rooftop.

When I gave the attendant the code word, the door opened just wide enough for me to slip through and was barred again immediately behind me.

"Hello, Blenniss. It is good to see you again."

"My lady waits with the children in the courtyard."

"Thank you. I will find the way. We have much to discuss. Please see that we are not disturbed. It would be best if the children were not present."

"Perhaps tea in the sitting room would be more private? I could see to the children in the garden."

"Yes, that would be best." I dreaded the task ahead of me. How does one tell a woman that her husband has been murdered, that her children will never see their father again? Oh Earth, am I strong enough for this?

Blenniss showed me into a small room lined with eight chairs, two against each wall. In the centre stood a low round table covered with a snowy linen cloth. On it sat a game of Bluff, half completed.

"I will tell my lady that you are here."

I had barely seated myself in one of the carved chairs, each with an embroidered seat cushion, when Nairin rushed in.

"What news?! How fares Rellnost? Oh, I miss him so. And Lord Merlost, is he all right?"

"Rellnost is well, my lady. We have much to discuss. Blenniss brings tea. She will see that the children do not disturb us."

Nairin paled as she realized I had said nothing about her husband and quickly sank into the chair beside mine. I knew she had caught the message behind my omission and that I had done so to give her a chance to steel herself. "Of course. I forget my manners." She sat stiffly, fidgeting with the rings on her fingers, fighting for composure as she prepared herself for what she knew must come.

We waited in silence until Blenniss brought the tea and honey cakes and set them on the table between us.

I smelled the tea. Chamomile. Good. Blenniss had chosen a calming herb. It would not hurt my own frayed senses either. I helped myself to one of the cakes as Nairin poured.

"How fare Wartin and Leyla, my lady?"

"They miss their home and their father and especially the freedom to ride their ponies and play out of doors. But they behave very well and attend to their studies. I am most grateful for our safety."

"That is well, my lady. I am glad to hear it. I do understand how confined they must feel." I took a sip of tea. "I go home to see Rellnost when I leave here, my lady, but I have been assured that he is well. He does suffer from homesickness and misses you but that is to be expected. I will return in two days with a more personal recounting."

"Thank you...and my lord?" Nairin's cup shook. I could barely hear her anxious whisper.

I put a comforting hand on her knee. "I am sorry, my lady. He is gone."

"How?"

"I do not know the details. Only that he died in prison. But my source is true. There can be no doubt."

I waited as Nairin stubbornly blinked back the tears that filled her eyes then kept my voice low and soothing. "Lieth must look to Rellnost, now, my lady."

"He is only a boy!" Nairin buried her face in her hands and finally allowed her tears to flow for her son, as she had not for her lord and husband...only ten years old and not ready for such a burden.

"We must speak of his future, my lady. There are choices. If his lordship can be taken back from the usurpers, a regency must be established for him." I hesitated. "Or...he could renounce his title and you could all find a safe haven here in Bargia. Lord Gaelen has extended that invitation if you wish it. This is much to think on, my lady."

Nairin drew herself up in her chair and I watched fierce determination fill her eyes. "I must see my son."

"I wish that were possible, my lady. Alas, it could compromise his safety and all of ours as well." My words hung like lead between us. "I will return in two days. When I come back I must hear your wishes. If you decide to declare a regency Lord Gaelen will wish to consult with you about who should act in his place. His regent and his council will need to be chosen with great care and plans must be made for placing him back in Lieth and taking back control...if that is even advisable."

"I see." Nairin's voice took on a tone of rigid determination. As any good mother would, somewhere she found the strength she needed to do what she must for her son. The display of fortitude boded well for Rellnost and his future.

It had been his father, Lord Merlost's, weakness as a leader that had led to the situation they now found themselves in. Merlost had come to power prematurely when his father died of the Red Fever that had ravaged the entire One Isle seventeen years ago. Merlost had come home from a journey to find Lieth in chaos, his father dead, and those left behind unable to make decisions. His father, Lord Wernost had ruled as suspicious autocrat, jealously guarding his power. He had not even seen fit to train his heir and so had left young Merlost ill prepared for lordship. Now Nairin and the children bore the fruit of Merlost's ineptitude.

Nairin rose. With clenched fists she declared, "Rellnost must have his birthright."

When she said nothing more I rose and went to the door. As I turned in the open door I saw that Nairin stood rigid, her mouth set in an angry determined line.

"In two days then, my lady," I said softly and turned and went in search of Blenniss to see me out and bar the door behind me.

I looked up as I stepped into the street just in time to see the kestrel leave her perch and begin to circle overhead again. *Hello little one. Why are you still here?*

I am for you.

I welcome your company, little one, but your place is the forest.

I am for you, came the stubborn response.

The small raptor followed me in wide circles until I reached my parents small cottage. When the welcome sight of smoke curling lazily up from the chimney made me quicken my step I looked up and told the kestrel that I was home now.

I hunt. I wait, came the reply.

HOME

I wondered at this and decided that if the bird was still with me when I left on the morrow I would need to give her a name. But before I had time to ponder this further the door flew open and my mother rushed out onto the muddy path to embrace me, only a sweater over her shoulders and indoor boots on her feet.

"You are home! Oh, thank Earth you are safe. Come and eat. Tell us all. I have been so worried about you." Her face crumpled as she looked toward my hand. "Your father told me...oh, Liannis. If only you had been able to wear the whites. No one harms a seer."

"That has been true, Mama, but I am not certain it will always be so, or that it would have saved me. I do know that I would not have been able to get Nairin and the children to safety if I were known as a seer."

I gave my mother a squeeze. "My fingers will heal, Mama. And you know I cannot wear the whites until I have a sign from Earth." I smiled to soften the harshness of my words. My mother had such a tender heart and anything that threatened her only child affected her like a personal blow.

As we stepped through the door my father added his own long embrace. "Welcome home, daughter." The formality of the words could not hide the feeling behind them.

My father seldom voiced his feelings but I knew how deep his love went...and how far he would go to protect me if he could. Even though I was a girl and would not normally have learned such skills, he had taught me everything he could about survival and self-defence, even to the use of the dagger and sword. As a young man he had discovered a way to insert a small blade, commissioned just for that purpose, in a belt between the two layers of leather. He shared that secret only with Mama and me. Thus, if ever found I myself in danger and stripped of the small dagger I kept at my waist, I would still have a blade to rely on. He had also passed on all he knew of herb lore and tending wounds. Through all of this he had shown infinite patience.

My gifts as a seer made me an uncommonly insightful child. The occasions when he or Mama needed to admonish me had been few and always delivered calmly and patiently. Neither of them had ever raised their voices to their sensitive daughter. Nor had I often given them reason to. My home provided an oasis of calm in my turbulent world.

Sensing that Rellnost, sitting disconsolate on a stool by the table, was about to lose face by bursting into tears, I turned from my father to greet him. "Rellnost, I am glad to see you well. I think you have put on some bulk since I left you here. Father tells me you are training well. That is good, for you shall need those skills soon when you become lord of Lieth."

"I want to see my mother! I want to go home." He spat the words at me as his hands clenched tight together on the table.

My mother opened her mouth to rebuke him but I stopped her with a look.

"Rellnost, I truly wish I could make that happen. I know that your mother wishes it, too, for I just came from her and she wept that she could not see you. But before you go to sleep tonight, I think you will understand why it cannot be. Through no fault of your own it is necessary for you to become a man too soon. It will take all the courage you have. You will not have the luxury of an easy youth like other young men your age."

"I can be a man. I am almost old enough already." Rellnost squared his shoulders and put on a haughty expression that only served to emphasize his youth.

I knew enough not to laugh. "Then I know you will be strong enough to hear what I must tell you." My heart ached that this boy must learn of the death of his father alone, with no one who loved him nearby to share his grief with. I watched as his look turned anxious. "But first we must have supper. I am famished and it smells wonderful. Mama, have you learned a new dish?" My mother had, at best, always been a mediocre cook, having learned all she knew from my father early in their relationship. But she continued to try new dishes with singular determination. She had shone with pride when around my tenth birthday she finally mastered bread. It had been a welcome staple ever since.

She beamed. "Yes, I learned that a tiny bit of honey added to the onions when I fry them enhances their flavour. I do it before I add it to the stew. It does smell good, does it not? And I found fresh leeks and fiddlehead ferns to add to the pot."

Papa gave her a fond look. "And we have fresh bread with honey for later."

"Please do not make me suffer any longer. Let me eat!" I laughed when Mama threw her hands up in mock embarrassment and hurried to place the kettle on the table where spoons and knives sat ready. Soon we were all seated and she ladled the steaming stew into the waiting clay bowls. The bread, fresh butter and the promised honey waited on the shelf on one wall behind us. Mugs of milk from our only cow rounded out the meal. To me the simple fare tasted wonderful. I was home.

45

Over supper we three adults kept the conversation going, bringing each other up to date in a general way, saving more painful topics for later when we could speak privately. We included Rellnost with questions and tales of his progress since he had been at the cottage and reassurances about his mother and siblings. I noted his efforts not to press me for more about his father with approval.

When we had finished supper I turned to him. "Rellnost, you have shown great patience and good manners over dinner. Now I will tell you all you wish to know."

"You have said nothing of my lord father. It is bad news is it not?" Rellnost's face scrunched up with anxiety and he squeezed his hands between his knees to keep them from twisting.

"I am afraid you are right, Rellnost. Your father was killed by his captors. You are lord of Lieth now." I paced a hand on his arm.

Rellnost jerked away from my touch as though he had been burned. "No! I do not believe you. Did you see his body? You were not there. I want to go home."

My mother started to reach toward him to try to comfort him but I stopped her with a small shake of my head. I let my silence speak for itself and when Rellnost's outburst had spent itself out he looked at me, full of anguish.

"Your mother has already been told. She wants very badly to be here with you so you may weep together. It is good to grieve, Rellnost. Even hardened soldiers weep when they lose someone they love."

I sent him waves of comfort without touching him, urging him to loosen the tight control he held to. When his lip trembled and unshed tears welled in his eyes I said, "Come, let me be your mother's arms and her shoulder." I reached for him once more and this time he crumpled into my arms like the boy he still was. I did my best to absorb much of his anguish and send him calm. Oh Earth, why must I feel so much pain. Why have you chosen me? I do not think I can bear it. I am too weak.

Mama, too, shed tears of sympathy. They slid silently down her cheeks. My father placed a silent hand on her arm.

Rellnost eventually pulled away from me, his tears spent. In a voice still thick from crying he asked, "Will I ever truly be lord? We are not in Lieth and those that killed my father are in power."

I shook my head. "I do not know. But for now you must act as though it will be. You must learn all you need. I have promised to speak with Lady Nairin in two days time. She is thinking about whether to attempt to set up a regency for you and who might best represent you."

I met Rellnost's eyes and held them. "Rellnost, this is something you must think on as well. Before I speak with your mother I would like to know if this is what you want. If you decide to pursue your birthright it will take all the determination and strength you can muster. You must search deep inside yourself to decide if you have what it will ask of you. You will be a boy no longer. Think carefully on it, Rellnost. Do not answer me now. I will speak with you again to try to answer any questions you might think of before I take your answer to Lady Nairin."

Rellnost's eyes had gone wide as I spoke. He squared his shoulders and drew himself up. After a silence during which I did not let go his gaze, he said solemnly, "I will be ready."

"I believe you will."

By now it was well past dark. My father spoke up. "Rellnost, you have had a trying day. I think you need to go to bed now."

Rellnost's eyes narrowed as though he would challenge Papa, then he seemed to think better of it. "Yes sir." He got up from his stool and climbed the ladder into the loft where they had made a bed for him.

I recalled the day my father had realized his fey daughter needed a space of her own. It happened on my eighth birthday. I had looked at him and told him matter-of-factly that I would sleep in the kitchen because I needed to dream my own dreams, not his. The next day he had gone out to survey our cabin and told my mother he could build a small loft over the back half. I claimed my new space only a moon later, overjoyed with my new riches.

I understood my father's wisdom in allowing Rellnost to keep my room even while I visited. It was a show of respect for his status as future lord. I would make do with blankets and a pillow on the rough table in the kitchen, the only space big enough to accommodate me. Even the floor had no space big enough for me to stretch out.

My father asked, "Shall we go to the shed to speak privately?"

"That will not be necessary." I gave him a knowing smile. "He will sleep. It is warmer here. Do you have tea Mama? Are there any of the white pine needles left? It is my favourite. "

"You know I always save some for you." Her quick smile told me she welcomed the distraction. The events of the day had taken their toll on her sensitive nature. She bustled about making the tea and putting out some aged sheep's cheese beside the left over bread. I looked at her rough hands and smiled to myself. My mother had been raised to the soft life of the court. But she wore her calloused and chapped hands as badges of honour. She had chosen this life and it suited her well.

Lady Marja had told the story more than once. When Brensa and Klast first decided to join together and Klast had found this cottage, Brensa had taken to gardening with a will. She had shown off her work worn hands to Marja with pride declaring she had never been suited to fine needlework anyway. Marja had told me it was the first time her dearest friend had truly smiled since her ordeal in the cave at the hands of the rapists who had captured her, mistaking her for Lady Marja. My father had rescued her and brought her back to Marja but Mama's recovery had been slow until she and Papa joined.

Even before the steaming mugs sat in front of each of us, I made a mock show of cocking my head to listen for Rellnost, smiling to share the joke. Of course they both knew it was not necessary for me to listen that way, but it was a long standing joke we shared and now it lightened the mood for us. "He sleeps. He will not hear us." Their answering smiles warmed me reminding me once more that I was truly home.

We talked well into the night. I told them all I knew of what had transpired since I had brought Rellnost to them for safekeeping, including the parts I had not had time to tell when I had so hastily dropped Rellnost off with my father outside the city; my flight to safety with Nairin and the children.

"Nairin almost refused to allow me to take Rellnost from her and leave with the other two in the care of the driver. It took a great deal of persuasion, even a push with my gift. And you know I do not like to use that part of my abilities. I always try to let people use their own minds."

I dwelt as briefly as possible on my torture at the hands of the traitors who wished me to divulge the children's whereabouts and how I had persuaded the young guard to let me go, my headlong flight into the forest in the cold and snow, not knowing where I went.

When I got to my rescue and forced stay with Corrin and his men, Mama wrung her hands. "Thank Earth they found you. Oh, Liannis, I could not bear it if I were to lose you."

I gave them my impressions of Corrin's character, recounted my conversation with Nairin and my approval of the strength Rellnost had shown tonight, which I thought boded well for his future.

"But that is only your own impression of him, not sent by Earth?" My father's worried frown betrayed that he hoped my answer would contradict him.

"It is only my own, Papa."

"And Earth has not shown when you may wear the whites?" asked my mother, her tone both worried and hopeful.

"No Mama. Perhaps I need to do more to earn them."

She shook her head, a spark of anger darkening her face. "You have always done all that is asked of you. Your studies were almost complete when Liethis died. I cannot believe Earth would make you wait. It is unjust."

"When I am ready Earth will show me, Mama. Do not fear. She will keep me safe until then." But secretly I also wondered what more I must do before I would be permitted the garb of a true seer. I longed to be able to show my true identity. I hated this hiding, which felt like a deception.

14

DAUGHTER

I stood barefoot in my night-dress, the lush new grass ticked my ankles and dripped wet drops of bright dew onto my feet. I wiggled my toes in delight. Spring! Earth's promise of renewal.

I looked up from my feet to see a pair of women approach. Though each walked with the strong stride of someone in the peak of health, one looked much younger than the other. As they drew near I saw smiles on both their faces and the younger waived in greeting. With a rush of joy I recognized Liethis. This Liethis was dressed, not in seer's white, but in a gown of azure as blue as the sky, with bright flowers in yellow and green embroidered about the hem and sleeves. When they came within reach I could see that Liethis' eyes still shone with her familiar wisdom and love, but her body, so ravaged in life by the coughing disease that had claimed her, now looked strong and lithe as a willow.

She laughed gaily at the question forming in my mind. "Earth is kind to those who serve her. She has taken me back into her embrace and made me young and whole again. Look!" And she spun in a graceful arc, her arms flung out in a joyous dance, her thick chestnut braid flowing behind in a mirror of the curve. The sight filled me with a surge of joy.

As Liethis arced away, the woman with her once more drew my attention. This one I did not recognize. Though her body appeared strong and lithe, her eyes gave an impression of infinite age. When she looked into mine I saw such love, wisdom and sorrow there that I understood who this must be. Earth had come to me in her woman form. The smile she gave me suffused me with a love so vast words cannot describe it.

"Daughter. You have done well." Without my knowing how they came to be there, for they had not been there before, I saw in Earth's arms the white robes of a full seer. "Liethis has no need of these now. They are yours." She held them out to me and smiled once more.

"Mother." I could say no more, too awed to speak.

Earth's smile faded to a profound sadness. "Do not thank me yet daughter, for she who wears the whites will face many trials. A seer's fate is never easy." Her smile returned. "But wear them in health. Be assured I will never be far." She reached the robes toward me. When our hands touched I sensed immense power wrapped in total love and acceptance. Then Earth lifted one hand and touched my right temple. "Remember." She repeated the gesture to my left temple. "Believe."

At her touch speech deserted me. Then Earth dropped her hands and I stood once more before her. "Yours is a very special gift, Liannis. I know you will use it well. I am proud of you." She nodded her understanding. I had received the answer to my question.

Earth gave me one more smile and turned away.

Liethis waved farewell, and she, too, smiling, turned to follow Earth back the way they had come.

I once again found myself alone in the grass, this time with the white robes held firmly in my arms.

15

MORNING

I woke to the sounds of my mother scouring the breakfast dishes. I almost fell off the table when I jumped up. "Mama, I am late. Has Papa left to meet with Lord Gaelen yet?" I saw that my mother had set a bowl of porridge for me to the side of the hearth to keep warm and that a pot of tea rested beside it.

She looked over her shoulder. "No dearest, your father has gone to milk the cow before leaving. You have time to eat. Rellnost is in the shed with him."

"But how did you all eat with me occupying the table?"

She laughed. "Why with our bowls on our laps, of course." Then, more seriously, "I could see that you were dreaming and felt it important not to wake you."

"Yes, I was. It was a wonderful dream, Mama. Liethis came to me, and Earth in her woman form. Liethis was young again and very happy. And Earth greeted me with such love. I cannot describe it. But you will be pleased to hear that I will very soon wear the whites. In my dream the grass stood only a little higher than it does now. I think I will visit Liethis' cabin and retrieve her robes. It seems I am to start with those."

I beamed at my mother and reached for the bowl she handed me. "I wish to go with Papa today to see Lord Gaelen and tell him. I know he will be relieved, too."

"What wonderful news!" Mama's looked as though a great burden had lifted from her. "And I am sure Klast will be glad of your company. But will you return tonight?"

The longing in her voice told me how she had missed me. "Yes, and tomorrow, too, Mama,." I hugged her. "I have missed you both terribly."

When I stepped outside after breaking my fast, my attention immediately rose to the top of the tall pine that stood paces away from the cabin door. There, the little kestrel swooped down to greet me. *Hunting good. Full. We go now?*

I am full, too. Yes, we go now. I have a name for you, little one. I shall call you Kira for the beautiful sound you make. Do you like that?

Kira am for you.

I am glad for your company Kira.

Kira gave an affirmative whistle that sounded remarkably like her name. I mind-spoke her my pleasure for her company.

"And what makes you so happy this morning, daughter?" My father emerged from the shed with a bucket of milk, Rellnost trailing behind him, the curry brush still in his hand.

I pointed upward. "Meet my new friend, Papa. Her name is Kira." The bird flew in a proud circle and whistled again. "It seems she has attached herself to me."

He looked up. "So it seems."

"Papa, I wish to go with you today to speak with Lord Gaelen. I have had the sign we have all waited for. I am to wear the whites."

My father did not normally show his feelings. His reputation for reserve was legendary. Yet now, his look of relief showed so openly it made me laugh. "Why, Papa, I think that pleases you." That brought a rare smile from him.

"Indeed. And I will welcome your company today. Perhaps Lord Gaelen will also wish to have you join our discussion."

Rellnost stood staring open-mouthed during this interchange. Now he burst out, "What do you mean whites? Are you a seer?"

Papa intervened before I could answer. "I think you are not finished with your chores. We will speak of this tonight after we return. And I want to hear your answer to the strategy question I gave you."

"But...?

"Not now Rellnost. Duty first..."

Rellnost hesitated a moment longer, but when it became obvious that he would receive nothing more he turned and reluctantly went back into the shed.

We rode companionably back to the castle, my father on his roan and I on the docile mare Corrin had loaned me. I had no mount of my own. That would need to be rectified now that I could wear seer's robes.

Kira made to follow us. I mind spoke her. I go to the city, Kira. I return before dark. Be free until then. Kira seemed puzzled for a moment then sent me I hunt and flew off. I smiled to myself, and when my father raised one eyebrow at me, I explained my conversation with the bird.

"So you have a familiar. I know Liethis sometimes spoke with birds as well, though I do not think any stayed with her." He gave me another of his rare smiles. "It seems you have discovered another gift. You told me in a vision the night you were conceived that you would be very special. I will never forget that vision." He grew serious again. "I hope your gifts do not become too great a burden for you. I have never heard of a seer as powerful as you."

He stared straight ahead but I could feel his worry. He could hide his feelings from all others. It was his greatest asset as a spy. But he could not hide from me.

"Earth has chosen me for this Papa. She does not waste her gifts." It was the only reassurance I could give him.

16

A GIFT

We arrived early, just before the midday meal. Instead of going to the conference chamber the guard led us through to Lord Gaelen's private chambers. Lady Marja hugged me warmly but even after all this time she still greeted my father with reserve. When they first met Marja had mistrusted him immensely because of his presence as a spy at the court of her father, Lord Cataniast and had been instrumental in the successful campaign against him. Marja had resented Lord Gaelen's close ties with and trust of him. But when he had rescued Mama from the brigands who had raped her, the two had come to an uneasy truce for my mother's sake.

Marja bade us be seated and called for food to be brought. To my delight Gaelen brought his son Lionn with him. I had not seen my childhood friend for months and even though he had been present at the meeting yesterday, I had not had any opportunity to speak with him.

"Sennia will not be able to join us, Liannis. She is visiting friends in the country for an eightday. I know she will be sorry she missed your visit."

When Lionn hugged me I reached up to rub his cheek. "So, you are old enough to shave now? Maybe you will be a man some day after all."

"I do not see you in whites yet," he quipped back, grinning.

"And if I should wear them, my oh-so-superior friend, will you look up to me as you ought?" The playful banter lifted any strangeness I still felt about my homecoming. To Lionn I would always be just another sister, only two years older than Sennia, his blood sister. He had always held it over me that he was my elder, even if only by less than a year.

"Hmmm. I will be your Lord...so you will have to look up to me." His grin grew wider. "I declare a draw."

"Then you had better begin shaving every day." I put on my most haughty face but could not hold it and burst into a laugh. "Perhaps this would be a good time to announce my news so you may all hear it at once." I waited, glowing in the indulgent smiles of the adults and watched Lionn raise one eyebrow in a mirror of his father.

My news was too important to be treated as a jest so I composed myself before continuing.

"I have good news. Earth gave me the sign last night in a dream that I am now ready to wear the seer's whites. It seems that I must retrieve those Liethis wore. I no longer need to keep my gift secret."

Lionn and Marja both burst out together, "That is wonderful!"

Gaelen grew more thoughtful. "I congratulate you, Liannis. This is indeed good news." He paused. "I have missed having a court seer since Liethis died. This will make many things easier."

"My lord, while I will provide what assistance I may, I regret that I cannot ally myself with Bargia alone as Liethis did. As you know, my gift is much stronger than hers. Earth has shown me that it must be used in the service of all the One Isle, not Bargia alone. I fear I am destined to spend much time away from home."

Gaelen broke off a chunk of bread and took his time chewing. "I admit what you say is not unexpected. I know of no seer in history whose gift matches yours. Liethis saw true but your visions are stronger and I suspect that you truth read more easily. Perhaps that is why it is so much harder for you to live among many others." He grew quiet again, staring into his ale as he swirled it slowly around in the mug. "I expect that with the trials facing the demesnes of both Lieth and Gharn, into which Bargia will no doubt be required to play a part, that Earth has need of you beyond Bargia. No single demesne can lay claim on you."

My father and Lady Marja nodded. Lionn looked slightly disappointed. I caught his thought. "I suppose I must be satisfied with seeing little of her from now on. I will miss her."

Though eavesdropping on others' thoughts is forbidden I still have not perfected the blocking techniques that prevent stray thoughts aimed at me from coming through.

Gaelen took another draft of his ale before speaking again, his eyes twinkling. "But a seer needs a good mount. I have been saving one just for this occasion. I trust you will have time after our discussion to take a walk to the paddock with me?"

I hesitated, not knowing what to say, not only out of gratitude for his generosity, but because I did not wish to seem ungrateful. Both he and my father regarded me, puzzled. I swallowed and decided I had best be frank, trusting Gaelen would understand.

"My lord, I have always been grateful for your generosity. And it is true that I will need a mount...but the choice must be made by the horse. The bond is a lifelong one and we must be able to mind-speak one another. It is possible that the one you have chosen for me will not agree or does not mind-speak well."

I held my breath, waiting. He looked surprised but recovered smoothly. "Well then, I hope that our paddock holds the successful candidate. Else we shall need to widen our search."

I let out the breath I had been holding. So did everyone else, it seemed. "I am glad you understand, my lord. I look forward to that meeting." But I wondered if the paddock actually held the right candidate. Would one of those horses choose me? Or would Earth decide I did not merit such a bond?

Gaelen smiled and rose. "Well, we have much to discuss. Lionn, my friends, let us go to the council chamber so we may be assured of privacy."

Marja rose with us to embrace me again. "Will we see you again before you are called away? And will you tell Brensa how much I miss her?"

"I do not know how long I will remain in Bargia but I think it will be several days yet. Do not think you may be rid of me so easily! Mama misses you terribly, too. Perhaps we may arrange for her to visit here, now that I am home for awhile and able to stay with our guest."

"I would like that very much."

17

CONFERENCE

As we three walked to the council chamber behind Gaelen, I asked, "Papa, will you have time to accompany me to Liethis' cabin to retrieve her whites?"

"I would not miss it...but perhaps your mother would like to go and one of us must remain behind at the cabin."

"Perhaps that is better. She has been stuck at home since Rellnost arrived. I could even bring her here afterward for a long visit, perhaps a day or two."

"Yes...if Lord Gaelen can miss me for a few days."

Gaelen looked over his shoulder. "Klast, my friend. You retired a year ago but I think you still spend as many hours serving me as before. Even now you attend to our guest's education. I can live without you for a while. If I need you urgently I will ride out to see you."

"Or," Lionn piped up, "I could go with you, Liannis, after you bring Brensa to visit Mother. I would very much like to spend some time with you as well."

As we reached the door of the council chamber I sent my senses ahead into the room. While I could tell that the room was unoccupied something felt wrong. "No! Lord Gaelen, wait!"

He must have heard the urgency in my voice. He snatched his hand from the latch and whirled to face me.

"There is no one in the chamber, my lord, but I sense something that feels wrong. I suggest you have someone precede you, and have them take great care. I do not know if there is truly danger here but I mistrust it."

My father had placed himself in Gaelen's way even before I finished my first warning, blocking the door. He looked to me. "You cannot tell us more?"

"No. I only know that it is not living."

"Klast, wait until I send for someone else."

But my father had already slid back the bar. He moved to the wall beside the door, motioning us behind him. With his sword he pried up the latch and very slowly eased it open. As soon as the door came free of the frame three arrows thunked into it and quivered for a moment. Then nothing. He looked at me again, questioning.

Gaelen looked worried but Lionn gaped in shock.

I let my senses scan the chamber again. "I sense no more. We may enter now."

My father insisted he precede us. In a moment he reappeared and told us that all appeared safe. He pulled the arrows from the door and examined them. "Poison" He looked at me. "It is well you were with us," and turned to Gaelen "...else you might now lie dying, my lord. I must find out how this was done." His eyes narrowed to grim slits. "My lord, only Janest and myself know the secret of the other entry to this chamber. I would stake my life on Janest's loyalty. We must find out how someone learned of it. This could only have been accomplished by that door."

Gaelen and Lionn both looked as shaken as I felt.

My father checked the door very carefully when he closed and barred it. "I have barred the other as well, my lord. I think we may speak safely now." He took the chair opposite mine closest to Gaelen's.

"What other door? Father, do you not think I should have been told of it?" Lionn asked. "Where is it?"

"Seventeen years of peace in Bargia. I have come to take it for granted." Gaelen passed his hand over his eyes and pinched the bridge of his nose, a gesture I had learned to recognize as worry or fatigue. "Come Lionn, I will show you. The last time it saw use was when Klast and I questioned Sinnath. It is a secret usually known only to the lord and two closest advisors. You would have learned of it eventually."

"Shall I send for Janest? We need to sound him out with Liannis present. While I do not doubt his loyalty, I cannot forget when Sinnath betrayed your trust."

My father referred to Sinnath, the traitor who had tried to have Lady Marja killed. Sinnath had been one of Gaelen's father's most trusted advisors, just as Janest was now. Janest was the only advisor on Gaelen's council who still remained of those Gaelen had inherited from his father. I could tell that the idea that Janest might betray him as Sinnath had made him sick to his stomach. Both he and my father trusted Janest completely.

"I will truth-read him, my lord, if you wish, but it might be wise to wait until I have my whites. It will help him understand why I am present without explaining to him. I hope he is innocent and that he does not hold your questions against you."

"If he is innocent, and I hope to Earth he is, then he, too, will remember Sinnath and understand." I had never seen Gaelen look so downcast. "Go and get your whites Liannis. And I think you need a sword beside you, so Lionn shall go with you. You may bring your mother to visit Marja. Klast, my friend, I think it is time to step up Rellnost's training."

My father nodded agreement.

"Now, to the reason for our meeting today. Liannis, do you see any reason to avoid assisting Dugal in his campaign? I do not think we can undertake one in Lieth at present. Much more discussion needs to take place with Nairin and even Rellnost before that decision can be made."

"Dugal is young and untried, but his claim is legitimate and he has gathered considerable support. He is headstrong and passionate. The three who came with him believe in him and are completely loyal. Though it is an opinion only, I believe he will make a good lord and a strong ally if he regains his birthright and finds the right men to advise and support him. But Earth has not given me any sign. These are my opinions only from the short time I have spent with him."

My father spoke up. "I think he will need as much assistance from Bargia in choosing his advisors as he does in taking Gharn back from the traitors. Do you think he will listen to such advice?"

I understood what he meant. As usual, my father had gone straight to the heart of the matter, for what would be gained if Dugal were to regain his lordship only to flounder without strong and wise men to advise him? In spite of my sex my father had instructed me in history, politics and strategy. Such discussions had been his version of bedtime tales. Even as a little girl, he had encouraged me to participate. My mother would try to discourage him, saying that I was too young for such talk, but I loved it and so she would give up, shaking her head fondly. Often Lionn joined in during one of his frequent visits.

I shook my head. "That I cannot say."

"I think that it is preferable to deal with the known than the unknown. So, as we know more about Dugal than those who usurp his seat, I believe it best to convince the council that we must support his claim. Klast, what do you think, my friend?"

"I concur, my lord. It is the lesser of two undesirable choices."

"Father, since Dugal and I are close in age I might be able to assist. In any case I think we should become friends as we are to be allies. It will strengthen his ties to Bargia."

Gaelen nodded approvingly then studied his hands silently. After several moments he sighed, raised his head, squared his shoulders and rose from his seat.

"Well then. If we are finished there is a paddock full of horses. Possibly one of them may decide it is a seer's mount. Come."

"My lord. After the events of this afternoon I think it advisable to have guards about you...and Lionn as well."

"Perhaps later, my friend. Right now I have a seer and the former head of my personal guard in attendance." The smile he gave us both looked strained. I saw it mirrored in both Lionn and my father.

18

WHITE ON WHITE

Behind the lord's special stables lay a fenced paddock where Gaelen kept a small number of young horses. These he and his stable-master had handpicked, bought from the horse breeders who came several times a year to the trader's field just inside the city gates.

Over the years Gaelen had encouraged my father to walk by his side as his closest friend. But today he kept just a step behind, vigilant. Lionn, too, gave pride of place over to me and hovered to the other side. I kept my senses open as well but we passed almost unnoticed as people went about their business.

The stable-master spotted us as we approached and strode over to meet us. "My lord, we have a new addition. See the bay over there to the right? He will make a fine addition to your cavalry. Smooth gait, strong hocks and just the right amount of fire."

Gaelen shook his hand as he searched and found the right horse. "I see you still have him blindfolded. He must be new indeed."

"Yes, my lord. Bought him from a man from Lieth just yesterday. New breeder."

I watched my father and Gaelen briefly look at each other and knew they had not missed the reference to Lieth. It sent a prickling sensation that raised the hair on my neck.

"Very good. You remember Liannis? She has earned a mount of her own. I thought one of these might suit."

"Shall I give the merits of each , my lord?"

"No, I think we can manage nicely on our own. I am familiar with them. You may go about your duties. Thank you, Kersh."

I turned my attention to the field as Kersh walked away. Behind me, I heard my father tell Gaelen he would check out the trader.

"I would like to enter the field, if I may, my lord."

Gaelen nodded and Lionn opened the gate and stepped inside along with me. I stopped him with a touch on his arm. "No, Lionn. I must do this alone."

Before me grazed possibly the ten finest beasts in all of Bargia. Would one of them be mine? The excitement of that thought made it take more effort than usual to still my mind and open my senses. *Who will come to me?* I sent out. Only three horses looked up. One went back to his grazing. Two started toward me. *Welcome friends. How fine you both are.*

The chestnut tossed her head as though the compliment was only her due.

The white, just back behind her, looked directly at me, then nipped the flank of the chestnut. I clearly sensed disdain from her. Vain. She shouldered her rival aside and reached me a nose ahead of the chestnut. I laughed with delight. The chestnut nudged my shoulder. I sensed impatience and pride but not much mind speak. The white stood very still, her nose just touching my hand. *Youngling. Too proud.* Her thoughts entered my mind clearly.

You do not like her?

Stubborn. Child. She whuffed in disdain. *Does not listen.*

But you do listen.

I listen. I choose.

You choose?

Choose you. Friend. Not child.

I need a friend. I also need to ride. Will you carry me?

She took her time, snuffled my head, my body and finally placed her chin on my shoulder. *Friend. I carry.* Then she eyed me and I sensed distaste. *Need back thing? Mouth thing? Not like.*

I am sorry. I fear others will not understand if you do not wear the saddle and bridle. My kind does not usually have the ability to speak with yours.

She thought about that. *See all with them. Not like. I carry. But do not pull mouth thing. Hurts.*

I promise I will not hurt you. I am Liannis. Do you have a name?

Cloud.

Thank you, Cloud. We will be good friends.

Cloud simply whuffled her agreement and rested her chin back on my shoulder. I stroked her neck as I rested my forehead against it.

Apples?

I will find some.

When I broke away it seemed I lost something precious. I turned and looked at Lionn leaning over the rail. "Cloud has asked for apples. I did not think to bring any. Are there some in the stables?"

Lionn gaped. "Asked? She asked for apples?"

"Yes. Do we have any?"

He did his best to recover. "I am sure there are some in the stables. Kersh always keeps some for training. Um. I will see what I can find."

"Wait." my father interrupted. "Liannis, do you sense any danger?"

"No, Papa. I think we are safe."

Lionn ran for the stables. I took the time to take a closer look at

Cloud. She was almost pure white but her hocks and muzzle showed just a hint of grey. Just around her forelegs I detected the beginnings of pale grey markings. So, that is how she chose her name. She was a dapple. Those grey marks would deepen and spread over the years until she was covered with them. Eventually, in her old age she would become almost totally grey. I thought her the most beautiful horse I had ever seen. I loved her.

Lionn came running back, his hands full of last fall's shrivelled apples and handed them to me. "Cloud? Did you name her or did she tell you that?"

I grinned at him. "She told me, of course."

He shook his head, incredulous. Gaelen just smiled and even my father had a half smile.

Gaelen spoke up. "So, Liannis. It seems Cloud has chosen you. She is the one I had picked for you as well, more for her colour and ease of gait. Of course she could not speak to me. But Cloud is yours. May you have many years together."

"My lord. I do not know how I can thank you." Suddenly decorum had no place here. I threw my arms around him and hugged him.

Gaelen laughed as he returned the embrace, his troubles forgotten for the moment. "You are welcome. I have no doubt that I shall be repaid many times over in the years to come."

Cloud mind-spoke me, impatient. *Apples now. Smell apples.*

I quickly turned back to her and held one to her nose. I am sorry Cloud. Here. Six apples. All for you.

She whuffed at me, sounding for all the world like a miffed old woman. I bit back my laugh, knowing she would be insulted.

"Lionn go and ask Kersh for a proper bridle and saddle. I expect Liannis will wish to take Cloud home."

"Kersh is watching us Father. I told him Cloud had asked for apples." A sheepish look came over him. "Oh, I think he must know you are a seer by now. I am sorry. I forgot myself."

"One sign of maturity is being able to stay alert even when surprised by events. You ought to know this by now Lionn." Gaelen shook his head.

"I know Father. I will try to remember."

"See that you do or it may cost you your life or that of your companions."

Lionn looked chagrined. My father stepped in. "I think this lesson will stay with Lionn, my lord. It is the first time he has been in a situation where it might have made a difference."

Lionn gave him a grateful look. "It will, sir, it will."

Kersh chose that moment to bring the tack for Cloud. "This is what she came with, my lord. I bargained for it when I bought her." He held out a beautifully tooled saddle in a pale tan and a matching bridle. Under it, on his arm lay a wool blanket in unbleached white.

Cloud whuffed to get my attention. *Hurt mouth. Liannis promised not to pull.*

I will not forget my promise.

19

TRUCE

I had forgotten the little kestrel in my excitement over finding Cloud. Now, as I mounted my new horse I heard an indignant whistle from above. Kira was flying tight circles high overhead. *Not like horse. Kira am for you.*

Feeling somewhat guilty, I answered, *Hello, Kira. I am happy to see you.*

Not like horse.

Cloud is also my friend. She will carry me. But you are my far eyes, my far seeing friend.

Horse make you forget Kira.

I am sorry, little one. I will not forget you again. I wondered what would smooth Kira's feathers. *Cloud carries me. Shall I ask if she will carry Kira? Do you wish to ride?*

Kira flew off in disdain.

Knowing that she would return eventually, I mind-spoke Cloud. *Thank you for carrying me. Your gait is very smooth. When we get home I will have carrots for you.* I got the impression that Cloud thought this no more than her due and told myself I must be careful not to injure her pride or take her for granted.

As we approached Liethis' cabin, Kira reappeared. *Will you show me what you see, little one?*

Kira agreed but her tone remained aloof.

I surveyed the area carefully and concluded that no others waited nearby. We remained safe for now. I thanked Kira and as I made to return to my own vision she huffed, *Kira ride Liannis.*

I will ask Cloud if she will carry us both. We are here now. Will you wait?

I hunt. She soared off as I dismounted and told Cloud to enjoy the new grass while Lionn and I went inside.

Carrots?

Not until we go home. This is not home.

A wave of nostalgia came over me as I entered the cabin where I had spent so many happy moons learning how to use my gifts. But Liethis' presence had gone and only dust remained. The gust of air when I opened the door lifted the dust into sparkling swirls as the sun danced off the motes. I left the door open to let the light in and remove the stale mustiness that lingered from being shut all winter.

Inside, the cabin looked just as it had when I left it after Liethis' death. Nothing had been moved or taken. Had any ordinary person died and left a cabin such as this, it would soon have found other tenants. But Liethis was a seer and so the cabin had been left untouched, out of respect.

"I have never been here." Lionn's voice betrayed his awe. "So this is where Liethis lived."

"Yes. I wonder if one day I will live here." I walked about and touched the things that had been so familiar to me; the hearth, its kettle still hanging on its hook, now covered in dust, the rough platform that had served as our bed, now bare of straw or blankets, the shelf on the wall with its few pieces of pewter and clay, and the two candle holders. The table sat, now bare of the linen cloth that had always covered it. On the side wall stood the large chest that was the target of my visit today. I knelt by it and ran my hands over its smooth, worn surface. Then I tugged at the wooden peg that held down the latch and lifted the lid. Inside, carefully layered with cedar chips to keep out the moths, lay Liethis' blankets, the cloths for the table, her night-shifts, and on top of these, the treasured whites. I lifted them out reverently and closed the chest back up.

Lionn looked at me and when he spoke I sensed a new respect. "So, it is real. You are a true seer now." He looked both awed and troubled at the same time.

"Yes." I sensed the same feelings in myself and understood. "It is time to leave our childhood behind, Lionn. I don the robes of a true seer and you have just had your first taste of the dangers that await a lord of the demesne."

Lionn nodded slowly and I sensed a sadness from him.

"Lionn, you will always be my best friend. That will not change, my friend and my brother."

He nodded again with a small smile. "But you belong to the One Isle now, as I do to Bargia. It changes things."

"Yes." We stood in silence for a moment. I looked at the whites in my arms and remembered my dream. Outside, Cloud munched on the new grass. It did not reach her hocks yet. "Lionn, I cannot don these for a few days yet. Let us close up and I will take them home in my panniers."

He raised his eyebrows in surprise, then shrugged and nodded.

Both our minds were too full for conversation on the way home. When I saw Kira overhead I decided I had best see how Cloud felt about having a falcon ride on my shoulder. Somehow I needed to stop the rivalry Kira felt.

How had I acquired two such proud friends?

Lionn noticed me give my head a small shake and quirked his brow in question at me in a mirror of his father's gesture. I shook my head and concentrated on Cloud. *Cloud, I have a request...I have another friend. She wishes to ride on my shoulder.* I waited for her curiosity to get the best of her. She pictured another person on my shoulder and knew that could not be what I meant. *Friend?*

I smiled at her puzzlement. *Yes, a very small friend. A bird. A kestrel. Her name is Kira and she lets me use her eyes to see far.*

At first I thought she would refuse. She shut her thoughts off from me. After some time I asked, *Cloud?*

Bird rides on Liannis, not on Cloud, came the grudging reply.

Thank you. I will give you an extra brushing tonight. I allowed myself a sigh of relief then sought Kira. *Kira. Cloud says you may ride on my shoulder.*

She circled several more times, gave a whistle and slowly settled on my left shoulder. Her claws pricked through the wool of my cloak and I told myself I must get a leather perch for her. My father could make something, I was sure.

68

GONE

We stopped off at the city where Lionn left me and Papa joined me for the ride home. The plan was that I would ride back tomorrow with Mama to visit with Lady Marja while Papa stayed with Rellnost

Though I could sense no immediate danger to us as we made our way to the cabin I could not shake a sense of foreboding. The image of those three arrows in the door still stood stark in my mind. I listened as far as my gift would allow as we approached the path that led to the clearing where our home stood.

Not until my father and I cleared the forest did the reason for my feeling become clear.

"Rellnost!" I shouted over my shoulder as I spurred Cloud into a gallop. "He is gone!"

I spotted my mother racing out to meet us at a dead run, waving her arms wildly to get our attention. Both my father and I reached her at the same time.

"He is gone! I do not know how long but I sent him to milk the cow, and when he did not return I went to look for him. He has taken my Kenna."

"Then he could be anywhere." My father uttered a low curse, a measure of how worried he was, as he never spoke thus in front of my mother. "Brensa, stay here in case he returns. Liannis come with me. We must find him." His eyes narrowed suddenly as another thought struck him. "Is he alive?"

I reached out for Rellnost's aura. "Yes, and he lies in that direction. He seems alone. I do not sense others near him." I could see the red sparks in Rellnost's aura that indicated fear and excitement, but no pain. "He remains safe for now."

We had already left my mother behind and galloped in the direction I had indicated, my father two lengths ahead of me. Then he slowed his horse, waiting for me to catch up.

"You lead until I find his trail."

Kira had fled into the sky with my first cry. Now I sent my thought to her. *Little one, I need to find a boy on a horse. He goes to the city. Can you see him?*

Kira circled once, shrilled her klee, klee, and veered off to search.

My father caught my eye and nodded a grim smile of understanding. We kept on in the direction my senses led us.

Papa caught Rellnost's trail at the edge of the forest, confirming what I already suspected. It headed in the direction of the city. "Looks to be about a span old, just starting to dry at the edges. The sun is getting low. It will be harder to follow soon."

I simply nodded and followed. My father was the best tracker in all of the One Isle. If anyone could keep the trail he could. The shadows had almost lengthened into true dusk when Kira's cry made me look up. Have you found him, little one?

Boy stopped. Stands by horse. On path. Men on path. Not see boy. Close.

Thank you, Kira. Lead us to him.

I relayed this information to my father as I followed Kira's lead.

He shouldered himself ahead of me. "I go first. If there is danger I must be ready to fight." He drew his sword out of its scabbard in readiness. By now we had to trust our mounts to find their footing as it had become too dark to see the details of the trial.

Kira circled ahead. There. *Men find boy.*

My father spurred his horse on as the first loud shouts and laughter reached our ears. "You stay back," he ordered over his shoulder.

"Unhand me you brigands! I will have you hanged for this."

"You and whose men, brat. I dinna see anyone riding t'rescue ye."

"Mighty fine mare," came another voice. "Sh'll fetch a fine sum."

"Hey! Wha...?" A clash of steel and a thud.

"Klast, help!" Rellnost cried.

By the time I reached the scene my father had disarmed and knocked one bandit unconscious, his dagger by his side where it had fallen from his fingers. The other faced my father with a knife held at Rellnost's throat.

Rellnost held him self stock still, his eyes wide with fear.

"Let the boy go and I will let you live to see Lord Gaelen's justice. Hurt him and you are both dead men."

"Wha's he to you, old man? We found 'im. The horse be ours."

"He is my grandson and that horse belongs to my wife. Let the boy go."

The man on the ground stirred. I ran and grabbed the knife, placing myself between him and the others.

Without taking his eyes off his opponent my father growled to me, "Hit him on the head again. You know where."

I did indeed know where. My father had taught me the use of weapons and self defence. But I had never actually needed to use those skills. Hitting a defenceless man did not sit well with me. The man stirred again, louder this time and tried to lift his head.

"Hit him! Now!"

As the man's eyes registered my presence, I hesitated no longer. Using the handle of the knife I gave him a practiced *tock* on his temple and watched his eyes roll into his head as he fell bonelessly back. It was the first time I had ever deliberately hurt someone. My stomach lurched in protest.

"Keep Kenna back, Cloud. You stay back, too."

Cloud moved to shoulder Kenna out of the way while Kira circled, whistling her worry.

"Liannis, stay back."

But it looked too much like a standoff. I circled to get behind Rellnost's captor, making sure my newly acquired knife remained visible. The movement caught the bandit's attention for a split second. It was enough. My father's sword pricked at his temple and I saw a small line of red roll down his cheek. His eyes went wide.

"Drop the knife and let him go." The knife fell.

My father grabbed Rellnost and shoved him out of the way. I caught him as he stumbled and pulled him over to the horses.

By the time we reached them the bandit lay on the ground, his face in the dirt and my father's foot on his neck.

"Liannis, the rope on my saddle."

I left Rellnost trembling beside our horses and handed my father the rope. Soon both men were trussed up and hanging face down, one in front of my fathers' saddle and the other across Kenna's back.

Rellnost climbed up in front of me, once I had Cloud's permission.

"Take him home. I will see to these two."

I nodded and turned back. Rellnost said not a word the entire ride, but his trembling had subsided by the time we saw the smoke from our chimney.

My mother ran to meet us. "Liannis! Oh, thank Earth. Is your father all right? What happened? Where is he?"

"He is fine, Mama. He has gone to take two prisoners to the dungeon. I expect he will return in the morning with Kenna."

"Prisoners?" She wrung her hands, her face pinched with worry.

"Let us go inside, Mama. I will tell you while we eat. I am hungry." Feeding us always calmed my mother down. It kept her hands and her mind busy. She nodded quickly and we followed her inside.

71

I looked at Rellnost. "I think you will tell your story to all of us at once. My father needs to hear it first-hand."

He gave a meek nod.

"Now drink some milk and go to bed. You have caused enough trouble today."

He took the mug from my mother, downed it without a word and ascended the ladder to the loft.

"He did not even milk Bess, poor thing. I had to do it myself." Mama shook her head in disbelief as she set down a bowl of stew and a mug of tea in front of me.

21

HARD NEWS

Neither Mama nor I had gone to bed yet when Papa arrived home. When I heard the horses outside I bade Mama wait and went out to the shed to help him stable and groom them. I wanted a few moments alone with him to get his news so he could speak freely outside my mother's hearing. He always shielded her as much as possible from anything that might distress her.

Had Papa had a choice at the time, Rellnost would never have been left in my parent's care. Papa wanted to keep Mama away from such dangerous intrigue. But at the time, no other reasonable solution had presented itself. Secrecy surrounding Rellnost's whereabouts was paramount, and no one else could both train him and maintain that secrecy.

Now I curried Kenna and waited for him to speak. That took some time, and when he finally did speak he avoided my eyes.

"Gaelen agrees the brigands must hang...before they have any opportunity to speak with anyone." He sighed deeply. "If not for Rellnost's identity these deaths might have been avoided."

The usual sentence for such robberies is two years on a work gang repairing the castle walls or working the harvests.

"I am to supervise the hangings the day after tomorrow." Papa raised his head and sent me a grim look. "You may be sure Rellnost will learn how his rashness has caused such unnecessary deaths. And this will change our plans concerning him and his family as well. He can no longer stay here. I cannot allow him to put Brensa in such danger."

I nodded understanding and waited, knowing more would come.

He bent back to his work. "Gaelen has decided, and I agree, that Rellnost is not ready to make any decisions regarding setting up a regency on his behalf. He does not show the strength of character to be a leader, nor the maturity necessary. Perhaps this will come in the future with training. But I fear he has too much of his grandfather, Lord Wernost, in him. He is too headstrong and more concerned with power and status than his responsibilities." He looked up at me again. "I have not said so to you, and your mother would never complain, being too soft of heart, but Rellnost has treated Brensa rudely from the start. He shows no gratitude for the efforts being made on his behalf. He makes demands that tell me he feels she is his servant, and not that he is a guest in our home, and a guest of Bargia and Lord Gaelen. Unless that attitude changes I fear he will never make a good lord."

He had gone back to his grooming and spoken quietly. I knew what it cost him to tell me this. It was I who had brought Rellnost here. He regretted that he must disappoint me.

"I understand, Papa. For his own sake, too, other lodging must be found for him. This location is no longer safe for any of you."

He hung up the curry-brush and we both reached for some hay before he continued.

"Gaelen has decided he will support Dugal's claim first. It will give Rellnost another year to show if he has the makings of a leader." When he met my eyes I nodded for him to continue. "And Gaelen wishes you to be present when we bring this news to Lady Nairin. He fears she will not take it well. Of course she and her children will continue to be honoured guests. And when it becomes known that they will mount no immediate challenge to those who killed Merlost, perhaps they can be afforded more freedom in time, though their safety must still be safeguarded."

"How soon does Lord Gaelen want her to be told?"

"Tomorrow."

"So soon?"

"Yes, and Rellnost will be coming. He needs to hear it at the same time."

"But..."

Papa made a cutting gesture with his hand. "Rellnost wishes to see her and she him. He needs to be away from here. And he needs to be present when Lord Gaelen presents the news to Lady Nairin." His voice took on its 'I will not be swayed' tone. "Liannis, Rellnost needs to learn now, not later, that his actions have consequences, and not for himself alone. It is a lesson every leader must learn. His parents have indulged him too much and neglected his training."

I nodded sadly as Papa reached for the latch to the cabin. He was right. I just wished it could be different.

As we entered he looked at my mother and raised an eyebrow in question, cocking his head in the direction of the loft.

"Asleep," she said and handed him a mug of tea. A plate of cold fowl and a chunk of bread awaited him on the table.

"He is," I agreed.

"He will be gone tomorrow, Brensa. He will be a danger to you no longer. Gaelen has decided not to support his claim for the time being. He is not ready."

"Klast I think he just wanted to see his mother. He is still a boy."

"Boy or no, he wants to be Lord some day. He is old enough to learn that he must think before he acts." And that was that. After a few bites he gave her a rueful smile and said, more kindly, "He needs to learn quickly, Brensa, or he will never attain his birthright. He must leave boyhood behind. By his age Gaelen had already learned so much more."

"I know, but I wish he had more time. His life has been hard." She went to stand behind Papa and kneaded his shoulders. My mother had a small gift of healing and my father groaned in gratitude as his muscles began to lose their tension.

I rose and grabbed my blanket and pillow. "I will sleep in the shed tonight. I will be warm enough with the animals there."

Mama looked about to protest, but when Papa nodded, she changed her mind. We all understood that Papa needed to stay in to cabin to guard it or he would have given me his place. And I would be more comfortable in the shed than on the table.

22

TO BARGIA CITY

In accordance with everyone's mood, the morning dawned cold and wet. A penetrating drizzle soon had us reaching for our oiled leather capes.

Rellnost went disguised as a girl in my mother's cloak, she being closest to him in size, hood firmly up around his chin to hide his short hair and a skirt over his trousers. This did nothing to improve his mood but he knew better than to protest too much.

My father had given him no explanation other than we were going to see his mother, but his meagre belongings had been packed in my father's saddle-bags, so I think he knew he would not be coming back. Nor did he ask any questions. I saw them in his eyes when he looked at me from time to time, but I shook my head and he held his tongue. He rode perched in front of my father, whose grim, silent presence told him he would get nothing from that quarter.

When we passed the spot where he had been ambushed his eyes flashed for a moment with remembered fear, telling me he understood just how close he had come to losing his life and how foolish his flight had been.

As we entered the city I watched him take it all in, his head swivelling back and forth with avid interest, his sulk and fear forgotten. When his hood threatened to slip from his head my father growled at him, and he hastily pulled it back up and tightened it under his chin. But he kept his head up and it seemed he was trying to memorize our route. Much good it would do him. My father led us in such a roundabout way even an experienced soldier would not be able to recall it. He had not been Gaelen's best spy and head of his personal guard without becoming expert at such skills. I knew the area well and even I had trouble following our path.

Once inside the city walls I broke off from them and went ahead to prepare Nairin. I knew Gaelen waited inside the castle to meet my father. The four would join us in a few moments, approaching by a more obscure way. Papa had not been able to talk him into an armed escort yet since the incident with the arrows, so he was taking no chances with his safety.

On inspecting the council chamber they had decided that the only way the assassin could have left was by the hidden door behind the tapestry, which they had discovered unlocked. One concession Gaelen now agreed to was that a solid bar be added in front of it. Previously it had had only a weak latch, as they assumed no one knew of its existence.

Gaelen had also posted two guards outside the council chamber with orders to report anyone who came and went, no matter how legitimate their business.

Papa had told me he was still working on getting Gaelen to agree to at least one elite guard as escort for both he and Lionn when they left the castle's protective walls. That had been my father's duty years ago, when Gaelen had first come to power. But we had enjoyed peace for so long that Gaelen had abandoned the precaution, over my father's continued protests.

I guided Cloud through the familiar streets by thought, holding the reins loosely so that no one would think it strange, and dismounted in front of the house where Nairin and the children stayed. At my rap and the code word, the door opened. Blenniss admitted me, quickly shutting and locking it again behind me. "My Lady is still at table drinking her morning tea."

"That is fine, Blenniss. I will find her there. How are the children?" I knew she had a soft spot for Leyla.

"They are well but wishing they could spend more time out of doors, now that the weather is getting warmer." She dimpled a smile. "Leyla has learned a new song. She has a sweet voice."

I returned her smile. "They are lucky to have you here with them, Blenniss. And you may expect Lord Gaelen, who will be coming with Rellnost and Klast in a few moments. Please admit them. They know the pass code."

Blenniss nodded, opened the door to the eating room, announced me and withdrew.

Nairin rose to greet me, eyebrows raised in surprise. "Liannis! It is good to see you. What brings you so early?" Her face fell. "Earth, not bad news I hope. Is Rellnost well?"

"Rellnost is fine, my lady. In fact he is on his way to see you here, along with Lord Gaelen."

Her face lit up at that, then became full of concern again as I recounted Rellnost's escapade of the previous day, her hand flying to her mouth at the part where he had been held at knifepoint.

Before she could respond the door opened and Blenniss announced Lord Gaelen. My father followed with a restraining hand firmly on Rellnost's shoulder to prevent him from darting forward into his mother's arms. He glared in fury but kept his silence. I wondered what Papa had said to him to prevent the litany of complaints I had expected to hear.

Nairin curtseyed. "My lord, please be welcome. You honour me. Blenniss, please bring refreshments for our guests." Her duty done, she turned at last to Rellnost as my father removed his hand. "Rellnost! Earth, how I have missed you." She opened her arms and Rellnost allowed himself to be hugged, glancing over his shoulder at my father to make sure it was permitted.

"Mama, I missed you too." His voice quavered but he held back his tears.

Nairin, too, brought her composure under control, though the two clung to each other for a time. Finally, remembering her duty, Nairin broke away and faced Gaelen. "My lord, Liannis, please be seated."

My father, with that uncanny ability of his to appear so inconsequential as to render him almost invisible had already retreated into a corner. He stood there at ease, observing all that went on, in detail, so that he could speak with Gaelen about it later and offer him his impressions. I knew he also kept himself ready to defend Gaelen should that be necessary, though by his disinterested appearance others would not see that.

Before we were all well seated Blenniss knocked, and at Nairin's, "Enter," brought in a tray laden with honey cakes, fresh butter, soft cheese and dark fragrant bread. She was followed by the scullery maid bearing another tray with cups and a large pot of sage tea. Both scurried out as soon as the trays had been placed on the table.

Nairin busied herself with pouring and had Rellnost hand around the filled cups. Then, no longer able to avoid it, she sat back with her own cup and addressed Gaelen. "My lord, while I am honoured by your presence, from what Liannis has already told me, I understand that this is not a social visit. I am aware of what happened yesterday and that this meeting concerns Rellnost." She gave her son an admonishing look. "Rellnost will sit and listen. He will speak only when asked."

Rellnost flashed her a surprised, angry look then lowered his eyes and played with his fingers.

"Indeed, my lady. I fear that what I have to say will disappoint you." Gaelen explained in detail all of the behaviours and attitudes Rellnost had shown that led to Gaelen's conclusion that he was not ready to pursue lordship and that even a regency would not be advisable at this time.

I watched Nairin sag more and more as Gaelen spoke. She could see the logic and the truth in what he told her, but it was evident that it was not what she wanted to hear.

"So, my lady, I have decided that for the time being I cannot support a campaign against your enemies in Lieth. Perhaps a year from now, or two, that may change. First, Rellnost needs much further training. Even then I will need to see him develop strength of character and maturity. I must be convinced that risking my people in battle will result in better government in Lieth and in greater peace for both our peoples. But I have pledged myself to your safety and that of your children. You will remain as guests of my court and I will welcome the opportunity to see to the education and training of both your sons."

Rellnost could hold still no longer. "But I am Lord of Lieth!"

Nairin rounded on him. "No Rellnost! You are merely a guest, here on the sufferance of Lord Gaelen, to whom we all owe our lives. Try to remember that!" Nairin's voice had risen to such an angry pitch that Rellnost reacted with a shocked jerk. His mother had apparently never spoken to him in this way.

Nairin turned back to Gaelen and sighed. "Thank you, my lord. I am afraid I have indulged my son too much. His father spoke of the need for his training but would not gainsay me when I argued to allow him to be a boy a little longer. Now I see our error." She turned to Rellnost, who looked about to protest, but at a stern look from her, waited to hear what she would say. "Rellnost, you have heard. I have done you a grave disservice by giving in to you too much. Now I will do my duty, painful though I find it, and give you into Lord Gaelen's care, to train and educate you as a lord ought to be."

Rellnost's eyes widened in surprise at first. Then his expression became hurt and angry. He jumped up and looked about to challenge her, his fists clenched and his body rigid.

Before he could speak his mother made a cutting motion with her hand to silence him. "No, my son. This is as it must be. If you are ever to reclaim your place as Lord of Lieth, you must become a man. I have spoiled you. I have made it more difficult for you to learn that lords cannot always have what they wish. Good leaders do what is best for their people, not what they wish for themselves." She shook her head sadly. "And I am ashamed that you have placed me in the position where I must apologize to Klast and Brensa for your lack of gratitude. Such behaviour is inexcusable." Tears filled her eyes and she blinked them back angrily. "Know that I blame myself for this. And that I love you. I will always love you. You are my son. That will never change. But it is decided. You cannot change my mind. I must do now what I ought to have done long since."

"But..."

She cut him off with an impatient gesture. "No, Rellnost. It is as it should be. Do not shame me further with childish complaints."

She squared her shoulders and faced Gaelen. "My lord, where will you take him?"

"My lady, you have been separated from your son these three eightdays. I think we may keep you all safe together for a day or two. His training can wait until then. Spend some time together. I expect you will have much to say to each other. Then he will join the other lads in the barracks to begin he training as a soldier."

Rellnost gawked in surprise at the temporary reprieve. Nairin's eyes filled with fresh tears. This time she could not hold them back. "Thank you, my lord. We are most grateful. You may be sure that I will speak to him again of what I expect from him."

Gaelen rose, indicating the meeting over. Nairin and I followed while my father once more came to stand behind Gaelen. "In two days time then, my lady...Rellnost."

23

CAMPAIGN

"Klast, when we reach the castle find Lord Dugal and meet us in the council chamber. He is to come alone."

"My lord, I will send someone for him and accompany you. The council chamber may not be secure."

Gaelen smiled as he met his eyes. "As you wish my friend. Though I think Liannis could tell if there were danger present."

"Earth does not show me everything, my lord," I protested. "I think it is a wise precaution. There is much unrest. Two of our neighbours are under siege by traitors. This can have unpredictable effects on Earth's power to keep me abreast and to keep you and your family safe. You must not rely on me overmuch." I thought a moment before deciding it would not be too bold of me to add, "I agree with my father. You would be wise to go escorted by an armed guard, two of your elite as you used to do. And Lionn as well. The people are aware of events in Gharn and will soon hear about Lieth, so will not take it amiss."

Gaelen started to protest but my father cut him off. "Liannis is right, my lord. The people know that you are no coward. They will not see it as lack of confidence...and do not forget that treachery can be found even among your closest. Until we find who is responsible for the incident in the council chamber we cannot be certain it is not one of our own."

My father referred again to Sinnath, the trusted advisor to Gaelen's father who turned traitor when Gaelen came to power. It had been a hard lesson for him.

Gaelen hailed a passing maid as we entered the castle and ordered food and ale for the meeting.

My father hailed a guard who hurried off to fetch Dugal. Papa stopped another. "Guard, is Lionn at weapons practice?"

"Yes, my lord."

"Summon him immediately to the council chamber."

As we passed through the Great Hall, Lady Marja came to meet us. "I am glad to catch you all together. Liannis, Sennia has just returned with Mikost and Nellis from her eightday in Catania. I hope we can all dine together soon. They were so disappointed to have missed you last time. You are away so much it is seldom we are all in the same place at the same time." She slipped her arm through Gaelen's and smiled up at him. "And you must tell Lionn to come as well. It will be like old times."

Gaelen returned her smile fondly. Theirs had, in spite of an inauspicious beginning, become a true love match, and he found it hard to refuse her.

"An excellent idea my love." He turned to me. "And now that Rellnost is no longer in your care, Klast, you and Brensa must come as well. I am sure she will enjoy being at court again after so long away alone."

I looked at my father. As usual, his face remained inscrutable to all save me. Only I could detect the wry twitch at the corner of his eyes that told me he understood how I had been neatly cornered.

"I am sure we will all look forward to it, my lady," I smiled. "All of my favourite people in one chamber. Will tomorrow be all right?"

Marja beamed. "I shall tell the cook to make the egg custard that you like so well Liannis...and honey cakes for Brensa." She still had a lively grace about her when she moved, that made her seem younger than her years in spite of the grey that peppered her russet hair. Mama had been her maid and best friend even before she met Gaelen. So it had been natural that when Lionn and I were born less than a year apart we should become playmates. I loved her as I would a dear aunt. Now that I had learned to dampen the barrage of noise in my head from so many people around, I could endure a day or two at court again.

Gaelen surprised me with sudden foresight as he asked, "Would you prefer to use Liethis' old chamber for our visit? I know it shuts out some of the pain for you."

Marja grew immediately contrite. "Of course, Liannis. I forgot for a moment how hard it is for you here at court."

I smiled, relieved. "Thank you, my lord that would be helpful. And do not feel badly, my lady. It is hard to think of things that one does not personally experience. I truly do look forward to a visit."

As we left the Great Hall I asked, "My lord, do you wish me to be present when you meet with Dugal? If so, I think it might help if I donned my whites first. They are still in my panniers. I have not had time to remove them." Two days of sun had helped the grass grow to the length in my vision so I knew I could wear them.

"Yes, I think that is wise. Can you meet us there when you are ready?"

I nodded and hurried to the stables. Finally. My whites. I felt elated and apprehensive at the same time. This began a whole new chapter in my life. I hoped I could live up to the responsibility that came with the honour.

24

STRATEGY

I watched Dugal enter the council chamber just as I approached, so he did not see me. When I took my seat at the table he gawked openly, unable to hide his surprise.

I laughed. "Yes, Lord Dugal, I am a seer. Now you know why I had to travel with you when you came to Bargia. My apprenticeship is over. Once again, I thank you and your men for rescuing me. You have done Earth a great service."

Gaelen gave him no time to respond. "So you see, Lord Dugal, how Liannis' confidence in you has affected our willingness to hear your cause. She has assured us that you can be trusted."

Dugal bent forward in a formal sitting bow. "My lord, Liannis, I am most grateful. It seems I am once again surprised."

Gaelen nodded. "I have asked you here today to say that I will put my personal recommendation behind your request to support your claim." When Dugal's face split into an eager grin Gaelen cut him off. "That does not mean that my advisors will support my decision. While I do believe I can convince them to it, this is not my decision alone. I learned long ago, when not much older than you in fact, that it is best to listen to sound advice. Then, decisions that may be unpopular with the people will have the full support of the council. That support carries a good deal of weight."

I understood the lesson in his speech. Gaelen was subtly teaching Dugal about leadership.

Dugal sobered. This time he thought a moment before answering. "My lord, any help I receive will be met with gratitude. What can I do to help my cause?"

I sensed Gaelen's and my father's satisfaction. Dugal had taken the hint quickly.

"I need to know all you can tell me about the traitors and who their supporters are. Also, how many men you can call on to fight at your signal. How well armed and trained are they? What is your sense of the mood of your people in Gharn? Do they favour you or your enemies?"

When Dugal had told us all he could I raised my hand to be heard. "My lord, Lord Dugal, I must remind you that all battles, even when justified, cause Earth pain. War upsets the Balance and when the Balance is disrupted we may expect unpleasant results. I do not know what those may be but we may be sure that they will occur. Please remember this when you plan your strategy. Bloodshed always has consequences." I could almost feel Earth's pain already at the mere contemplation of battle.

All three nodded soberly. When Gaelen was satisfied that he had all the information Dugal could give, he rose. "Thank you. I will present this to the council."

My father checked the hall before we left. "About that personal escort, my lord."

Gaelen sighed. "I will see to it." He called out to the guard at the end of the hall. "Gorn."

"My lord?"

"Find Kerroll and tell him I need to speak to him."

"Yes, my lord." Gorn hurried away.

"Does that satisfy you, my friend?" He gave my father a wry look.

Papa remained serious. "Only if it results in my seeing an armed escort with you and Lionn next time I see either of you."

I hid my smile behind my hand.

Gaelen's eyes twinkled. "Only one?" he teased.

Papa caught the joke. "Well, I do think three would be better, but if you can only spare one I suppose it will have to do." This time he, too, managed a small smile.

As we entered the Great Hall, and my father and I headed out for home, Gaelen said, "I would like you both present at the council meeting tomorrow." We both nodded.

"Oh, and you look very official in your whites, Liannis. It is good to have a seer to call on again."

25

INVASION

My decision to make Liethis' old cabin my home was met with mixed feelings. Mama wanted me closer to her. She would miss me and knew that my duties would make my visits home farther apart now that I wore the whites. Papa on the other hand agreed. My presence at home would bring unwanted visitors. Their home had been chosen precisely because it afforded much needed privacy for my father. Not only did his extremely solitary nature require it, but it helped to keep his cover as a spy secret and so lent a measure of safety.

Though he seldom went on missions for Lord Gaelen any more, the decision to support Dugal and invade Gharn on his behalf made it likely my father's services would be required. He was no longer a young man. The knowledge that he might be needed filled me with foreboding, though I could not have said why. Earth had not shown me anything. I tried to tell myself I felt only normal concern.

Gaelen also felt it best. Liethis' cabin lay on a known path outside the city and was easier to reach should he need my services.

As I settled into my new home, Cloud and Kira grew accustomed to each other and formed a grudging truce. Kira now rode on a pad of hardened leather which cupped my shoulder and was held in place by a thong. My father had fashioned it for me after seeing the deep scratches her sharp talons left when she took off in flight.

Bargia's troops left for Gharn a mere eightday after the meeting with Dugal. They planned to meet with some of Dugal's supporters hiding deep in the woods just inside the western border of Gharn, near my rescuers' safe-house. Another band would be ready on the south side, in a copse where they could not be seen from the city walls. Dugal would also have men inside. They were to make certain the gates opened long enough to get men inside before the alarm went out and his enemies could gather support.

A small band would approach the wall at each gate unseen by night and hide against its base waiting for it to open. If four gates opened, resistance would be futile, three and victory remained almost a certainty, only two and we would be in difficulty as no one could predict the outcome.

Earth gave me no hints how it would go. Perhaps she did not know herself. War always caused her such pain.

I sent Kira out periodically to help me see the progress of Gaelen's troops. After a few forays learned I the limits of our mind-speak and the range of our combined sight. In order to see clearly when Gaelen approached, I decided to follow at a safe distance. I set up a temporary camp deep in the woods a short ride from the city of Gharn, still just within the border of Bargia. I warned Kira each time I sent her out to stay high, as men might capture her, falconers or those who could sell her to one. She had grown accustomed to my father, Lionn and Gaelen and had lost much of her natural fear of humans. It worried me.

My gift of seeing made it impossible for me to be near the fighting so Kira became my source of information. Through her eyes I could see and still avoid some of the flood of emotions and impressions that battered me when among large groups. In spite of her limited intelligence she soon caught on to our routine and learned what I needed from her. She preened with delight when I praised her.

When Gaelen's force approached the meeting place with Dugal, I sent Kira ahead to scan the woods where his men waited. What I saw made my heart sink. While their numbers were close to what Dugal predicted, the men looked poorly armed and disorganized. I hoped the men inside the gates knew their duty and were better prepared.

So much hung on these men. The attack would begin at dawn in two days. And still Earth remained quiet.

That night I sought the auras of Dugal, Larn, Farsh and Merrist. I found Dugal with Merrist at the meeting place. Farsh and Larn however, had slipped inside the city, Larn near the main gate, the west one, and Farsh at the second busiest in the south. Both their auras bore sparks of red and orange from their heightened anticipation. At least they would be alert and ready. I wondered who Dugal had at the north and east gates. Were they loyal?

Sleep eluded me the night before the attack. Dawn found me checking in once more on my friends and those I loved. When I could wait no longer I sent Kira to fly over each of the gates. *Stay high little one. Do not get too close.*

Within minutes I could see the west gate, the one that was usually the most heavily guarded. I felt a wash of relief when I saw that it stood open. The men outside the wall poured into the city and became immediately engaged in hand to hand combat. Across the open space between the forest and the wall I could see a cadre of mounted soldiers, followed by a cloud of dust as their mounts surged toward the gate, long swords raised. Gaelen's men took the lead. Dugal's few, less well trained horsemen followed close behind. Just as they attained the gate I saw three bleeding guards make a vain attempt to close it. They were cut down. Kira circled unaware of the stabbing pain the scene caused me.

She arced to the south gate, just as I had instructed her. There the gate remained closed and my heart lurched in fear. Outside the gate about twenty men hid in the shadow of the wall. When the gate did not open they began to crowd in front of it shouting. Inside the gate a smaller group of men fought. All wore the gold and green tunics of Gharn, making it impossible to tell which side they were on. Unaware of how important the outcome of that skirmish was, Kira circled once more, this time to the eastern gate. This one stood open, and here too, men in both the gold and green of Gharn and the yellow and blue of Bargia fought. No cavalry entered here. There had been no place to hide them.

I spotted Lionn, his back against the guard hut, matching swords with an older man in gold and green. Lionn parried a tired thrust and ran the man through, then rushed to the aid of a Bargian in blue and yellow, his sword dripping.

Again Kira flew off, this time to the final gate, the north gate. This gate saw little traffic and as such was both poorly maintained and inadequately guarded. The wood looked dry and brittle, with cracks of light showing through between the planks. Yet it stood closed. Inside, a small group of about ten men in green and gold fought each other. As soon as one managed to get close enough to the gate to open it, another engaged him to prevent it. Outside, the waiting men conferred. Then, as a unit, they began to surge toward the gate and throw their shoulders into it. With each thrust I could see the gate bow inward. Then, through Kira's keen ears, I heard a loud crack. One plank had broken. As soon as the men outside saw this a shout went up and one thrust his sword into the break and lifted the bar off its bracket. The gate swung inward and the waiting soldiers surged forward.

Kira flew back to me. I wanted her to go back to the south gate to see if the gate had finally opened, but that had not been in my instructions to her, and she was too excited by all the noise to listen to new ones.

Hunt, she declared and began to scan the ground for mice.

Reluctantly, I let her go. I knew the long flight had depleted her energy and she needed to feed. I would have to wait for further information. I, too, felt tired and hungry so I went back to my shelter where tea and porridge awaited me.

I did one last thing before settling down for my meal. I searched for my father's aura. Gaelen had given him orders when we left to stay clear of the fighting, telling him he needed one trusted advisor well and able, and that he could not risk having Klast injured or killed.

"You have done your share of fighting and spying for me. Your use to me as advisor is too great to risk losing you."

In his usual fashion my father had protested, but Gaelen had remained adamant and my father had to obey. So he had accompanied Gaelen only until they reached the woods at Gharn's border and promised to do nothing more than border scouting.

I found his aura immediately, much to my surprise. The reason soon became apparent. He melted out of the woods beside my lean-to and gave me a sheepish smile.

"Hello daughter. I came to see how you fared." He looked at my small fire. "Is that tea I see by the fire?"

"Papa, it is so good to see you." After a bear hug he let me go and produced a mug and a small parcel from his pack wrapped tightly in oiled leather. "Honey...from a hive I found on the way." He handed them both to me, his eyes crinkling at my pleased grin. From his other hand dangled a pair of rabbits. "I will skin these and we will have meat for supper. You may prepare the spit."

"Save the entrails for Kira. Then she will not need to hunt when I next send her out." I filled the mugs with tea and set them aside while I stoked up the fire and found some suitable branches for the spit.

We shared my tea and porridge in companionable silence, as we watched the meat roast, its aroma filling our nostrils with the promise of filling fare.

Without looking at me, unsuccessfully feigning nonchalance, he asked. "What news have you? How do Gaelen and Lionn fare?" He looked sideways at me waiting for my answer.

"I have seen nothing for at least a span, now. Kira hunts and so I cannot send her back yet. But I will tell you what she has shown me thus far. I must tell you that Dugal's troops were ill prepared. Understandable, since he has not been present to see to their training, but it means the outcome is much less certain." I shared with him all Kira had shown me. He interrupted only once to ask for more detail about the numbers and condition of Dugal's men.

Darkness fell as we talked, and when the moon began to rise behind the branches of the trees, Kira flew back. *Man back? Good man? Come down?*

Yes, Kira, this is a good man. You may come down. Good hunt?

Good. Kira full. Sleep. She flew down and settled on her perch on a stick I had set in the ground away from the fire.

Yes, sleep little one. You have done well today. I watched her tuck her head under her small wing, fluff her feathers and give a small chirrup.

My father shook his head mildly in wonder. "I have never seen such a bond before."

"Yes, but I worry that she may become too tame, that she will place herself in danger to please me."

Papa nodded his understanding. Then he rose to check on the horses, banked the fire, and we lay out our blankets. I slept soundly, secure in the knowledge that my father was with me. We were both safe, at least for this night.

26

MERRIST

When I woke at dawn tea already sat to the side of the fire and the left-over porridge from the evening before had been warmed up.

His senses as keen as ever, my father noticed immediately when I woke, and reached for a mug to pour me tea. "Good morning, Daughter. You slept soundly." His mouth quirked in a teasing smile.

I took the proffered mug. "Yes, you were here. I knew I was safe." I looked around. "Where is Kira?"

"Making a meal of the rabbit entrails." He handed me a bowl. "Here, eat. I must go."

"I can send Kira out before you leave. She may tell you more than you will find yourself."

"Then do so quickly. I plan to meet with Gaelen by midday."

Kira, will you fly for me, little one?

Kira chirped in indignation at having her meal interrupted but came obediently to my shoulder. I gave her instructions to fly over the city of Gharn and show me what she saw. But fly high. Do not get caught.

"I must head toward the city, Liannis. Will she find you if we ride there?"

"She will find me wherever I am, Papa."

"Then ride with me as we wait for her to return."

He gave me a leg up onto Cloud. Neither his keen senses nor my sight hinted at any danger and so we rode easily, enjoying the warmth of the sun on our backs after the chill of the night.

See? Kira had reached the wall around the city.

Yes. Show me what you see.

The sight that met me made me sway in my saddle and almost lose my seat. My father grabbed my arm to steady me and waited.

Devastation littered the streets. In the public square pyres burned, one for each side. More bodies waited nearby for their turn in the flames. I strained to see the colours of their tunics. Who had suffered the greatest losses? I could not tell. I saw too many of both the gold and green of Gharn and the blue and yellow of Bargia; far too many. But I did not see fighting. Whatever the outcome, it was over. Here and there citizens put out the last of the fires. Soldiers wearing both colours moved about, seeming to give orders and organize the cleanup. Good. That meant that at least we had prevailed; but at what cost? To one side of the central square guards wearing both colours kept a small group of men standing. Some in gold and green tunics, some in common dress.

"Dugal has prevailed. We have victory." I knew my tone showed my horror. They were the only words I could force out. *Find friends, Kira.*

Kira over-flew the entire city. While I saw familiar faces among the cleanup crew and guards, some with bandaged arms and heads, she could find none of those I cared most for. *Not here? Inside?*

Yes, they must be inside. Thank you little one. You may come back.

Breaking the link I turned to my father and told him what Kira had shown me. "Now I must see if I can find their auras. Can you wait? I cannot ride while I seek them."

He nodded, grim-faced. "I must. I have to know before I go to them."

He helped me off Cloud and I sat in the grass. Breathing deeply to compose myself I asked Earth to show me those I sought. I found Gaelen and Lionn together and sensed horses nearby. Perhaps they were saddling up for the meeting with my father. Gaelen seemed unhurt, though his aura showed an overlay of grey, no doubt from fatigue. Lionn's aura looked strong but was shot with red, possibly the result of an injury, though the knowledge that he accompanied Gaelen suggested it was not serious. I found Dugal in the castle, Larn and Farsh close by. All showed the grey of fatigue, and Farsh seemed injured. Dugal and Larn showed no signs of injury. Merrist was not with them so I sent my probe further to find him. There! His usual cool green showed shot through with the bright red of pain and orange of fear, the signs of serious injury. That he was separated from his friends also told me that his injuries kept him off his feet. Poor, gentle-hearted Merrist, innocent no longer. My heart wept for him.

I opened my eyes to see my father's face filled with alarm and concern. Some of it was for me, I knew. These efforts always took a toll on me. "They all live," I managed and took a deep draft of the water-skin he handed to me. Then I told him, in detail, all I had learned.

His relief was almost palpable. Then he took in my exhaustion. "Daughter, I have no choice. My duty to Gaelen makes it necessary to leave you. Will you be all right?"

I managed a tired smile. "Yes Papa. I have done this many times. I will recover. Go, and send back what news you can. Especially about Merrist. I fear for him." It did not occur to me to wonder why he mattered so much.

Though I knew Papa would not be fooled, yet I made the attempt not to show how exhausted the seeing had left me as I waved goodbye and watched him disappear toward Gharn City. When he blurred into the dust on the horizon, I turned Cloud back toward my small camp. By now the sun rose high and its heat lulled me into lethargy. My head nodded and I left it to Cloud to find our way back. Kira had by now flown back to me and settled on her perch on my shoulder.

A blaze of fire shot through my leg and I felt myself slide from Cloud's back, unable to break my fall as unconsciousness claimed me. I did not feel the earth as I landed.

* * *

Merrist lay on the rough table, a piece of wood between his teeth. Two burly men held him down by the shoulders, another held his right leg. Even so, he bucked, swinging his head wildly from side to side as foam flew from his mouth around the wood. Then I saw the reason. A fourth man wielded a saw just below his left knee. Above the knee a twist of rope, knotted tightly, staunched the flow of blood. Nearby in a fire, a man waited with a sword heated to red, to cauterize the wound when the cutting finished. At the third stroke Merrist fell lax and silent, no longer aware. The men who held him loosened their grip slightly but remained alert, lest he wake again. At the back of the chamber I spotted Larn weeping unashamedly. No doubt he had been sent by Dugal to stay with their friend.

The surgeon worked swiftly. He handed the severed stump to a waiting guard, who took it out to the pyre, and gestured to the other who nodded, grabbed the sword and brought it to the surgeon. At the first touch Merrist woke long enough to buck, scream and swoon again. The bleeding staunched, the surgeon quickly packed a clean cloth around the stump and bandaged it tightly. He nodded to Larn, who, with the help of another, moved Merrist onto a board that served as a stretcher and bore him out.

I followed their progress as they moved him to a small chamber inside the castle, where they tucked him carefully into a feather-bed.

Another man followed them in and placed a sac of herbs next to the brazier. Poppy for sleep, he said, and willow bark for pain, to be made into a tea and given to Merrist as soon as he woke.

Larn nodded understanding and took a stool by the bed to keep watch. He looked haggard and the horror had not yet left his face.

* * *

I came to with my face drenched in tears, the last vestiges of pain in my leg from the vision not yet fully faded. Cloud nudged me with her wet nose and Kira hopped anxiously about chirruping in distress. The sun blazed in my eyes and my mouth felt like cotton. The effort to raise my head set it to pounding, but I had to see. To my great relief I confirmed that my leg was still whole. And it appeared my fall had not damaged me aside from a few bruises. With that knowledge the last of the pain ebbed.

Water. I needed water. My water-skin still hung from the saddle. Cloud could not untie it for me and it was too heavy for Kira. But Cloud seemed to intuit my need without even mind-speak because she lowered herself beside me so that I could reach it without getting up. I took a long drink and rolled back onto the grass. I will be all right. Cloud, give me shade, please. I sensed both animals calm down and I fell promptly asleep.

I woke to Cloud nudging me firmly. A look at the sky told me that darkness would soon hide our path back to camp. But Cloud assured me she could find the way. As I remained too weak to mount her the regular way, she lowered herself beside me and let me pull myself onto her back by holding onto her mane. I clung to her neck, my face buried in it as she bore me back to camp. Kira, unable to sit her usual perch, circled above us emitting the occasional worried chirrup to keep me awake when she sensed I was about to fall off again.

Back at camp, too fatigued to eat, I fell into a deep sleep until the smell of fresh meat roasting woke me. That could only mean one thing. "Good morning Papa." I enjoyed the satisfaction of having caught him off-guard as he turned in surprise to see me awake. Then the impact of my vision hit me again. I half rose in alarm. "Merrist..."

"He lives, though he will never be a soldier again. What did Earth show you?"

"I saw the amputation. Earth, what will become of him now?"

He shrugged. "I know not. I do not think Dugal will allow him to starve. He will learn some useful task." He roughed his cheeks with his hands as if to wipe away his weariness. His face looked grey, and I thought he had aged ten years overnight. "I think he still does not fully understand that the leg is gone. He has been in and out of awareness with fever. The biggest concern now is that it may fester and even more will need to be taken. Now he still has a stump that a wooden peg may be attached to. Such a shame. I like the lad."

"He was so kind to me and so disappointed to find I am a seer. I know he fancied himself in love with me. Poor Merrist. Why can men not honour Earth by finding solutions that do not shed blood? It is not only themselves they harm, but every drop shed in anger, wounds Earth, too." I pricked back tears of both compassion and sadness.

"I fear it is in our nature to take by force what we cannot have by right. It has always been thus."

I shook my head, partly in denial, partly in sadness that he might be right. "Perhaps that is why Earth is a goddess. Men need her feminine attributes to balance men's nature to control rather than seek harmony." I rubbed my leg where the memory of my vision still lingered. "But I wish we did not hurt her so."

"Perhaps." His agreement was more noncommittal than assent. He handed me my bowl filled with meat and porridge and a mug of fresh white pine needle tea.

I inhaled the aroma from the cup gratefully. "You remembered, too. I thought only Mama knew this is my favourite."

"I thought you knew better than to underestimate me." He kept his face stern but I detected the teasing glitter in his eyes and grinned back.

We ate in silence before I asked him to tell me what he had learned in the city.

"That is why I have returned. Gaelen and Dugal want me to bring you there so you can be present at the council meetings. We need your ability to truth-read and any impressions you can gather there. Gaelen remembered to explain your need for a stone chamber in the heart of the castle, so you may get at least some sleep. One will be ready for you when we arrive." His face grew graver. "I am sorry, Liannis. I know how difficult it will be for you in the city after so much bloodshed and anger. It cannot be helped."

I sighed, resigned. I had known this would come. "Then I had best eat a lot now, for I will not be able to swallow much there."

He nodded understanding and pulled another hind leg off the roasted rabbit and handed it to me.

"At least I will be able to look in on poor Merrist." I said.

Our meal finished, we gathered up my small camp, loaded the horses and rode to the city. We spoke very little, my father too weary for conversation, and I thinking ahead to what I must face.

27

GHARN CITY

I could feel the waves of pain, horror and hate even before we reached the gate of Gharn City. It was well that I had eaten spans before. Otherwise I could not have held my meal. My stomach roiled and my head pounded. I longed to flee. Earth, keep me strong. It became a silent chant as we approached.

Kira you must stay high. It is not safe for you near me in the city. Cloud, you must let the groom stable and curry you. Both let me know this did not sit well with them but agreed to obey.

Kira flew off toward the top of a watchtower where she settled to wait. I told her she could hunt as I would be a long time but I did not see her budge.

When we got to the stables, a young groom took both our mounts, though not before Cloud had made her displeasure clear, causing the young groom to blanch. My father led me directly into the castle where a guard took in my whites and made haste to lead us to the council chamber.

"Welcome. Lord Dugal is expecting you both. Please follow me."

I nodded my thanks and slowed my steps in order to take in my surroundings. The castle proved similar to the others I had been in, those of Lieth, Catania and Bargia. The main entrance opened into a large Grand Hall with a stairway to either side leading to the lord's apartments and the chambers for the guests and workers in the castle. Pennants in the gold and green of Gharn still hung from the ceiling, but half the draperies and tapestries that ought to adorn the walls lay in tattered heaps on the floor, some obviously beyond repair. Pallets lined the floor along the outer walls. On them lay the injured, tended by two healer women. Debris from the previous day's battle littered the central area and we had to walk around it to reach the door on the left which opened into the passage to the council chamber.

Gharn was one of the younger cities on the One Isle. It relieved me to see little damage from fire as here the buildings were mostly of stone. My father had told me how badly Catania had been damaged by fire when Bargia had invaded it before my birth. Catania had the longest history and was more densely built up, with many buildings of wood rather than stone.

Two guards stood alert and ready outside the door of the council chamber, and I noticed that one wore the blue and yellow tunic of Bargia.

Good. Gaelen is taking no chances. Farsh, his arm in a sling, recognized us and immediately opened the door to admit us. "Lady, Klast, Lord Dugal is expecting you." His smile of greeting held a hint of triumph.

"Thank you, Farsh. It is good to see you again."

Dugal, seated at the head of the table, rose as soon as he spotted us. "Liannis, you honour us. Please be seated."

The others around the table, seeing the honour Lord Dugal gave me, hurried to stand as well. Only Gaelen remained seated, knowing how it embarrassed me, and gave a broad smile in greeting. My father went to stand behind him as I walked to the last empty chair. I noted that Larn had a place of honour denoting his position as head of Dugal's personal guard. He wore a fresh gold and green tunic and a proud, serious mien. It was no doubt the first time he had the right to wear the official colours. Dugal, too. wore a tunic of gold and green, his richly embroidered with a wolf's head on each shoulder, gold on the green side and green on the gold. His torque of office adorned his throat. It made him look even younger.

I made the decision to set things right. "Please, Lord Dugal. You do me too much honour. Please remain seated in future. I am not comfortable with such formality." I sat and they all followed.

"I will try to remember that. Gharn has not had a seer here since long before I was born. I know they are held in high esteem."

"A seer is the servant of Earth, a woman like any in all other respects. She bears no title. As for me, I prefer as little fuss as possible. I have only recently come into my full gifts and am not yet accustomed to the notice the whites bring. Liethis, my mentor, also tried to attract as little attention as possible, as do all true seers." I smiled and tried to keep my voice light to soften the impact of such a strong speech to a lord.

I counted eight men seated around the table. Aside from Dugal, Gaelen and Lionn, whose arm was held in a sling, five were from Gharn and two from Bargia. Gaelen appeared to be the eldest and he could not be forty yet. To my dismay none of the Gharnians looked to have reached even thirty years. Had there been no one among his father's men that could still be trusted? With no one of experience among his advisors, Dugal's decisions could lack the caution that wisdom brings. It seemed he had chosen none from the old rule. I sighed and determined to keep quiet until I had a better grasp of the situation.

As the man next to me poured ale for me, I saw my father pick up Gaelen's goblet and first sniff, then taste it on the tip of is finger. His eyes met mine and I acknowledged his small nod of warning. He nodded to Gaelen. "It is safe, my lord. I detect no poison."

I had detected no hint of danger in the room either so I addressed Dugal and Gaelen. "I think we are safe here today."

Several pairs of shoulders relaxed. Dugal took a large swallow of ale, cleared his throat and began. "Thank you Liannis. I am happy that you are able to be here today. Among our prisoners we have two of the traitors that mutinied against my father. I wish to interrogate them this afternoon and hope you will truth-read them for me. Anything you could add to our consultation will be appreciated. While we have achieved victory, and Gharn is mine as it should be, our losses were high. It will take both knowledge and wisdom to hold Gharn, and to foil any attempts to reverse our victory. I scarcely know where to begin so I am grateful for the continuing support Lord Gaelen is providing."

Gaelen raised his hand to interrupt. "Lord Dugal, it is also in the interest of Bargia to maintain stability in Gharn. There is much to do here to insure it. Bargia wants a strong ally in Gharn and we see our support as much in our own interest as in yours." He smiled at Dugal but I sensed a warning in his words and tone. He wanted Dugal to know that he would not sit idly by while Dugal made decisions that would endanger Bargia.

By his sobering expression I knew that Dugal had heard it, too. "Indeed, Lord Gaelen, I will not forget my promise to Bargia."

I raised my hand to get Dugal's attention. All eyes turned to me, and for a moment I felt exposed. I took a deep breath. "Lord Dugal, I see that all those around this table from Gharn are very young. Are there no older men you trust to advise you, some with experience in governing?"

Dugal blushed. I sensed the question pricked him and that it had been raised before now. "I am aware of this problem Liannis. I knew, even before Lord Gaelen pointed it out to me, that I will need loyal and experienced advisors with the wisdom to guide me in those areas where my training is incomplete. I know I have much to learn. That is another reason I am glad you are here. Several of the men waiting in the prison were members of my father's court. Two were advisors. But I have no way of telling if they are loyal to me or not. I hope that when I interrogate them you will be able to tell me who I can trust."

"I will be happy to assist. But I warn you that my gift is not always complete. Seers do not have perfect sight...though I can tell if someone is telling the truth as they see it, and I will strive to sense what I can. I am glad that you seek loyal men from among your father's court. It will also show the people that you do not seek to destroy all that went before. The people need to observe you restoring order and sometimes the familiar is comforting."

Both Dugal and Gaelen smiled. Gaelen added, "Thank you Liannis. Once again you show wisdom beyond your years."

28

INTERROGATION

"Are we all ready to see the prisoners?" Dugal looked around and stopped at me. At my nodded assent he turned to Larn. "Have Kerran, Sherroll and Burrist brought in first, together as suggested by Lord Gaelen, so we may observe their reactions to each other as well as our questions."

"Yes, my lord." Larn saluted smartly and left. Dugal himself barred the door behind him and sat down again, his face troubled. "I do hope we find at least one of these three loyal. I will do what is necessary, but it will go hard if I must execute them all, especially Burrist as he was like an uncle to me. I have always thought him devoted to my father." He sighed heavily then pulled himself back erect. "It will take some time for Larn to return. Perhaps this is a good time to have food and drink brought. Antin, go to the kitchen and tell Vernia to bring food and fresh ale." As Antin left he added to the rest of us, "Vernia is the young woman who warned me to flee. I owe her a great debt."

I detected a hint of embarrassment that no one else could see. At the mention of her name a prickle of foreboding washed over me. I wondered if she would expect more than a position in the kitchen in gratitude, and decided to try to get a sense of her as well as the prisoners. I also decided to speak to my father about her later. He would know if Dugal needed to be warned.

Soon Farsh admitted three young women laden with roast fowl, three different cheeses, two breads, one dark and one light, honey, butter and two fresh jugs of ale. I had no trouble telling which one was Vernia. Not only was she better dressed than the other two but she wore an air of authority beyond her status. She moved with a calculated sensuality and seemed almost possessive of Dugal, showing no deference to him.

I saw Gaelen's brow knit slightly, showing that he had seen it, too. My father, of course, would not have missed it either, but he remained inscrutable as always. I relaxed. This problem would not require prodding from me.

A small wave of unguarded feeling washed over me and I looked over at Lionn in surprise. He stared at Vernia with unabashed admiration. Vernia noticed too, and a current passed between them that told me this story would not end here. Drat. Now we have another problem to worry about. This girl sets her sights too high. I do not trust her. I looked at my father and he gave me the slightest of nods to show he had seen it, too.

Shortly after the maids left, Larn and two other guards returned with their three prisoners, hobbled and hands tied, looking unkempt and dishevelled. They were escorted to three waiting stools. Only one still wore the green and gold tunic of the Gharnian court and guard.

"Have they been checked for hidden weapons?" Dugal asked Larn, who nodded.

"Yes, my lord. Even their belts have been replaced with cord."

"Then you remain behind them. You other two may go but remain outside to return them when we are done."

The two left and Larn positioned himself behind the stools. The man at the end of the table moved his chair to the side to leave an open view of the prisoners. All three stared at me. Two squirmed uneasily, including the one in uniform.

Dugal stood, took a deep breath, and squared his shoulders before addressing the prisoners. "I see that you are surprised to see a seer at our table. She is here at my invitation. I need to know who I can trust. She will truth-read your answers. Start by giving your names so that our visitors from Bargia - Lord Gaelen, Lionn, his heir, and his men will know who you are." He nodded to the farthest to begin.

"I am Burrist, my lord, advisor to your father and I welcome the opportunity to be truth-read." He had been one of the nervous ones, but now he calmed and nodded respectfully to me.

The second, the one in uniform, had become deeply afraid on seeing me. His voice shook as he answered. "I am Sherroll, also advisor to your father." He avoided both my and Dugal's gaze, his eyes darting about the room as if looking for a safe place to hide.

The third cleared his throat. "I am Kerran, head of the elite guard. My family has been under house arrest since the coup that cost Lord Dennist his life." After bowing to Dugal from his sitting position he looked directly at me as if to make sure I understood. *They held my family to force me to remain. I had no choice.*

I did not let on I had heard his thoughts.

"Since you seem so eager to speak, let us begin with you." Dugal looked grim. He could not completely hide his uncertainty and looked to Gaelen briefly before continuing. "Did you know of the plot against my father before the traitors struck?"

"No, my lord, though only days before, I became suspicious when I approached members of the council and they became suddenly silent. That struck me as unusual. I tried to find out more but the coup happened only two days later and it was too late."

"What did you do when they struck, and afterward?"

100

Kerran shook his head and I could hear regret and shame in his voice. "My lord, I was with my family when they struck, my wife in labour with our third child. I had just been handed my newborn son when guards burst in. I had no weapons to hand. They searched the house and captured every one they could find, then told us we were not to leave, that we were under arrest, all of us. Finally, one guard told us your father had been killed and that Seltan now ruled. No one would answer my questions and I did not find out the extent of the coup until late the next day." He looked at me again, his eyes pleading with me to believe him. "They took me away from my family and brought me before Seltan." He nodded to Sherroll, who almost recoiled from him. "Sherroll and Varst were with him. They told me that I had a choice. I and my family would be thrown into prison until a trial where I would be found guilty of treason and executed. My family would then be exiled by escort, with only the clothes on their backs and left outside to fend for themselves as best they could...or they would remain under house arrest as hostages against my compliance and I would retain my current position as head of the elite guard. They told me they wanted the people to see things remaining as normal as possible and if they saw me going about freely it would buy them time to organize their control." He shook his head again. "Forgive me, my lord...I had no choice...my family..." His voice broke. "I have not seen them since that day."

I did not doubt his sincerity, but could he be trusted to remain loyal to Dugal in the event of another uprising? My head pounded and I sipped ale carefully, unable to swallow any food and wanting to make sure my attention did not become clouded. As Kerran fell silent Dugal turned to Gaelen. "Have you any questions for him, Lord Gaelen?"

When Gaelen shook his head, Dugal turned his attention to the oldest man. "Burrist, the same questions."

Burrist inclined his head respectfully. "My lord, I, too, knew only days before that Seltan and Varst were plotting against your father. Varst caught me alone one the evening as I prepared to go home. He told me that several members of the court and council were unhappy with Lord Dennist's rule and wanted to speak with me. He suggested that I come to a meeting. Deeply concerned, I decided to see what I could find out. All the way, Varst asked questions that sounded me out on my views. I tried to be as vague as I could and became more and more worried. By the time we reached the others, Varst was sounding annoyed with me. I soon found out why. The meeting room held Seltan, Sherroll, members of Lord Dennist's personal guard and some of his elite guard."

101

I saw Sherroll jerk slightly at his name and felt his fear heighten. "Liar!" He tried to rise but Larn pushed him roughly back onto his stool. Farsh, seeing this, had also already risen half out his chair, knife in hand.

Burrist seemed not to notice, continuing without hesitation. "I knew my life and that of Lord Dennist depended on how that group would judge me. They plotted treason and if I stood against them they would kill me rather than risk being found out. So I feigned surprise at first and gradually let them persuade me to their side. I knew when I left the meeting that not all of them had been convinced I could be trusted. I knew I was followed so I walked home as I normally would have. Then, in the night, I slipped out and had a guard wake Lord Dennist. I told him all I had learned. Unfortunately I had only part of the plan. Lord Dennist thought he could handle it by waiting until morning and sending guards to arrest those at the meeting. Some of those guards knew of the plot and sided with the traitors. My warning had come too late. When I saw there was nothing I could do I used the confusion in the city as cover to get my wife and my self out of Gharn city to our summer home. From there I sent a message to Seltan that, while I would not oppose him, neither could I support him as part of his council. I would not seek to influence others to any course. Since I had left enough doubt at the meeting about my feelings toward Lord Dennist, they agreed to leave me in peace as long as I did not return to the city. I think they believed I had not enough influence to cause problems."

He stopped, took a deep breath and gathered his thoughts. "My lord, since that time I have worked secretly to gather support for a counter coup." He met Dugal's gaze. "I had heard that you escaped and I tried to find you. But I am no spy, and since I could not leave my home without arousing suspicion, felt it best not to act openly until your whereabouts became known and I could contact you." A small smile crept into his eyes and his mouth quirked. "You hid well, my lord. I never did find you."

When Dugal did not return his smile, he grew serious again. "My lord, some of the men who fought in the city to help restore you are those I recruited." He held his head high and met my gaze steadily as his explanation ended.

Dugal remained silent for a long time. I could sense his indecision.

Gaelen quietly suggested, "You have yet another prisoner, Lord Dugal."

Dugal started slightly, hesitated an instant, then, shooting a grateful look at Gaelen, drew himself up and faced Sherroll. "Now you. The same questions."

I had watched Sherroll while Dugal had remained silent. He sweated profusely and fear rolled off him in waves. But Sherroll was a shrewd man, used to power as advisor to Lord Dennist, and not about to give it up without a fight. I could sense the moment he decided to brazen it out. "My lord, you have just heard the words of a coward, one who fled as soon as he saw trouble, rather than do his duty." At first scathing, his tone grew challenging. "Burrist is correct in one thing. I was present at that meeting, but as a spy for Lord Dennist. He knew something was amiss and sent me as his most trusted friend, to find out what I could. It did not surprise me to see Varst bring Burrist in. He always sought more power than he deserved. I never did trust him."

He sent Burrist a scornful look before turning back to Dugal. "My lord." He lowered his voice and continued in a conspiratorial tone. "Even after the coup, it was I who stayed, I who remained to gather information which I could send to your followers, Lord Dugal, information which might help bring you back where you belong. You know how long I served your esteemed father. Why, was it not I who tutored you in strategy? Surely you see..."

I heard no more. I felt faint and began to slip from my chair, unable, any longer, to hold the barriers around me that kept some of the pain at bay. From far away I sensed my father catch me before I fell to the floor and heard concerned voices exclaiming as the world fell away and darkness claimed me.

29

INTERLUDE

I came to with a feather bed supporting my back, a cool cloth on my forehead and my father chaffing my wrists. As my eyes tried to focus I heard him sigh with relief.

"Liannis, are you well? You caused quite a stir."

My head still throbbed, but here, deep within the castle, in my stone chamber, the intrusive impressions did not clamour quite as loudly. Before I could answer, my father raised my head and held a cup of fresh water to my lips. Its coolness refreshed me and helped to clear my mind. "I will be well, Papa. Thank you. The pain became too much for me but it is better here."

Anxious to know what had happened after I lost consciousness I tried to sit up but he pushed me gently back.

"Rest, daughter. I heard Gaelen advise Dugal to end things for today. When you feel ready I will send for him and Gaelen to meet privately with us." He set the cup on the table beside me. "But I think we already know most of what is needed, even without your input. Your reaction alone told much."

"I must see Merrist. I must know how his wound heals." I tried to get up but he pushed me back again.

"No Liannis, I have sent for beef tea and dark bread. You have not eaten since we neared the city. We will not leave here until you have eaten."

"We?"

"Yes, we, since your mother is not here to see to you. I will not stand by while you use up all your strength. That is, unfortunately, a trait you have learned from me. I well know the toll it takes. We..." He emphasized the word, looking sternly at me. "We will not leave until I know you have eaten and rested."

I tried to smile at this display, so unlike the restrained, serious man I knew. The sternness was for effect only. But my smile turned into a wan imitation. "But you know I cannot keep food down amid so much suffering."

Papa crossed his arms. "Then we will be here a long time."

The knock came at the door before I could protest that he had other duties. He kept his hand on the latch without opening it and asked, "Who is there?"

A timid voice answered, "Sir, I bring the food you sent for."

He opened the door a crack. Then, the maid's identity confirmed, opened it further to take the tray and closed it firmly again without admitting the terrified girl. Before he poured a mug of broth for me he sniffed it carefully and tasted a drop on his tongue. He nodded at me, satisfied, poured a mug for us both and handed one to me. "Sip it slowly, daughter, and it will stay down."

I obeyed, grateful that the decision had been taken out of my hands.

He handed me a small hunk of bread. "Slowly, small bites, chew them well and alternate with the broth."

I nodded, too weary to speak, and did as I was told. My stomach protested a few times but the food stayed down. I could feel my strength returning. When he deemed I had eaten enough he took the mug from me and said, "Now sleep. I will sleep here on the floor beside you."

I lay back and he tucked the blanket under my chin in an awkward imitation of my mother. By now the only light in the chamber came from the embers in the hearth. Merrist would wait until morning. "I am so glad you are with me Papa. Good night."

"Good night, daughter."

I slept.

30

RELLNOST

Rellnost wielded his practice sword with ill-contained fury. His partner clearly had better skill and looked embarrassed as he hesitated to allow Rellnost to save face. Rellnost understood the ruse and resented the older boy's kindness.

Without warning, and completely against the rules, he lashed at his opponent's arm with all his strength.

The lad had not expected it and missed the chance to parry. He cried out, dropped his sword and clutched his arm, which dangled crookedly at his side.

At first Rellnost's face held a brief look of triumph, then, as he took in the weapons master's anger, drained of colour.

Seeing that the other lad clearly had a broken arm, the weapon's master whirled on Rellnost and said, between clenched teeth, "You will stand here until I return to deal with you." Then he turned his back on Rellnost, now seething with rage at being spoken to in such a way, and gently led the lad away, helping him support the arm as best he could.

I wondered if the arm would ever heal straight enough for the lad to wield a sword again.

Rellnost remained standing. Once or twice he seemed to consider leaving then change his mind again. He was afraid. And he was furious.

Darkness fell, and still the weapons master did not return. Rellnost grew hungry and tired. He wanted a hot meal and his soft bed. Unlike the other young boys in the barracks, he had been assigned a chamber of his own with a feather bed. It had been allowed, under protest, due to his demands for special treatment for his 'exalted' rank. Some of the fury he felt now, he directed at himself. Some part of him knew he had gone too far. There would be consequences, ones he did not want to think about. He directed the rest of his rage at all and sundry who dared deprive him of the deference he knew was his due as lord of Lieth. Rellnost was at war with himself.

* * *

I woke to sun streaming in the window slit and my father seated calmly beside my bed.

"Good morning." A mug of tea found its way into my hand. "Do I want to know what you dreamed?" Papa asked.

I nodded and told him what I had seen between bites of porridge with milk and honey. It tasted wonderful and did not threaten to leave again. When Papa tried to have me eat some soft cheese and bread I declined, knowing that it would push my battered stomach beyond its capacity.

"He will need to be watched more closely. I have always thought he ought not to have special privileges. It is good for neither him nor the rest of the lads."

"I agree, Papa. Perhaps now that will change. Bargia cannot support his bid to gain his lordship until he learns the lessons of what makes a good leader...and until he learns to control his temper."

"Do you think he will learn it?"

"I do not know, Papa. Earth has not shown me."

As I ate I slowly gathered my barriers against the influx of impressions from all the people in the city around me again. Gratefully, I could feel my ability returning. I knew I would need it for the visit with Merrist and the consultations with Dugal that would follow.

"You may leave now, Papa, while I clean up and fix my hair. Then I want to see Merrist."

He assessed me shrewdly. "All right, but I will accompany you. I do not trust you not to work beyond your strength."

"Do Lord Gaelen and Lord Dugal not need you?"

"They will wait."

I got up and hugged him. "Then I will welcome your company." I felt, rather than saw, his smile as he left.

31

MERRIST

A guard took us to the chamber where Merrist lay. Unlike the other wounded soldiers he had been given a small room of his own. When we entered, Farsh, who had been keeping vigil by his friend's side, stood up, a look of surprise crossing his face. "Lady..." He stammered a little as if not sure how to address me or what further to say. Apparently he had not expected me to make a personal visit to Merrist, now that I was a 'seer'.

"Hello, Farsh. It is good to see you well. How fares our friend Merrist? I know he lost part of his leg." I asked the question more to set Farsh at ease than because I wished to know the answer. I could see immediately that Merrist looked flushed with fever and, though asleep, his face was pinched in pain.

"He lives, though I am not certain that will not change. He is very fevered, lady, and has no will to live." His voice took on a hopeful tone. "Do you think you can help him?"

"I am no healer, Farsh. The only thing I can do for him is speak to him and give him hope that he can still live a good life, even without full use of his leg."

Farsh opened his hands wide, his tone pleading. "He says all he was good for was soldiering, lady, and he cannot do that without two good legs."

"Yes, I understand that is what he believes. I will do my best to convince him otherwise." I looked at my father, who had placed his hand on Merrist's brow to check his fever.

"I need to see the wound." Papa lifted the blanket and, at Farsh's quick attempt to stop him, turned and asserted, "Farsh, I have tended many battle wounds. You may trust your friend to my care. I will not harm him."

I intervened. "Farsh, would you mind leaving us alone with Merrist for a time?" I sent him a reassuring smile. "I am sure you must be hungry. We will sit with Merrist until you have returned from a good meal."

Though he gave my father a dubious look he hastened to comply. Papa had already turned back to Merrist and was in the process of unwinding his bandages. Merrist groaned but did not waken. I sniffed his breath. "Poppy," I told him.

My father shook his head in disgust. He did not approve of the use of poppy juice, saying it slowed healing and that men craved it after if they had been given it for too long. When the last of the bandage came off he sucked in his breath. "Liannis, I need warm water and clean cloths. The wound is starting to fester. If that is not halted we will either lose the rest of the leg or lose Merrist altogether...and a bowl in which to make a poultice."

I hastened to get him what he needed. Out of the corner of my eye I saw him untie the pouch he always carried on his belt. I had never seen him without it. In it could be found a wide array of herbals and medicinal plants. My father had learned much about the healing arts during his years travelling as a spy. He had even studied for a time with a healer woman. Merrist would now get the best care possible.

Merrist's small chamber had no hearth, so when I returned with the water I brought another maid with me. She bore a small brazier, and a small bucket of live embers to keep the water hot.

"Thank you, Sella," I thought a moment. "Do you think you could also find a pot to make tea and three mugs?"

The maid gave a nervous nod and hurried off. Within moments she was back with the pot and mugs. I smiled my thanks and she scurried away. That was one disadvantage of wearing whites. People who were unaccustomed to seers tended to be nervous around them. I sighed. I would also need to take Farsh to task for calling me □Lady'. I wanted to be known as myself, Liannis first, and seer as only my work.

I watched silently and handed my father the items he requested as he cleaned Merrist's stump. The leg had been cut just below the knee. I examined the wound as my father tended it. It oozed pus in spots and looked fiery red. I knew it would be hot to the touch.

For the next span we kept warm, salted, wet cloths on the wound to draw out the pus. When the cloths became red with fresh blood, telling him all the pus had been drawn out my father made a mash of goldenseal and honey and placed it over the wound, under the clean bandage he wound around it.

I was just putting some willow bark and valerian into the pot to make tea when Merrist stirred, moaning. My father drew the blanket back up to cover the leg and looked at me to take his place.

"Merrist. It is Liannis. Can you hear me?"

Merrist moaned again and his eyes fluttered.

"I have tea for you. We have tended your leg and put on fresh bandages. Try to wake up now."

He moaned again but I could see him make an effort. I kept up my patter until he managed to open his eyes and focus on me.

"Liannis." Tears leaked from the corners of his eyes and rolled into his ears. He turned from me in shame. I could barely make out his hoarse whisper. "I do not want you to see me."

"Yet, here I am, Merrist. Someone needs to make sure you look after yourself." I tried to keep my voice light. "We have changed your dressings. Are you in much pain? My father has some willow bark tea ready which is good for pain and fever. "

"Please, just go."

My father broke in. "Merrist, I have seen many men with battle wounds such as yours. They, too, wanted to be left to die...yes, I know that is what you are thinking, though you do not say it in front of Liannis. But Liannis does not want you to die."

So. He is using Merrist's affection for me to reach him. I watched Merrist stiffen slightly, then slowly turn his head to look, not at me, but at my father.

His voice shook with effort, anger and hopelessness. "Then you must tell her to stop. I am half a man. I have no future. I do not need her pity."

My father's voice took on a military tone, one I know had made many men cower. "No future? You are mistaken, boy."

My father had used his most commanding voice and I knew the use of the word "boy" was meant to stir Merrist into greater anger. I waited as he continued.

"You do not want pity? Then be a man. Self-pity is a coward's way. Liannis never told me you were a coward."

It worked. Merrist flushed and his eyes flashed with hopeless fury. "Then tell me what a man with only one leg can do. A man must walk to work. Crutches will not let me use my hands. So what good am I?"

Meanwhile, I thought hard. What could I say that might help? An idea struck me, one that would be good for both of us. But I knew my father had not finished so I kept my silence.

"Crutches? No, not crutches. If you have the courage, and can handle some pain, you will walk...and without crutches. Do you have the courage to deal with a little pain, Merrist, or are you truly a coward? Will you listen, or shall we leave you to wallow in your self-pity?" He put as much scorn on the last as he could.

"How?" Merrist still sounded angry but now he was also curious. He eyed my father with a mix of suspicion and hope.

"A leg of wood. I have seen such. They work. Not comfortable, but it will allow you to move without crutches. You will not soldier again, of course, but there are other useful occupations where a limp will not hinder much."

Merrist became stubborn. "But soldiering is all I know. It is all I ever wanted to do." He turned away.

Now I interrupted. "Merrist, I have a plan. Will you listen?"

I knew he would not refuse me. His feelings for me were too strong to allow him to deny me. He turned his face away again and said, dully, "I will listen."

I plunged ahead, my plan still only half formed. "Merrist, since donning my whites I have moved into my mentor Liethis' cabin. But I have a problem. My work takes me away too much of the time to look after the garden and to keep the cabin and shed in good repair. I need someone to look after things for me so that I may be free to come and go as I need to. There is already an extra pallet as I stayed with her while I apprenticed."

"I do not want your charity."

"Merrist, it is not charity. I knew I would need to find someone. I just have not had the time to pursue it yet. I already know you to be honourable. If you do not think such work beneath you..." I let my voice trail off.

My father nodded approval.

Merrist remained silent for a while. When he turned to meet my eyes for the first time I read uncertainty and hope there. We were making progress.

"But your reputation? I should sleep in the shed with the horses. Even then there will be talk."

I allowed myself a moment of triumph.

My father beat me to the answer, saying almost exactly what I would have, but his opinion would be more convincing. "Liannis is a seer. All know that seers do not take a mate. No one will question this and if they do others will set them straight."

I shot him a grateful look and got back the tiniest of smiles. Conspirators. That is what we were. And we were winning.

Merrist thought a while again, and asked, "But can a leg really be made for me? I have never seen such."

"I have. They work well but can be painful. They are made of wood and leather, like a peg with a cup at the top and straps to hold it in place. They must be padded with moss in the cup to cushion the stump."

"Where would I find someone who knows how to make such a device?"

"If I tell you, will you agree to Liannis' plan?"

Merrist looked at me. "Do you have the time to wait for me to heal and get such a device?"

"I still spend a good deal of time at my parents' cottage. I have some time. And I would rather hire someone I know I can trust."

I watched determination and hope replace uncertainty. "Then I will gladly agree. It will be an honour to serve you."

"Good." My father said. "I know how to fashion such a device. I have seen them close to hand and know how they work." He turned to me. "Liannis, I think Merrist can be moved. He needs to get better care than the surgeon here or the healer women can give him."

I nodded, following his train of thought. "Merrist, moving you to Bargia will cause a good deal of pain. Have you the strength for it?"

I could not help but notice that he did not use the word courage this time, though we all knew that is what he meant. It gave Merrist a chance to agree without seeming to need to save face.

Merrist blanched. "I will do whatever is necessary, sir. You may rely on me." His voice had taken a stronger tone, a soldier's voice in response to his commander.

"Then you will be taken to our home. My wife, Brensa, Liannis' mother, has a small gift of healing. She will know what to do. And I will be able to start making your new leg and fitting it for you. But understand that it will be some time yet before you are able to try walking with it. Your leg must heal completely first." He held Merrist's eyes. "When you first try it the pain will seem unbearable. It must be done in small stages to build callous on the stump."

"I will do what is necessary, sir." Merrist made a valiant attempt to keep his voice calm but I detected a small tremor.

Poor Merrist. He would have a difficult time ahead of him.

"Good, then start by drinking this tea. It will taste foul, but it will help the pain and fever and also help you sleep. We will be back to look after your bandages. Until then, drink as much of this as you can and try to eat the food we will have sent in for you...and no more poppy juice. It is poison to the mind and will slow healing."

"Yes, sir."

"It will be well Merrist, I promise." At his hesitant smile I sensed I spoke true.

32

VERNIA

We sat in Dugal's private apartment sharing our meal before reconvening in the council chamber; Dugal, Lord Gaelen, Lionn, my father and I. Neither Dugal nor Lionn liked what we had to say.

"But she saved my life! How can you now say she cannot be trusted?" Dugal looked mutinous.

"And what evidence have you, Liannis? You saw her only a few moments." Lionn shot at me, not bothering to hide his resentment

My father spoke up. "I, too, sensed something amiss in her. Lord Gaelen well knows my abilities to read people, as do you Lionn. Had Liannis not sensed something I would have brought it up myself."

"I do not know just what it is," I said, "but I know I sensed something wrong about her. And I certainly would not trust a woman who sets her sights on more than one high born man. Perhaps it is only ambition I saw, but ambition can lead to betrayal. If she does not get what she wants in one way she may well try another." I shrugged my shoulders and opened my hands, unable to offer anything more solid.

"Lord Dugal," Gaelen added. "Much has occurred in Gharn since your father's death. Such events can often change a person. It is possible that she could be trusted then, but that something has happened to change her."

"I did not see her try to engage Lionn." Dugal sounded almost petulant.

Lionn blushed and remained silent, confirming to the rest of us that something had indeed happened.

I decided to press the point. Too much was at stake.

"Lionn, do you deny that anything passed between you?"

His blush deepened and he tried to look away, but he knew I would be able to tell if he dissembled. "She was most happy to see me when I sought her out in the kitchen last evening. I planned to see her again tonight." He looked at Dugal. "I did not know she still meant something to you, Lord Dugal. I will not see her again if you wish it."

Now it was Dugal's turn to blush. "Did you lie with her?"

Lionn shook his head. "No, my lord."

I heard the unspoken, *but she invited me to her chamber tonight.*

Dugal let out his breath.

Gaelen took the lead. "Lord Dugal, you are young and virile. No one expects you to sleep alone every night. But history has shown us that there are women who seek power by giving birth to a lord's bastard. Wars have been fought over such situations. It is important to be very discrete in your liaisons. Now that you fill the lord's chair you need to keep such possibilities always in your mind."

Dugal looked about to protest when my father broke in. "My lord, while in this, too, it is necessary to show wisdom in your choices, may I suggest that you assuage your appetites with those women who work under the protection of an innkeeper in one of the better inns? They are usually clean, do not seek attachments and have no wish to bear children...and are very good at avoiding such."

I knew he referred to a high class of prostitute who chose this work rather than submit to joining with a man and becoming his chattel.

Dugal's mouth dropped in surprise. "You suggest I visit whores?"

"It is a better option than fighting your own children and their mothers, or wondering when one will begin to plot against you." My father kept his voice calm and serious, though I knew he had never liked the idea of exposing himself to pillow talk and did not, as a rule, trust prostitutes. He looked at Lionn. "You, too, need to show wisdom, Lionn. This is not the time or place to explore your passions."

Lionn blushed again.

Dugal still struggled to regain his composure.

Gaelen added, "Lionn, you will show discipline while we are in Gharn. A leader must be able to control his appetites. He is not free to indulge every whim. A leader thinks of his duty first and his pleasure only when it will not endanger his people."

That was too much for Lionn. He hung his head in submission. "Yes, my lord."

Although directed at Lionn, the message was clearly meant for Dugal as well. It was one of the lessons he had missed due to his father's untimely death.

Dugal took it in and nodded slowly, "I can see that I must be more careful. Vernia will see no more of my bedchamber."

Gaelen changed the subject, deeming the matter closed, at least for now. "That is wise, my lord. Are we expected in the council chamber yet?"

When Dugal rose, we all followed him to there. The others already waited outside the locked door. My father looked at me in question and I let my senses probe the room. Finding nothing suspicious I nodded. Dugal bade the guard unlock it and we all resumed our seats from the previous day.

33

CONFERENCE

"We have all had the opportunity to think about the testimonies we heard yesterday." Dugal wasted no time addressing the issue. "I wish to hear the opinions of each of you before asking Liannis to tell us her findings. My future council members sit in this chamber and I must choose those who show the greatest insight. I want to hear not only what you think but also how you came to your conclusions."

That strategy had been agreed on last evening between Dugal, Gaelen and my father when he left me sleeping. He had told me of it this morning as we walked to see Merrist.

"Larn, you first."

Larn drew himself up, doing his best to look mature and formal. As I knew him to be both loyal and intelligent I thought him a good choice for council. But like Dugal he had much to learn. "My lord. I have confirmed that Kerran's family has spent the time since the coup under house arrest. As such, I believe his claim that he did not act against your father of his own will. Whether he could have done more to prevent Lord Dennist's death I cannot say. I think we need to reduce his influence with the guard until we can better determine his loyalty."

Dugal nodded but both my father and Gaelen kept their faces inscrutable.

Others might see Dugal's reactions and temper their answers accordingly. Gaelen saw the danger, too. "Lord Dugal, a moment in private please?"

They moved to the corner and when they came back to their seats I could see that Dugal had taken on a stern expression. I felt for him. He had so much to learn and no time to learn it. But he put his best effort into it, and I had no doubt that if he could hold on to his position long enough he would be a good lord to his people.

Dugal inclined his head to Larn to continue.

"Both Sherroll and Burrist have opposing stories about their involvement. Each story could be believable. But since Sherroll stayed behind and has had continued association with the traitors I find his story less so. I do not trust him at all." He sounded more uncertain now and a frown line appeared between his brows. "I think Burrist would not have remained outside the city in partial exile if he had been involved with treason. Before we decide on his future I think we need to find out if the rest of his story, about trying to help you, is true."

When Dugal did not give him the approving nod he expected, Larn remained standing.

But Dugal had taken Gaelen to heart and his expression did not change. "Thank you Larn. Biel, you are next."

While Biel's conclusions matched Larn's he rambled more and sounded much less certain. To greater or lesser degrees the next two young men had much the same answers and showed differing degrees of confidence.

Farsh came last. To my surprise, he spoke with confidence. He had learned a good deal, it seemed, since he had feared Dugal's wrath for saving me. "My lord. I am in agreement with Larn. Sherroll is a traitor and must not be allowed to influence you. As I sat beside him during his testimony I could smell his fear. Do not laugh. I could. And a man who tells the truth does not fear that much."

The surprised looks and smirks disappeared from the faces around the table, a few behind hands to hide their disbelief.

I knew that what he said was true. It is possible to smell fear. My father had told me of it many times. I had sensed it in the past as well but had never been sure if it was smell or my gift that told me this.

Farsh continued after sending the disbelievers a glare. "As for Kerran, I believe him. My concern for the future would be to determine, if possible, what he would do if he had to choose between loyalty to yourself or his family. And I believe Burrist. My father, may Earth hold him, knew Burrist well and always spoke highly of him. I think we may trust him." He sat down without waiting for a response.

I sensed Larn and Farsh had passed their test and would sit on the council. They would miss their friend Merrist, but then Merrist's gentle nature made him a poor choice anyway.

"Lord Gaelen, would you give us your impressions, please, and then Lionn and lastly, Klast."

I noted how Dugal ordered the three according to rank. At least his training had not lacked in diplomacy and manners.

For Lionn, too, though his future did not depend on it, this was a test and I think he knew it. He stood erect and chose his words with care. "Lord Dugal, my opinion must be based on what I have observed here alone, as I have no previous knowledge of these men, either by experience or reputation."

I detected a small sigh of relief from Gaelen. His son had learned caution, at least in this.

"I concur with the others in that I do not believe Sherroll's story. He was fearful and would not meet anyone's eyes during his testimony. On

116

the other hand, both Kerran and Burrist spoke with apparent sincerity, and I thought Kerran showed regret. While I do not know if I would keep him as head of my guard I do think his intention is to be loyal. Burrist, too, seemed sincere, though his story must be checked before I would hand him back the power that comes with a seat on council." He bowed slightly to Dugal and resumed is seat.

Gaelen cleared his throat but remained seated. As Lord he had no need to show deference. "Lord Dugal, you appear to have astute and loyal men in this chamber. I congratulate you. It will make your choices easier to know that all present have the potential to serve you well. The opinion appears unanimous where Sherroll is concerned. He cannot be trusted and I agree that he is very likely among the prime traitors. Knowing that the other two are already dead will make what you decide simpler. I, too, believe Kerran's tale. As a father I can attest to how difficult some decisions are when they put a man's family at risk. While I would not reinstate him as head of the elite guard immediately, neither would I think it amiss to give him the opportunity to prove himself again. I think that Burrist, too, told the truth. If Liannis concurs and she sees him as loyal it is my opinion that his voice on the council will provide the caution of age and prove a valuable asset. But only if Liannis and Klast agree that he is completely loyal." He gave each of us a searching look as he spoke our names, then inclined his head at Dugal and relaxed back into his chair.

My father, already standing in his usual position behind Gaelen, stepped into better view. "Lord Dugal, as you know I have a lifetime of experience judging men's words and actions and have a reputation for accuracy. While Liannis must have the final word, as she has truth-read all three, I believe Lord Gaelen has the right of it. I have nothing more to add to what he has advised." He stepped back into position again, ever the vigilant protector.

Now all eyes turned to me. Unlike the others, I chose to remain seated and leaned forward so all could see me clearly. "Lord Dugal, I agree with Lord Gaelen that you have loyal men in this room, all of whom love you well."

Dugal relaxed and allowed himself a smile of relief. I saw Gaelen notice and stifle a small smile of his own. Dugal had heeded him well and the test had ended.

I continued. "Sherroll is not only a traitor, but I sensed that he had a pivotal role in the coup. I caught one unspoken thought from him during Burrist's testimony and believe it was he who cut your lord father down."

At this Dugal could no longer mask himself. "He will pay with his life." Dugal's voice shook with fury and he gripped the edge of the table so hard his knuckles went white.

"That is fitting. But please do not ask me to be present for his execution. As it is, I find it very difficult to be here amid so much pain and strong feeling." I waited for him to acknowledge this before continuing. "Kerran spoke true. I saw no deception in him. He is deeply ashamed that he could not act against the traitors and believes that he will never again be trusted. His only hope is for leniency so that he may take his family out of Gharn to start a new life as he is able."

Dugal seemed surprised by this, but Gaelen nodded understanding.

"Burrist, too, spoke true," I went on, "even about his efforts on your behalf. While I still advise finding evidence to that effect to convince the people of this, I see him as completely loyal and trustworthy." I sat back and waited.

Gaelen spoke up. "Lord Dugal, may I suggest that we speak privately with Liannis and Klast to go over what we have heard so that you may choose your advisory council?"

"An excellent suggestion, Lord Gaelen. We can remove to my private chambers and have food brought as we consult." He looked at me. "Will you be more comfortable there than here, or would you prefer we meet in your chamber?"

"I would welcome a meeting in my chamber, Lord Dugal. Thank you for remembering."

"Then we shall reconvene there." Dugal rose, indicating the meeting over.

DECISIONS

I had, by now, been in the city for almost two days and the press of feelings had become almost unbearable, but the extra stone around us in my chamber with its location deep within the castle, dampened the noise enough that I could eat a light meal and drink tea. I saw both my father and Gaelen watch what I ate. "I am managing." I assured them.

This time Vernia had not been among those bringing in the meal. I decided I would suggest to Gaelen that he find out what Dugal had done about her. While I did not trust her too close to Dugal, neither did I think it wise to anger her unduly lest she turn against him.

The food was delicious and the others all fell to with good appetites. Since Lionn was not a candidate for Dugal's advisory council he had been invited to join us. I could not tell if he would rather have accompanied the younger men or not. He, too, was learning to control his face. That would make Gaelen happy, I knew.

When we had all eaten our fill and the others refilled their mugs with ale, Dugal began. "I think there is little doubt, now, of the status of our three prisoners. I will deal with Sherroll. His execution will be swift and public. Before we decide on the other two I would like to hear your opinions on the remaining choices for my council." He looked at me first. "Liannis, do you have strong impressions about any of them?"

"I do, Lord Dugal. I am sure you will be relieved to hear that you have two very strong candidates in Larn and Farsh. Both showed insight and strength. Their loyalty is beyond question, and in spite of their youth, I have seen a surprising growth in maturity since we first met. And also, because of their youth, they will be with you for many years. Of the others, Biel is loyal, but lacks focus and I question his ability to make sound decisions under pressure."

As I thought about the three prisoners, a scene, sent by Earth, flashed briefly in my mind.

* * *

An older Kerran sat on Dugal's left at the table in the council chamber enjoying ale and sharing a laugh with the others

* * *

"Lord Dugal, may I suggest that you consider Kerran as a member of the council, rather than keep him in your guard? Earth has just sent me a sign. I do not think you will be disappointed."

Dugal's eyes widened in surprise. I saw Gaelen raise his eyebrows as well, while Lionn looked frankly astounded. My father did not let his reaction show.

"Liannis," Dugal began, "Do you suggest that I let this man, who has worked for the enemy, sit on my council before he has had a chance to prove himself? I mean no disrespect, but this strikes me a foolhardy."

"I agree that it would appear so on the surface, Lord Dugal. Let me clarify that my seeing shows a council somewhat older than you all are today...perhaps five years from now. But he sits at your left hand and with a closeness that speaks of long familiarity. I cannot say when this must take place but I see no barriers to it happening soon."

Gaelen looked at my father, "Klast, what do you think of this?"

"I have never known Liannis to err in her seeing, even as a child. If she says Kerran belongs on the council, then it is possible that to delay in heeding Earth's message would have unlooked for consequences."

Lionn nodded vigorously. "That is so, Lord Dugal. We have known each other all our lives. She sees true."

Gaelen agreed. "That has been my experience also. Though I do not see harm in a short wait. Earth does not demand immediate obedience. We are thinking beings and so must use her gifts wisely to make decisions with clarity and understanding. Once we have spoken with Kerran further the decision may become more clear."

Dugal's resistance faded away at this and his shoulders relaxed. "Then we have some time to know him better, you think?"

"I agree with Lord Gaelen that this is wise as well," I continued. "But let me add my other reasoning. Kerran has, as you say, been in constant contact with the traitors and those who worked with them and may still be sympathetic to them. The knowledge he has may prove valuable in learning who to trust and who may yet have plans to usurp you. But I see no harm in a short wait to give him an opportunity to prove his loyalty, if only to help others see it as well."

"May I suggest, Lord Dugal," Gaelen broke in, "that you use Kerran to flush out the remaining traitors who yet walk free? It will allow him to prove himself to you, and to others who will have a natural distrust of him. Then you will have the evidence you seek to support his appointment to your council."

"Thank you Lord Gaelen. That does seem a sound course."

"Earth's message also confirms that you will still hold your position several years from now." I smiled. "A good sign, do you not agree?"

"Then let us toast to good fortune." Dugal poured fresh ale into all our mugs and lifted his high.

"Good fortune!" We all shouted in unison, raising our mugs and taking a long pull. The mood lightened as we basked in the glow of the omen. Success in Gharn was assured, at least for a few years.

The celebration lasted only until Gaelen reminded us that we had not yet decided on Burrist's fate. "Klast how much time do you think is needed to confirm Burrist's claim of support. His age and his apparent ability to stay calm under pressure and make decisions based on reason rather than emotion make him an excellent candidate for council. And I think it wise to act quickly where he is concerned to reduce speculation that could undermine his credibility."

Dugal nodded. "I have already told Larn to send out men to gather evidence of his claims but I have no spies with experience whom I already trust. I welcome any advice you have."

"Klast is my most experienced and trusted spy. If he is agreeable..." Gaelen looked at my father. "Klast this is not to be taken as an order. You have earned your peace with your family."

"If I may direct only and remain outside the field, my lord?"

I knew my father would never hesitate to do as Gaelen wished. It was a measure of the depth of their friendship that he was even able to suggest such a condition, rather than simply agree without question.

"I think that would be best," Gaelen agreed. "Then we can spread a wider net. You will remain in Gharn to instruct Lord Dugal's men. They will report to you, and you will report directly to Lord Dugal...if that is agreeable to you, Lord Dugal" When Dugal nodded assent he turned back to my father. "But it will mean a delay in returning home, my friend."

My father merely inclined his head.

"That is decided then. Lord Dugal, I suggest that you take full advantage of Klast's knowledge and skills. He has been my closest and most trusted advisor and spy since the day I came into power. There is no man who understands what you face better than he."

I had an idea. "My lords. To remain in the city is becoming unbearable for me. And Merrist needs to be brought to our home for mending. It will give my mother some ease if I return home a while, and my presence will let you focus on your work, Papa, knowing I am with Mama. Also, it gives me a chance to see to them both until you return...that is unless Earth has work for me to do before then."

Dugal gave me a grateful nod before turning to Gaelen.

"My lord, I have not adequately expressed my gratitude for what you have done for me and for Gharn. I know you must return to Bargia to see to your own people and to comfort those who lost loved ones in the fight to reclaim my seat. I know I have learned much and have much more yet to learn, but with Klast to assist I am confident that we will find the right way."

35

KIRA

A faint cry pierced my mind. *Help! Caught! Dark! Afraid!*

Kira! A wave of panic assailed me. Where was she? Had she been caught? How? When? How would I get her back? My stomach clenched and I stopped where I was so suddenly that my father was a step ahead before he noticed.

"Liannis, What is it?"

I only heard the question from far away. *Kira, little one, where are you?*

Dark. Leg caught. Kira sounded terrified, her voice plaintive.

Why dark?

Man covered eyes. Afraid.

Do you know where you are?

City. Dark. Afraid. Leg caught.

I will find you, little one. I promise. But it will take time. Do not be afraid. I will come.

"Oh, Papa, Kira has been caught! I think a falconer has her. She says her eyes are covered and her leg is caught. She has no idea where she is other than she is in the city. Papa, we have to rescue her. This is my fault. I let her get too tame." And I burst into tears.

I sobbed into his shoulder. When I calmed enough to think again I pushed myself away. "Papa, I cannot leave here until I have her back. She is like my child."

"I know, Liannis. And we will find her."

I knew he had already been thinking of a plan because his questions to me were ordered and clear.

"Liannis, can you tell from her mind-speak when you are getting closer?"

"Yes, that is why I had to get close to the city before the battle, so I would be able to hear her."

"Then we will find her together. I will find out where the falconers keep their birds. There cannot be too many. You will mind-speak Kira as we approach each one." He took me firmly by my upper arms. "We will find her. They will not harm her. They will want to train her and that takes time. We will find her, I promise."

His assurance and knowing we had a plan calmed me. Papa had never made a promise he could not keep.

"Then let us hurry. She is so afraid." I reached out to Kira. *We come little one. We will find you. Be calm.*

Dark. The answer did not seem quite so afraid as before. I knew I could never break her trust. Merrist would have to wait.

We each went in different directions to inquire where the falconers resided and agreed to meet in the market square at midday. I tried to keep up a constant stream of reassurance to Kira.

I knew that falconers kept newly captured birds tied to a perch and kept their heads hooded for a time before taking them out to train. This allowed the birds to tame somewhat and to become accustomed to being hand fed. We had a few days before Kira's position changed. But I was determined to find her today. I would not sleep until she was safe again. I knew that my father would not either.

When we met in the square my father handed me his water-skin. "Watered wine. You need to keep up your strength." I managed a few swallows before handing it back and accepting the chunk of dark bread he held out to me. "I know it is hard but I want you to eat this in small bites as we walk."

I declined. "It will not stay down, Papa." I followed him out of the square in the direction of an area where shops that sold items that took time to make, such as tack, clothing and pewter stood. My inquiries, too, had sent me in this direction.

The shops that sold food items such as bread, cheese, meats and ale nestled on the opposite side of the square. Today the square stood open and bare. Tomorrow on market day it would be ringed with booths and thronged with men and women in search of their wares.

"What names have you found, Liannis?"

"Only two, Papa. Fortan and Kirsh. They both have shops in this direction."

"I have those and one other, Gerrist. He is closest so let us start with him." He led the way with unerring confidence.

Had it been me leading it would have taken twice as long. I mind-spoke Kira again. *Be brave, little one. We come. Are you all right?*

Hungry. Dark. Leg hurts, came the petulant reply.

Gerrist had a small shed where he housed his birds. About ten perches, poles set into the dirt floor, with cross pieces to which leg chains were attached, filled the crowded space. He also strapped the wings of the larger raptors so they would not flap and injure the others as the perches stood closer than wingspan apart. It reeked of dung and rotting entrails. While I let my father do the talking for now, I determined to speak of it afterward. This cruelty had to stop. It became clear immediately, that

124

Kira was not here, for which part of me was grateful. The thought of her in the hands of such a man horrified me. Oh Earth, why must men do such things? Where does such cruelty come from?

Fortan's roost was cleaner, the perches further apart and the shed much airier. I still hated to see the beautiful birds captive but I knew that nothing I said would stop the sport of falconing. Men trained these birds to hunt for small prey. They wagered about which birds would bring in the most prey, would find prey quickest and which did the least damage to their catches. Bringing them back unharmed, against the natural instinct of a hunter, gave the trainer bragging rights about the success of his methods and the intelligence of his birds.

I questioned each bird with my senses. They appeared to be calm, and only the most recent one still dreamed of freedom. I resigned myself to their plight and the knowledge that these ones at least were well cared for. But Kira was not here either and my anxiety rose with the knowledge that we had only one more address to check. *Little one? Are many birds with you? What do you feel around you?*

Big bird. Hungry, too. And horse. Smell horse. Dark. Hungry. The last was a plaintive cry.

We come, little one. We will find you. Then you will hunt.

What worried me was that her voice was no nearer than before. The third falconer's address was not far away and after that we had nothing but Kira's voice to go by. I said nothing, hoping against hope that we would find her at the next place. We were met with disappointment. This establishment was bigger than the last, but well managed. The birds were well cared for and calm. We left almost immediately.

Kira, speak to me little one. Her voice came from nearby, I knew, but where?

"Papa, I know she is near. But I cannot tell exactly where. My mind-speak is not keen enough." My voice rose in panic and I fought back frustrated tears.

He responded by accosting the nearest man walking by. "My good man. We seek a man who has acquired a new kestrel. We wish to buy the bird. Kestrels are rare and we understand one has been captured near here."

The man merely shook his head. "I dinna know nought 'bout birds." And he walked on.

It took three more such tries before one woman said her husband had talked about a friend who had bragged about the easy catch he had made.

We hurried to the address. *Kira?*

You not come. Hungry, Dark. Hurt.

125

We do come, little one. It is hard to find you. But we will. Do not fear. I promise we will not stop until we find you.

We came to a small hovel with a shed attached to the back. The gardens were overgrown with weeds. The roof badly needed re-thatching, the door sagged on its leather hinges and the oiled leather over the windows had cracked in places.

Kira?

Come.

We come.

36

RESCUE

"This is the place, Papa," I whispered.

Her voice was so close now I felt as though I could touch her. My heart wrenched with the thought of Kira in the clutches of someone who showed so little care for his property.

A thin woman met us outside the door. "What d' ye want?" Her voice shook and she twisted her apron nervously in her hands. When she took in my white robes she shrank back into the doorway, then hesitated as if more afraid to go back in than to face me. Something was very wrong here.

"We seek a newly caught kestrel and have information that one can be found here."

"I dinna know 'bout no bird."

"Mistress, I know you lie. I am, as you can see, a seer. I have truth-read you."

"Get out of the way woman." A man shoved her roughly inside and came out to face us, a leg of fowl still in his greasy hand. "What d'ye want with my bird, heh? And how do ye know I have one?"

"That kestrel is mine."

My rage gave power to my voice and for an instant I saw him flinch. He recovered quickly. "Now I caught that bird fair. It be a rare un. Worth summat. Methinks ye wants te steal it, eh? Rob a poor man coz ye c'n fool 'im with th' whites. I dinna b'lieve ye be a seer." He sneered.

My father gave me a small hand signal to desist and let him take care of it. I did so with difficulty. I wanted to rip the liar's tongue out. Not a proper sentiment for a seer.

"We can prove the bird belongs to Liannis."

"I dinna b'lieve ye."

I could not wait. I headed for the shed where I knew she must be.

he man tried to get in front of me and block the way but my father caught him in a vise-like grip and lifted him off the ground. A look of surprise came over the man's face. As with most bullies, he was unaccustomed to being defied.

I opened the shed and went in. I spotted Kira right away. There were only two perches here. A large falcon was tethered to the other. I could tell it was in pain. I would deal with that after seeing to Kira. As I moved to her perch my father stopped me.

"Liannis, we must show this man that the bird does belong to you.

We cannot have him accuse us of theft."

"But..."

"Can you think of a way to prove she belongs to you?" He looked at me, his eyes warning me to think before I acted.

I took a deep breath to steady myself. "I think she will answer to her name."

My father nodded. "How?"

"She will speak when I call her name."

"Then have her do so."

Kira, when I say your name you must answer me out loud. Do you understand?

Hurt. Hungry.

I know little one. You will be free soon. Will you do as I ask?

Her answer was a petulant mind-speak grumble, but I knew she would do as I asked.

The wait had given the man confidence and he now leered at me, hands on hips, and rocked back on his heels, thumbs hooked into his belt.

"Ye canna do it, eh?"

A coldness washed over me. Later I would understand it for the hate that Papa talked about feeling towards those that had killed his father when he was only nine. It frightened me to have such rage come over me so strongly. I could understand, now, what drove men to kill.

"She will answer." I said. "And when she does I will make you pay for what you did to her and to the other animals in your care...and to your wife."

My voice must have carried some of Earth's power because he recoiled as if he had been struck. He recovered with a failed attempt at a swagger. "Show me."

"Kira, little one, speak to me."

Kira gave a strained "Klee."

The man blustered, "That be just accident."

"Kira, speak again, two times, please."

"Klee, klee." Her voice sounded a little stronger.

As I hurried over to free her, the man made a last attempt to bluff it out. "But I caught 'er, fair. She be worth summat. Ye better pay fer 'er."

Before the words were out my father had him by his shirt and up against the wall. In his most menacing growl he said, "It is you who will pay, slime. You will spend time in Lord Dugal's prison. Lord Dugal does not look kindly on theft, or on cruelty to animals. And I will personally see to it that you never hurt a woman again." He looked at me as I took the hood off Kira's head. "Liannis, hand me that rope to tie him with."

"I must free Kira first."

Kira's wings had been tied down with a rag but what enraged me most was the device around her leg that chained her to the perch. It had barbs on the inside which bit into her flesh. Fortunately for Kira it had been made for a somewhat larger bird and so had only pricked her. But a bird any larger would have been pierced by the barbs enough to draw blood. If left on it would soon fester. The thought made me ill. I retched into the stale, sour straw on the floor.

As soon as Kira was free I held her to my chest and crooned to her to soothe her, tears of rage and sorrow coursing unheeded down my cheeks and dripping onto her feathers. With my free hand I tossed the rope to my father. "Papa, when he is tied please see to the falcon. He is in pain."

Kira calmed and agreed to wait to hunt until I could feed her myself, to keep her safe near me. Her fear of being caught again helped to gain her agreement in spite of her hunger.

We go home soon, Kira, I promised her.

She chirred into my chest, somewhat mollified. *Eat?*

Yes, I will find something to eat.

My father examined the falcon. His voice took on a dangerous tone as he told me, "Liannis, go and comfort the poor woman. I will deal with this."

I obeyed, relieved that I could get away from the man and the poor raptor.

"Missus, may I enter?" I eased open the door and peered in.

The woman cowered in a corner of the dank shack. A grimy hand clutching hers was all I could see of the small child that hid behind her skirts.

"Do not fear, missus. We mean you no harm." Waves of alarm met me, and I understood that it was not me she feared but her husband. "Please believe me when I say we will see to it that your man will never harm you again. My father is the lord's man and he will take him to prison for theft. Nor does Lord Dugal take kindly to cruelty to either animals or women and children. He will mete a fitting punishment for him." Somehow I knew this to be true.

"But who will feed us. How will I find work to feed my child?"

I had not thought about that but I knew I could not leave this woman and her daughter without protection so I made a rash promise. "You and your child will be given a better life. I promise." And I vowed to make sure that I would somehow keep that promise. Then I remembered that my father had thought we might need to pay the falconer to get Kira back, and that he still had that coin in his belt pouch. It would feed the two until I found a better solution for them.

I heard him open the door. "Papa, do you still have the coin to pay for Kira. I think it is owed this woman."

He nodded understanding and reached into the pouch. "Indeed. She is a valuable bird. Here, missus."

I saw that the amount he took out far exceeded what we had planned to pay.

When she drew back in fear I took it from him and placed it on the rough plank that served as a table. "Here, missus. This will keep you and your child until help can be found for you. I promise you need never go hungry again. Lord Dugal's man will come for you soon. Do not leave or you will miss him."

"Your man is coming with us," Papa added. "Have no fear that he will return."

She just stared at us, mouth open in astonishment, eyes wide.

Papa gave her a short nod, and I tried to smile reassurance as we left. She had not moved. Once outside Papa told me, "Wait here."

When he returned from the shed he had the liver and entrails of the falcon in his hands. He placed these on the ground and said, "Let Kira feed. It will make the death of that poor bird less a waste." At my reproachful look he added, "I am sorry, Liannis. He was beyond help."

I nodded, swallowing, unable to speak lest tears overtake me.

When we neared the castle I asked, "Papa, do you think I ought to let Kira go, to tell her to leave me? I feel responsible for what happened to her and worry that she may be caught again."

"Did you not tell me she had been sent to you by Earth?"

"Yes."

"And do you think Earth would have done that if she did not think it best?"

"No, but I worry about her. I wonder if I am being fair to her...though I would sorely miss her if she were no longer with me."

"Then perhaps you ought to ask her if she still wishes to stay, or if she thinks her work is done. Surely Earth will let Kira know what she wishes."

I nodded, relieved. "Thank you, Papa. You are right, as usual. That is what I shall do, though I will wait until we are outside the city."

GOING HOME

Cloud was as happy to see me as I her. To her it meant exercise but to me it meant going home. I knew the journey would be a slow one. That, too, gave me pleasure. I would be out of the city, enjoying the countryside...and away from the pain that being around so many people always gave me. I might even be able to enjoy eating again in a day or two.

My father had fashioned a means of attaching a litter made of planks and rope to the reins of Merrist's horse. It meant a bumpy and uncomfortable ride for him, but as a soldier he had been inured to discomfort and took the idea in stride.

Upon removing his bandages once more to clean his wound prior to departure we found that it had begun to heal. The redness and swelling had gone down and Merrist showed no more signs of the fever that signified disease. His outlook had improved as well. He questioned my father in detail about the wooden leg and how it worked. Even hearing that it would be several eightdays before he could even attempt to put weight on his stump did not sour his mood. Merrist had always shown a sunny disposition and so I looked forward to his company.

Gaelen and Lionn, along with a cadre of their men, had left the day before while we searched for Kira.

I declined the offer of an armed escort, opting instead for four panniers full of provisions so I would not need to hunt for meat. We strapped two of these to Merrist's horse. I sensed no danger to us and felt that my whites offered better protection than an armed guard.

Gaelen had promised to let my mother know that we were on our way.

JOURNEY

During my three days in the city the countryside had undergone an unusual change. This early in summer the fields ought to have been verdant and lush. But when I looked now, the grasses already showed tips of brown. This normally did not happen until high summer, when the rains fell further apart. An apple orchard outside the city walls had already lost almost all its blossom without forming fruit.

I tried to remember when we had last had rain. When I realized it had been near two eightdays I became concerned. The planted fields showed the beginning signs of drought.

Was this the result of Earth's pain from the conflicts in Gharn and Lieth? The last time Earth had been injured by war she had been unable to prevent the Red Fever, the plague that had killed so many just before I was born,

I felt glad that the problem in Gharn had been mostly resolved. Things looked stable there for now. That left Lieth. But judging by Rellnost's behaviour, I saw no speedy resolution there.

Merrist found the makeshift litter very uncomfortable, painful even. Every bump jolted him and though I watched him bravely bite back most cries of pain, he could not hide it from me. Another solution needed to be found. He declared that if he could only get astride his horse, Warrior, he could ride. But the terrain we crossed consisted of low rolling hills, and meadows and the occasional orchard. Our route had been planned to avoid contact with others as much as possible, both to avoid the inevitable questions from those we met and because both of us craved solitude at this time.

Warrior stood higher than most horses, bred for strength and endurance, and to carry heavy men in battle. Merrist stoutly told me that he felt strong enough to ride if only he could get up into the saddle. Injured as he was, he did not have the ability to climb Warrior unassisted. The landscape offered no mounting blocks or even rocks to stand on. And I had not the strength to lift him, even had he been able to help.

The first day we stopped to make camp by early afternoon. Merrist could go no further. I could see his mood darkening as I lit a small fire and set about getting our supper on. Attempts at conversation were met with one word answers or short grunts. While our meal boiled I heated two more pots, one for willow bark tea for pain, the other with salted water to clean Merrist's wounds while changing his bandages.

"Useless, that is what I am."

"Merrist, you are still weak from your injury and have had a difficult day. You must be patient with yourself."

"Bah! I cannot even ride. All I can do is lie here and let you act nursemaid to me. I cannot even start a fire."

I looked at him a moment. "I have been thinking about how you may get onto Warrior. I agree that you will be more comfortable if you can ride and I have an idea."

He raised his eyebrows at me, his interest piqued, but said nothing.

"Give me a moment," I said. "I need to mind-speak Cloud."

His eyebrows rose even higher. "What do you mean, mind-speak?"

I smiled. "I can speak with both Cloud and Kira and often even other animals. It is part of the seer's gift."

"Oh!" He had clearly not heard of this. His astonishment made him forget his pain for a moment.

I smiled inwardly and turned to Cloud. *Cloud?*

Yes.

Do you think we can get Warrior to kneel so that Merrist can climb him? Warrior will need to get as low as possible. I can try to mind-speak him but it will be better if you explain as I do not know if he will understand me.

Warrior not as smart as Cloud.

That is so, but he is a good horse. Cloud's pride sometimes made her taciturn. On occasion I had to mollify her.

Hmph. I will try to explain.

Thank you. I sensed Cloud connecting to Warrior but could not hear their thoughts.

He understands. Will do it. Now?

No, tomorrow, when we are ready to leave again. Thank you, Cloud. You may graze now. I never hobbled Cloud. Because we could mind-speak she understood that she must never roam out of range of my call. But Warrior did need to be hobbled. I asked Cloud to stay close so that Warrior would not try to follow her and get frustrated. She agreed but not without expressing her annoyance. She was not past reminding me that she served me freely and could leave if she chose. Though I knew she would never really do so I made sure to stroke her pride occasionally. I watched her head toward a tussock of grass that looked greener than the rest and set myself to preparing our blankets. Then I banked the fire so that we would still have embers in the morning to start our porridge and tea.

Merrist watched me silently. I had thought he would fall asleep but his interest had been piqued and he kept himself alert until I sat down beside him.

The sun still shone bright though it hung low in the west. I knew the sunset would be brilliant when it sank so I saw no signs of rain. Dry weather would make travelling more comfortable but I wished to Earth it would rain so the crops could grow.

Merrist gave me a questioning look as I sat to explain my conversation with Cloud.

"Merrist, if we can get you onto Warrior are you certain that you can remain astride him? We will need to ride several spans each day, though we have some time and need not hurry. If we stop as we did today, do you think you can manage?"

"I will manage. You will see."

"Then Cloud thinks she can show Warrior how to get as low to the ground as possible. If he holds still I think I can help you onto his back. The hardest part for both of you will be to get Warrior's feet back under him so he can stand up with you on his back." I hesitated. "It will cause you great pain to get up and down. I am still not certain it is a good idea. We must not re-injure your leg."

He masked his fear with a determined look, though he could not hide the slight tremor in his voice. "I will do it. If Klast says I will need to learn to endure pain to walk again, then I best begin now. I must not become soft."

"Then sleep now, for you will need your strength."

He nodded.

"But first, more tea for your pain. I am pleased to see you no longer crave the poppy juice." I handed him the willow bark tea which had cooled by now. He swallowed it in one draft and after handing me the mug back, grimacing at the bitter taste, lay down and rolled his blanket around himself.

He slept within moments, and I sat alone watching the sunset. The earth held the heat from the sun and I sat, relaxed, my hands combing the blades of grass around me, and waited. But if Earth had a message for me she chose not to reveal it that night. At full darkness I lay upon my blanket and slept a dreamless sleep until dawn.

Merrist slept on, while I quietly woke the fire and set our breakfast to boil. As I worked I reviewed what needed to happen with Cloud again. Her attitude was almost contemptuous, assuring me that she knew perfectly well what to do, and that she had already told Warrior. But she also told me that if it did not work, the fault would lie with Warrior and not with herself. She told me that while his heart was great he lacked understanding. I reminded her that a good heart was all that Merrist needed in a horse and that Warrior would do his best. Her grudging agreement made me smile to myself.

Merrist stirred just as I decided to wake him to clean his bandages before breaking our fast. When I unwrapped his leg, the beginnings of bruising from the bumps of the previous day's travel confirmed that we had to get him on his horse somehow. I knew that the bruises I discovered on his thigh would be repeated all over his back and other leg as well, even his arms. This would not do at all.

When I finished dressing his leg and tried to hand him a mug of tea he shook his head. "Um, Liannis, er...could you help me up so I can lean against Warrior and, um, would you turn your back?" His face blushed crimson and his eyes would not meet mine.

I understood immediately, chagrined that I had not thought of it before I changed his dressings. The tea from the night before would be pressing on his bladder. I nodded, pretending not to notice his embarrassment and bent down so that he could put his arm around my shoulder.

He grabbed a handful of Warrior's mane with his other hand as soon as I had him high enough to reach it, and pulled him self up the rest of the way.

I quickly withdrew to fill our bowls. "Let me know when you are ready to sit back down."

"I am ready."

When I rounded Warrior to help him back down he still clutched a handful of mane. His good leg shook with the effort of holding himself upright and it struck me how much strength he had lost from his illness. I bit back the question of whether he would be able to ride, knowing it would hurt his pride.

"Our porridge is ready. Then I will need some time to break camp while you drink an extra mug of tea. It will be some spans before we can make more."

I deliberately took my time packing up our few things so that Merrist could recover before we left. When it came time to mount I suggested, "Merrist, you will not be able to dismount until we reach our next stop. Since you have had two mugs of tea I suggest you relieve yourself once more before you climb Warrior."

He blushed again but nodded assent. Both Cloud and Warrior stood ready.

I helped Merrist stand and turned away, turning back only when I heard his, "Ready."

I let Merrist lean on me while Cloud told Warrior to get down as low as he could without rolling over. At the same time I had Merrist tell Warrior to "kneel" so that he would learn the command from him. That way, after a few tries he would no longer need Cloud to be present. That would be good for both Merrist and Cloud. She needed to see that Warrior could learn.

I am not much taller than my mother, and she is one of the smallest women I know. Even with Warrior's chest on the ground and with Merrist doing all he could to help, it took all my strength to support Merrist long enough for him to pull himself on top of Warrior, lift his stump over Warrior's back and settle into the saddle. By the time Warrior rose to his feet, with Merrist clinging to his mane with all the strength he had left, I was in a sweat and trembling with the effort. When I looked at Merrist I saw blood on his lip where he had bitten it to stop from crying out.

"Bravely done." I gave him my brightest smile. "How does it feel? Better than the litter?"

"I will manage," he hissed between clenched teeth.

I thought it best not to express my doubts.

At midday, swaying in the saddle, Merrist broke his silence to tell me, "Tie me on so that I do not fall. I can hold no longer."

At his challenging glower I knew better than to suggest we stop for the day. He needed to believe he would not hold us up. I did as he asked. He slumped over Warrior's back, cheek on his neck, asleep despite the pain. I wondered how soon I could make camp without hurting his pride more than it suffered already.

Getting Merrist off Warrior proved as hard as getting him on. Merrist was so weak from his exertions that his good leg buckled when he tried to stand, and I had to lower him to the ground by sliding him down Warrior's side. He collapsed into an exhausted heap on the blanket I had readied underneath him. I just managed to get some cold willow bark tea into him before he fell asleep so I decided to leave him be until dusk so that he would have the strength to eat.

The next days repeated the pattern, but each day Merrist lasted a little longer before I had to strap him onto Warrior. The sixth day he remained in the saddle until late afternoon.

I spotted the first trees that marked the border of Bargia. That night we slept under the cover of the oaks at the forest's edge. I built a larger fire and boiled a stew with the dried meat we had, and some leeks, wild carrots and mushrooms I found among the trees. After dry journey bread and reheated beans, it tasted like a feast. We both ate well and slept soundly. I still had had no dreams or other message from Earth and wondered what she had in store for all of us. Nor did I see any clouds that might foretell rain.

39

WILL YOU GO?

When we came close enough that I felt we would arrive in two days time I called to Kira. She had flown high most of the way and we had not had much mind-speak since we left Gharn. At that time I had told her she could be free if she wished. She had not answered and had not come to her perch at night so I worried that she would leave me, that she would no longer feel safe enough to stay by me. If that were so I was prepared to let her go, but the thought of losing her weighed heavy on me. So I gave her time as we travelled to make her own decision. I knew she would stay if I asked it of her but I could not, in fairness, do that.

Kira? Little one?

Her answering cry came almost immediately though I could tell she flew a way off. But she let me know she was coming.

Thank you, little one. I have a question. Do you wish to fly free?

I am for you.

You wish to stay with me?

I am for you. I sensed both stubbornness and hurt in her reply.

Thank you, Kira. You are very brave and I am very glad you wish to stay. My heart felt full and I blinked back tears of relief. *I have a special job for you. Will you carry a message to small woman?* She knew my mother by this phrase but could not comprehend our relationship. Nor did names mean anything to her.

Carry?

I had never asked her to carry anything before so the request puzzled her. *Yes. If I tie a message to your leg with you take it to small woman? It will not be heavy. She will take it off your leg.* I sensed a frisson of fear but she showed her devotion to me.

I carry. Small woman take off leg.

Thank you, little one. Come down and I will attach it. I took a small scrap of leather and with a stick blackened in our fire wrote "home in two days". Kira came to her perch and I rolled the scrap tightly and fastened it to her leg with a piece of wool yarn. That way, if she did not reach home, the yarn would wear so that it would eventually fall off. Leather would hamper her hunting if she could not get to my mother. I stroked her feathers to calm her, telling her again how brave she was. *Home to the cabin. Small woman will be there. Stay high. Wait until she is alone. Do not let anyone see.*

Kira chirruped her understanding and lifted off.

She returned by early morning the next day. *Small woman take thing off leg. Good hunting. Full.* She came down and settled on her old perch on my shoulder. My little one had returned. That happy thought filled me with gratitude.

To my surprise, Lionn rode up early the next afternoon. "Brensa got Kira's message. Father sent me to meet you. You have been longer than he expected. He wanted to make sure all was well. We have been home for four days already."

"We are well, Lionn. Just making sure we do not over-tax Merrist's endurance. But it is good to see you. What news from Bargia?"

"Everyone is well. But we need rain for the crops. And Rellnost's attitude is not showing any improvement. He is a very angry young man. His tutors are concerned that he will not learn compassion or patience. It does not bode well for him. I wish Klast were here. He may be the only one who can reach him."

I nodded. What he told me fit with what my vision had shown me. It did indeed not bode well. And my father would not be back for some time yet.

Lionn changed the subject. "Your mother, and mine, are both eager to see you. As soon as we get within a half day from home I will go ahead and fetch Mother to the cabin. She says she is bringing a feast and lots of extra food as she is sure you have not taken care of yourself." He grinned. "How does it feel to have two mothers fussing over you?"

My answering grin matched his. "It feels wonderful. Now I know I am home."

Lionn turned to Merrist. "Merrist, you look stronger. I am surprised to see you riding."

Merrist nodded, doing his best to hide his weariness. "It beats that contraption Klast made. And Warrior is used to me so it works well."

Lionn had a skin filled with fresh venison stew which we all devoured with gusto that night. Merrist fell asleep soon after, but Lionn and I sat by the fire until well after dark catching up over some white pine needle tea. Out here, away from the city with the need for me to keep my barriers closed against the press of impressions, we could sit at ease and just enjoy each other's company, as we had when we were children. These were rare moments, and I wanted to enjoy every one.

139

40

HOME

Lionn rode ahead after we had broken our fast the next morning and he had helped Merrist into the saddle. His added height and strength made it look so easy. I was glad he would be waiting at home to help get Merrist into our cabin when we arrived. And then the long healing could truly begin. I knew it would go more quickly with the added benefit of my mother's healing gift. Though small, it would still make a difference.

As we broke into the clearing where our cabin stood, Kira flew ahead and whistled her "Klee, klee." to announce our arrival. Two welcome figures burst out the door.

Marja, being the taller, beat my mother. "Liannis, it is good to see you."

I slid from Cloud's back into a bear hug, followed by the same from my mother.

Then Mama turned her attention to Merrist, who sat looking shy and uncomfortable atop Warrior.

"Brensa, forgive my lack of manners. I am unable to dismount." He gestured to his leg.

Mama took charge with quiet efficiency. "No matter, Merrist, we will soon have you down. Ride right up to the door. I have a bed ready for you inside, or a chair, if that is what you wish. I think the rocker will be comfortable for you, if you are not ready to lie down yet."

I gave up Merrist's care to her and led Cloud into the shed that served as a stable to give her a well deserved carrot and take the curry brush to her neglected coat..

Lionn helped get Merrist inside the cabin then tried to bring Warrior into the shed to curry and feed him. "He will need to sleep outside," he laughed. "There is no room in here for him." He backed Warrior out again and returned for an armful of hay and bucket of oats. "Bring me the brush when you are finished."

I laughed. "Yes, Warrior is one of the largest war horses I have ever seen. This shed was never meant for a war horse." I asked Cloud, and she agreed that she, too, would like to remain outdoors.

As soon Lionn had left a low moo sounded behind me and a wet nose nudged my neck. Our cow, Bess, was asking to be milked. I welcomed the chance to spend some time doing that homely chore. As I rested my head on her side while my fingers relieved her of her precious gift I relaxed and could feel her do so as well. But I could not help but notice that she gave less milk than the year before, another sign of the dearth of lush forage. I wondered again what we needed to do to bring back some Balance so that Earth could provide for us as she wished to.

I searched for Kira before I went in. *Go hunt, little one. All is well.* She chirruped happily and flew off.

The sight that greeted me when I went in with my bucket of milk made me forget my troubles for the moment and smile. Lady Marja had indeed brought a feast and it laid spread across our crude table. And my favourite people surrounded it. Only Lord Gaelen and my father were missing. Everyone looked happy, and even Merrist looked comfortable sitting in the rocking chair with a blanket wrapped around him and a pillow behind his head, though I saw him nod and fight to stay awake.

"He insisted on staying up," my mother told me. "Your young man has a strong heart."

My young man?

Merrist gave me a worried look. "I told Brensa about your plan to have me work for you. I hope you do not mind."

While I still felt there was more than that to my mother's remark, I decided not to pursue it. "Of course. I am pleased that you told her." I looked about our crowded room and laughed. "It seems I shall have to sit on the bed to eat. Oh, it is so good to be home."

"Here." Marja handed me a full platter. "You look near starved."

My mother had another platter in her hand and looked at Merrist. "Merrist, what can I put on your plate?"

He gave a shy grin. "All of it please. The smell is driving me wild."

"Good. It will help you get your strength back." Obviously pleased, she began to load his platter so full even a bear would not be able to eat it all.

I met Marja's eyes, and we exchanged knowing smiles. Nothing suited my mother more than taking care of someone in need. I wondered if it was part of her healing gift. Whatever the cause, she never failed to put hurt spirits at ease.

We spent a happy evening together and as dusk fell, said goodbye to Marja and Lionn. Merrist had long since fallen asleep in the chair.

"I will come to see you at the castle and to speak with Lord Gaelen the day after tomorrow," I assured them as we watched them off.

The happy aura still lingered in the cabin after they had gone. After tucking Merrist into my parent's bed Mama and I talked long into the night over endless mugs of tea and caught up on all that had happened since I had left for Gharn. For this night, at least, a great weight had gone from my heart. This was home, my sanctuary, the one place I could always count on being looked after and able to rest from my duties.

Then Mama went to sleep in the rocker to stay close to Merrist and I climbed the ladder to my bed in the loft only scant spans before dawn.

41

MISSION

By the time my father returned home two eightdays later, Merrist's stump had healed well. Only bright red scars remained where his leg had been cut and cauterized and some of the scabs had already begun to come loose, though my mother forbade Merrist from removing them. He grew restive and wanted to be up and about.

Mama gave him the task of rubbing his stump, now that the bandages remained off, first with a rough cloth, then with coarser stuff such as moss and hay. She explained that this would begin the process of toughening the skin to prepare for the wooden cup.

Merrist also exercised Warrior, now able to mount him without assistance from us. Warrior knew the routine and knelt easily on command. Merrist refused help getting around and crawled with his hands and good knee wherever he needed to go. I made him a leather knee patch so that he did not wear holes in his breeches.

On his return, with Merrist watching every step of the process, my father chose a sturdy straight piece of oak from the woodpile out back. After measuring carefully, and making sure it was free of knots, he showed Merrist how to begin shaping one end to fit his stump. While Merrist whittled it into a rough semblance of a peg with a cup at the top, Papa found some leather and fashioned the straps that would attach the peg to Merrist's leg.

I could see Merrist's mood improving with the active role he had in creating his own device.

Papa told me that the woman we had rescued when we found Kira now had a position in the kitchen of Gharn castle.

Inquiries had uncovered several accusations of theft and assault. These made it possible to sentence her husband to a lengthy term in the dungeons after which he would be exiled from Gharn. The woman and her daughter now had a chance for a peaceful life.

During this quiet period at home, my father and I also met with Gaelen and Lionn, and once with the entire advisory council. I learned that Rellnost's attitude had not improved. He showed increasing anger and arrogance, and resisted following the orders of his tutors and instructors.

All agreed that attempting to set him in power in Lieth would cause serious problems. Now that the campaign in Gharn had been successfully completed it was time to check out the situation in Lieth.

When the other council members had left Gaelen turned to me. "Liannis, I want you to go to Lieth to see what you can find out. Who is in charge there? How are the people faring? What can Earth show you that normal eyes and ears do not receive? Now that you wear the whites you should be safe from harm."

"I will do so gladly, my lord."

"And I shall go with her," my father declared in a tone that brooked no argument.

I had to try anyway. "Papa, that is not necessary."

Gaelen tried, too. "Klast, I cannot ask this of you. You are not getting any younger and have long since earned your rest. I can send another spy or two into Lieth with Liannis."

"Besides, you have become too well known, Papa. You will be recognized. They could kill you. I will be safe but that is no longer true for you."

"Yet, I will go, Liannis. You will be safer that way and there are things I can find out that you cannot."

"As I said, my friend, there are others who can find those things out."

My father grew stubborn, and I understood that he trusted no one else to protect me. "Not with my skills."

After a silence he added, "I will go disguised as your man servant, to look after your horse and such." A wicked twinkle came into his eyes, no doubt at the irony of this reversal of roles. He stood up and even without any change in clothing, stooped slightly, and regarded me with his head lowered in submission. "Meet Hurst."

I could not help but laugh at the transformation. He had not lost any skill at all. With the added years since he had actually gone as a spy he looked even more the part of a slightly feeble-minded, slow moving old man.

Gaelen, too, shook his head and chuckled. "All right, Klast, you win. But please be careful. You no longer see, or move, as well as you used to. But this disguise does give you the opportunity to speak with Liannis along the way about what you find."

I did not feel entirely pleased with this arrangement as my father had not spied for Gaelen for many years, but had to allow that I would welcome his company and would feel safer with him beside me. I did not know how many in Lieth would recognize me as the young woman who had spirited away Nairin and her children. Even in my whites they might seek to eliminate me.

"How long will we be gone, do you think?" I asked.

"No more than three eightdays. One for travel and two there."

"Then we had best leave tomorrow."

"Agreed."

On the ride home I asked, "And what of Merrist while we are away?"

"I will finish his leg tonight. All that remains is to smooth out the inside of the cup and attach the straps. I will teach both him and Brensa how to bandage the stump and line the cup with soft moss for padding."

"I fear that he will re-injure himself in his eagerness to walk again."

"Brensa can judge whether he is doing too much. I will set a training plan for him." He studied me with a questioning look then apparently decided not to pursue his thought.

I did not ask, afraid that he perceived that I cared about Merrist almost too much. I needed to discipline myself against such attachments. A time away would help. A seer's life could be lonely.

We rode the rest of way home in silence, each absorbed with our own thoughts.

My father had led home a non-descript dun gelding from Gaelen's stables that, while sturdy, had seen hard use and showed its years. His own roan was far too fine for a man in his disguise as Hurst.

Of course, I rode Cloud, who proved keen for an adventure. Kira, too, was eager. Though more wary, now, of approaching strange men, she had recovered from her ordeal well and no longer felt any fear of accompanying me.

That night had brought torrential rains which caused the river to overflow its banks. Wild winds ripped large branches off trees at the edge of the forest, littering the clearing. Even from the view outside our cabin I knew that some crops in the area would be damaged. Yet I felt some relief knowing that the ones that survived the deluge would have moisture to grow for a while. I could only wonder about what effects the storm may have had in the city.

Papa surveyed the damage around our cabin before we departed. He left firm orders that Mama was not to attempt to clean up the mess, and that that went for Merrist, too. I wondered if either of them would heed him.

42

LIETH

By the time we reached Lieth City the sun beat down hot and dry and the land had once again lost its green. Grasses broke, brittle and dusty beneath our horses' hooves, stunted and sere. If Earth were to recover in time to bring enough rain to grow even meagre crops something had to be done quickly.

I knew Gaelen kept enough stored grain to keep the people of Bargia from starving this winter, but I doubted that the same would be true for Gharn or Lieth. Catania, since it was ruled by Lord Gaelen as well, and governed by his appointed advisor, would also have planned for such a disaster. But if they were asked to sell their supplies I feared all the people of the One Isle would know hunger.

More than once, along the way, Papa had to admonish me to stop giggling as he practiced his disguise as my man servant.

I tried to explain that it struck me funny to see him taking his role so seriously when we had not yet arrived.

But he told me that I needed to practice telling him what to do, as it did not come naturally to me. He insisted that I call him Hurst, the name he had chosen. It felt awkward but I understood the need. If I accidentally called him ☐Papa' while in Lieth it would give him away.

We entered Lieth by the east gate on the fourth day late in the afternoon. As we followed the directions to the castle, given by the guards at the gate, I wondered again if anyone would recognize me as the maid who had served Lady Nairin only moons ago. If I were, it would make our mission much more dangerous. My station as seer would ordinarily offer me protection from harm but if I were seen as a traitor that might not save me. It made me grateful that my father had been adamant that he accompany me.

We chose an inn close to the castle and rented two small, adjoining rooms there. I would have preferred a room surrounded by stone deep within the castle but that would mean my father could not stay near me. And it would have made it more likely someone would recognize me. Fortunately the city seemed only mildly uneasy so the noise did not press on me as much as it might have.

My father took Cloud and Dornel, his horse, to the stable attached to the inn to groom them and see to their feed. Cloud only agreed to let my father look after her with reluctance.

I had suggested to Kira that she stay outside the city but I sensed her perched high up on a nearby roof peak. *Stay high, little one. Do not get caught.*

The innkeeper and his wife fussed about making me comfortable. A seer as a guest brought status to the inn. I would have preferred to keep my presence quiet but thought it best to allow the extra attention. It might prove an advantage if we found ourselves under suspicion later.

Even though he had a room of his own, I knew that my father would sleep on the floor outside my door as soon as the other guests had retired and he would not arouse notice. And even then, he would keep one ear alert. It was another of his remarkable skills learned both as a captive boy and as a spy.

We had agreed that Papa would eat dinner at my table at the inn but that, as my servant, he would wake up ahead of me and attend to the horses before breaking fast with me. We listened to the drone of conversation in the main room while we ate our mutton stew and bread and shared a crock of good ale. The stew tasted wonderful after our makeshift meals. The mutton, young and mild, swam in a rich broth of onions, with barley to thicken it. The bread, though dark, proved soft and fragrant.

My whites had drawn a good deal of attention and I had the sense that the inn had more guests than usual for dinner.

At the end of our meal the innkeeper's wife brought out a small bowl of dried apples, raisins and plums. "For our honoured guest." She dipped a hasty curtsey and eyed me to see if her offering would be well received.

My father kept his eyes lowered and slouched in his seat, appearing indifferent and submissive, as I looked up at our hostess. "How wonderful! I am sure I will enjoy your gift." I wondered what I could do to avoid such special treatment in the future. This could prove a problem. As the woman still waited beside our table with an anxious, expectant look, I chose a slice of dried apple and took a bite. It was still soft for this time of year. I smiled at the woman. "Delicious, thank you."

Her shoulders relaxed and she beamed at me as she dipped another curtsey and backed away, then turned and retreated back to the kitchen. I looked at my father and caught a tiny quirk of amusement. This was my problem. It almost made me want to kick him under the table.

But he no longer looked at me but surveyed the room with practiced eyes and ears. Knowing that he needed time to assess the mood of the people and to gather information I made myself linger over the last of my meal and enjoy the fruit. I saved a few pieces for him in my pocket for later. It would not do to have people see me share my special treat with

147

my servant. I would have to find a way to stop this before things got out of hand.

When we had finished our meal I wrote a message on a piece of rolled leather, which I instructed "Hurst" to take to the castle and to tell the guard that 'Liannis, seer', requested a meeting with Garneth, the name of the man who now sat in the lord's seat. Hurst grunted assent and as he rose slowly to do as I bade him I raised my voice to say, "Now no one else but Garneth, mind. And bring back a reply. "

He gave me a resentful glare, hunched his shoulders and shuffled off, for all the world a slow, somewhat lazy servant.

I hid my smile behind my hand. After he had gone I requested a tub and hot water for a bath to be taken in my room. Tomorrow I would meet Garneth and I wanted to make a strong impression on him and his cronies. Besides, I loved baths and had not been able to take one since we left Bargia. When the maid, Morna, came with the tub I offered her two pieces of the fruits the innkeeper's wife had given me. I made sure to touch her hand as she took them to get an impression of her. Her delight was genuine and I sensed no guile in her. She might prove useful if I needed information or had to send someone with a message.

A soft knock told me Papa had returned. When I opened the door he said, in a voice that would be heard by several others, "Lord Garneth says come to th' castle at midday. He be seein' ye then."

"Thank you Hurst, you may go to bed after you have checked on the horses...and no more ale, mind." I knew he would be sure to let the others see his resentment and would order a crock in spite of my warning and make a show of sitting there drinking it. I hoped it would help him glean some information. He would dump the ale out when no one could see.

This was the first time I had seen him ply his craft as a spy. He used such subtle skill that even I had to remind myself that he was anything other than what he pretended. No wonder he had always had such success. Just the same, he was no longer a young man and I worried about his safety. I could not shake that small sense of foreboding each time I thought of the danger he put himself in.

When he returned from seeing to our mounts he made sure to make some noise as he shut his door so I would know. I relaxed and went to sleep. Earth visited me with my first dream in many nights.

* * *

"Mama, I am hungry."

"I know Luca, but there is no more. The guards will bring more when you can see the sky turning red through the window slit." The

woman raised a hand in helplessness and let it drop into her lap again, her eyes drooping once more to the floor at her feet.

Four women and several children shared the large cell in the dungeon. They had been there for some time. All wore shabby filthy rags, though vestiges of embroidery showed through the grime. Their hair hung lank and matted onto thin shoulders. Most sat on the stone shelves that lined the walls and served as beds, listless, staring dully at the floor. Here and there one wrapped a filthy blanket around slumped shoulders. One woman draped an arm around a small child who lay with a cheek resting on her lap. Two older children used a chunk of stone to scratch out the lines of a game they played on one of the walls. Here and there, bits of straw, blackened from long use on the floor, lay scattered about.

The child who had complained turned toward the small sliver of light that found its way into the dim cell. It created a thin slice of light which moved slowly across the floor, growing thinner as evening neared, and it made its way up the far wall before disappearing. He uttered no more complaint, just kept his gaze on the sliver of sun, face expressionless.

* * *

I woke with the stench of that dreary, hopeless place still in my nostrils. My mouth felt dry and my stomach ached with hollow emptiness. The feelings of helplessness I had sensed from those held in that prison hung about me like a pall. I felt like I was slowly suffocating and my very bones seemed so heavy I could hardly get up off my bed.

I moaned and the sound of my own voice brought me back to the present. I reached for the pitcher of water on the small table by my bed and drank a long draft of the cool, fresh water. Oh, Earth, who are these people? What must I do to help them? Women and children...what circumstances sent them to this melancholy abyss? I rose and knocked quietly on my door to alert my father before silently opening it to admit him.

As I had known he would, he had slept at the foot of my door and came instantly awake. The first hint of pink lit the horizon, telling me that dawn had not quite arrived. We had only a few moments to talk so I filled him in as quickly as I could.

"I will see what I can find out at the dungeons today. You go to your meeting and see what you can find out there."

"By their dress they appear to have been wealthy, not thieves or petty criminals. And surely the children are blameless? They must be the wives and children of men loyal to Merlost. What threat can they pose now? Papa, do you think we can rescue them if I cannot persuade Garneth to let them go? They look near death from starvation."

Papa shook his head. "I do not know who they are, Liannis, but we will find out. And then we can decide what may be done, if anything, but not before. We cannot risk our mission to rescue those Garneth has placed in prison, even if they be deserving."

"I do not think Earth would have sent me this without reason. These people mean something to our future. And I do not think any children belong in prison, no matter what their parents may have done."

"Probably, but we must be certain, lest we make things worse."

I sighed, knowing he was right and anxious to find out as soon as possible, so we could decide what needed to be done and do it. "Be careful, Papa. It is long since you did this kind of work. I need my man servant in one piece."

Papa transformed himself back into Hurst, opened the door and backed out saying, "I be seein t' yer table now, lady." He flashed me a wicked grin before leaving me to smile my response at the closed door.

I dressed with care in a clean gown of light linen and plaited my hair into a single braid which I let hang down my back. Wearing my hair this way reminded me of Liethis, my wonderful teacher, and gave me more confidence. With nothing further to occupy me in my chamber I took a deep, steadying breath and followed my father to the table in the main room, where a bowl of thick porridge and a mug of steaming tea awaited me.

He slouched on the bench with his back to the wall, seeming indifferent.

I knew better. Not the smallest thing escaped his notice. A shiver of fear passed over me at the thought of him spying in the dungeons. If anyone saw him they would surely know he had no business there. Oh, Earth, keep him safe! Underneath the table, where no one would see, he nudged my leg with his boot. Though I had thought I had shown nothing, yet he had seen and tried to reassure me.

43

GARNETH

My whites made the guards at the gate nervous but they still had me wait while one went to confirm that Garneth expected me. To question the word of a seer is an insult, but it seemed they had orders to let no one past without direct permission from Garneth, now called Lord Garneth, or his closest advisors. Perhaps not enough time had passed since the coup to trust that they would not find themselves in the same position Merlost had.

While both my father and I had already noticed an underlying unease among the inhabitants of the city, entering the gate to the castle made it more apparent. Very few people looked relaxed. Most hurried about their business and avoided meeting the eyes of those they passed. Guards posted about shifted hands to touch their swords, as if to make sure they were still there close to hand.

Where I had expected to simply follow a single guard to our meeting, two escorted me, one in front and one behind. The castle had the feel of a place under siege. Thoughts of my dream came back to me making me wonder if I would soon join the prisoners. My biggest fear was that someone would recognize me. If that happened I knew that my chances of learning what I needed to know, or effecting any change for those poor women and children, would dwindle. Earth, help me now. Show me what I need to see.

Outside the meeting room one guard stayed behind with me, while the other rapped a coded knock and was admitted inside. Neither guard had spoken a word to me along the way. The one who waited with me still kept silent, shifting from foot to foot and avoiding meeting my eyes. We waited a long time before the door finally opened and I was ordered to enter.

I saw immediately that no chair sat empty waiting for me, another direct slight. The guard who opened the door, the same one who had escorted me here, left quickly and another inside closed and barred the door. I remained silent to one side waiting to be told where I might stand.

The council chamber held the usual long table but only three chairs of the customary twenty remained. The three who occupied them appeared both hostile and uneasy.

I breathed a small sigh of relief when none of them looked familiar.

"Stand at the end of the table where we can all see you." This came from the centre one at the head of the table so I presumed he must be

Garneth...but no, this was a test. Garneth sat to the right of this one. I nodded to the real Garneth. "As you wish, Lord Garneth."

He raised one eyebrow at the other and without a word they traded places.

"You claim to be a seer." Garneth made it sound more like an accusation than a request for confirmation.

"I am."

The man to his left smirked. His name came to me. I turned to him, deciding to be bold. "You doubt me, Baylin?"

Garneth answered in a bored drawl. "It would have been easy for you to learn our names. This proves nothing."

"And should I also have learned the names of the two guards who brought me here and the one who now stands at the door? The dark one goes by Griel, the other, Morler and this one is Berl. Berl, you have a long scar on your chest from where your own sword grazed you when you fell from your horse."

Berl gasped.

The three men sat straighter, ready to take me more seriously. The one who had smirked asked, "Is this so?"

Berl nodded, shaken. "Yes, it is."

"So, seer, tell us why you have come." The sneer from Garneth's previous questions had diminished now but was still present. "Which demesne do you serve and what does Earth tell you about Lieth?" He leaned toward me, forearms resting on the table in front of him. While he did his best to look relaxed and confident I sensed my revelation had unsettled him.

"No demesne may claim me. I serve all of the One Isle. I have had no visions about the future of Lieth at this time. If I had I would gladly share them. I am merely here to learn first hand how Lieth fares since its new rule."

All three looked surprised. Then I could sense anger rising in Garneth. He half rose out of his seat and demanded, "All seers serve only one demesne, one lord. Who do you serve?"

I waited, trying to appear calm as he settled back into his chair. "Yet I speak true, I serve no lord. Earth has chosen a different path for me. I do her will only. That takes me where she guides me and may involve any demesne."

It took effort to keep my voice level and stand at ease. "I have been given a vision by Earth just this last night. She has shown me a dungeon, a large cell. In it a group of women and children languished. They were dressed in garments that hung on their bodies, the poor fit indicating loss of weight. The gowns still bore signs of rich embroidery through the grime, with colours only available to the wealthy. I saw a babe near death, no longer having even the strength to cry, his mother's milk dried up. Another, a small girl, sat listless, hunger having robbed her of the will to move about. A golden haired boy watched the sliver of light coming through the window slit waiting for it to tell him when his one daily bit of food was on the way. All looked ill. Tell me, Lord Garneth. What crime did that babe dying in his mother's arms commit? Did he murder someone in their sleep? Did that small boy steal gold from your coffers? Did the women take up arms against your council?" My voice had risen as I spoke.

Baylin, and Korliss to Garneth's right, exchanged furtive glances. Garneth, however, did not even blink, and his eyes never left mine.

The only hint I could see that he felt any reaction was a tightening of the muscles in his jaw. I hoped it was a sign of nervousness and I wished for a moment that my father were here. He would have known instantly where each man stood. I had only my young skills to rely on. Then I remembered I could truth-read. In my anxiety I had almost forgotten.

"They should consider themselves fortunate that they have not been beheaded and their children exiled. Is that not the usual sentence for traitors?" Garneth raised one eyebrow at me in mock question, a sly smile playing about his mouth.

"Lord Garneth, you are aware that I can truth-read. Why do you persist in this sham? All in this chamber know that these are not traitors." I had a sudden flash of certainty. "They are the wives and children of the men you deposed. They have committed no crime, unless being family to those you removed to gain power is a crime."

Garneth's look darkened and he opened his mouth to speak but I cut him off. "I make no judgment about whether that coup was conducted for the right reasons, or was necessary. I merely suggest that holding these families in this way is cruel and unjustifiable. These women and children can do you no harm. They have no more power. They do not deserve such treatment. What can you offer that shows good will and may improve their circumstances?"

Garneth finally sat back in his chair and a small glimmer of guilt stole across his face. He sat still a moment, then leaned toward me again, his arms on the table in front of him, hands wide in acknowledgement. "It seems you are indeed what you say. Perhaps their situation can be improved. But I cannot set them free. So what do you suggest?" He lifted his hands to me in question and leaned back again, as though waiting for my solution.

153

My anger welled up and I pressed it down with difficulty before continuing. If I did not move with extreme care this impasse might be broken with disastrous results. I forced a smile. "I would not presume to tell a ruler what he must do. I only ask what may be done to ease the plight of these unfortunates." I forced a smile and opened my hands in entreaty.

I sensed Garneth weighing his decision. Apparently he felt this would not be a good time to risk the wrath of a seer. "Seer, I was not aware that these prisoners were so poorly fed. I cannot set them free. But I give you my pledge that they shall have all they need to eat and that they shall be moved to a cleaner brighter cell. Will that satisfy you?"

A small concession and I caught his lie that he had not known. But I knew that future relations with this man and his cronies were important, so I bent my head in acquiescence. "It is less than I hoped, my lord, but I am grateful for this much for them."

He returned with his own tight smile. "Now tell me, seer, surely Earth has some small predictions for Lieth."

"I am sorry, my lord. Earth has shown me nothing in this regard. But I do suspect all will remain quiet, for a time at least, as I know that Nairin and her children remain safe...though not in any position to challenge you at this time. And I do see, even without any vision, that all peoples of the One Isle would do well to prepare for drought and poor harvests. We will all know hunger this winter. In this Earth does not show favourites. Look to your people, Lord Garneth."

"Do not presume to tell me my duty seer. Unlike Merlost, I know how to govern."

I inclined my head again. "Earth shall judge all lords on that score. I merely seek to lessen the suffering that is sure to come."

Garneth gave a curt nod and rose to indicate the audience was over.

I moved to the door and was led out again to the castle gate. I had done what I could. The rest was up to Garneth. Somehow, I felt it would not be enough. My mood remained dark as I approached the inn.

44

WHERE IS PAPA?

I did not worry over much when I did not see my father at the inn on my return, but when darkness fell and all the dinner patrons had left the main room, I became alarmed. No one at the inn had seen him. I tended to the horses myself to keep my mind from spiralling out of control with fear. He still had not appeared when I had curried and fed both Cloud and Papa's poor mount and had mucked out their stables. Then, thoroughly dirty, I had a bath brought to my room.

Before shutting myself in to take a hasty bath, I made sure the innkeeper, and all who worked there, were aware that I was concerned that Hurst had met with some unfortunate incident, and that any information of his whereabouts would be most welcome. I had, I told them, had to rescue him before when he had been lured into inns and plied with too much drink. He was slow, I explained, and easily taken advantage of. I wanted him back safe.

Then, bath over and with nothing more to busy myself with, I did what often gave me information. I went to sleep, hoping for a message from Earth. I did not wait long.

* * *

Hurst scrabbled close to the slit that passed for a window. When his body blocked the meagre shaft of sun a tremulous voice cried out. "Mama, a bad man."

Then nothing. Hurst went right to the slit and called out. "Who be here?"

An older child answered, apparently less fearful. "We have been here for a long time. Our fathers were killed. Can you get us out? Or bring food? We are very hungry."

Just as Hurst asked to speak to one of the women, an alert guard spotted him and called out, "Hey, you there, get away from there. What are you doing? No one is allowed here."

When my father made to run off, the guard collared him and dragged him away.

Then I saw my father manacled in a cell. His appearance had changed as soon as the guard left. I watched him reach behind him for the small blade that he kept between the two layers of leather in his belt. That blade, commissioned to his specifications years before my birth, had saved his skin many times. He soon had his manacles unlocked and began to work on the lock on his cell door. By now it had grown so dark

155

that I caught only fleeting glimpses of movement. I heard the cell door creak open then shut again. The lock clicked closed.

My next view showed the guard who had arrested and questioned him about to leave the dungeons. My father slipped behind him and efficiently knocked him senseless. He would have no witnesses to his escape.

* * *

I woke with a start. Darkness still filled my small chamber and only a sliver of moonlight lit a pale square on the floor beside my cot. A tiny rustle caught my attention at the same moment that I felt two fingers on my lips.

"Shhhh," Papa whispered before he removed his fingers.

I wanted to throw my arms around him and cry out my relief but his furtiveness and the memory of my dream told me to keep still.

"I cannot remain as Hurst," my father explained. "I have made sure that all rumours have him dead and his body hidden by thieves. In the afternoon, when you have decided I will not return, a man will come to the inn looking for work. He will walk with a limp, wear a green hat and speak in a gruff voice. You will hire him as your new servant. You will both leave and go back to Bargia. Gaelen needs news of what passes here in Lieth."

I nodded my understanding, knowing he would sense the movement. Then, unable to lie still any longer I sat up and wrapped my arms around his neck.

He returned the hug then quickly let go. "Dawn is almost here. I must go now." He slipped out without a sound.

Sleep eluded me now so I rose, dressed and made sure I had everything packed, ready to leave. As dawn lit the horizon, I went to the stables to feed the horses and tell Cloud we would leave soon.

Good. Need to run. Want sun.

We return to Bargia. There will be enough sun but we will walk, not run.

She answered with a disdainful snort. I laughed, in spite of the gravity of the situation.

At breakfast I inquired once more about Hurst. I made my tone more angry and impatient than before. Of course, no one had heard of him. I ate alone, making sure to send impatient glances at the door and shaking my head several times. When the serving maid asked if I needed anything more I asked for tea and said, "It looks like Hurst has done it this time. I will not take him back. He has disappeared too many times and come back so drunk he was useless. Do you know of anyone who could take

156

his place? The work is not hard but he must be trustworthy. I will not put up with fools any longer."

She shook her head. "But I will inquire."

"Thank you. And I plan to leave tomorrow. I have duties that call me away, with or without a servant. Can you see to food for a seven day journey - bread, cheese, tea, beans, some dried meat and one small ham?"

"Certainly, lady, I will have it ready when you break your fast tomorrow."

I nodded my thanks and she hurried away.

Just as I finished my tea and made to rise to leave two guards in uniform tunics came through the door. They looked around and headed straight for me. I sat back down and waited.

"Where is your man?"

"I have no idea. The lout is likely sitting at a drinking hole getting soused. I have already told the maid I am looking for a replacement." I breathed a sigh of relief that the maid could verify this.

"We arrested him nosing around the dungeon and put him in a cell. But this morning he was gone and his cell still locked. What do you know of this, seer?"

I feigned surprise. "The dungeon? What could he possibly want there?" I shook my head in disgust. "He always was unpredictable. The dungeon, you say. I have no idea what he was doing there." I made my voice angrier. "But if you find him you may do with him what you wish. I no longer have need of his services." I shook my head again. "It explains why he did not return at dinner last evening."

The guards, not knowing how to respond, blustered and muttered something about reporting it if I see or hear from him.

I gave them my solemn promise to do so.

They questioned the terrified maid, who confirmed what I said, then left.

I breathed a huge sigh of relief.

45

HOMEWARD

That first day we left at dawn to put as much distance between ourselves and Lieth City before nightfall as we could. We kept away from open spaces as much as possible. Kira flew overhead, keeping watch for pursuit. We pushed on until well past dark and ate a cold meal before I rolled into my blanket. I fell into an exhausted sleep, safe in the certainty that Papa kept watch, one eye and ear always alert. His years of training, and work as a spy, never left him. I knew that he had been taken by surprise only once, but that time he had actually wanted to be caught anyway.

From time to time, as we made our way, Kira settled on her perch on my shoulder to rest. I made sure we had fresh meat for her, usually the entrails of the rabbits my father trapped at night as we slept. She communicated her pleasure at being with me again with contented chirrups. *Not like big place. Too long alone.*

I am sorry you felt alone, Kira. And I am glad to see you. It is good to travel together.

The worry that Garneth or his guards would see though our ploy and come after us put speed into our flight, even after that first day. We saw the welcome sights of Bargia in two days less time than it had taken to reach Lieth.

We stopped at home to let Mama know we were safe before heading into the city.

Taking in our dirty clothes and fatigue she knew all had not gone well. She hugged us both fiercely and asked, "Will you at least have time for a bath and a meal before you meet Gaelen?"

It was not until after I saw my father give her a tired nod that I noticed Merrist standing behind her, a crutch under each arm and a shy, lopsided grin on his face.

My delight at seeing him upright must have shown even before I spoke because the grin widened even more.

"Merrist! You are walking!" I hurried over and gave him an impetuous hug before realizing what I had done. I retreated hastily, while he blushed to his roots. I decided there was nothing for it but to put a good face on it, opened my arms wide to include them all and declared, "Oh, but it feels so good to be home." I hoped they would all put it down to that.

I noticed that Merrist handled his crutches well as we went back into the cabin. Papa and I sank into our chairs and let my mother's happy prattle wash over us, soothing our frayed senses and removing the need to talk.

"Merrist is doing well, do you not agree? He has worked very hard to regain his strength and has learned to do so much while using his crutches. And he practices with the new leg every day...too much if you ask me, but he will not leave off. Three days ago he climbed up onto the roof and repaired the weak spots. It will still need new sod before winter, though." She turned to look at my father with a smile. "He has hauled water from the stream for my garden, too. The rains still have not come, and the stream is beginning to run dry. I do not know what I shall do for water. There is none left in the barrels. The well still has water but I sent a rope down tied to a stone to check and it has only three feet of water in it. I have never seen it so low." She turned to me, a worried look on her face. "Liannis, have you any news about rain?"

I shook my head. Movement from the bed where Merrist sat drew my attention. I became alarmed as he unwound the last layers of bandaging from his stump. Some showed the bright red of fresh blood. He tried to shield his stump from me but I saw before he could cover it.

My father saw it, too, and reacted quicker than I could, his look darkening to a thunder that made me glad I was not the one receiving it. "Merrist, let me see that."

I almost held my breath as I waited for the result of his examination. When it came it was surprisingly gentle.

"I see that you have taken my urging to heart. You have worked hard, as Brensa said, too hard. But this looks clean and shows no signs of pus."

He probed some more as my mother piped in. "Well, of course it looks clean. What kind of nurse do you take me for?" She tsked indignantly and my father gave her one of his rare smiles over his shoulder.

"You have taken better care than I could have. Your healing gift is beyond question."

She hmphed again but we all could see the twinkle in her eye. "It is just that young Merrist must do twice what you set for him. Nothing I say will slow him down."

Merrist gave a small, shy shrug in mute apology. "What else could I do," it seemed to say.

I smiled back. "Papa is hard to ignore, even when he is not present. He says toughen your stump and it is done, whether good for you or not."

159

My father looked completely absorbed in his task again. "Tell me how much pain you feel when you put pressure on it? How much time are you on it every day?"

"I started sooner than Brensa wanted me to. I probably should have heeded her but I wanted so badly to try it out...and to show you." Merrist looked sheepish. "At first all I could do was to stand and place it in the wooden leg. We had to figure out together how to wind the bandages and how much moss to put in. That took a few tries. But yesterday I managed to walk from the cabin to the stream with just one crutch. I did it again today. But it hurts like fire, like someone pounded it with a meat hammer to make it tender."

"I do not doubt it. Your courage does you credit. But I want you off it for the next two days. Then you may try the walk to the stream every other day, not every day. It needs time to recover between each try or it will become too damaged to heal." When Merrist grimaced his disappointment Papa added. "Merrist, the goal is to walk, not to lose the rest of your leg."

Merrist's face fell, chagrined, and he nodded. "I suppose I am impatient when I should be grateful."

"Hmmm. When I am not here I know Brensa will cosset and coddle you." Mama shot Papa an exaggerated indignant look but said nothing, knowing it to be true. "But you wish to go too far too fast. Perhaps a good guide would be to do what is midway between."

A small furry bundle shot past my legs and jumped into Merrist's lap, bringing a low chuckle from him. A loud purring followed as the cat settled with proprietary content into a lazy stretch across his legs and closed his eyes as Merrist stroked his chin.

Well, that had not taken long. The young cat, an offspring of my first cat, No-tail, had shown a preference for me before Merrist arrived. Fickle creature. I gave Merrist a rueful look and received an apologetic smile in return.

"Dinner is ready!"

All attention went to Mama.

46

NEWS

We entered the city gates about a span past dawn and, after stabling our mounts, made our way to the castle to seek Gaelen. A young guard at the castle gate told us where we would find him.

We watched him spar with Lionn for a few moments until he noticed our presence. "Lionn is as good as Gaelen now, do you not agree."

My father nodded. "And Gaelen has lost none of his skill, in spite of his age."

The two men strode over to us. "It is good to see you both back, Klast, Liannis." He clasped our arms in turn.

Lionn, close behind did the same, ending in a hug for me, grinning the grin that had delighted me ever since I had known him. "I will surpass him soon! I can feel it!"

Both looked to my father.

Gaelen's grin matched his son's. "Klast, what do you think?"

"I saw an even match. You will need to work hard, my lord, to stay ahead of him, I think."

Lionn let out a great whoop and tossed his leather shield in the air.

Even my father smiled.

As we made our way back to the castle Gaelen wasted no time. "So, what news from Lieth, my friend?"

"There is much, my lord."

"Is it news that can be shared with Marja over tea? Marja will be happy to see you both back safe."

"It is serious but not secret. And Lady Marja has often had good ideas that the rest of us do not think of."

This was high praise from my father, as their relationship had always trod a careful path. Though they now trusted and respected each other, that trust had been hard won.

As soon as one of the maids in the castle saw us, she hurried over. "Will you wish to see Lady Marja, my lord?"

"Indeed. Will you also have tea and food brought to our chambers...or no, the garden, I think. It is pleasant there."

The maid dipped a quick curtsey, "Yes, my lord," and hurried off.

As soon as everyone held their mug of tea and had helped themselves to bread, cold fowl and soft cheese, Gaelen cleared his throat. "Forgive my impatience but I am eager to hear your report."

Papa inclined his head to me to take the lead.

"My lord, the situation in Lieth is not good. Garneth has declared himself Lord and has only two men close by him who act as advisors. They are Baylin and Senth. Garneth trusts only these two. My whites did get me an audience, but Garneth's attitude toward me was both suspicious and arrogant. He acted as though he disbelieved me and even showed contempt. I chose my mien and my words carefully lest I find myself in prison."

I took a breath to collect my thoughts. "There is more. I had a vision in which I saw women and children languishing in the dungeon." This got the rapt attention of all three as they leaned toward me in unison. "These were the families of the advisors to Lord Merlost. They had not enough food, their clothes hung in rags and at least one babe will surely die even if their conditions change immediately. I expect even more are beyond hope of recovery. It is my opinion that he plans to leave them there to die."

Marja's hands covered her mouth in horror and sympathy. Gaelen's mouth became a grim line. Lionn's lips mirrored his father's and a deep frown line stood between his brows.

"I did speak to Garneth about this. The only thing he agreed to was to increase their food. He feigned surprised about their conditions. My lord, something needs to be done, and soon, if these innocents are to survive."

No one ate now. All had gone still as I spoke.

"I will let Papa tell the rest. He has seen the prison and has more to tell."

All attention moved to my father. He had just opened his mouth to speak when someone knocked at the garden door.

Gaelen held up his hand to tell Papa to wait and looked at me. I nodded that it was safe so he went to open it. "This may be important as I left instructions that we must not be disturbed."

Gaelen admitted a guard whose dusty and tired appearance told us he had travelled fast and hard.

Gaelen handed him a mug of tea. "Sit down and rest. Take some food. Tell me, does your news require immediate action or can you take the time to eat before you speak?"

"The news is important, my lord" he said between gulps, "but a span will make little difference." The guard nodded gratefully as he sank onto a bench and began to wolf down meat and bread.

"Perhaps you can tell us your name while you eat."

"Bannin, my lord, and pardon. I ought to have given it before."

"No pardon necessary, Bannin, you have ridden hard and are no doubt fatigued."

Bannin nodded his gratitude, his mouth too full to speak. As soon as he had swallowed he went on. "Kerran sent me, my lord, upon discovering a possible conspiracy against Lord Dugal. He said Lord Dugal knows of it and that I was to come to you." He took another long draft from his refilled mug before continuing. Suddenly becoming aware of Marja's and my presence, he halted, a worried expression clouding his face. "My lord, ought I to give this report in front of your lady and the seer?"

This brought a small smile from Gaelen. "Lady Marja and Liannis have long acted as advisors Bannin. I do not keep news from them and value their opinions. Continue."

Bannin nodded, relieved. "My lord, we do not yet know the details of this plot but we suspect that someone in the castle, who has Lord Dugal's ear and moves freely about it, is taking information to someone outside the city. Lord Dugal's spies have found that too many things discussed in the council are spoken of in the taverns and inns. And two men thought to be among those responsible for the plot against Lord Dugal's father have left the city."

I heard no more.

* * *

My sight flew to Gharn. A young woman looked to both sides and over her shoulder, then slipped out the castle gate and through the narrow streets before disappearing around a corner...

Vernia. The name flashed into my memory as I recognized the figure in my vision.

* * *

I opened my eyes to find four pairs fastened on me, those of the guard round with surprise and alarm.

Marja recovered first and quickly thrust a fresh mug of tea into my cold hands which I drank in two drafts, grateful for the liberal dose of honey.

Gaelen quirked one brow at me in question.

I shook my head. "What I saw is best told in private, my lord." I turned to Bannin. "Is your report finished?" He nodded, still awed by what he had seen. "Then, my lord, if he could wait while I tell what I saw...?"

"Bannin, you may go and refresh yourself. We will send for you when we are ready."

163

After the garden door once more insured our privacy, I conveyed what I had seen.

Gaelen frowned. "But how is Vernia getting this information?"

Papa spoke up. "Vernia is a very persuasive woman and is angry that she has lost Dugal's ear. It does not surprise me that she has used her skills in this way. And Dugal, though he agreed to exclude her, did not seem completely convinced. Do not be surprised if it is Dugal's ear she bends. He is still not immune to her wiles."

"Surely not, Klast. He swore he would not trust her again."

"Hmmm." My father did not sound in the least convinced.

"I agree, my lord. Even when we discussed her in Gharn I sensed that we had not done with her. I fear Dugal has a hard lesson to learn." I could not help remembering how reluctant Dugal had been to shut Vernia out.

"Well, regardless of who she is receiving pillow talk from, something must be done to uncover and stop this plot." Gaelen looked at my father, the apology already on his face. "Klast, may I request your services? It seems that, once again, I must break my promise to let you retire."

It was the first time I had seen any reluctance from my father whenever Gaelen asked anything from him. It gave me a chill.

His answer, though, was the same as ever. "As you wish, my lord. I am always ready to serve you."

Gaelen had not noticed the hesitation. "Thank you, my friend."

"And I shall go with him," I announced.

"No, Liannis, this is best done alone so I can remain unseen and unknown. This does not require the skills of a seer."

Having nothing I could use as argument against my father's logic I said nothing to him, my stomach a lump of lead within me. Instead, I turned to Gaelen. "My lord, is there no one else you can send?"

Papa did not give him time to respond. "Liannis, you know I am the best choice. I will go."

We spent another span discussing the situation in Lieth that the news from Gharn had interrupted. Gaelen decided to call a meeting of the advisory council for the next morning. He asked both of us to attend.

Our ride home was silent and sombre. Neither Cloud not Kira penetrated my thoughts.

47

COUNCIL

My father planned to leave for Lieth right after the council meeting. He had given strict instructions to Merrist on the training of his leg. Mama had given him a tearful hug and bade him to be careful. We both knew he was getting old for this and that this mission could become dangerous. The weight I felt yesterday still sat heavy in my stomach, and I feared its meaning. But Earth remained silent.

I decided that until Earth showed me a different task, I ought to remain with Mama and Merrist. Something made me want to stay nearby. My uneasiness was not for my father alone.

When we arrived at the council chamber Janest, the only remaining member of the council that had supported Gaelen through the crisis of Sinnath's treason, greeted me warmly. It saddened me to see how much he had aged since our last meeting and that he had begun to look frail, and more dishevelled than ever. But his mind remained keen, and his eyes still sparked with curiosity. I felt glad that Gaelen still had him to rely on, the oldest voice of experience and wisdom among the younger men.

Gaelen had chosen his other three advisors with care. Brest, the eldest, sat at his right. His military training showed in his stiff posture, his broad shoulders and well muscled arms. His attitude matched his appearance. He held the position of head of the army and the guard, and had his finger on the pulse of each. His was the voice of caution and tradition.

To Gaelen's left sat Grolsh, youngest member of the council, son of one of the oldest and wealthiest families in Bargia. His light build, his excess energy which made it impossible for him to sit still, and the eagerness with which his eyes darted about to take everything in, made him appear almost a child. But Grolsh had a way of seeing possibilities that others missed and offering solutions that were as apt as they were innovative. I could almost imagine that this was how Janest had been as a young man. I liked him immensely and returned his quick smile with my own.

Kamdeth, the last member, owned a number of warehouses and had a reputation as a shrewd business man. His family, too, had lived in Bargia for generations. He knew every trader family from every demesne and employed traders in every city on the One Isle. One of the most influential men in Bargia, he took great pains with his appearance, always wearing the best fabrics in the most elegant cuts. He kept his straight dark hair in a tail and wore a short beard to make him self appear older.

Lionn rounded out the group.

I had truth-read each man and knew their loyalty to be unassailable.

The two issues that Gaelen had convened them for were quickly decided. A delegation, of which Kamdeth would be a member, would leave for Lieth to negotiate an agreement of trade for grain during the expected famine and to plead for the release of the women and children in the dungeon. If they could get Garneth to agree, Bargia would offer them asylum.

I had strong doubts that Garneth would let them out of his sight, but perhaps he would at least agree to improve their circumstances. But Kamdeth felt confident that the offer of grain would stir Garneth to agree.

The delegation would include two additional members from the business faction, one commander from the army and one spy who would also act as another member of the guard.

Gaelen had just concluded telling the news from Gharn, and had informed the council he had chosen Klast to find out what he could there, when we heard an urgent knocking. A muffled, "My lord, my lord!" penetrated the thick planks of the door.

My father instantly stood between Gaelen and the door, hand on his sword, and looked at me. I nodded that I could sense no danger. Gaelen indicated to Kamdeth to open the door.

The young guard that rushed in could barely speak, his alarm making him stutter. "My lord...it is Rellnost...he...we were...at the hunt...and..." He stopped, afraid to continue.

* * *

With each word a scene appeared, vivid in my mind. Rellnost, on his horse, in a rage, screaming, brandishing his sword wildly. A large buck, bleeding from the neck, fleeing from the clearing into the trees, his broad antlers momentarily caught in the branches of the low shrubs at the edge of the forest. Rellnost, shouting, "He's mine!" and beating his horse into wide eyed panic with the flat of his sword.

The horse plunged headlong into the trees. A branch struck the beast in an eye making it rear back. It threw the unprepared Rellnost off, head first, sword flying out of his grasp. The middle of his back hit a large dead branch on the ground. I heard a sickening crack as his spine broke. The horse, panicked and blinded by the pain in its eye, backed up and kicked Rellnost in the side of his head, which began to bleed profusely. Rellnost lay unmoving on the sere grass. By now the others had caught

166

up and crowded around him. Their leader gesticulated to the young guard to send for help.

* * *

I raised my hand to interrupt. "I have seen it. His back is broken and he has a serious wound to his head. His horse threw him. But only he is to blame. I will prepare Nairin...I fear he will not live, and if he does he will wish himself dead. This is what Earth has shown me." I allowed myself to bury my face in my hands for a moment, unable to look at anyone, near tears for Nairin and trying to gather courage for what I must face. Then I forced my head back up

Shocked eyes fastened on me, not the least those of the guard, whose mouth hung open below eyes so wide the whites showed all around.

Gaelen recovered first. "Has help been sent to bring him back?"

"Yes, my lord."

"Go back and bring news as soon as he arrives here. Liannis, you may go to Nairin, Klast, your presence is not necessary. Go to Gharn. The council will meet again tomorrow when we are more certain of Rellnost's condition."

The meeting ended, each of us went our designated ways. I barely had time to get a departing hug from my father and to hear his usual admonishment to look after my mother.

Nairin did not weep at the news of her son's accident. Her face told me that she had expected something like this. Yet, Rellnost was still her child, and her anguish showed through in spite of her self-control. She went immediately to his side and took his still hand tenderly into her own. When she finally looked at me tears stood in her eyes but she held them back. "He was such a happy child until the others were born. I remember his small form in my arms as I put him to my breast." Only then did two great tears slide down her cheeks and leave dark splotches on her gown.

I nodded understanding, knowing that to touch her would cause her to lose her hard held control. "I know how much you care for him, my lady. He is your son, he always will be. Love him now, in his last days. It will reach him, even in his silence. It will ease his passing." I touched her shoulder, turned so that I would not see her weep, and left them alone. I knew what I said was true. I also knew he would never wake. Earth wanted him back in her bosom. I wondered, as I left, what greater disaster his death would prevent. It was not mine to know.

That night I sat on the sod roof of my parent's home to think, as I had done since childhood, my refuge under the stars. Earth, what must I do to stop this chaos? How much must the people suffer for our wars in Gharn and Lieth? What will happen in Lieth? How will we live thorough the coming famine? Mother, I am lost. I wept tears of grief for Nairin and for the sense of hopelessness that threatened to overwhelm me.

No answers came and I had to be content in the belief that Earth would let me see what I needed to know. That she would show me at the right time. But I had never felt so alone.

Kira had come to sit beside me on a branch I had set into the sod of the roof for her. She chirruped softly as if to comfort me.

Thank you, little one. I reached over to stroke her soft feathers, which soothed me somewhat. A thought struck me that made me sit up for a moment. Could she do it? I sagged again. No, she would not be able to find him, especially as he would be in disguise. My father's fate would remain unknown to me.

Kira chirruped again and looked at me with one keen eye. She seemed to want to tell me something. *Sad?*

Yes, Kira. And worried.

Kira help?

No, little one, not this time. It is too far. But I am glad you are here. You are my friend.

Friend, yes. Stay with seer, yes.

Yes. Thank you. Stay with me.

48

NAIRIN

Nairin neither ate nor slept as she kept vigil beside Rellnost's bed. I looked in on her daily. She knew nothing could be done for him. He never woke, but Nairin sang him the lullabies she had when he was small and tenderly changed the cold compresses on his forehead. When I looked in on her daily, her face remained tight and no expression showed through, but when she sang to him she let silent tears leak from her eyes and drip unheeded onto the blankets where she hovered over her dying son.

It took three days for Rellnost to die. While I visited them each day, Nairin took no comfort from my presence or that of any other.

Gaelen decided to delay sending the delegation to Lieth until after Rellnost's death and burial. I reluctantly agreed with him. Once Rellnost had been buried, Gaelen planned to consult with Nairin about her wishes for both hers and her children's future. Her wishes could affect the plans for the delegation.

Nairin agreed to speak with myself and Gaelen the day after Rellnost had been given back into Earth's embrace. She shed no more tears in our presence but set herself to her duty with stoic strength. I could not help but admire her.

To spare Nairin from needing to come to the council chambers and to face the entire council Gaelen advised them that only he and I would visit her and would bring back her message.

Blennis brought in tea and cakes as soon as we arrived, then discretely closed the door behind her as she left. Nairin, pale, dressed in her plainest gown, hair in a severe knot at the nape of her neck, poured with studied poise, only a slight tremor of her hands hinting at the emotion she fought to control. Only I truly sensed what she felt.

As soon as we all sat with cakes in our hands, Gaelen cleared his throat. He kept his voice low. "Nairin, I apologize that this meeting cannot wait longer. Please forgive this intrusion so close upon the heels of the loss of your son. Believe that if it were not of the utmost importance I would have waited."

Nairin nodded, silent.

"We have had troubling news from Lieth which I must share with you. Garneth, who now calls himself Lord of Lieth, has imprisoned in the dungeons under the most cruel conditions the wives and children of several of Lord Merlost's supporters. Those men have all been killed. As we speak, certain of the children may have already died. Liannis did extract a promise of more food for them but suspects he has no intentions of keeping that promise."

Nairin's hand had come to her face and trembled in front of her mouth. She could no longer hold back her anguish. "My friends, my poor friends."

I placed a calming hand on her arm, and she drew herself erect again, regaining her fragile composure.

Gaelen's voice grew even softer. "Nairin, I think you have some idea what it is we will ask of you."

She gave a mute nod.

"Garneth knows, now, that you and your children are our guests. Perhaps he has already had news of Rellnost's death, or will in the next day or two. Even before we heard of Rellnost's accident I planned to send a delegation to Lieth to see what could be done for your friends. But Rellnost's death changes things. I waited to send that delegation until I had spoken to you. I need to know if you wish to go forward with making a claim for Lieth on behalf of Wartin." Gaelen paused and when Nairin merely gave him a bleak look of comprehension, continued.

"My lady. I do understand what a sacrifice this is. My lady, I believe that we can make a strong argument on behalf of your friends if we can convince Garneth that you have no desire to wrest control back from him, either for yourself or your younger son. But this is a decision only you can make, and we will support whatever you decide. The delegation will attempt to secure better conditions for the women and children with an offer of trade for grain this winter when his stores run out as a result of the drought that is upon us."

Nairin looked at the untouched cake in her lap for a long time.

When Gaelen made to speak again I shook my head at him. Nairin needed to make the most important decision of her life, with no time to think, and on the heels of her child's death. Gaelen nodded and sat back to wait.

After several moments Nairin raised her head and faced Gaelen dry eyed. "Lord Gaelen, the debt my children and I owe you can never be repaid. I had hoped that Rellnost would show the qualities of leadership that would make a bid to reclaim Lieth worthwhile. He was my son and I shall never stop loving him, but we all know that he lacked those qualities and showed no signs of improvement. His death only brings my decision closer. If you can continue to give me and my remaining two children asylum in Bargia, I will renounce any claim to Lieth on their behalf. If this oath will serve to help my poor friends left behind I will be grateful that I am able to bring about some small good from Rellnost's death. Tell Garneth he need fear no challenge from me or my children." She held Gaelen's gaze steadily for a long moment then let her eyes drop back to her hands.

I took the cake from her stiff fingers and replaced it with the mug of still warm tea, which I had taken the liberty of lacing with honey. She put it to her lips without lifting her eyes.

If Gaelen's voice had slipped any lower we would not have heard him. It made me remember what had caused me to hold such admiration for him, both as a leader and as a person.

I know that the compassion he put into his words reached Nairin, even though she showed no outward sign.

"Lady Nairin, the cost to you these past months is greater than most of us are asked to face in a lifetime...your lord and husband, your home, your freedom and now your son and the hope he represented. I can only begin to imagine the pain you must feel. Lieth has lost a fine Lady. Your sacrifice today will save many lives...both, perhaps those of your friends and their children...but more, the lives of those whose blood would have been shed in any attempt to regain Lieth. We all owe you a debt that cannot be repaid. I hope Earth will accept your gift and use it as one step toward restoring the balance that will bring us all back to peace and health."

When she raised bleak eyes in acknowledgement, he rose and knelt on one knee in front of her. Taking both hands between his he asked, "Nairin of Lieth, do you pledge fealty to me on behalf of yourself and your children?"

"My lord." Her eyes rounded in shock. "It is I who must kneel."

"No my lady, I honour the gift you have given Bargia this day. Now, may I have your oath?"

"With all my heart, my lord." Though her voice shook she spoke clearly as befitted the lady she was.

"Then, as soon as I feel confident that Garneth believes this, I will set you up in a house of your own where you, Wartin and Leyla may live in freedom. You shall want for nothing." Gaelen let go her hands and rose. When Nairin followed he embraced her with the dual kiss of new family, a rare gesture, unexpected even by me.

Now Nairin did lose her composure and her hot tears blossomed dark on her grey gown. She whispered, "My lord..."

Gaelen raised a hand to silence her. "No thanks are due, my lady. I shall inform Lady Marja. You are as family now. I think you will need the company of a woman while I am away in Lieth."

171

Nairin nodded mutely, gratitude mixing with awe on her face.

Nothing I could do would offer greater comfort than what Gaelen had already done, so I merely nodded my sympathy as we left, swallowing to try to clear the lump in my throat. Neither of us spoke as we made our way back to the castle.

49

DREAMS

I sent Kira ahead to let Mama see I would soon be home. When I entered the clearing around our cabin I saw Merrist standing almost at its edge, leaning on a walking stick. His shy, proud grin, as he watched Cloud and me approach, warmed me, and I returned it with one of my own.

"Merrist! All this way with just a walking stick? What does Mama say about that?"

His grin widened. "I am sure you can guess. She cossets me and fusses over me but she smiles as she does it. I think she knows it will do no good."

I got off Cloud and let him lean his other hand on her side as we walked back to the cabin. A quick sensing told me he had probably pushed too hard, making the walk back very painful. I wondered when we would be able to return to Liethis', or rather, my cabin, when Merrist would be able to start his new duties as my caretaker. I suspected it would be sooner rather than later. He was making rapid progress.

That night, after Mama and Merrist had gone to sleep, I climbed up to my familiar spot on the roof. Soon one young cat found a place, in the hammock created by my skirt stretched over my knees, and promptly fell asleep. Kira sat beside me, and I stroked her soft feathers, their silky smoothness calming beneath my fingers, as I searched for my father's aura. I knew how fast he could travel and suspected that by now he would be near the outskirts of Gharn. By tomorrow he would meet with Dugal and be about his mission. When I found him it relieved me to see that his aura remained a strong purple sliding into blue. A few sparks of red told me that he was alert to danger and would keep his senses alive even when asleep. Even so, it did not dispel the heaviness I felt about this mission and his safety.

Before climbing down to find my bed I asked Earth once again to help me see and understand.

Mostly I do not dream ordinary dreams. Earth sends me the dreams I need to tell me what I need to know. Or perhaps I simply do not remember the ones that are not important. I do not know. That night I had two dreams, one clearly meant to tell me something...but the other remained a puzzle. In it Merrist and I sat close to the hearth fire in my cabin. We had aged a few years. On a braided rug, between us and the fire, played a small child of about two. Both of us smiled at her with obvious indulgence. I wore a regular gown, though my whites hung close to hand on a peg by the door. The ease with which Merrist and I sat together spoke of long familiarity. But who was this strange child with us, and how did she come to be in our care? I pondered this for a long time when I woke but could make no sense of it. If it had any meaning Earth would show me when it became important for me to know.

I had less difficulty understanding the second dream. Dugal standing on a dais in the central square, watching grim faced, hands clenched behind his back. On another platform across from his stood Vernia, with a noose around her neck, her feet on the trapdoor that spelled her death. Two men stood tied to a post behind her, awaiting their turn. Behind Dugal, I saw Larn, Burrist and Kerran. I searched for my father but could not find him.

This dream told me the plot against Dugal would be broken and the traitors brought to justice. And that the men closest to Dugal remained true. But why could I not find my father? Had he already left for home? Had something befallen him? With no answer the knot in my stomach grew tighter. Oh Earth, keep him safe.

50

RAIN

I woke to the sound of rain pelting the small window of our cabin. But I knew it came too late. Harvest season had already arrived, and the stooks of grain which would normally have covered the fields now looked like lonely, drooping sentinels, too far apart. But perhaps the maize, which ripened later in the fall, would still provide some food during the winter.

We had no grain crops in Mama's little garden, only herbs and vegetables which had been lovingly tended by her, with water hauled from our shallow well after the creek dried up. For the last eightday even that had not been possible. The water in the well had become murky, and when Merrist had tested its depth, it barely covered the bucket. Mama loved her garden and the thought that we might have to leave it behind and go into the city, for lack of water to drink and cook with, worried her. So she welcomed the rain that would save her tubers, turnips and healing herbs. And it would replenish the well so she would not be forced to leave her beloved home.

The torrents kept on for almost two eightdays, with only two days in between that settled down into a lazy drizzle. Merrist and I pulled the bean plants and hung them from every possible space in the rafters of both the cabin and the shed. We hoped the pods would still dry and not go mouldy before they could be shelled and stored. Merrist had done a good job making the roofs of both cabin and shed tight so that we stayed dry. He built a careful fire, in a ring of stones on the floor of the shed, which helped to dispel the dampness there. Shelling and winnowing would have to wait until dry weather returned. Each day, all three of us came in from our work sodden and muddy, but now that the well had filled again, we at least had water to bathe.

While grateful that my family would not go hungry this winter, I knew that others would not fare so well. Though Gaelen's foresight and careful preparations would see the people of Bargia through, with its stores of grain, maize and beans in the warehouses from last year's harvest, they would need to be managed with care. I had warned Dugal, and so he, too, had some stores in Gharn, though not enough. In Lieth the situation would be dire indeed.

Hunting had also become scarcer, as the deer and wild boar retreated deeper into the forests seeking forage. Even the numbers of rabbits had dwindled, and those that were caught had little meat or fat on them. Many people would be forced to kill their chickens and sheep to survive, and they would be left without the means to buy more. Cows' udders had dried up and stopped giving milk, so no new cheeses could be made. Famine would ravage the people this winter bringing both death and disease.

If things were to improve for the next year, I knew that we would have to assist Earth by bringing stability to Gharn and Lieth. I knew that the discord that existed, and the blood that had been shed, had brought about Earth's inability to provide good weather for our crops. Only by helping to bring back the Balance would Earth recover enough to heal herself. Only then could she bring about the conditions that would sustain health and prosperity for her people. It saddened me that so few understood that connection.

Each night, after the others had gone to bed, I sought out my father's aura. It told me that he lived, but I worried about his health as its colour lost its brightness. This could mean that either fatigue plagued him, or that he was ill. I hoped it was only fatigue. But I knew that even if he were ill he would press himself to the utmost as long as he had not completed his mission and would press on until he arrived home.

Then, after so many nights without dreams or visions, two days before the rains stopped, his aura changed. It became overlaid with a grey pall and the purple-blue looked more shot with red and bits of black. This meant either serious injury or illness, and that he was very weak.

My first inclination was to pack up Cloud and head out to find him. It took effort to make myself stop and think through the best course of action. I had other duties and knew that Papa would disapprove if I went in a headlong search for him without considering these. I slowed my breathing and tried to think, asking Earth for help.

* * *

He lay rolled in his blanket under a narrow overhang of rock. His back rested against the side of his horse, offering a measure of warmth and sheltering him from the wind and rain. I could not see any evidence of a fire, and assumed that he had either not the strength to build one or the rains had made things too wet to start one.

I could see no one else and gathered he travelled alone. And I sensed that he was on his way back to Bargia. He preferred to travel alone as he always made better time and need not feel responsible for the safety of his companions. He knew, better than anyone I had ever met, how to use the gifts of the forests and fields to stay strong and healthy.

As dawn began to bring light into the grey of the night he stirred and rose. I could see the effort it took. He needed to hold on to his horse and pull himself up by stages. I could detect no injuries, so it must be illness that felled him. I watched as he levered himself onto his horse's back before allowing the horse to stand. He had not taken any time to eat, nor had he drunk anything. I wondered if this resulted from a decision to avoid something bad or from the illness affecting his ability to think. I soon had my answer. I watched him take great care to strap himself in so that if he slept he would not fall off. His mind was still clear then...for now.

* * *

When I woke the sky showed the first lessening of grey before colours showed visible, and knew that my vision had shown me my father in his actual state. Mama and Merrist still slept, but now I had a plan and set about packing the few things I would need for travel. By the time full dawn arrived I had mind-spoken both Cloud and Kira and told them my plans. Mama woke just as I tried to slip out to the cabin to pack my panniers and saddle Cloud.

I had already decided I would relate as little as possible about my father's condition. I told Mama only that Earth had sent me a message. That I must ride to meet Papa and accompany him the rest of the way home. Perhaps he had news that could not wait. Yes, he was already on his way, though I did not know how far. Yes, food and skins of fresh water would be welcome, as I did not trust the water in the swollen creeks and rivers. No, I would not have time to cook, so travel food, lots of it, would be all I could take. No, I did not know how long I would be gone.

So far, I had not had to tell a lie, but her last question, the one she had been afraid to ask until the end, made me pause. Had I seen how he fared?

I took a deep breath and steeled myself. "Mama, he lives but I think he is ill. But he still rides." So the truth then, but as little as possible.

Mama looked at me, narrowing her eyes, and became very still. "Liannis, what are you not telling me? How bad is it?"

"I do not know for certain, Mama. He is ill. I hope that he is not so far away that I will reach him soon and bring him home. I can say no more." I ought to have known she would see there was more I had not told her.

Her voice shook with fear and urgency. "Bring him home alive, Liannis. I will save him if he is alive."

"That is my plan, Mama." I hugged her tight then turned to Merrist. "I want you to go to the city and tell Lord Gaelen where I have gone, and

177

that Papa is ill. Ask Lady Marja if she can come here to be with Mama. Then ask Lord Gaelen if he needs your services until I return. You are strong enough now that you no longer need a nursemaid and he may have need of another courier. Tell Gaelen we will return by the west way through the forest, the same way we first came to Bargia together. If Gaelen agrees, you may seek to meet us. Bring another man if he can spare one." By the time I finished speaking Cloud had been packed and I led her out.

Merrist whistled for Warrior, saddle in hand, and soon sat astride. With nothing left to keep her busy, Mama wrung her hands as she watched us both depart. Merrist did not look back, but I turned at the edge of the clearing to give her one last wave. Her return wave looked forlorn and worried, as she watched, drenched to the skin, her hair stuck to her face in dripping tendrils.

51

PAPA

I sought out Papa's aura often to make sure I did not lose his direction and travelled as quickly as the muddy terrain allowed. It was weak but remained steady.

The mud clung to Cloud's hoofs and hocks and made it hard for her to pull them free. I chaffed at the slowness of our pace but knew I could urge Cloud no faster without risking a broken ankle. She grumbled at me a few times, but seemed to sense the urgency of the situation and did not try to slow her pace. Kira sat on her perch on my shoulder, not wishing to fly or hunt in the rain. The water dripped off her feathers and ran down my neck, making the oiled leathers I wore to keep out the rain almost useless. Yet her company comforted me so I did not ask her to fly off.

I wondered what Gaelen would do now that Merrist had brought him the news. I hoped he would send an escort to find us, as I expected that by the time I found my father we might need assistance to get back home. While Gaelen did not know our exact route, he had travelled to Gharn with my father before and knew the general direction. And I expected our tracks would be easy to follow, once found.

It worried me that I did not know the exact nature of my father's illness or distress. Earth had shown me no more, so the only comfort I had was to see that his aura had not declined even further. I wondered how far he had come before I had the vision, and if he had managed to travel much further. If he were closer to Gharn it might be wiser to return there, though I knew Papa would never agree to that. He would insist on going home to Mama, and a large part of me understood that he would heal much better there.

Before he and Mama had joined, when Mama had been Lady Marja's personal maid, she had rescued a kitten that had seemed beyond saving. Marja had discovered that Mama had a small gift of healing when she had nursed the kitten back to health. That kitten's offspring now roamed our land and warmed our laps. Papa needed Mama's healing gift now, as well as her love. That thought helped me decide to not even bring up the option of returning to Gharn. I needed to bring him home.

That night I set up a shelter with some pine branches leaned against the trunk of an oak. It kept out most of the rain, and exhaustion helped me to sleep a few spans. When I woke to the greying of the dawn, the rain had slowed to a fine drizzle. Kira had gone off to hunt, and returned just as I packed the last of my travel food into my pannier. She fluttered

179

back and forth until her antics caught my attention. In my worry I had not noticed her excitement.

What is it, little one?

Found quiet man. Quiet man is the name she had given my father, perhaps because he spoke so little.

What!? Where?

Long way. I show.

Show me with your eyes.

She gave me her memory of my father, lying against his horse in the rain. This was not good. He always took care for his safety and shelter. This meant he was in deep trouble.

Where, Kira? Show me where to find him.

I found him at dusk, still sitting half upright, leaning against the side of his horse, his chin sunk to his chest. It relieved me a little that he lifted his eyes and recognized me as I approached. At least his mind remained alert. But he did not try to rise to meet me, merely raising his hand. I rushed to his side but the first words were his.

"I knew you would come. Do you have fresh water?"

I halted in mid-stride and turned back to grab my water-skin. When I held it to his lips, he drank only a small amount and pushed the skin back to me. "The water here is fouled. I could not drink it, so must start with small amounts now." He tried to make his voice cheerful but I could see the effort talking took. His skin was dry to the touch and he looked paler than I had ever seen him. His clothes were damp through, but there was nothing I could do for that right now. We needed a fire.

"I will make a fire, Papa and make some tea and soup."

He nodded and closed his eyes.

It took a while to find branches dry enough to light. As soon as I accomplished that I set about spreading my oiled skins and blanket to give him a dry patch to lie on, and helped him over to it. I lay his saddle bag under his head, covered him as best I could, and soon heard from his soft snoring that he had fallen asleep. That gave me time to set a pot on to boil, into which I sliced a few onions and tubers, along with a piece of the dried meat my mother had sent with me. I checked on my father and gave him another drink. When he assured me he would be all right, I went back into the now dimming woods to forage some fresh greens. I had to give up after only a small handful as I could no longer see. At least the rain had stopped, and the night looked to be clear.

The addition of my meagre find soon brought a delicious aroma from the soup pot. By full dark we would have a hot meal. In the second pot I made a tea of chamomile, white pine needles and willow bark...to soothe, and to help against fever.

Even in illness Papa could not sleep long. He watched the last of my preparations and managed to sit upright long enough to drink the tea and eat some of the broth from the soup. When I urged him to eat some of the meat and vegetables he shook his head. "My body will reject it. I cannot keep it down. But the tea is good. You used the right herbs."

When he showed no inclination to go back to sleep, I asked him what had happened, if he knew what was wrong with him, and what would help him recover.

"The last two days before I left Gharn the rain must have fouled the water in the well we used. I think the camp cook did not boil it enough when he made tea. By the time I left I could eat nothing and had only one skin full of clean water. My bowels went to liquid. I have been travelling two days with nothing to drink since I emptied my skin. I had not the strength to start a fire any more, so continued without food or drink that last two days."

His story used up the last of his strength, and he lay down again to sleep.

"I will get you home, Papa. Mama will make you well."

His only reply was a tired, sad smile before his eyes closed.

His tale only increased my worry. Bad water could make it hard for a body to keep liquids or food in. If his bowels remained like water, and he could not eat or drink enough, he would die from lack of fluids. My only consolation was that he had kept the tea down, though he had drunk only a small cup. If his condition did not improve by morning I needed to get him home as quickly as possible. Only my mother could add the healing touch that might help him recover. Oh, Earth, keep him until I can get him home. He has served you well. Help him now. Whether she heard, I did not know. I wrapped myself against my father's back, under the blanket, to add my warmth to his, and tried to sleep.

He shivered against me and I could tell that he was fevered. Sleep eluded me, so well before dawn I crawled out from under and stirred the embers back to life. I reheated the tea from the night before, adding more willow bark for fever. He would not like its bitter taste but I knew he would drink it. After all, it was he who had taught me the healing properties of all the plants and herbs that could be found on the One Isle. I had never met a healer who knew more than he did. At the last, I added more pine needles, remembering that they often speeded healing as well. If it was too strong, so be it.

When I turned to check on him I found Papa watching me through fever glazed eyes. His skin had taken on a slight sheen from his fever, and his lips had cracks and flakes of dry skin hung on them in places.

He sniffed the tea, made a face and sipped at it dutifully, but when I tried to feed him some broth he pushed it weakly away.

Oh Earth, he is too weak to ride. How will I get him home? Panic threatened to overtake me. How could I get him on his horse? When would help come? He needed to be home now.

The look he gave me showed that he understood how dire his situation was. "My horse. I will ride," he croaked.

I would have protested that he did not have the strength, but I knew that if we stayed here he would never see home again. I led his horse to him and had him kneel. My father raised himself to sitting, gasping with the effort. I did my best to help him mount, and at his insistence, tied him into the saddle. "Take me home, Liannis. Do not stop...no matter what."

I nodded in mute misery, mounted Cloud and we set off. My father leaned against his horse's neck and I could see that he drifted in and out of awareness.

Help arrived in the form of a three man guard escort. They took turns holding him in front of them on their mounts. We rode through the night, stopping only to rest the horses and heat tea, which I made my father sip in small amounts at regular pauses. We ate travel food as we rode.

We entered the clearing outside our cabin just after dawn. Mama noticed immediately and flew out the door to meet us. By the time we had Papa off his horse Merrist had made the bed ready and built up the fire. They peeled off his clothes and wrapped him in dry blankets. Now he was in Mama's care. I could do no more.

52

BRENSA

As soon as she saw his condition my mother pushed aside her fear. She began to croon and to stroke my father's head and arms, her touch light but deft. She sat on the bed with his head cradled in her lap. Though her attention seemed distant, focused on something I could not see, she was still able to tell us what to do and to respond to questions. This was her healing gift at work. I had seen her do this before if one of our animals became ill, or when our cow had unexpectedly stopped giving milk and her udder had become swollen and tender.

The last spans before arriving home, my father had no longer answered us and seemed out of reach, though he appeared to have understood when we lifted him into bed, and made an effort to help. I hoped, to Earth, it meant we were not too late, and my mother could save him.

Throughout the night my mother kept up her ministrations, while Merrist and I took turns preparing medicinal teas and broth, and trying to get my father to swallow some. In between we tried to rest.

About the middle of the night Merrist looked at me and shook his head. "Liannis, you have been gone four days, had almost no sleep, and have had the burden of caring for your father mostly without assistance. You can barely stand upright, and your hands shake when you hold the tea. Go to bed. I can do these small tasks that Brensa requires."

When I shook my head and began to protest, he gently raised his fingers to my lips to stop me. "No, Liannis. Go to sleep. I love him, too, and will not fail him."

"But..." I stopped when I could not come up with a thought coherent enough to form an argument.

He shook his head again. "Liannis, I will tell you if anything changes. Go to sleep ... please."

I knew he was right but I still did not want to go. I took another long look at my parents. My mother nodded slightly. "Merrist is right. He can do what is needed. Go to sleep."

With great reluctance I set one foot in front of the other and slowly mounted the ladder to my bed. Earth did not visit me in dreams or visions. When I woke I thought it was only morning, but Merrist informed me that I had slept for over a full day, and it was now the following morning.

Mama stood at the hearth dishing out a bowl of thick porridge, which Merrist took out of her hands even before she had finished. As he grabbed a spoon and handed it to me, he told her, "Brensa, it is your turn now. You have not slept and Klast's fever is less. If he needs you we will tell you."

"He is right, Mama. Please use my bed so you will not be disturbed."

"I will sleep here with him." Mama started to sit on the bed but I stopped her.

"Mama, please use my bed. I will be with him...please." I took her elbow to guide her to the ladder. She looked from me, to Papa, and back to me again. She nodded slightly, her eyes bleak, and made the climb to my bed.

I discovered my appetite had returned and I was ravenous. I wolfed down that bowl of porridge and a second, as well as two mugs of tea but not before I had checked on my father. His forehead still had a clammy sheen but felt cooler than the last time. He breathed evenly and seemed to be in a normal healing sleep.

"He woke a couple of times and knew us. He kept some broth and tea down and managed to piss some in that jar. Brensa says that means things are working, at least...oh, and Lord Gaelen and Lady Marja both came to check on Klast yesterday. When they saw the situation they left again. They said they would return tomorrow but to send word right away if things got worse...which they have not," he added as an afterthought.

"You should have wakened me! I should have heard them." At Merrist's admonishing shake of his head, I collected myself. "I suppose it would have changed nothing. I have no more news for them." I sighed, sank to the side of the bed and examined my father once more, knowing I would see no change but feeling the need to do it anyway.

I turned to Merrist. "You need sleep, too, Merrist. I can care for him now."

He looked as if he were about to protest, then seemed to change his mind. "All right, wake me as soon as something changes." I nodded and he left for his bed in the shed. He turned at the door. "I will see to the horses and cow before I sleep."

I nodded silent thanks, and he was gone. When I turned back to my father I found him looking at me, a small smile on his lips. "A good man, Merrist."

"Yes he is. I am glad to have his help." I rose to get more broth. He was able to sit up and take it from me, though his hands shook like leaves in a wind so I had to steady the cup. When I brought tea he needed help holding the second mug.

As I plumped his pillow and made him comfortable again, he whispered, "I think I might live. Your mother has saved my life again."

I hugged him and told him to go back to sleep. As his eyes closed and his breathing took on his sleeping rhythm I had time to wonder what he meant by 'again'. He had never been tended by my mother during a mortal illness before.

Then I understood. He was not referring to his physical life but to the healing of his spirit. It made me smile, for the first time in many days, remembering the story my mother had told me about their courtship and early joining. Theirs was a true love story, one that not many ever found. It had healed both of them from the scars of their pasts. I felt a small pang of envy knowing such a relationship was forbidden me.

I suddenly thought of Merrist then pushed that thought away. The infatuation he had for me so many moons ago had developed into a quiet devotion. And that is how it would have to stay.

Just as I reached for the kettle to pour myself more tea, I heard horses arriving and went to the door, closing it behind me quickly in hopes I could keep our visitors outside so my father would not waken. That hope was in vain. I ought to have known that he would sleep very lightly now that his fever had diminished. I heard him call out before I had a chance to close the door.

Merrist also emerged from the shed to greet our visitors. When we all turned to go inside, we found my mother already winding a scarf around her unruly curls, at the door ready to greet her guests. She invited us in and set about stoking the fire to brew more tea. Her rest had been short, but it seemed that seeing my father somewhat improved and awake, and having her closest friends around her, had banished her fatigue, at least for now. Some colour had even returned to her face.

This time Marja and Lionn had come. Lionn said Gaelen had a courier from Gharn he needed to meet with. They also told us the delegation to Lieth had returned.

We all listened closely, especially my father, who missed nothing in spite of his weakness.

"They did not bring back all the news we had hoped for," Lionn began. "Garneth remained suspicious and aloof. He maintained that you are Bargia's seer, Liannis, and that you work only for Bargia's advantage."

But," Marja broke in, "he did agree to release the women and children if we would take them off his hands. I am told he seemed eager to rid himself of them. That is why the delegation took so long to return. Gaelen had already decided to send out a cadre of soldiers to find out what happened and to retrieve them. They were going to leave tomorrow morning. But the delegation returned with the women and children just yesterday at dusk. Oh, Liannis, you did not exaggerate." Marja's voice rose in sympathy. "They tell me three children and one woman died, one of the children while travelling."

"Yes and my father met with the delegation last night. Garneth demands that we send two warehouses worth of grain immediately as a gesture of good will. And that we swear never to let the women and children enter Lieth again. He made a threat, too, that if any one of them ever became involved in an uprising against Lieth he would hold Bargia responsible and see it as the act of an enemy."

Lionn and Marja almost spoke over each other in their eagerness to tell us what they had learned. Lionn kept to the political side, but Marja, with her usual compassion, wanted to share the news of the poor exiles. I kept a close eye on my father, as did Mama, but while he made no attempt to speak and closed his eyes a few times, he remained awake and alert, ever the dutiful lord's man. We knew better than to protest.

We learned that the exiles were now housed in the castle, in an apartment away from the centre, so they could be given the best care possible while allowing some privacy. They all showed signs of starvation, and many had loose teeth and hair falling out. One child could still die, and Marja said the healer woman, who had been summoned to care for them, was not sure the rest would all recover. That depended a lot on hope, she had told Marja.

"That man is a beast," Marja finally spat out. I silently agreed. We would not be done with him yet. And Earth would continue to suffer.

"Has Gaelen been given the news from Gharn? Do you need a report from me to take back?" My father's voice came out in a croak, causing my mother to jump up with tea for him again.

"He has all he needs for the present, Klast. We have heard that the plot has been uncovered and the traitors brought to justice. Lord Dugal plans to visit Bargia before full winter to discuss what trade may be made for some of our stores of grain."

Papa nodded. "He is a good man and cares for his people. He will learn quickly."

Marja narrowed her eyes, as she regarded my father, and rose. "Come Lionn, our friends all need rest." She embraced my mother. "I hope you will put the cakes and cheeses to good use."

"To be sure Marja thank you. Perhaps Klast will even be able to eat a little bread and cheese tomorrow."

Merrist walked, with the help of just his cane, to the shed to help with the horses. My father already slept again, and my mother looked grey with fatigue. I led her gently to the ladder to my room in the loft. "Back to sleep Mama, I will see to things here."

She rewarded me with a small smile. "He will live," she whispered before climbing up again. And I knew she was right...but how well would he recover?

53

REPRISE

By Harvest Festival Papa had recovered enough to make the short ride into the city, so Mama could visit with her friends and enjoy some of the activities. But even three eightdays after I had found him he still had little strength, and the robust man I had relied on all my life had become gaunt and frail. I knew, beyond doubt, that without my mother's ministrations and healing gift, and his indomitable will to live, he would have died. I also knew that he would never again be the man he had been. And Gaelen would never again be able to rely on him for his services as he had until now. But he lived, and for my mother's sake as well as my own, I thanked Earth for this, and none of us voiced our grief over his loss of strength. We all saw, and we knew that we saw, and that was enough.

While my father rested and my mother visited with Lady Marja, I asked Sennia to tour the city with me, to watch the preparations for tomorrow's Harvest Festival activities. Tomorrow marked the One Isle's most important festival day. Usually, harvests would have been mostly brought in, stores of fruit and vegetables set in for the winter. People came to celebrate their optimism for surviving the coming winter, until the spring equinox announced the arrival of a new year. With that would come the time to plant anew and rejoice that they had successfully come through another long, cold season.

Kira had come along but at my admonishment remained aloft, circling above the rooftops until she found a perch on one of the castle's peaks. She preferred to ride on my shoulder but when I reminded her of her time in captivity she agreed to remain high out of reach. I still thought it best that no one outside of my friends and family be aware that we could mind-speak each other and that she acted as my eyes on occasion.

I looked at Sennia, now fifteen years old and considered on the cusp of womanhood, as we walked the edge of the central square together. Her hair had a copper sheen, somewhat lighter than Marja's had been before streaks of grey began to appear at her temples. Sennia stood even taller than Marja by two fingers and she carried herself with a poise and dignity that belied her youth. Headstrong and vivacious, her sharp eyes missed nothing and she exuded a lust for life that rubbed off on those in her company. I felt my spirits lift as she pointed out the various stands and exclaimed over the goods that we would sample there when the sun reached its midday point tomorrow.

I imagined Marja must have been much like this when she was young. No wonder Gaelen had been smitten with her.

Sennia returned my smile with a bright one of her own. "Liannis, I am so glad we have this time together. I have missed you. My studies take up so much of my time and your work takes you away."

"Yes, I am glad to be here, with you and with all of us together."

"Look, there! See that stall being set up?"

I looked where she pointed and nodded.

"You remember the man who made those sweet buns we love so much, the ones with the raisins and honey. This is his son. He is old enough now to assist him. I have bought those buns at their shop, and Brest's, that is his name, are every bit as good as his father's. I can't wait to get one tomorrow."

"And I." I pointed to a table being set up with a canopy of bright linen to keep off the sun, as it would be on the sunny side of the square. "Sennia, I am not familiar with that one. Do you know what will be sold there?" The cheerful aura that always accompanied the festival made it easier for me to keep my barriers in place so I could enjoy the day.

The man setting up the table noticed us and gave us a huge grin. "Ladies, I am Marenth."

We walked over. "Marenth, you are new to our festival. What wares will you have for us?"

He gave us a mysterious smile, put one finger to the side of his nose and teased, "Prepare to be dazzled, but not until tomorrow."

I smiled and shook my head as Sennia laughed gaily, "Indeed we shall Marenth. Until tomorrow then." She took my hand and tugged me to the next alley off the square. Here owners who would not have goods on the central square, which was kept for food and baked goods, wine and ale, set up tables outside their small shops. These sold beads, fabrics and such.

When we wandered back into the square I saw fire pits set up with spits, wood stacked carefully nearby, awaiting the kindling that would light them. I knew that long before dawn this night, the families who owned these stalls would have fires going and children turning the spits roasting deer, sheep, foul and other meats and probably at least one wild boar.

We headed back to the castle as the lengthening shadows told us that dinner would soon be served. "Sennia, I am so glad we could do this together today. It was just what I needed to lift my spirits."

Sennia squeezed my hand as we entered the gates. Marja met us in the Great Hall and urged us to hurry to their apartments where the aromas of roasting meats and fragrant bread met us at the door.

Papa had already found a chair and I noted with relief that he had gained some colour during the afternoon. His ride this morning had not over-taxed him. When he made to rise as we came in Sennia stopped him with a firm gesture. "No Klast, do not get up, unless it is to reach for that stew at the far side of the table. I am not a lady yet, only the daughter of one." Another of her gay laughs had us all at ease as we filled our platters and found chairs around the chamber.

I had no illusions that this supper would not end in serious discussion. It had been a long time since all of us had sat together. When the talk veered to topics of concern I was glad that Gaelen did not suggest Sennia leave. At fifteen she needed to learn all she could about the issues that could affect our futures, and to participate in discussions and decision making. While as a woman Sennia would never sit on council, Gaelen had many times acknowledged that Marja's opinions and suggestions had been very helpful and that she acted as his advisor outside of the council. Sennia must learn to do the same for her man when she joined. Until now she had taken lessons from tutors in history, strategy, ciphers and how to run a castle. She had also trained, at my father's insistence and firm agreement from Marja, in the use of dagger and small blade. She, too, kept a small blade between the layers of leather of her belt. If she ever found herself in danger she could defend herself.

Gaelen opened the discussion. "What concerns do you all have for the celebrations tomorrow? What have you sensed about the mood of the people, about their worries for the coming winter, the harvest and hardships that will come?"

Marja responded first. "Gaelen, they know you have planned well and believe that they will survive. I have sensed no unrest."

"But they are not aware how low our stores are, nor do they understand the depth of our commitments to Gharn, and even the agreement with Lieth." Papa said. "They believe, based on past experiences that you will succeed against all odds, my lord. They do not understand that you are limited by situations beyond your control. Their loyalty has not been tested. Do not fall into the trap of forgetting that the winds change when people grow hungry."

As my father spoke it felt as though a cloud darkened the room. Except, possibly, for Sennia, we all knew he spoke true. We knew how quickly the moods of the people could change when confronted with a situation beyond their control.

Lionn looked sombre. "I do not think Bargians will lose faith so quickly. Some still remember the Red Plague and how Lord Gaelen and Lady Marja took care of the people. But I fear Lord Dugal may not fare so well when he has not the years behind him to build trust and loyalty."

Gaelen and Marja both nodded.

Sennia broke in. "But Dugal has shown them that he is strong. Will not his people understand that he has not had the time to organize and prepare? And we have promised them supplies from our own stores of grain to aid them."

"That will help, I agree Sennia, and I hope it will be sufficient to take him through the winter and that spring will bring good weather, good planting and new hope," Gaelen agreed, "but we will need to be ready to offer assistance if he needs it."

"Earth has shown me nothing to suggest we need be concerned about Gharn." I added. "But even without a message from Earth it is easy to see that our greatest concern lies in Lieth. Garneth is ill prepared for the hunger that Lieth will see. He has done nothing to control the stores of grain and acts as though he has nothing to fear. He shows no regard for the lives of the people and lives to excess while they suffer. I fear that the two warehouses of grain we send will never reach the people. And he hides in the castle with his two advisors and does not go among the people to see how they fare. He trusts no one and believes only what he wishes to hear. I fear our troubles with Lieth are only beginning."

Gaelen nodded agreement. "And he does not trust our promise and Nairin's that we will not try to regain rule of Lieth. Nairin and her children are no longer sequestered. Even though I have given them freedom of the city, I keep a guard with them at all times to defend against assassination. I know Nairin fears this as well for she takes great care to keep her children close."

"Yet there is no more that can be done. We are as prepared as possible." Marja stood. "Tomorrow is Harvest Festival. Let us all have that one day to forget our worries and enjoy ourselves. We must show the people that we are confident."

I noted as we left for our respective chambers that Papa looked grey again. Mama took his elbow and steered him firmly to their chamber. I knew he would have stayed to speak with Gaelen and was glad she had come so he would get the rest he needed.

I noted the look of sadness Gaelen sent after his friend's back. When I met his eyes he gave a sad shake of his head and looked away. Gaelen felt some responsibility for my father's condition, as he had promised him he would not send him into such danger again several years ago. But we both knew my father would have insisted on going on the mission even if Gaelen had tried to prevent him. And Papa would never blame Gaelen. He had been free to decline and had chosen to go. As far as my father was concerned that was the end of it.

I dreamt that night of people all over the One Isle, rich and poor alike, taking small gifts of a handful of grain, a scrap of fabric from a loom, the bones of a rabbit taken from a stew, an apple, all the small tokens of gratitude to Earth, and burying them with reverence, or placing them behind a stone in a wall. Some acted alone. Others took great care to teach a child why and how this must be done. These were peaceful dreams, ones that showed me Earth saw and received these gifts with gratitude. That she recognized the love in them, the circle renewed and strengthened. I woke refreshed and ready to face the celebrations.

54

SHOOT

Harvest Festival morning dawned crisp and sunny. By the time Mama and I had settled Papa in a sunny spot in Marja's garden and made our way into the square to join Sennia and Marja, the happy sounds of revellers filled the air. Hawkers shouted their wares trying to entice tasters and buyers, musicians played on the raised dance platform, bards roamed the edges and into the side alleys singing and playing their lutes. Bright banners and ribbons flew from stands and buildings. Down the side alleys I could see the small tents of the fortune tellers, the sellers of love amulets and trinkets, and the open doors of artisan's shops. The aromas of roasting and baking competed with each other for the attention of the revellers. For today, at least, no one worried about famines or hungry winters.

Normally I avoided crowds and found the press of thoughts and feelings oppressive, but this morning most were happy and so I could tolerate it. For Mama's sake I was happy to do so.

We soon spotted Nairin with her children. She strolled the square accompanied by the exiles from Lieth. It was the first time I had seen her smile since Rellnost's death. The women laughed as they chatted together and watched their offspring chase each other around their mothers' skirts. I noted that the children did not stray far from the women; still not as free from care as such youngsters ought to be. I hoped this would be a healing day for all of them.

Lionn and two soldiers, assigned to guard them, followed at a discreet distance.

Marja noticed them, too. "It is good to see our friends from Lieth able to enjoy this day." She caught Nairin's eye and waved gaily at her. A grateful smile accompanied Nairin's answering wave.

"I would like to meet Nairin." Mama looked at Marja who nodded and we began to make our way through the crowd toward her.

We passed a stand that offered some honey buns Mama favoured and stopped to sample one. A man at the next stand gave us an exaggerated bow and held out slices of new cheese, which we accepted with an equal show of delight. We approached Nairin's group with sticky hands and full mouths. This is what Harvest Festival was for...to celebrate together one last time before the cold of winter kept us by our hearth fires.

When we had almost reached Nairin's group I caught a movement out of the corner of my eye that made me stop, hands outstretched toward them. "No!"

* * *

Time no longer followed its normal pace. All sound fell away. I watched in horror as a man drew a dagger from his belt, shoved Nairin and Leyla aside and grabbed Wartin by the hair, pulling him toward himself. At the same time I watched Nairin's mouth open to scream and Leyla fall to the ground, eyes wide with shock. To the left, close behind, I saw Lionn's sword halfway out of its scabbard, his dreamlike lunge already halfway to their sides. A stranger, also with sword drawn, made to intercept Lionn.

* * *

The sound of clashing swords and a shout of fury broke the silence of my vision and time resumed its normal pace. Lionn ran his sword through his opponent and whirled to meet Wartin's assailant. He and the other two soldiers with him had the assassin hemmed in. The man held his dagger to Wartin's throat, choosing to hold him hostage rather than finishing his mission by killing the boy. It became a standoff.

Nairin fell to her knees facing the assassin. "Please, do not kill him. He is no threat to you. He has done no wrong. Oh, Earth, do not take him from me. I beg you...I have lost one son already...please, I beg you." Words failed her then and she stretched out her hands toward them in mute supplication.

No one moved. It seemed the whole square held its breath. Then I saw Lionn's glance flick upward to a rooftop behind Wartin and the assassin. There stood an archer, bow ready, arrow nocked. Lionn gave a curt nod, almost too small to be noticed. The assassin still stood rigid, looking at Nairin, so no one but me noticed.

His arrow flew true. A surprised look came over the assassin's face as his head split open and he fell lifeless to the cobblestones, Wartin underneath him. Lionn rushed forward and rolled the man off the boy, Nairin on his heels. Wartin scrambled up trembling and found himself swept into his mother's panicked embrace.

Only then did I have time to register that Lionn's sleeve stuck to his arm, red with blood. The stain grew even as I watched. He did not seem to notice until he saw Wartin safe in his mother's arms, the crisis passed.

Mama rushed to him, her hands ready to staunch the flow. As soon as her hands made contact she stilled, deep in concentration. The spread slowed to a slow seep. She dropped her hands, exhausted, and stepped back to make room for the surgeon who had come running with bandages. She met my eyes and nodded. Lionn would be all right.

As the surgeon led Lionn away, arm bandaged, the hush that had fallen over the square gradually died. The noise that had been so cheerful before was now replaced by animated chatter as citizens compared what they thought they had seen. In an effort to call their attention back to the celebrations hawkers once more began to call their wares. By the time Nairin had been carefully escorted back to her residence with her children and friends, Mama Marja and I had reached the castle. I just saw Gaelen's back as he hurried to follow Lionn and I heard him shout, "There must be others. Find them!"

We retreated to the garden where my father still sunned himself. The pain behind my eyes almost blocked my vision and I needed to sit down. No longer did happy sounds keep it at bay. But disaster had been averted for now. Nairin and her children remained safe.

As soon as Papa had been told what had happened I excused myself and went to my chamber deep within the castle to lie down and try to regain control of the pain. Gaelen and a pale Lionn passed me in the doorway as I left, an anxious Marja and Sennia rising to greet them.

55

AN INVITATION

By morning the pain in my head no longer made being with others unbearable. Earth had not visited me with dreams that night. I had time to wonder why I had not had a warning about the attempt on Wartin's life. I began to doubt my gift and worry that I had done something wrong or missed a message sent by other means.

I rejoined my family and friends for the morning meal of porridge, tea and dark bread, fragrant with currants and nuts, before leaving for home. Merrist joined us from where he had stayed in the guards' barracks, and then went out to see that our horses stood ready to leave. I looked forward to the ride home, just the four of us, Cloud beneath me and Kira above or on my shoulder. Only back home would I recover completely from the pain that still lurked behind my eyes.

Just as we stood to leave, a messenger arrived from Gharn. Lord Dugal sent a formal invitation to Lord Gaelen, Lady Marja, Lionn and Sennia of Bargia to visit his court before the snows of winter made travel difficult. And would Lord Gaelen extend the invitation to Klast, Brensa and Liannis as well.

Sennia clapped her hands with excitement. "Oh, yes, let us go. I have heard so much about Lord Dugal and have yet to meet him." She turned to me. "Liannis, is he truly as handsome as they say?"

Having just turned fifteen years of age, though Sennia stood at the cusp of womanhood, she still had one foot in girlish things. The other showed signs of awareness and maturity beyond her years. This moment proved one of the former and made me smile remembering the impetuous child who had wanted to follow Lionn and me about and do everything we did, even though two years younger.

I looked at her now with new eyes. A young woman a knuckle taller than her mother, though she might surpass Marja's impressive height before she stopped growing. The same thick hair a shade lighter than Marja's rich russet, just as headstrong, with the same uncanny way of cutting through to the truth in sticky situations. A young woman just coming into her full beauty, she would soon have many suitors. And, knowing Sennia, she would rebuff them as quickly as they approached, waiting for the 'right one'. I smiled, as I imagined a disdainful Sienna sweeping past a string of young men, all lying in the dust behind her, hearts bleeding. Not that Sienna would be unkind, only that she lacked tact and would cut them with her directness not aware of the effect she had on them.

"Well...?"

The prompt brought me back from my musing. I decided to tease her a bit. "Sennia, you know I do not look at men in that way. Have you forgotten that I am a seer?" But I could not hide my mirth and she saw through me. She put her hands on her hips and gave an exaggerated huff.

I relented. "I think many would find him very pleasing to look at. He is considerably shorter than your father, though strongly built and with broad shoulders and a straight back." I let a tease creep back into my voice. "But I am sure he has many ladies vying for his attentions. He would have no interest in a girl as young as you."

Sennia took the bait with glee. "Young girl indeed. You know as well as I do that I am now old enough to be joined. That makes me a woman." She tossed her head coyly. "And he will not resist my charms, I assure you," which caused us all to laugh.

Gaelen brought us back to the invitation. "I think the problems Lieth still presents us with make it best for me to remain in Bargia, and Lionn, too."

I watched Lionn sag with disappointment then quickly recover before Gaelen could see.

"But I think," Gaelen went on, "that the ladies ought to go. They have not been to Gharn since Dugal came into power. An official visit will strengthen our ties and let everyone see that we are allies and friends."

"I will make ready to accompany them." As the words left my father's mouth I watched my mother's face crumple.

Before she could protest Gaelen broke in. "No Klast. An escort of regular guards will suffice. Your special talents are not needed for this."

Mama relaxed again. We all knew that such a trek would put my father's fragile health at risk and Gaelen had found a way for him to save face.

"I do not know if I will go." I thought aloud. "Let me know when you wish to leave. I will decide then."

"And I will most certainly remain at home with Klast," Mama declared in a tone that brooked no argument. "I have no desire to leave Bargia." She gave my father a glare as if to dare him to disagree. He merely nodded agreement, a small smile at the corners of his lips. My mother had a core of inner strength that belied her small stature. It was what had made Papa fall in love with her. When he had no good reason to deny her he almost always gave in to her, content to please her when he

197

could. I think he still had moments of wonder that she should love him so fiercely.

Come now. Tired of letting One Leg hold me here. Want to go home.

I laughed aloud, causing all eyes to send a questioning look my way. "Cloud is impatient for me to come and ride her so she can get rid of Merrist. She tolerates him for my sake but we are testing her patience."

Papa nodded and he and Mama rose and followed me out.

I caught Merrist's face before he lowered his eyes. His joy at seeing me again made me realize that he was still in love with me. I wondered if I should send him away now that he had healed enough to find some useful work. I was very fond of him but knew that I must never let that feeling grow. The inner conflict such attachment caused would prove disastrous for any seer.

None of us spoke on the ride home, each occupied with his own thoughts. My father, I knew, berated himself for not being strong enough to serve Gaelen in the way he knew best. I think all of us realized his travelling days had come to an end. He would never regain the strength he once had. Mama had confided to me that this caused some mixed feelings. On one hand she would no longer need to fear his death due to mishap or murder. On the other, she knew how his inactivity would bring feelings of uselessness that would make him unhappy. Even though he had lived well past the average man's age we all knew he would not retire with an easy mind.

56

EARTH

In spite of the cold I sat long into the night on the roof, Kira settled beside me and two cats nestled in the warm refuge made by the blanket I wrapped around me. Finally the warmth of the small furry bodies and the soft feel of Kira's feathers beneath my fingers calmed me enough that I felt I would sleep so I crawled down and sought my small bed.

* * *

A bright fire burned in the hearth of Liethis', or now my, cottage. I chopped vegetables to add to the small kettle boiling above the flames. The door burst open and a red cheeked Merrist stumped in, his arms full of wood. I quickly moved to shut the door behind him as he made his way to the hearth and stacked the wood beside it. He looked at me, grinning, and sniffed appreciatively. "Smells good. Is that the rabbit you snared yesterday?"

I nodded and gave him a teasing sideways glance. "Is that all you smell?"

He concentrated a moment sniffing again. "Where are you hiding the honey cakes?"

I laughed. "I wondered if I could fool you. They are on the top shelf. But you cannot have any until this evening. I expect company. Earth says a messenger is on the way. We must have something for him. And he will likely stay the night. Can you see to a bed in the shed for him?"

"Yes. It is cold nights now. I have already piled extra straw in the loft and suppose I can spare one of my blankets. The horses add some heat so we should be warm enough." He sent me a questioning look. "Did Earth tell you why the messenger is coming?"

I nodded. "He has news of the visit to Gharn. Lady Marja and the others have returned to Bargia and wish to see us. We will need to leave with the messenger in the morning."

Merrist's face lit up. He always looked forward to a trip into the city. "The horses will welcome the exercise."

* * *

Dugal sat astride a magnificent, coal black stallion. His face and those of his ten guard escort were red with cold. They had the hoods on their cloaks pulled tight over their heads and each one wore a colourful scarf wound around his neck. Thick shearling mittens covered their hands. The horses walked ankle deep in powdery snow. Dugal clapped

199

his hands together to bring some warmth back into them then wiped a drip from his icy nose. His eyes danced as he urged his comrades on.

"Come on. No more complaining. At this pace we will sit before a warm fire tonight and sleep in feather beds." The men answered with various half-hearted grunts and mocking groans but they seemed in good spirits.

I looked more closely at the man riding beside Dugal and recognized Larn. "I do not know of any woman worthy of such a trek in the middle of winter. I think you are mad and the woman has beguiled you. We should turn back and return to our own fires."

"I am sure you are correct Larn," Dugal laughed back. "But imagine her face when she sees I have come."

Larn grunted derisively. "If she knew you as I do, she would send you back at once with nary a smile for your trouble."

Both men grinned at each other and Dugal spurred his horse ahead leaving the others to follow through the snow kicked up by his horse's hooves.

* * *

When I woke I pondered the meaning of these dreams. The first told me that Earth wanted Merrist to stay with me. I still did not understand why this should be important though I could not dispute the meaning.

The second clearly showed Dugal in love and on his way to court his lady. But it told me nothing about who the lady was, or if she would return his affection.

I soon found myself asleep again. This time the recurring dream, of Merrist and I watching a young child play on the floor of the cabin.

This dream gave me an odd feeling of rightness that left no doubt that it would happen just as I saw it. When I woke again dawn began to light the horizon. No one stirred yet so I lay a few moments wondering why I had been sent the same dream again and what that could possibly mean. It must be important. But who was this child, this young girl that I felt such love for? Finding no answers, I shook my head and got dressed. Patience, I told myself, Earth will show you when the right time comes.

By the time I had dressed and descended from my loft Merrist had already come in from his bed in the shed. As he took his stool at the table to eat his porridge I could not help but see that his movements looked stiff. The shed, while not freezing in the company of the cow, still did not offer enough heat to keep Merrist's leg from aching.

My parent's home had started as one small room to which Papa had added the loft when he saw that sleeping on the table no longer served my needs. We had no room for guests and as soon as Merrist's leg had healed sufficiently he had gone to sleep in the shed.

I had assumed that, when he and I went to my cabin, Merrist would sleep in the shed there with the horses. Now I could see that would not work. Oh, he would never complain, but I could not ask him to suffer the cold. The alternative seemed no better. If he shared the cabin with me it would not only cause unwelcome rumours about a seer with a possible lover, but would also add an additional strain to our relationship that I did not know how to resolve.

Merrist understood the impossibility of his infatuation and I trusted him never to overstep the bounds of propriety, but I feared it would make things difficult for him. I wondered for a moment if this was what Earth intended. That Merrist, living in such close quarters with me, would see that he ought to strike out on his own. But somehow that did not feel right. The repeated dream showed us both older. I pictured again the small girl with the fiery curls sitting with her doll on our cabin floor.

I watched my parents and Merrist closely as we finished our tea and understood that the time had come for Merrist and me to go home, my home, the cabin I had shared for so many winters with Liethis.

Mama needed to have Papa to herself, and Papa required solitude to aid his recovery. And Merrist no longer needed my mother's care or my father's training.

My father showed no surprise as I announced that we would leave as soon as we had packed. Mama protested that she had little to send with us, no fresh bread or cakes on such short notice, only a pot of stew, but I stood firm. "We will visit often, Mama. You know you will see us again soon."

57

BACK HOME

I enjoyed the ride home. Merrist respected my need for silence and said little so I took in the changes since the last time I had come this way. The fall rains had brought some green back into the grasses. Where grains had grown in the fields I saw stubble awaiting the snow that would soon soften its harshness. Most trees had already shed their leaves. Only the oaks still held on to theirs, though these now showed brown in place of green. They gave stark contrast to the deep green of the pines and spruces. Here and there, rabbits scampered across our path, in a hurry to get out of sight lest they become prey.

Kira offered me her bird's eye view from above. It gave me a unique perspective of the land, the patchwork fields, an orchard here and there, now bare of fruit or leaf, rolling grassland and scrub leading into dense forest. I loved this country, even at this cold, wet season. I hoped the rains Earth had sent would replenish the land enough to receive seed come spring. A second season of drought would be beyond even Gaelen's skills to plan around.

When I left Kira's eyes to come back to my own she bade me farewell with a cheerful "klee" and left to hunt.

A glance at Merrist told me that he, too, enjoyed the ride. Watching him reminded me of the dream in which I had seen his old friends Dugal and Larn riding through the snow to court a maid.

"Merrist, do you miss your old friends, your old life? You thought you would be a soldier and would serve Lord Dugal all your life. Do you miss that life?"

Merrist sighed, and I heard in it a deep regret, but when he spoke his words surprised me. I did not need to truth-read him to hear the honesty in them when.

"We both know I was never cut out to be a soldier. That was the dream of a boy in love with the idea of greatness and fame serving his liege lord. I do miss my friends terribly sometimes, and my home in Gharn. Then I look at what has happened in the last moons and see that I have a new life, a life of service of a different kind but no less important. I have new friends now in you and your parents, in Lord Gaelen, and am proud to serve you now." He grew silent for a moment than continued. "Do I miss my old life and my leg? Yes, of course. But I am content with the new life I have been given. I do not yearn for the old. I do not even wish for my leg back. If I had it I could no longer serve you. I think this is what Earth intended for me. That I serve you so that you can serve others."

In that moment I knew that Merrist had become a man. The boy had gone. And I understood that we would find a way to live that worked for us both. If rumours came of it so be it. We, and Earth, would know the truth.

As soon as we arrived I went inside to start a fire in the hearth, and Merrist looked after the comfort of the horses. By the time he came in, the small cabin already welcomed him with a bright blaze.

"I have put some extra straw around my bed in the shed. With the two horses inside I should be fine. It is still tight. I looked around and can see no new holes that need fixing."

His words made me realize that I had not shared my new plan with Merrist. I decided not to put it off any longer.

"Merrist, it is too cold in the shed. I saw how your leg pained you this morning. We will need to find a space in the cabin for you." I gave my small abode a critical eye looking for a likely place to put another bed. Of course. The corner where I had slept when I stayed with Liethis now held baskets of herbs but could be cleared away again. I began to tug the baskets out of the way but found the first one taken from my hand.

"No, Liannis. It is not seemly for me to share the same roof. I am comfort-able in the shed."

The picture from my dream flashed in front of me and told me my next words spoke true. "No Merrist. Earth has shown me that we must share the cabin. I cannot allow you to suffer the cold of the shed."

Merrist's eyes grew round with surprise. "Earth has shown you this? Truly?"

"Yes. It is strange to me as well but it is so." I smiled at him to reassure him. "So you will be warm this winter, Merrist." I pointed to the corner. "And that is where you shall make your bed, just as I did when I stayed with Liethis."

After another puzzled look at me he shrugged and took the basket he had taken from me to the wall underneath the shelf that held my pots and dishes. The corner cleared, he went to the shed to retrieve his blankets and arrange them in their new spot.

By that time I had warmed the stew Mama had sent with me.

Over the next several days our lives found a rhythm that felt natural. Merrist spent most of his time chopping and piling wood at the back of the cabin. I sorted the herbs and did what I could to wrest Liethis' old garden from the weeds. My hand grew chapped and red from that work but by the time the ground froze I knew it would be ready for spring.

The snows started the third day after our arrival but that did not keep visitors from coming to seek the assistance of a seer. Some I could help with simple advice, others Earth gave me messages for, and still others had to be sent away without what they sought. That was the way of it. People knew this and had no other expectations. Their gifts of eggs, meat, oats and beans and the occasional piece of cheese replenished our supplies. I no longer worried that we would not have enough to eat. The donations might become smaller as winter wore on but I knew we would not suffer hunger.

What surprised me was that no one seemed to notice the pallet in the corner. Perhaps they thought I kept it for guests. Merrist did stay out of the cabin when I received my guests so perhaps they had no reason to think he did not stay in the shed. Soon I stopped checking for reactions.

Two eigthtdays after our arrival I told Merist, "Prepare the shed for an overnight guest. A messenger is on the way with a request that I visit Gaelen in Bargia City. The women have returned from Gharn and wish to share their news."

He raised on eyebrow in mild surprise then nodded understanding. He was getting used to living with a seer.

Just as Liethis used to do, I had a hot meal prepared for our guest. Merrist had made a stall in the shed ready for the man's horse and had some oats on hand to feed it. The look of astonishment on the messenger's face when he saw that I had anticipated his arrival brought back memories of similar looks from those that came to Liethis.

The memory warmed me and let me know that Earth never stopped caring for her people. If only we could ease her burden as well. If only the people could see that it was their hate and conflict that made it so hard for Earth. When wounded she found it difficult to create the conditions that allowed bountiful harvests, and health and prosperity.

Dawn found us saddled and ready to depart. That night had been the first time Merrist's sleeping arrangements had come under scrutiny. While the man pretended not to take note I sensed his questions and his decision not to pursue them. I decided then that I had best explain my dream, and the decision to share the cabin, with Gaelen and Marja. I thought it best they know before they heard questions about my true calling by way of rumours.

Light, new snow blanketed the land in a soft sparkling cover and made the whole world look clean and new. No wind blew the warmth of the sun away, and we remained warm even when we stopped, at the top of a hill overlooking the land, to eat our midday meal. I took this as a sign that Earth's wounds had begun to heal. That blanket would soon thicken as the land slept through the cold moons of winter until the sun once more woke the grasses and trees.

The sun sent its longest shadows across the land by the time we saw the gates of the city. Dusk came early this time of year. As soon as full dark descended the guards would close the gates for the night. We made it inside with less than a span to spare, though I dare say the guard would have opened the gates at seeing a seer there.

Merrist and the messenger took our mounts to the stables. Merrist would join the guards in the barracks for the night while I sought the company of my friends.

58

BARGIA

My parents met us at the castle as we arrived in time for supper. After the long ride in the cold, the blazing hearth and hot food tasted even better than usual. Gaelen indulged Sennia as she regaled us with tales of their stay in Gharn. The serious talk could wait.

"Lord Dugal treated us most graciously. He held two banquets for us, each with music and dancing...and oh, he is a good dancer." A small frown formed between her brows. "But you are correct, Liannis. He is shorter than I am." The frown disappeared as quickly as it had come. "But in spite of that he is handsome, and very attentive. And we even had some serious discussions about the future of Gharn and the alliance with Bargia. And he took what I had to say seriously. I know most men think women know nothing of such matters. But it reminded me of you Father, and Mother, and how you always discuss things together." She grew serious for a moment. "I think I will never join with a man who cannot take me seriously and share his thoughts with me." She brightened again, the changes as quick as a squirrel finding places to bury his nuts. "And the food...oh, Liannis they had these sweet cakes, all of nuts and honey in the lightest pastry. Dugal promised me he would ask the cook to teach me how to make them next time I visit. And you will be pleased to hear that Gharn is very stable now, no more trouble with traitors or people questioning Lord Dugal's ability to rule."

When she had finally run out of breath we turned our attention to the rest of the news of the visit.

"Dugal listens to his advisors and shows all the signs of becoming a great leader. The council has agreed to the measures he has taken to guard the food supply this winter. He sends his thanks for the shipment of spelt and oats. He thinks meat will still be in good supply as they are closer to the dense forests than we, and hunting will still be possible."

Marja, too, had been impressed with the progress Dugal had made. "And Larn is ever beside him to advise caution when he begins to show too much enthusiasm for an idea that has not been fully explored." Marja smiled at Gaelen. "It is almost like watching you and Klast, in those early days, my love."

Gaelen nodded and looked at my father. "Then I know Dugal is well served."

Papa inclined his head in acknowledgement and changed the subject. "I think it will be wise for Lionn to pay Dugal a visit in the spring. The two of them need to strengthen their alliance, and friendship is the best way to achieve that."

Lion looked pleased at the suggestion but grew thoughtful before asking, "But will I be needed to help with the conflict we expect with Lieth?"

"We will not know that until spring." A frown creased Gaelen's brow. "That situation will no doubt cause more difficulty. We may need to call on Dugal for support if we need to start a campaign to bring them under control. If that is so I may send you to Gharn to call in Dugal's oath. I hope we will be given another year before that becomes necessary. I doubt it can be avoided completely, given his actions until now, but the famine may weaken his forces too much to rise against us so soon." Gaelen sent me a questioning look. "Has Earth sent anything in this regard?"

I shook my head. "Not yet. I trust I will learn what I need in time to do what we must."

"Did the news reach you, Liannis that we caught three men from Lieth trying to escape the city after the attempt on Wartin's life?" At my shake of the head he went on to explain. "Two waited outside the gates. The guards caught them there and stayed hidden until the third came to meet them. They feared to go back to Lieth with their mission unfulfilled and so thought to hide in the countryside until spring. They planned to hold a family hostage for the winter for food and shelter."

"Surely they knew such a plan would never succeed? Someone would see them and report it?"

"I think they feared Garneth more than us. We do not know if Garneth has heard of the failed attempt. I expect he will know simply by the lack of the return of his men. Perhaps he expected them to be caught. They have met their just ends."

The sudden image of three men dangling from a hangman's noose made me shudder. While just, such violent deaths always caused me pain. I pushed the image from me and returned my attention back to the present.

"How fare Nairin and the children? I expect such an experience would make them fearful again, just when they were beginning to recover."

"Yes, Nairin hardly lets the children out of her sight. She no longer feels free to walk about the city and only receives those visitors she knows well. I have increased the guard on their house. She has declined my offer of a larger escort if she wishes to go out. I hope that when full winter makes travel difficult she will avail herself of the offer. I suspect we will see nothing more from Lieth until spring." Gaelen shook his head in frustration. "And then I fear we will hear more than we wish."

"I have visited her twice, Liannis," Marja answered, "as has Sennia since our return. I hope she will accept an invitation to visit the castle soon and share a meal with us. And she sings Lionn's praises for his efforts to save Wartin." The look she sent Lionn showed both pride and concern.

Lionn, how is your arm? I asked. "Has the wound healed well?"

Lionn flexed his arm to demonstrate. "Good as before. All that blood got me more sympathy than I deserved." He flashed a wicked grin. "But I sure am enjoying the attention of the young women. Lionn, hero of the day."

Mama laughed and changed the subject. "Liannis, how is Merrist's leg? Is it paining him less? If he is here I could look at it in the morning."

"I am certain he will be very happy to see you, Mama, though he is doing much better. I do not think your care will improve his leg any more. He still feels pain though he takes pains to hide that from me...as if he could."

"Good. I will expect him to break fast with us in the morning then."

I caught an image of Merrist, sitting in the barracks with the other men, but looking decidedly lonely. He no longer fit in there. I watched him listen to their boisterous tales and sensed how being there accented how much had changed for him. I decided that I would need to make other arrangements in the future. Then I saw him smile slightly to himself, unnoticed by the others. His thought came to me clearly. Let them boast of their short conquests and their prowess with the whores. I serve the woman I love. I have the nobler station.

Silence and several pairs of eyes met me when I returned from my reverie. I shook my head. "Nothing important."

Only Papa quirked a brow in question.

59

WINTER

As winter deepened, visits from those seeking my help thinned. People hunkered close to home. Travel even the distances to our cabin carried risk of a squall that could disorient the traveller. He could become lost and die a cold death. But now and then a petitioner made his way to see me. If I felt, or if Earth showed me, that it would be dangerous to return the same day I put them up in the shed until I knew the weather remained safe to travel through.

One morning I woke to an urgent sense of peril. I knew someone would arrive at our door by midday and that his need was great.

Merrist rose as soon as I stirred and went to stoke the fire in the hearth. I waited until we sat with our porridge to tell him what I knew.

"Merrist, we will need to travel with a visitor today. Please prepare the horses. They must have an extra blanket and we will need to take oats for them. I will prepare food for the journey and extra for those we will travel to. I will call Kira to come along. We may need her eyes. The weather will worsen by the time our guest arrives but we cannot delay."

Merrist merely raised his eyebrows as he took this in then nodded. "How many days shall I prepare for?" He rose from his stool, placed his bowl and spoon in the dish-bowl and reached for his cloak.

"I think we will be gone two days but best take enough for three."

Another quiet nod and Merrist hurried into the cold and pulled the door tight behind him. I looked at the closed door and thanked Earth, not for the first or last time, for sending Merrist. He never questioned my decisions, trusting that my gift of sight would never lead us astray. His solid presence and quiet company, rather than causing me distraction or intruding with his thoughts, helped keep me from worry and kept our lives flowing with an easy rhythm.

I busied myself with preparing as much food as the horses could carry, beans, cut oats, root vegetables and a small ham. I had the panniers filled by the time Merrist came in. He took them wordlessly out to tie on to the saddles.

When he returned the second time he closed the door and announced, "I see a dark spot through the snow. I will go out and help our visitor in." Before I had time to nod he had already gone.

I poked the fire to bring up the flames. The man would need warming before we could leave...and a bowl of hot porridge and cup of tea. I sensed that he was so cold that he could barely keep going. While I waited I summoned Kira. *Kira, little one, we must go into the snow. Come with me. If I need to I may ask you to be my eyes.*

I come. Hunt good. Full now. Wind strong. Hard to fly. Hard to see. Kira try.

I smiled at the eagerness in her tone. She would not let some wind and snow keep her from an adventure. That pleasant thought ended abruptly to the opening of the door as Merrist supported a man covered with snow from head to boot.

I hurried over to assist him to the fire. He tried to resist our efforts to get his cloak and boots off to dry. As he stuttered out his request that we go immediately to his cabin to see to his wife, I sensed there was more than he told.

"My wife...her baby lies backward and the midwife canna come. You mus' come t' help 'er or she will die." The man's eyes darted back and forth, meeting mine only briefly and darting away again to another part of the room, back to Merrist and on to something else. He clearly held *something* back. Sensing that this could be important I decided to truth-read him.

"Amest, what is it that you are not telling me?"

"N...nothin', lady." His eyes darted to mine and away again his face growing more anxious.

"Amest, I am truth-reading you and I know you are hiding something important. What is it?"

He grew even more agitated, his eyes wide with fear. "I canna say."

I sensed this last to have some truth. "What prevents you from telling?"

"Please, lady, dinna ask. Truly, I canna tell."

A picture came into my mind of a woman, who looked due to give birth, sitting on a cot holding another small child close. She and the child looked fearful.

On a stool opposite her sat a burly man dressed in dark leathers, with a sword in one hand and eating a leg of fowl with the other, grease in his dark beard. On the floor beside him sat a mug with steam rising from it.

"Who is the man with your wife and child?"

"He will kill 'em if ye dinna come." The man's voice grew pleading and he shook with fear, both of me, I sensed, and for his family.

"Who is he and what does he want?"

"You, lady, he wants you. He be from Lieth. I know no more. Please...my wife, my son...he will kill 'em."

"Do you know why he did not come to me?"

"N...no, lady."

That much rang true. I knew I would get no more from him. I put a mug of tea into his hands and told him to drink it as I filled a bowl with porridge. I handed it to him with a spoon as I took his empty mug and sat down to think.

"He must have been told I might sense his coming and be prepared for him and believed that I would come if someone was in danger because of me. Garneth would guess that from my efforts on behalf of his prisoners." I sighed.

Amest tried again, "Lady, please, we mus' go back. If I dinna bring ye he will kill us all."

"Yes, I believe you, Amest. But I must think on how to stop him."

"I still know how to wield a sword," Merrist piped up, "And I have kept mine ready, as you know. Perhaps the surprise of another man with a weapon will help. I will keep him busy until you get the others to safety. Then you may truth-read him before I kill him."

"But 'e 'as a sword, too," Amest spoke up. "How will ye best him? Ye can hardly walk. He be strong. 'e will kill you, too." The last almost sounded like a wail. Amest clearly did not like this idea.

I thought again. The image of Merrist and I sitting together with the young child came to me and I knew Earth had plans for me and would protect us both. So I made up my mind. "We will go with you, Amest. A plan will come to us before we reach your home. Earth will protect us. Merrist, I do think it a good idea to bring your sword. I think we will all be happy that you have tried to keep up your skills before this day is over."

Merrist nodded. "The horses are ready." He reached toward a peg on the wall, took his sword and belt down and strapped them on.

I nodded to Amest. "Get dressed again. We will leave now."

He looked only mildly relieved but grabbed his boots in obedience.

As soon as we had mounted I called Kira to me. She came and settled on to her perch on my shoulder. Amest knew the way, at least for now, so I did not send Kira aloft. She needed to save her energy for later. In this wild swirl of snow I had no doubt that we would need her.

At Merrist's suggestion we all tied ourselves to each other with rope in a line so that we would not lose each other. As we left I marvelled that Amest had found us. We could not see ten paces. Amest led and Merrist stayed beside me at the beginning.

"Liannis, do you think it will be dark before we reach his cabin? Even Kira cannot see in the dark."

"Earth will keep us safe. I think that when we do not arrive before dusk the man will think we wait until morning, or that we have become lost in the snow and will not survive the night. Perhaps he will be relieved that he will not need to harm me and let his guard down. It will give us a small advantage."

"Do you have a plan?"

"Not yet, but one will come to me."

Amest did not even look back. The wind and snow had muffled our speech so that he had not heard us.

"Merrist, I need to close my eyes to think. Can you stay close and see that I do not fall off if I go to sleep?"

"Of course. But I hope you do not fall off as it will be difficult to stop all three horses and get you up again." Merrist's gave a look full of concern.

"It will be well. We will succeed." I hoped the smile I gave him looked reassuring. He shook his head slightly and sighed. Apparently I had failed.

I closed my eyes and asked Earth to guide me. If she wanted me to take this journey surely she would show me what to do. I did not wait long before I heard her in my mind.

* * *

Daughter. It will be well. When you arrive the man will leave the cabin to relieve himself. He thinks you will not come today and will leave his sword in the cabin. He will look for you in the front. Call to him as you arrive. Let him see both you and Amest. Have Merrist go around the back, approach him from behind and capture him. Do not let Merrist kill him. He has information.

* * *

I thanked Earth and opened my eyes. Looking at Merrist I said, "We have a plan. All is well," and told him what I had learned. The relief on his face made me smile in spite of the cold that threatened to rob me of all feeling.

Just over a span after we left Amest stopped. As we caught up to him the panic in his face told me all I needed to know.

"Lady, I dinna know th' way. I be lost. We be undone!"

"No Amest," I assured him, "we are not yet undone." I lifted the end of my scarf that had covered Kira. "Kira will fly for us and show us the way."

His eyes widened then narrowed again in disbelief. "How can a hawk guide us? It doesna' know th' way. Even if it does we willna see it in th' snow." His shoulders sank in despair. "No lady, we die this day...my poor wife, she willna know why we dinna come...he will kill 'em both."

"No Amest. Kira will guide us. I have given her a picture of where we must go. She will show me what she sees. Do not fear. We will get there."

A small glimmer of hope shone through the doubt. I motioned him beside me and took the lead. With Cloud in the middle we formed a shallow vee against the white surrounding us.

Fly now?

Yes, Kira. You know what to seek?

Kira know. Fly. Seek. See what Kira see.

Take care. Do not get lost. If you cannot see come back. We can try again.

Kira see. Come back if not see.

That is good Kira.

Kira rose and disappeared from sight almost immediately. I worried for her even though I believed we would get there safely. Could she fly ahead? Was the wind too strong? Could she see through the snow? I need not have been concerned.

See? Snow down there. Fly higher than snow.

Very good Kira. I see. You fly above the snow. Let me see what you see.

Kira lent me her eyes and I got a clear picture of the terrain below her. Ahead, to the left stood a copse of trees I recognized, which told me we had not strayed far from our path. I corrected our direction slightly toward those trees and shouted over the wind to my companions.

"There is a copse of trees over there ahead. We will rest there for a while and eat something. The horses need a rest, too. Kira flies above the snow and sees the way." I called Kira back down to me, while we rested and ate, so she would not use all her strength. She seemed quite pleased with herself.

Cloud had a different opinion. *Bird should fly. I do not want her to ride. I want oats and my stall. I do not like this.* Her grumbling sounded only half-hearted. Cloud knew our trek must be important and would never refuse me. But I got a handful of oats from our sack and gave each of the horses some. Cloud acted miffed that a strange horse shared her oats.

I silenced her by asking *Would you prefer the horse fail and that you had to carry the man as well as me?*

She huffed back. *Man's horse weak...and stupid.* But she stopped grumbling and did not complain the rest of the way.

I allowed only a short rest as I knew we had to reach our destination before Kira could no longer see. The storm showed no signs of abating. Part of me hoped it would, but I knew that the snow would hide our approach and afford us the element of surprise. We did not want to give the man time to fetch his sword.

60

CONFRONTATION

By late afternoon the wind abated a little so the snow did not block our sight completely. We could see the blurred, dark blemish that was Amest's cabin as dusk began to lower her grey canopy over the world and Kira could no longer help us.

Just as Earth had described, the man who held Amest's family hostage came around the back of the cabin, head bent against the wind and snow. I could not see a sword in his hand, though the dark and snow made his image hard to discern and I could not be certain. I could only trust what Earth had told me. As planned, Merrist made his way quickly beside the cabin before the man spotted us. On my signal Merrist crept up to him behind.

"Man from Lieth!" I made my voice carry and put all the authority in my tone I could muster. "What does Garneth want with a seer?"

His head shot up, his hand moved to his side as though reaching for his sword as his gaze swung in our direction. When his hand did not find the expected weapon, he glanced briefly where it ought to have hung, then back to us. He moved into guard position and reached under his cloak for the dagger in his belt. But before he could accost us he felt the jab of Merrist's sword at the back of his neck.

"Drop the knife and raise your hands over your head!" Merrist snarled, "Or I will see that it leaves your body."

The man gave a start, stood stock still for a moment, then seeing that he had no choice, dropped the dagger in the snow and slowly raised his hands.

When I reached them I held my own small dagger ready while Merrist relieved him of a boot knife and felt all over his body and clothing for any other weapons. He had no more.

Amest had by this time untied the lead rope from himself and rushed into the cabin to his wife and child. I sensed the wave of joy and relief from all three of them at their reunion. The first part of our mission had been successfully accomplished.

Merrist trussed the man up with the ropes we had used to keep us together and we entered the cabin. The heat from the hearth felt almost too hot after the cold we had endured. I felt the tingling in my face, fingers and toes that told me how close we had come to frostbite. The fingers of my left hand throbbed where the nails had only now grown in to cover the ends.

Amest closed the door behind us, still holding his son in his arms. "Come, sit by th' fire. Maurin, make tea for our guests and give 'em food. We be near froze and be hungry."

Maurin hurried to comply, awkward from the bulk of her coming babe, and giving our prisoner the widest berth possible. She looked very near her time, but pale and thinner than I would have liked to see her. Her belly stuck out prominently, a taught ball on a stick. I suspected that food had been scarce this winter for this family. I worried that the shock of this experience might make the babe come early.

"Merrist, I think that chair will be a good place to tie our prisoner." As he shoved the man into the chair I stripped off my boots and cloak and went to help Maurin. As I stood beside her I touched her and sent as much calm into her as I could. She had no idea what I had done. She continued to glance at the man now and then, but she smiled shyly at me and went about her tasks less fearfully than before.

Watching her reminded me of the food we had brought with us. Merrist had the same thought and got up reaching for his boots. I saw him wince at the pain in his leg and realized how the cold must have affected him. It would be much worse than my fingers.

"The horses need bedding down and I will bring in the panniers." Merrist grabbed his cloak and thrust his sword at me to hold.

"Merrist, I will go."

"I will do my duty." While he kept his voice level, I felt a lance of anger. It was the first I had ever sensed from him. I recognized at once that my offer had wounded his pride. He had lost so much without any self-pity or complaint. Serving me was the only honourable work he could do and the only thing that allowed him to salvage his manhood. I wanted to tell him I understood, to apologize, but I knew that would only draw attention to it and make things worse. So I merely nodded. "Thank you, Merrist."

Many moons later I would look back on this moment as the one where my evaluation of Merrist as a man changed

Soon our fingers circled hot mugs of tea as the heat soothed out the last aches from them. Steam rose from our drying cloaks, sending cloudy tendrils up into the loft in dream-like wisps that thinned and disappeared as I watched.

Amest released his son and he scuttled over to help his mother get the food out of the panniers. Both exclaimed in delight over our gifts. Maurin declared she would repay me in the spring.

"We will need lodging for the night Maurin, perhaps two nights. That will be payment enough. And perhaps we may borrow Amest's horse to transfer our prisoner to Bargia City so that Lord Gaelen can interrogate him."

Maurin nodded gratefully but did not protest. They needed the food and I knew they had no means to repay me. This arrangement allowed them to save face.

The prisoner paled at this but he kept his face stolid. I could tell from the loud grumbling of his stomach that he was hungry, but we ignored him and he did not ask. I felt glad that he had been so well tied up because the heat and food, after so long in the bitter cold, sent a lethargy into our bodies that made it difficult to remain alert. Interrogation would have to wait. Perhaps we ought to leave it to Gaelen.

"Ye be welcome to th' horse as long as ye need 'im. He be a poor beast but will serve yon filth well enou'." Amest spat at the man, who remained impassive, silent and sullen.

"We will take him to Lord Gaelen tomorrow, if the wind dies and the snow stops so we can see. Merrist, can you take our prisoner to the shed with the horses for the night? And feed him some bread and cheese before you do. We need not feast him but he does need to eat if he is to survive the trek in the cold. He may have one blanket so he does not freeze."

"I think he should remain tied to the chair. If it is all right with you, Missus," he looked at Maurin.

She started in surprise then recovered. "Yes, that will give us all more space fer our blankets this night." She nodded in decision.

"Thank you Merrist. That is an excellent idea," I agreed.

He grabbed some cheese and a hunk of bread, stuffed them under the man's cloak and dragged him out without untying him. I wondered for a fleeting moment if his circulation had been cut off but dismissed the idea realising that Merrist knew what he was doing. He returned after some moments with our blankets, a grim look on his face. "He will be cold tonight but he will not freeze."

Amest spoke to Merrist. "We be right grateful fer what ye did to capture 'im. I watched. 'E had a dagger. Ye took 'im right smart, like a soldier. Ye knew what ye were about."

Merrist gave a crooked smile, shy acknowledgement of the praise.

I nodded agreement. "Yes, Merrist is a trained soldier. He lost his leg due to a battle injury, serving Lord Dugal of Gharn, but he does not let that get in the way of his duty." I kept my gaze on Amest as I spoke but I sensed the anger melt away that had simmered under the surface since the earlier comment. He would not lose sleep tonight.

61

TO BARGIA CITY

We all did our best to find enough space to lie down, wrapped in our blankets. The small cabin was cramped even with the chair gone, but our exhaustion from the day's efforts dictated that none of us lay awake long.

Light filtered in through the oiled leather that covered the one small window before anyone woke. I wakened to the sound of Merrist pulling on his boots. He put a finger to his lips when I looked at him and pointed to the door. He mouthed the word prisoner.

I pointed to the bread on the table to indicate he should take food. He understood and wrapped his cloak around some bread and cheese. On the way out he grabbed a mug of water.

I rose and checked on the weather. The storm had abated, and although the cold would bite us along the way, we would be able to see well and travel. The horses would still need to slow down due to the depth of snow, slowing our progress, but Both Merrist and I felt confident we would reach the gates by dark, since Amest's cabin was closer to Bargia City than ours.

After breaking our fast with full bowls of hot porridge we prepared to leave. Maurin tried to press some of the bread, meat, cheese and ale we had brought with us but I gave half of it back, insisting we had enough. We would not have too much, but neither would we starve. I sensed Maurin's relief that our gifts would remain and she and her family would have food to eat for a short while. I determined to visit again soon to make sure they had enough. Maurin would need to make milk for the babe.

The early morning shadows were still long across the sparkling carpet of snow when we waved our goodbyes. I told Maurin I saw no trouble for her with the birth, which relieved her greatly.

I mind-spoke Kira to tell her we would not need her eyes now and she could hunt freely. By midday we had travelled over halfway, so even though the skies had darkened with the promise of more snow I knew we would reach the city before it fell.

Merrist had informed me that our prisoner had not spoken a word, either last evening or this morning. He remained silent, his face grim, throughout the morning. All I could sense from him was sullen resignation mixed with occasional sparks of fear.

At midday I asked if he would try to run if I allowed his hands to be untied so he could feed himself. Even if he ran he would never survive so far from any food or shelter with not even a knife for protection.

His answer came as a sullen "No," so I nodded to Merrist to untie his hands. "But keep one hand tied to his mount's saddle. I planned to allow him to take the reins for part of the remainder of our journey. He would know that both Merrist and I could outrun him on our superior mounts so there would be no sense in trying to escape.

"I do think I should tie a lead from his horse to mine," Merrist insisted.

"Very well."

The shadows had reached their longest and the sky hung low and dark with snow as we approached the gates. Kira had ridden the last lap on my shoulder. I bade her fly out of reach.

Cloud picked up the pace when she saw the city gates. Merrist hung back with the prisoner as Amest's poor horse could barely place one hoof in front of the other any more.

"I will go ahead to prepare the guards at the gate. Our prisoner will need to be taken to a cell," I called back behind me.

Merrist caught up by the time the guard had heard our need and sent for an escort to take charge of the prisoner. The man still spoke no word as he was hauled from his horse, retied and taken away.

"I will take the horses to the stables and see to them." Merrist said. "Then if you have no further need of me I will go to the barracks for some hot food."

"No Merrist." I held up my hand for him to wait and asked the groom to look after all the horses. Merrist had earned a rest. "You are to come in with me, Merrist. Gaelen will need to hear your soldier's sense of what happened as well as mine."

He raised his eyebrows in momentary surprise, then, looking pleased, gave a short nod. "As you wish."

I mind-spoke Cloud. *You must allow the groom to handle you. Merrist and I have other duties.*

Warm stall tonight. Straw to sleep on. Oats to eat. She tried to grumble but I could hear the anticipation in her thoughts.

Marja met us in the great hall, already informed of or arrival. "Liannis, what a pleasant surprise to see you again. And you Merrist. You both look near frozen. Come quickly to our chambers and warm yourselves by the hearth. Sennia has gone to the kitchen for tea and food." Marja bustled us up the broad stairs. "Gaelen and Lionn will join us in a few moments."

It felt wonderful to be among friends again and I felt both my mind and body thaw. Even the constant barrage of impressions from all the people seemed muted. Bargia lay at peace for the time being.

Marja asked, "Will you be staying a while? I know your parents would love to see you."

"I do not know, my lady. If Gaelen wishes to have us stay through the interrogation of the prisoner we may. Do you think Papa is strong enough to make the journey into the city in the cold?"

Marja laughed. "I know he would not miss it. He has already come in twice since the snow fell. He seems stronger but still has a tremor and tires easily. Brensa hovers over him like a mother hen...ah, here is Gaelen. We can ask him what he wishes."

Now that Sennia had turned fifteen, Gaelen included her in all the discussions that Marja also participated in. That meant everything that took place outside of the council meetings and explanations of what occurred in them as well.

"I have already sent a guard to Klast to invite him and Brensa to join us." He smiled broadly at me, "even tough we may not need his advice. Neither one would forgive me otherwise." He nodded to Merrist. "Welcome, I am glad that Liannis thought to include you."

Marja broke in. "And you will sleep in a chamber in the castle. Your place is here with us and not in the barracks." Marja had remembered my request.

When Merrist made to protest Gaelen held up his hand. "No, Merrist. I concur. You have shown yourself above reproach and have outgrown the barracks. And I wish to include you in the future in our discussions. Your thoughts will add to our knowledge."

Merrist looked flustered and he blushed to the roots. "I am honoured, my lord", he stammered, "and at your service."

"Good, that is settled."

At that moment the door to the chambers opened and Sennia swept in, followed by two maids carrying tea, two kinds of fragrant fresh bread, three kinds of cheese, cold fowl, and pots of honey and butter. It made me realize how hungry I was when my mouth began to water. All conversation stopped as we filled our platters and Sennia poured tea.

Our tale came out between bites with Gaelen asking questions for clarification. Lionn and Marja added their own.

I watched Merrist stifle a yawn when the flow of talk lagged. Marja caught it, too and laughed, her duty as hostess coming to the fore. "Liannis, Merrist, whatever remains to be learned can wait until tomorrow. Liannis, your chamber is ready. Sennia, please show Merrist where he is to sleep this night."

"Thank you, Lady Marja, I know we will sleep well tonight. It has been a long day." I rose and went to the open door where Sennia already waited to show us out.

No dreams disturbed me that night. I woke to sunshine playing on my bed through the window slit of my chamber. The fire had died down to embers and the floor felt chill to my bare feet as I rose to stoke the fire up again before donning my gown and grooming my hair.

As I hurried, somewhat abashed that I had slept so long, I wondered if Merrist had wakened yet. I imagined his look of embarrassment if he were caught having outslept me. The thought brought a small smile to my lips as I knocked on the door to Gaelen and Marja's chambers.

"You look happy," Marja teased. "What is it that makes you smile so this morning?"

But I would not have the opportunity to tease Merrist. The tables had turned. "So, Liannis, do seers need more sleep than regular folk?" He had a new twinkle in his eye and a teasing lilt to his voice.

It seemed the shy lad had found a new level of confidence. I awed him no longer. Good. I liked that.

"You have caught me, Merrist. And I thought to catch you abed this morning. I shall have to try harder." My broad smile brought a light blush to his cheeks which both Marja and I pretended not to see.

62

INTERROGATION

We downed a quick meal of porridge, tea, black bread and honey just after dawn next morning, in readiness for our questioning of the assassin in the dungeon.

Just as we made to rise and leave I had a happier impression. "Marja, you will have more visitors by dark." The meaning of my dream about Dugal had suddenly become clear. "And Sennia, I think you will want to be here to greet them."

Sennia caught my secretive smile and jumped up. "What are you keeping from me, Liannis? Tell me... Oh, you are such a tease." She stomped her foot in a feigned show of petulance at my small shake of the head.

"Patience is a sign of adulthood, Sennia. I thought you had reached the age of womanhood." I slipped through the door as she gave an exaggerated sigh. "You ...!"

The warm exchange stayed with me until we left the castle and faced the grim task before us. I sensed the same resignation and distaste from my companions. Gaelen had never found interrogations easy. He hated to resort to torture. Though he never admitted it, I knew that after such incidents he occasionally lost his meal in the privy or behind a building. Lionn, too, had learned the same attitude from Gaelen, so the three of us made a gloomy trio. No one spoke until we reached the entrance to the dungeons.

"I wish Klast were here. He can make a man talk mostly with his stance and threats. I hope we will not need to resort to force." Gaelen shook his head as he watched the guard unlock the gate. "Which cell is he in Merkel?"

"Third on the left, my lord."

"Has he spoken?"

Not a word, far as I hear."

The furrow between Gaelen's brows deepened and he pinched the bridge of his nose in the familiar sign of worry.

"I fear he will tell us nothing, my lord," I said. "He has been obdurate and has not spoken at all since we captured him. Garneth sent his best this time." The pain in my head had increased to a piercing throb. I knew I had worse to look forward to.

Lionn noticed my pallor. "Liannis, you are whiter than your robes." He turned to Gaelen. "Perhaps we could try without her. You can see the pain she is in."

"No Lionn, I fear you will need me if we are to have any success at all. I will survive."

Gaelen nodded. "But I will make this swift. If he will not speak we will leave him here alone for a while. Liannis, do you sense any urgency here or do we have some time, do you think?"

"I have received no message from Earth, my lord, so I think we have some time. But as you know, Earth does not always show me everything. So we must always be ready. Garneth has shown he cannot be trusted and that he means me harm, as well as Nairin and the children. He is the first in history to attempt to harm a seer. A man so ruthless needs to be watched with great care." I had lowered my voice as we passed the guard room and entered the dark hall leading to the cells.

Lionn took a lit torch from its sconce and led the way. The soldier from the guard room followed, sword unsheathed in the event the man attempted to escape or harm us. He had no weapons, but such a strong man might overcome one of us.

He came abreast with Gaelen as we approached the door to the cell. "Let me enter first, my lord." He held his hand to the latch that locked the heavy bar in place.

"A good precaution, my lord." I nodded to the guard as Gaelen stepped back. "He waits for us and has girded himself against us. I cannot tell what he may do."

Lionn handed his father the dagger he had taken from his belt to pull back the bar, as it was so heavy he needed both hands. It gave a solid groan as it passed through the brackets that held it to the door, which opened with a rusty squeal that made me wince. The guard entered and stood to the side, sword ready.

Our prisoner sat on the bench at the back, stolid as ever, arms to his sides, loosely gripping the sides of the bench. The stare he sent Gaelen showed no emotion. Behind it I sensed his resolve grow, and knew we would learn nothing from him today.

"My Lord, he will not talk. I sense he will die first. Perhaps we ought to wait until Klast can join us."

Gaelen knew that my father would not make the trek in through the snow until afternoon so he raised one eyebrow at me in question. But he also knew I would be right, so he played along. "I see. Thank you, Liannis. You see true again. We will return. Klast will have ways to make him talk." He turned smartly on his heel and exited the cell. The guard barred the door again and, still looking surprised, followed us out.

When we had gone out of earshot I said, "Garneth will hear that we

223

have his man, and that I am unharmed. It will increase his belief that I am a true seer and make him fear me more. Perhaps he will attempt to kill me by more subtle means, poison perhaps, as the attempt to kidnap me has failed." I gave Gaelen a grim smile as he made to speak. "Yes, I will be very careful. I will read everything I eat and both Merrist and I will be extra vigilant. But I believe Earth will warn me. I can only serve her if I live."

At the entrance to the castle my spirits lifted when I sensed that Dugal could not be far away now. But I needed to get away from the noise in my head from the city. "My lord, I think I must rest in my chamber. You may call me back if you need me again." I grinned. "You will have some lively guests by dinner. Do not let Sennia go off. She will want to see Dugal."

I had spoken with Gaelen and Marja in private before going to the dungeon, explaining my dream and my conclusion that Dugal meant to court Sennia.

Gaelen had taken the news with alarm and expressed concern that Sennia was not mature enough to be betrothed yet.

Marja, on the other hand remained calm. "I agree, my love that she is not ready to join yet, but I think Dugal would make a good match for her. He is strong enough to balance her impulsiveness and we know him to be trustworthy. And he has shown good judgement, for the most part, and willingness to listen to good council when he has not."

"But she is only fifteen, too young to make such a decision!"

I could see that Gaelen might become intractable. Sennia was his weakness and if pressed he could get stubborn. I decided to interrupt.

"My lord, if I may."

His head swivelled in my direction and his face bore a look of surprise, as though he had forgotten I was in the chamber. His eyebrows drew together, but he gave me a silent nod, his mouth set in a determined line.

"My lord, while I cannot be certain, I think that Earth has shown me this to let me know that there is nothing to fear from Dugal's coming. It felt like a happy vision and I sensed nothing in it of foreboding. While I do think caution is wise I do not see that there is anything in this that requires strong intervention."

Marja broke in. "My dear, remember that I was not much older than Sennia when we met."

"You were seventeen! That is two years."

"Yes, but she is not betrothed yet, and even were she to become betrothed, I think we may suggest a period of waiting."

Gaelen softened only slightly. "Then we will tell her she may not become betrothed for a year, nor join for yet another." His mouth set in a thin line and I noticed that his fists had clenched at his sides.

"Gaelen," Marja put a hand on his forearm, "you know that Sennia is a headstrong and impetuous young woman. If we limit her too severely, I worry that she may take matters into her own hands. Do you want to risk that?"

Gaelen scowled but did not shake off Marja's hand. She knew him well and had learned just what would help him calm down enough to think clearly.

"Lord Gaelen," I added, "I agree with Lady Marja that we must not press Sennia too hard. Perhaps, if she is determined to join with Dugal...and if you do agree that Dugal is a good match for her...you might allow a betrothal. But also suggest that they wait at least until the campaign to deal with Lieth is ended before they join. It will allow some extra time and I think you can make a convincing argument that, in the event that Dugal is mortally wounded in that campaign, she will not want to be a young widow, with no experience. She would not be prepared to make the decisions for a demesne that is not even her own and where she has built no loyalties."

This was a viewpoint that Gaelen understood well. His shoulders lost their tension and he let the air out of his chest. "A good point, Liannis. One I think that both Dugal and Sennia will see merit in."

Marja nodded, satisfied that, for the moment, a serious problem had been averted. Her eyes spoke their gratitude to me.

63

LIETH

After a two day visit with my parents at their cabin Merrist and I headed home. The sky had cleared and the sun warmed our backs under a pale blue, cloudless sky.

We made slow progress due to the depth of the snow but neither horse seemed to mind. They lifted their feet high and pressed on with apparent good spirits. Indeed, Cloud expressed pleasure at the expanse of trackless snow ahead. To our left the trees at the edge of the forest lay wrapped in cloaks of sparkling white, the branches nearest us bent low with it, waiting for a breeze to remove its weight so they could spring back up into place. The only sounds to break the silence were the occasional call of a bird. Kira flew high above us, occasionally coming down to rest on her perch on my shoulder. She, too, made no sound.

It felt magical. Neither Merrist nor I spoke much, both affected by the beauty around us.

We had brought enough provisions for several days, my mother insisting we pack our panniers to the brim. One treat, packed at the bottom of mine, was a package of my favourite white pine needle tea. I smiled, feeling certain that she had given me her entire store on learning that I had used the last of mine.

So I felt no concern when it became clear that dark would fall upon us before we reached our cabin. That changed when I realised that our horses had not the strength to take us all the way without rest. We would have to spend the night out of doors. Warrior might have made it but Cloud told me she no longer had the stamina to lift one hoof in front of the other through the deep snow.

I looked at Merrist and knew that he had come to the same conclusion.

"Liannis, I think we need to head into the trees. We will have to make shelter there and spend the night. The horses can carry us no further. Even if we walk we will not reach the cabin."

I nodded, turning toward the trees at our left. "I have a small bag of oats that I always carry in my pannier. We can split that between Cloud and Warrior. It will sustain them until tomorrow."

As Merrist melted into the forest in search of a pine with low branches he could cut to build us a shelter, I divided up the oats and fed Cloud and Warrior. Then I pulled out some bread and meat for our cold meal. A small fire would melt the snow for tea. Though this situation differed considerably from the one Merrist and his friends had rescued me from last spring, I still felt apprehensive about spending a night in the cold. I did my best to shake off the tell-tale throb in my fingers.

After we had eaten Merrist showed me how our horses would provide some heat from their bodies if we arranged the branches over them on one side and against the tree on the other. I did not let on that my father had taught me the same tricks years ago.

Then Merrist went silent. By the awkward way he sat looking at his hands, I knew that something was on his mind. I waited for him to find the courage to speak. Finally he cleared his throat and looked at me sideways, his head still down.

"Um, Liannis...even with the heat from the horse it will still be very cold. I am concerned that the areas where you had frostbite will pain you and keep you awake." He cleared his throat again and looked away. "Um, you would be warmer if we shared our body heat...if we wrapped ourselves together in both our blankets...that is, if...um...you think that would be all right." He shot me a quick glance then looked at his hands again as if they were the most interesting objects on the One Isle.

The offer did not surprise me. I had been thinking along the same path and wondering whether I ought to make the same suggestion. Though it would be awkward, I trusted Merrist completely and had no fears he would do anything to jeopardize our relationship.

"That does seem like the best plan. It will help keep your leg warmer as well. Does it pain you greatly, now? I think it will be best if you remove the wooden one and massage the stump before we settle in."

Merrist blushed. "I think that will be necessary. I admit the last days have been hard on it. I am sorry, Liannis."

I managed a small laugh. "Merrist, I have seen your stump many times. This will be no different." But as I spoke I sensed that this time would indeed be different. I knew Earth had sent that knowledge and I wondered what it meant.

* * *

They escaped in ones, twos and family groups, rag-tag, thin and frightened. Some walked barefoot through the snow. Some carried what they could on their backs or in their arms. All looked desperate, hungry, and with little hope or strength.

Only a few rode donkeys or horses. The animals, too, looked thin, ribs showing and with bare spots where lack of food caused bald patches in their coats.

At the gates, soldiers made half-hearted attempts to stop them. They,

227

too, looked like they had not had a good meal in some time.

Parents tried to carry small children. Some left their babes in the snow, clearly dead but lovingly wrapped in what rags they had. Others were themselves the victims of the cold and hunger, and fell dying, into Earth's cold embrace, leaving children standing by, confused and unable to move away. Soon these joined their parents in their cold sleep. Horses froze, abandoned, those that were not killed for their life sustaining meat or warm blood.

Their general direction was toward Bargia. Pitiful few made it to that city's gates. Of those that did, many still succumbed to the privations that had sent them here. Bargians took them in, not all without reluctance. Here, too, food had been carefully rationed. More mouths to feed meant less for them and their children.

But Gaelen accepted all that managed to reach Bargia's gates, even those that could be found half a day's ride from it. He sent scouts out each morning after the first refugees knocked at the gate. He enforced this with determination and persuasion.

Nairin could be seen ministering to her people, looking almost as haggard. Even Wartin and little Leyla were pressed into service, no doubt a lesson they would remember well.

* * *

I woke with tears flowing onto Merrist's sleeve. Light filtered through the branches over our heads, telling me that I had slept well past dawn. I knew Merrist had no idea I had awakened when I felt his lips moving against the hair on the back of my head as he breathed, over and over. "Shhh, my love, shhhh. It is all right. It will be all right. Shhh. Shhh. It is just a dream, just a dream. Shhhh." I felt his free arm wrapped firmly around me from behind, in the position we had chosen when we settled down the night before. His body rocked back and forth gently, taking mine with it, like a parent soothing a small child.

In my state of half waking this felt like the safest cocoon any child could find himself in. Nothing bad could happen here...as long as I stayed asleep. But it could not last. As soon as my tears began to dry, Merrist noticed I had wakened and halted in mid-rock. His lips left my head and the arm that had held me so securely whipped away. I felt bereft and utterly alone, more alone than ever in my life. I choked back the tears that threatened to start anew, if now for a different reason.

Merrist had no idea of the turmoil he had put me in. He had already risen and pushed the covering of branches aside to cover his own discomposure. "You were dreaming. It must have been a sad one as you

228

were crying. A sending? Has Earth shown you something new? Can you tell me what she showed you?"

"Yes," I managed, "a sending." Cloud and Warrior rose, showering me with newly fallen snow. That removed the last vestiges of the spell. I jumped up and shook the snow from my blanket. "I am freezing. Do you think we can manage a fire for tea?"

Merrist nodded, his back still to me. "Already working on it." His voice sounded normal again. The sense of loss I felt had faded into the back of my heart, tucked into the place where those things best left unexamined dwelt. I busied myself with the activities of the morning.

64

REPRISE

Upon our return to my cabin our lives resumed the easy rhythm we had developed. I enjoyed the ebb and flow of weather, the trickle of visitors and the quiet. Every other eightday, Gaelen would send someone with extra food supplies, and to inquire if we needed anything. My assurances that we had enough had no effect.

The men and women seeking my help brought what they could. The donations grew smaller and supplies began to dwindle. I expected there would be little coming from them by the end of winter. So I carefully hoarded what we received against the time when our food would flow in the other direction, to those who would starve without our help.

Our next visitor with supplies from Gaelen and Marja arrived an eightday after our return to the cabin. He brought us news, both good and bad. Dugal had, indeed, come to court Sennia, and the day before he left for Gharn he asked if she would agree to join with him. Sennia accepted...both the proposal and, with obvious reluctance, Gaelen's insistence that they delay the joining until after the campaign against Lieth that spring would surely bring.

The prisoner still had not talked and Gaelen had had him hanged rather than risk his rescue. Though I knew that the decision to execute him was wise and not taken lightly, yet a shiver still ran down my spine. Another death Earth would pay for.

Even worse came the news that confirmed my dream. Refugees had begun to arrive from Lieth. Many died shortly after reaching the gates of Bargia, in spite of the efforts of Nairin and Marja to save them. The stories they brought of conditions in Lieth made me want to weep in despair and grief. While the dream had warned me, it had not prepared me for the breadth of suffering told to us that day.

Garneth had not taken any measures to insure that what little harvest they had would be rationed. Not even the wagons of grain sent by Gaelen reached the people. Much of it still sat in the warehouse, heavily guarded by Garneth's elite guard. Only these few, of all the citizens of Lieth, appeared to see no hunger. The castle had been barred to all but those closest to Garneth. Rumour held that the kitchens contained enough food to feed half the populace, and that Garneth and his cronies feasted every night, laughing at the plight of those outside the castle walls.

Some people had tried to leave early on, as soon as it became apparent that food would be scarce. But these had been stopped by the guards at the gate. The men were killed and the women and children thrown into the dungeons. When they died their corpses were left in the open to show what happened to 'traitors' who wanted to leave. But by winter solstice true hunger had set in. Most of the horses had been slaughtered and eaten.

When even the guards were not fed enough to keep from starving, they lost their zeal for preventing the people from leaving. It was said that even many of them doffed their uniforms and tried to get their families out.

But by now, winter had come in earnest. Travel was difficult in winter at the best of times. Now, without horses, with no food, already weak from starvation, it became near impossible. Those that followed the ones who had preceded them found their way littered with bodies; babes and small children, only, at first, then adults, many with children by their sides.

Most of those the scouts brought back each afternoon died from frost and starvation before they could take even one small meal. Many never woke once they fell asleep.

In the silence that followed our messenger's story, I felt Earth's pain like a deep wound that festered in my bowels. Oh Earth. How do you bear it? What must we do to help you heal? Can you ever, truly be whole again?

As quickly as the pain had come, it vanished again, leaving only a ghost of its former strength behind to remind me. My attention came back to the messenger who continued with his story.

"Lord Gaelen said to tell you that he believes the campaign against Lieth will go ahead in the spring. He says the victory ought to be easy, as the people of Lieth will be either too weak to fight, will refuse to support Garneth, or have already fled."

I saw Merrist nod in agreement, his face drawn. Then he shook his head sadly. "So much suffering, so many dead, and for what? Garneth's coup will come to nought and a whole demesne will need to be rebuilt."

Another silence fell upon our small cabin as our messenger nodded his sombre agreement. We remained with our own thoughts as we prepared for sleep. Even as we ate our porridge next morning, before bidding our visitor farewell, we spoke only as much as necessary.

65

LIETH

Two moons later the messenger's visit brought with it a summons to court. I had sensed it coming and Merrist and I met the man half way. Only a few patches of dirty snow still hunkered down under the north–facing branches of bushes and trees. While still muddy in spots, even the trail to the castle had dried to the state where our horses did not have their hooves sucked into it. Grass showed the beginning of bright green in between the tufts of brown left over from last fall.

Bargia had survived the winter well, as had Catania and even Gharn. Sunshine brought adults and children alike out of their homes. Travel was once again possible and I knew the guards at the gates would be busy checking traders' wagons. Traders passed from city to city with their wares; linens, baubles, honeycomb, furs...all manner of goods. But missing, or in very short supply, were smoked meats, sausages, nuts, and other foodstuffs. These had been consumed by the hungry populace.

When we arrived at the castle we were greeted by my mother as well as Marja and Sennia.

"Lord Gaelen and Lionn wait for you in the council chamber, Liannis. The whole council is there." Mama told me. "Papa too, he made the journey well."

"Gaelen told me to invite Merrist as well," Marja added.

This honour both surprised and pleased Merrist. I welcomed it, too, as it meant he had been accepted even beyond our inner circle. I now could speak freely with Merrist and discuss things with him that had previously been kept secret. It would remove a good deal of awkwardness between us.

When we entered the council chamber I saw that Dugal and Larn also sat around the table. Both of them grinned their welcome at us. I watched Merrist puff with pride and square his shoulders as his friends noted his presence.

What I heard confirmed what I had already sensed and what my dreams had told me. The possibility of travel brought an increase in the number of refugees from Lieth. With them came the tales of starvation, and death. Lieth, we learned had lost half its people.

Most had died of starvation. Children, and the frail and elderly, had been hardest hit. But Garneth and his guards had put many men to death for the crime of stealing food, or executed them for treason for speaking out against him. Lieth lay in utter chaos. Those that were left began to die of diseases that would normally have been minor annoyances. Their bodies no longer had the strength to fight them off. With no one left to bury the bodies that had begun to pile up, Garneth had ordered them thrown outside the walls of the city. Rats now feasted on them and entered the city, bringing more disease with them. The stench of the decay reached into the heart of the city. Garneth and his few remaining followers had locked themselves in the castle. It had one well within its walls and so they held their position as though in siege. Indeed, the new arrivals to Bargia believed that if Garneth dared to show himself outside the castle he would not survive long. Hatred would overcome the law against murder.

* * *

"Daughter."

"Mother, I am here."

"See, Daughter."

I surveyed Lieth, not with my own eyes, but with Earth's eyes. Lieth, soaked in blood, its streets oozed pus and rot. People near death, listless and without hope dragged themselves from place to place through mire that showed green and foul. The entire city lay as a festering boil upon Earth's surface. No cleansing sunlight fell upon it. The bodies piled outside its wall formed a putrid moat, with runnels of foul decay insinuating themselves into the countryside. The blight extended far beyond the city. Only well away from its walls could a few patches of fresh green fight for life.

With my vision came a sense of pain so severe I could barely breathe. The effort to contain the spread of this blight ate all my, no Earth's, energy. For the first time, I understood, in its full horror, why Earth could not sustain good weather and bring good harvests with such a wound upon her. Her powers had been crippled.

"Daughter."

"Mother, I see. I hear."

"This must be cleansed."

"Yes, Mother."

"It cannot be healed."

"Oh." The full weight of her words fell upon me like a physical blow. I recoiled from them.

"Only cleansed. This boil must be purged."

Earth returned me to my own sight and now stood before me as a woman. But this time she had none of the youthful vitality I remembered from my vision so long ago. Now her hair hung in lank, grey strands

233

about her shoulders. Her face looked gaunt and sallow, and pain narrowed her eyes. White clouds formed across her pupils and blocked much of her sight. She had become a bent, old woman. On her left forearm gaped a suppurating wound. It gave off a foul smell, the reek of disease and decay. Blood mixed with pus dripped slowly upon the ground at her feet. Where it fell, the earth lost its green and died. She indicated the wound with a nod.

"Only fire can cleanse this. Only fire can heal me."

A knot of dread clenched my stomach as the import of her words dawned on me. "Oh Mother, not that. Surely...?"

She shook her head, the movement making the lank strands sway. "You must tell Gaelen. Only fire."

"Yes, Mother. I understand."

* * *

Every pair of eyes in the council chamber fastened on me as I came back to awareness. Some showed shock, even fear, others only keen anticipation. But in those of Gaelen and my father I saw only concern and patience. They had seen me in trance before and knew the toll it took on me. They also knew that I would have important information to share with them that would most certainly affect the decisions they faced.

My father rose as soon as I met his eyes and brought a cup if cool water to my lips. I had not the strength to hold it myself. It revived me enough that I could croak out a request for another. I drank that second cup and managed a few bites of bread amid a silence no one dared break. All waited for me. I cleared my throat to begin, nodding to my father that I was all right so he could resume his seat.

"Earth has shown me terrible things."

My recounting met with stunned horror, mixed with outrage and some disbelief, or, more accurately, with confusion. When I had finished no one spoke. All waited for Gaelen to speak first, some out of respect, others because they did not know what to say.

Gaelen sat studying his hands for several moments. Then, after exchanging a look with my father he straightened in his chair. "Liannis, before opening discussion on this, can you tell me what Earth meant when she told you only fire could cleanse this wound."

This was the part I dreaded. "I can, my lord. She made it very plain. She meant the word fire very literally. Lieth must be purified by fire. Everything that is not stone must be burned to ash...the bodies, the contents of the homes and warehouses...everything that can burn, must. There is so much disease and rot there that the usual methods will not eradicate them. People will continue to die until this is done. Even the clothes the people wear must be burned and the people must bathe and their hair must be combed free of lice and other vermin before they may re-enter the city. Animals must be gathered into a field outside the city and kept there for a time until it can be determined if they carry disease. Those that show signs of illness or weakness must be slaughtered and burned, but not eaten. The fields around the city walls must also be burned in a wide circle around it."

Several people gasped. A few, notably Larn and Kamdeth, began to utter words of protest, tumbling over each other until Gaelen raised his hand for silence.

"Gentlemen, we have known, from what the refugees have told us, that Lieth is almost dead already."

I saw my father and a few others nod in agreement.

Gaelen continued, taking care to make eye contact with each man in the chamber. "We know that disease claimed many, due to the rot and the rats from the dead bodies that lay about. These rats will, no doubt, have entered the ware-houses and left the seeds of disease there. They and other vermin are also in the homes and cellars."

The men who had started to protest quieted and listened carefully as the realization of Gaelen's words sank in. Gaelen stopped, pinched the bridge of his nose in the gesture I knew so well, and sighed deeply before going on.

"I fear that Liannis is correct. Only fire will drive out those evils which have claimed Lieth for their own. But first we must roust Garneth from his hole."

Some men nodded but my father shook his head. Gaelen regarded him, one eyebrow raised in question.

"My lord. Perhaps the reverse is true. Perhaps it is fire which will drive him out of his hole. When he sees he no longer has a demesne to rule, he will have no reason to remain behind his barriers. And even if he does remain there he will, in time, run out of food. And it will be better for us to wait him out under siege in a city that no longer presents a danger to us of death by disease."

Once again silence fell upon the room, as though it held its collective breath, waiting for Gaelen to answer. He passed his hand across his eyes and scrubbed his face before addressing the council.

"Gentlemen, we have been given much to think on. I suggest we leave this for the rest of the day. Liannis needs to sleep to recover from her vision. The rest of us will benefit from time to reflect on what she has revealed. We will meet here again tomorrow after breaking our fast. Thank you." He rose before anyone could respond. The meeting had ended. As my father opened the door for him I heard Gaelen murmur, "Thank you my friend. See to your daughter."

But Merrist had already come to my side. I rose and found I needed to lean on him as my legs threatened to buckle. His arm around my waist sent warmth into my weakened body and soothed my agitation. I caught the small nod my father sent Merrist. The torch had been passed.

66

STRATEGIES

By morning sleep had revived me enough that I felt ravenous. Merrist joined us in Gaelen's apartments to break the fast. Mama and Papa rounded out the group with Gaelen, Marja, Lionn and Sennia.

Sennia expressed disappointment that Dugal had not been invited but Gaelen did not want the others around the council chamber to think that he knew more than they, or that Gaelen favoured his opinions. He promised her that Dugal would join us for dinner so Sennia swallowed her disappointment and joined us with good grace. But I watched her left hand cross to the third finger of the right where Dugal's heavy gold ring, set with a flawless turquoise stone, sat. I said nothing and let her think no one had noticed but I knew my father also had not missed it. It made me smile. Young love...so bright, so intense.

We lingered a little longer than usual over the meal. I sensed that we all needed the warm feelings there to sustain us through the darkness ahead. While I knew Gaelen had explained the events of the previous day to the women no one mentioned Lieth. It was as if we wanted to create a cocoon of goodness here. But duty called, and the spell broke as we rose to return to the council chamber.

It did not surprise me to find that only hushed conversation met my ears as we entered late. The news revealed from my vision left everyone glum and worried. When I took my seat and looked around the table not one person appeared well rested. Several sat with bleary eyes nursing either a mug of ale or hot tea. These and food had been delivered by a couple of maids before the meeting had been set to begin.

Gaelen did not even greet those gathered but went directly to the problem at hand. "Friends, you have all had a night to think and speak together about what we heard yesterday. By the end of this meeting we must have firm plans in place for proceeding with the campaign against Lieth. Winning will not be difficult. Purging the city will be more challenging. This is what needs to be carefully planned. We must not risk bringing disease and vermin into other demesnes and bringing plague, or worse, into our cities."

I saw cautious nods around the table but no one seemed inclined to speak so I swallowed and raised my hand.

"Liannis, have you more to add to yesterday's news?"

"No, my lord, but I, too, have thought on what that news means for how we must go forward. You are correct in thinking that plague is possible if we do not move with great care. And Earth told me that the only thing that could cleanse Lieth is fire, and that the entire city must burn. Often I gain clarity through my dreams and I believe I can expand on what I said yesterday. We have learned that less than half of Lieth's people remain. The rest have fled or perished. Earth has never demanded death of any people, so I am certain that she means to save those that remain there. So our task is to find a way to fire the city without killing her people. Yet, due to the disease that they could bring to other cities, they cannot be transported there. I believe that Earth means them to remain in Lieth."

Doubtful looks met me and were exchanged around the table. Larn spoke up with the question on all minds. "But if we fire the city where will the people stay while we do that and where will they go after? Many of their homes will be gone...and there will be no food left."

I could see that both Gaelen and my father had already thought of this for I watched Gaelen give my father a small nod. "Klast, what do you think? Can this be done...to quarantine Lieth, burn the city to the ground and send those that remain back? You are my best strategist. Tell us what you think."

My father waited a moment before speaking, choosing his words with care. "My lord, if we are to prosper again it must be done. We have no choice. But it cannot succeed without sacrifice from all of us. Bargia, Gharn and Catania we can count on, but I think we must also make formal requests to our other neighbours for gifts of grain and meat, whatever foods they can spare without causing starvation among their own citizens." At the rumble of protests that began he held up his hand for silence. "I understand that this will be difficult after the drought of last season. All of us see famine and death ahead if we do not protect what we have. Even our own people will resist giving our stores to Lieth when we need it for our own. Convincing those not sworn to our alliance will be even more difficult than firing Lieth."

Gaelen allowed the jumble of protests and questions to roll over one another for a few moments before rising. "Friends, I swear that before we leave today all of you will have an opportunity to speak. But before we hear your questions I want you all to hear what Liannis and I think, and to consider the ideas we and Klast have come up with. Lord Dugal, are you willing to wait?"

Gaelen had not gained such respect by ignoring diplomacy. I applauded his deference to Dugal as the only other lord present. Dugal did not need it but some of the others would be more willing to listen if they knew that Dugal gave his support.

238

"My lord, please give us your thoughts. I respect your experience and know of your past successes in times of crisis."

"Thank you." Gaelen turned to me. "Liannis, what do you see as the most important element in our plan?"

"My lord, Earth made it plain that Lieth is a wound. It festers and grows. The most important thing to do is to see that it cannot spread further." I stood to silence the wave of "but how," and "Impossible". "Earth told me to use fire. I propose that we begin with a ring of fire around the city. The area of field we burn must be so wide that the small vermin such as, mice, lice and other insects cannot cross it. Outside that ring we must set up a city of tents where the people can be kept in quarantine until Lieth is cleansed."

I watched Gaelen and my father nod approval and saw a few others begin to look thoughtful.

Dugal grasped the idea immediately and rose to speak. "Friends, I think I understand what Liannis is saying. If the people are quarantined in tents they cannot flee into our cities. By the time we are finished with Lieth, those that have survived their time in quarantine will be unlikely to spread disease any more. And when they re-enter Lieth they will have the freedom to rebuild it." He grew thoughtful as a consequence of what he had just said occurred to him. "But the people will need to be fed...and governed while they rebuild."

Janest stood. His hands trembled with the feebleness of age and he leaned against the table for support. But his eyes were as clear and keen as ever. I thanked him in my mind for speaking. So far he was the first, other than Gaelen, Dugal and my father. We needed support from the others for the plan to go ahead.

"My lord, I know you asked us to wait but I think I have something to add that may be helpful."

Gaelen smiled at him. I felt sure that only my father and I noticed the fondness in that smile toward the last surviving member of his original advisory council. "Then we need to hear you, Janest. Proceed."

"Lieth is one of the youngest demesnes on the One Isle. It has fewer buildings of wood and more of stone than the rest. I think that even after we fire what we must, enough stone buildings will remain to provide the remaining citizens with homes that can be repaired. Those that still have owners can return to them and rebuild. Those whose owners have perished can be allotted to others. Plans will need to be in place to insure that rebuilding goes forward in a proper manner."

"But," sputtered Larn, "most have not earned the privilege of living in such fine homes. Many are peasants and labourers." When Dugal sent

239

him a reproving scowl he stopped and began to examine his hands in embarrassment.

But I was glad that he had spoken as I expected others had the same thoughts. What right did a labourer have to live in a fine home when it had in all likelihood belonged to his now dead employer. It upset the order of things.

Gaelen rose to speak, unruffled. "You make a good point Larn, one that I am certain is in many of our minds. I believe the answer lies in how we set up governance. That responsibility will lie with Bargia as the conqueror of Lieth."

At first his remark took me by surprise, but in a flash I saw where he led us.

"As you all know, we have members of the former ruling family here in Bargia. As well, many of Lieth's former citizens have made Bargia their home. Bargia already rules Catania. I believe it unwise to increase the area under my rule beyond what I can govern effectively. I do not wish to govern Lieth once Lieth shows that it is again stable. I hope to see Lieth become, once more, independent. If Nairin proves willing, I propose a regency be set up there with her as acting regent for Wartin until he comes of age."

When protest began again about upsetting the lines of class difference Janest spoke again. "My friends, where do you propose the people sleep while Lieth is rebuilt? How will they be fed? How do you think to keep them where they belong when all their homes are no more? How will you prevent the riots when the people see good homes empty while they live in the streets? How do you think these things will be decided?" When the wave of outrage began he stood, stolid, a look on his face of a benign father who understood that his children had not quite reached maturity and only needed patience.

I intervened. "Gentlemen, what Janest says has merit. Earth has taught me many things. One is that, if we allow nature to find its course, all things find a way to exist together. Water seeks its level, the cycle of life and death keeps the forests green, and people, too, seek balance. True, some of the people who will move into the homes left standing will not know how to manage their new place. But out of them will arise some who show intelligence, skill and understanding. In time these will stand shoulder to shoulder with those who always lived there. Others, who grew up with wealth and status, will now show themselves unworthy of positions of influence. The loss of stability will see these men fall to their deserved state. In time balance will find its way. Those that deserve it will remain and those that do not will find themselves slowly weeded out. It is thus in nature and will be so in Lieth as well."

Some of the traditionalists had difficulty with my words. But Earth, or perhaps fate, had seen to it that the majority of those around the table were young. The idea remained thorny but did not meet with as much resistance as I had anticipated. Perhaps they saw that nothing could be done about it now and were willing to wait until after the capture and firing of Lieth to sort it out.

My father broke in. "Gentlemen, we have more immediate plans to make. The issue of governance can wait yet some time. We need to feed those that remain in Lieth until such time as they can once again grow their own food and hunt their own meat. I expect that will not happen until next summer, at least."

67

PRIORITIES

Gaelen sent messengers to the three remaining demesnes requesting grain, beans and whatever other foodstuffs they could spare. While we waited for responses plans went ahead.

But planting had to take place before men, beyond just the army, could be called on. We had survived one famine. A second would see half of us starve this coming winter. The added fear of another poor harvest made the plan to rescue Lieth unpopular with even the most ardent supporters of Gaelen and Dugal. But both leaders had garnered such respect and loyalty that people obeyed, though not without grumbling. No one among either lord's advisory council doubted that the consequences of failure in Lieth could bring about the fall of one or both lord's ruling houses. Very few understood, as I did, that failure would bring about far worse disasters. Earth's wound must heal in order to restore balance. And that task had been given to us.

So, while the people planted and hunted, Gaelen's and Dugal's troops gathered wagons, horses and canvas for tents. They emptied the coffers of both houses to pay for whatever food they could buy from the populace, and filled the wagons. They piled wagons with firewood for cooking, as well as with food, for time could not be spared each day to cut it along the way. They hired drivers to follow the army with the filled wagons and to help set up a city of tents each night in a circle, its perimeter guarded by soldiers. Shepherds were hired to follow the train with live sheep, for fresh meat.

Soon the fields outside the walls of Bargia filled with near two hundred wagons of all types and sizes, all laden with the goods that would sustain both those travelling to Lieth and the citizens of that city once we arrived. Never before in history has such an undertaking been attempted.

Planting had not yet finished when the long line, led by only a small part of the army, began to snake its way east. Progress, if that is what one could call it, occurred at a turtle's pace. Once finished, the remaining soldiers, those that had remained behind to help with planting, and as many other farmers, young business men's sons and healers as could be spared, would follow and catch up. These had orders to delay as long as possible so we would not have to feed them and use up our precious stores of food and wood.

A few tents had been erected outside the walls of Bargia City, at a separate spot, to receive any new refugees that managed to reach it. Here they would be looked after until the healers could determine that they carried no disease and would be allowed into the city. But the sad trickle of arrivals had all but ended, and any we found along our way would return to Lieth with us.

Cloud welcomed the daily exercise, even though she preferred a quicker pace. She often amused me with her derisive comments about the other horses. Sometimes her remarks became biting and I had to remind her that they worked just as hard as she did and deserved respect for that, even though they had not her ability to mind-speak.

Kira presented a problem. I felt torn between keeping her existence secret by sending her aloft and having no observable contact with her, and her desire to be with me. After three days during which she hovered close, her pleas softened me. I let her ride on her perch on my shoulder and made sure that everyone learned of her position as my familiar. My tent became a popular attraction as people gathered around me in the evenings to see the tame kestrel that obeyed my commands. After that she became a talisman of sorts and the sight of her circling above as we wound our way to Lieth. People began to see her presence as a sign from Earth that we would succeed. Those men who managed to bring down a rabbit or other small game began to bring the entrails for Kira to eat. I did not tell them that, as often as not, their offerings ended up in my fire after dark.

Merrist slept with the other men and tried too hard to keep up with them. After the fourth day, when he limped painfully over to ask me if I needed anything before he went to sleep, I insisted on seeing his stump. His guilty look told me what I needed to know even before he uncovered it. The entire area looked red and rubbed raw. Here and there sores had begun where blisters had broken.

"Merrist, is this how you look after the gift of walking? Do you want to lose the rest of your leg to the black rot that will set in if you do not take more care?" My worry made my reprimand sharper than I intended so that my words sounded harsh even to my own ears. But I could not help myself. "You are off duty until this heals. You will leave it bare and ride in one of the wagons. Merrist how could you let this happen? Your pride will be the death of you." My voice rose higher as I let my worry best me.

Merrist took my tirade without a word. He blushed to his roots, a guilty look on his face as he made a show of gathering his bandages together.

I beckoned to one of the men nearby who had watched with mouth agape. "Find a healer. And some water to boil." When he hesitated I barked, "Now!" As the man hurried away Merrist met my eyes. I blinked away the tears that would give away how helpless I felt.

"Liannis, I am sorry. You are right. I let pride get in the way of good sense." He shook his head and I felt a wave of sadness, loss and frustration from him. His manhood had again been challenged. He could not keep up with the others and so felt diminished, and he had been caught out by me.

I softened. "Merrist, everyone understands that you cannot do what the rest do. But I need you for other things. I cannot count the times I have looked to ask you to find someone, to discuss something that no one else will understand, to...oh, so many things that would require long explanations but that you have, through experience, grasped without those. And every time I look for you I am reminded that you are with the other men." A sudden truth flashed into my mind. Without thinking, I told him. "Merrist, I miss you when you are not beside me, and I worry that if you do not take care of your leg you will be taken from me. I cannot lose you. I depend on you too much."

I lowered my voice to just above a whisper so that only he could hear. "I wonder, perhaps, if you are Earth's gift to me. That she has sent you to see that I am not too lonely. It is a strange notion, but I sense truth in it. Merrist you are my best friend. Please do not do anything that will take you from me." I made a quick stab with my sleeve at the tear that threatened to roll down my cheek before I looked at him again.

His face had taken on a strange look. "Liannis, I am sworn to you for as long as you wish it." His words came to me soft, with a tone of wonder and something more that I dared not examine. "And I will do as you wish with my leg."

"The others will understand. They know what this costs you."

He gave his head a small shake. "It matters not. I was foolish to think I could keep up. I will stay closer to you from now on. That is where my true duty lies. I understand that now."

"Thank you. And I understand that it takes greater courage to admit that rather than try not to show weakness to the others."

After a silence during which I tried to sort out my thoughts I came to a decision and looked at him once more. "Merrist, as a child my parents kept as much pain from me as they could. My father was my champion. Then, during my apprenticeship, Liethis sheltered me so that I did not become overwhelmed as I came into my full powers. My powers are greater than Liethis' were. But with that greater power comes more pain from all that I sense. It is what makes it so difficult to block it when I am in the presence of many people. I believe you are here to help keep some of the pain at bay, so that it does not drive me mad. I think that if I did not have you with me I could not do Earth's work without losing my sanity. You help me find my inner balance. I truly need you."

"Liannis, I do not know why Earth has granted me so great an honour but I will do my best to fulfill that duty." His voice took on a sudden tenderness tinged with pain. "I will not leave you, Liannis. Never."

This time I let him see how his words moved me and made no attempt to wipe away the two silent tears that made their slow trails down my cheeks. "I know you will not, Merrist. And I am truly grateful."

The arrival of the healer woman ended any opportunity for further words.

68

CAMP

True to his word, Merrist left his wooden leg off for four days and rode Warrior beside Cloud a distance behind the rest. His presence as my guardian allowed me to stay somewhat behind the others for that time. Had he not, I would not have been able to eat due to the pain from being so close to so many others. My defences had grown stronger but even so I could not keep the press of noise completely at bay and was in constant pain. It affected my appetite. Merrist noticed and kept sending me worried glances.

At night when we made camp, though my small private tent was set well away from the rest, it only eased my discomfort a little. Merrist brought me bits of the best the cooks had to offer and watched me try to force some down.

"Liannis, you cannot afford to lose any more weight. Here, try some of this bean stew. The cook added a fresh rabbit. And I managed to wheedle a small jug of good wine from Junna, you know, the cook with the mole on her cheek, the friendly one."

"Yes, I know the one." I gave him a mischievous smile. "She has her eye on you, Merrist. Perhaps you ought to encourage her."

Merrist made a face. "Liannis, I wish to encourage no one. Leave off."

Part of me was glad that he showed no interest in other women. He could wed and still work for me. We could make room for him with a wife and children. But another part of me harboured the guilty relief, tinged with shame, that he still loved me and desired no other. I wondered, at times, why I could not release that notion but pressed the question aside and refused to examine it. I told myself, again, that seers did not join and that was an end to it. Perhaps this was a test sent by Earth.

Yet, in spite of this, the dream of watching a child in our cabin, with Merrist beside me, returned from time to time. I always woke from that dream with a strange contentment I did not understand, though the glow faded quickly when I woke.

The journey to Lieth rarely took more than five days. But this one lasted two eightdays and even when we reached the outskirts of Lieth it took two full days to set up a more permanent camp.

This campaign bore no resemblance to any other in history. Battle and swords would play almost no part here. This could not rightly even be called an invasion. In actuality, it was more a rescue mission.

It took a great deal of discussion and debate to come up with a strategy both councils could agree on. But each man in a leadership position knew every detail, so that when we finally approached the walls of Lieth City, everyone had their duties and carried them out smoothly. The tents were set out into two distinct areas, a smaller one for the soldiers, healers, cooks, the wagon masters and the rest of our retinue.

The other, larger area, isolated by a good distance would receive the citizens of Lieth. All but one of the healers would go to the Lieth camp and remain there until they felt confident that contagion presented no further danger. Patrols would keep people from crossing from one to the other. We divided our stores of food and supplies between both camps from the outset so there would be no need to cross back and forth.

This time, at my insistence, my small tent came to rest a good distance away from the others. Merrist set his blankets out on the ground beside it, refusing the offer for one of his own. It was almost summer and he declared that as a former soldier, he had no need of one. If it rained he would wrap himself in an oiled hide.

I never mentioned his leg again, but I could see from the diminishing limp, that it was healing well and would soon be back to normal, much to my relief. And since our little camp stood so far from the others, he used Warrior to go back and forth on his errands.

The clamour in my head, from all the thoughts and feelings of so many people, began to take its toll on me. I required more sleep, and ate less. I took to leaving on Cloud for much of the day when I knew my presence would not be needed at meetings, refusing even Merrist's company. He, and Gaelen as well, advised me against this, but I felt Earth would not allow me to fall into danger. I needed to solace to cope with the constant barrage that threatened to drive me mad.

It gave me an even greater sympathy for my father's need for solitude and his frequent absences from home. My mother had always accepted these without a word of complaint. She, too, understood how essential his periods of solitude were. He would be gone a few days, and when he returned, she would greet him with shining eyes that held not a trace of rebuke or resentment. It comforted me, at these times, to remember the special bond they had, and how their love had made my home such a happy one. At the same time, I missed having my father along on this mission, to discuss strategy and hear his unique observations. I knew that Gaelen missed it, too. He had relied on my father for so long.

69

TREMBLING

We all watched carefully for strangers while the men set up our various camps. Gaelen worried there might be assassins in our midst but I did not sense anything that spelled danger. Yet none of us doubted that we were watched and that Garneth knew our every move. But that was exactly what we wanted, that he should know our presence and fear his inevitable demise.

On the third morning, after breaking fast, Gaelen assembled his troops and gave them their last instructions. They must not use arms unless personally attacked. The people of Lieth must be evacuated to their camp where they would be fed, assessed for health problems, bathed and given the clean garments we had cobbled together for them. They would remain in that camp until the healers decided they posed no risk of contagion. Those strong enough would be given work cooking, gathering wood or hunting for game. They would return to their own camp each night. None would be allowed to enter the Bargian camp until the campaign ended and we all returned home.

Gaelen's men found the gates open with no one to guard them. They entered the city and used whatever means worked to get all the people and animals out. Some had already approached us as we set up camp. Most went willingly at the promise of food. Only a few had to be convinced with stronger persuasion.

Then the firing began. Soon thick black smoke darkened the sky all over the city. It belched from warehouses, billowed out of homes and businesses and roiled from stables thick with dung that had not been mucked out for several moons. The stench reached me even far from the walls of the city where our tent sat. Then tongues of flame of all colours topped the wall wherever we looked, red, orange, blue and even green.

What happened next sent people out of their tents screaming in fear and shock. The earth under our feet shook and trembled wildly, toppling many of the tents. The horses corralled in the field nearby reared and bucked, screaming. Many jumped the makeshift fence and ran wildly into the woods a span's ride away.

I felt my blood run cold as the sending overtook me.

* * *

"Feel daughter!"
Pain, oh, such pain as I could not have imagined. The wound on my

*arm burned with real flame. I watched, unable to quench the searing
pain. Nor did I wish to. This was the fire that would cleanse it and allow
the healing scars to form.*

I needed this pain.
Pain! Pain!
Would it ever stop?
Would it consume me?
Had it come too late?

* * *

When I came around, darkness had fallen. Merrist had managed to
bring me into my tent and lay me on my blankets. His worried look was
the first thing I saw. His one arm raised me up and a mug of cool water
wet my lips. I sucked at the draft as if my life depended on it, not one, but
three mugs before I could say a word.

At a nod to Merrist that I had enough he lay me gently down again,
waiting, the worry slowly ebbing from his face as he recognised the signs
that told him I would recover.

"What happened?" A strange question coming from me, the one who
usually explained things to everyone else.

"I do not know. I have not left your side and no one has come to our
tent. Perhaps they do not know we are inside. I have not built a fire as I
dared not leave you." Merrist hesitated. "Um, Liannis, look at your arm.
Does it hurt?"

I looked down and saw that the sleeve covering my right arm had
been pulled up past my elbow. The edges bore signs of scorching. I had
expected to still feel the pain from my vision. Often, when I experienced
Earth's messages I felt her pain as my own and that took a while to ebb.
But this was different. When I examined my arm I beheld a long red
streak the length of my forearm. It looked crusted and blistered and I
realised that the pain I still felt was, this time, very real."

"Liannis, this has never happened before. What is it? What does it
mean? What can I do for you?"

"I do not know, Merrist. I think, perhaps you ought to fetch a healer
and while you are gone ask what happened in the city. Maybe that will
give some answers." When he nodded and rose to obey I added, "But
leave me another mug of water. It seems I have lost a lot from the fire."

"Shall I build you a fire outside first? Are you cold?"

"No, I feel I may never be cold again."

After drinking the fourth mug of water I fell back into a deep,
dreamless sleep. I woke to the sound of footsteps approaching my tent

and managed to get to sitting before the flap opened to show Merrist's anxious face.

"I have Lord Gaelen and Lord Dugal with me as well as a healer. Are you well enough to see them?"

"Yes, please help me up and I will meet them all outside the tent. There is not enough space here."

His confident grip around my waist gave me both strength and comfort. I thanked Earth for his presence once again. How would I have managed without him?

70

RIFT

Gaelen waited to speak until the healer woman had clucked over my wound, rubbed a balm of goldenseal and honey on it and wrapped it in clean linen bandages. She gave instructions on how to dress it again tomorrow, placed the small jar of balm and more bandages beside me. She eyed me curiously again, shook her head slightly in puzzlement and took her leave, saying she would check on me in two days.

"Liannis," Gaelen began, "Merrist tells me that you are not aware of what has happened in Lieth." The look on his face told me how unusual he knew this was.

"No, my lord, I know nothing after the earth began to shift." I held up my bandaged arm. "It seems Earth has chosen another way to show me. Please tell me."

He nodded. "The ground shook, only a little at first but then more violently. Very few soldiers had remained inside the city and these came running out. I think we lost only one. Then, as we all watched, a crack appeared in the wall beside the near gate. We dared not approach for some time after the trembling stopped. When I finally sent a few to see what they could find out, they reported that they could see a crack in the ground starting at the gate and running as far as the smoke and heat allowed them to see. I had a few men circle the wall and they reported a similar crack and rift on the opposite side. The city still burns too much to enter to assess the extent of the damage." He gave me a searching look. "Liannis, have you any idea what would cause this?"

I shook my head.

"I am not certain. The only thing that comes to mind is that the heat from all the fires made it happen. I do know that this is what Earth needed to stop the wound she feels from growing even greater. My hope is that it did not come too late for her to heal." I looked at my arm. "I think she left me this wound so that I may see for myself if it is enough."

Dugal asked, "Have you ever heard of such a thing before...that the ground shook, or that a seer sustained a true wound?"

"No, but things are changing. And Earth depends on us to do our part. I think, perhaps, even she cannot live unless we care for her as well. She has shown me that she is sorely wounded and in pain." I glanced at my arm again. "I suspect I will feel pain in this until Lieth is cleansed."

Gaelen nodded. "As soon as the city has cooled enough to enter, we will roust Garneth out." A look of concern came across his face. "I think that may take some time if he has as much food as some say, unless we can find a way to infiltrate the castle. I will send my best men to see if it can be entered unseen. I would prefer to make him stand trial, but if that is not possible without a long siege we may need to resort to subtler means."

By the look of distaste I could tell that he meant assassination. I wondered if that would slow Earth's healing?

71

THE CITY

The rains began two nights later, torrents that left the tent cities a sodden, muddy morass. The cooks complained that they could not keep fires going long enough to make even porridge, let alone the meat stews and beans that would give us all energy and strength. But the rains put out the fires that still burned freely in the city.

Two days later the sun came out, and the restless people emerged to stretch and attempt their usual activities. From my vantage at the top of the small hill I could make out the happy noises of screeching children as they flung gobs of mud at each other in play. Tired parents, with enough to do setting the camp to rights, made only half-hearted attempts to stop them. The fear which had gripped us slowly faded, and the sounds of the children, together with the sun, helped to bring some optimism back. We had survived the worst Earth sent. Life went on.

The council had finally agreed with Gaelen's plan for dealing with Garneth. He chose an elite team of ten guards, and all four of the spies present, to scout Lieth, both to get a sense of the damage and what could be rebuilt, and to find a way into the castle. They returned just before dark.

While they were away Gaelen had a large tent set up close to mine, to use as a conference chamber, where we could consult unheard. I could not stop the thought that now Merrist would not need to sleep in the open any more.

Four trusted guards held watch at a distance out of earshot as our group convened to hear what our scouts had found.

How they had managed I do not know, but one of the guards called out before we started. "My lord, two maids request permission to approach."

I let my senses reach out and nodded. They presented no danger.

Dugal rose and opened the flap. "Ho, what is this?" A broad grin spread across his face as he stood back to admit the young women. A most welcome aroma accompanied them into the tent.

Gaelen and the others took in what they brought.

"Bread!"

"Ladies, do come in!"

"A feast. Dugal, I see why you opened up so quickly."

"Come in, come in. Do not keep us waiting."

Amid more good natured ribbing, the maids set down three large rounds of bread, still warm and dark with molasses, on a snowy linen cloth in the middle of the tent. One loaf even had some seeds and raisins in it. As well they brought a half round of cheese. We all fell to with gusto even before the tent flap closed behind them.

"I must see that I give the dark one my personal thanks tomorrow."

The men laughed with Larn as they caught his meaning.

"And I the other," quipped young Medlin, one of the scouts.

Gaelen brought them back to their duties with, "Just see to it that you are not so grateful they will not thank you when we all return home. These young women have enough trouble already."

Dugal took up from there when he realized that he had not thought of the possible consequences of careless dalliance for the young women. He still had much to learn. "Yes, I will not take it kindly if we cause these people even more hardship than they have experienced already. We have just rescued them, and they will be loath to withhold whatever you ask. They, too, may not think of where this may lead."

The grumbling that followed was mostly good natured. The reminder had not gone amiss.

"Friends." Gaelen brought them all back to the purpose of the meeting. "We have much to discuss and must to be ready by dawn to take action. Darkness is already upon us. If we are to sleep at all this night we need to work."

More good natured grumbles as the group settled.

"First, what is the state of the city? Can it be rebuilt? Or has the trembling we felt done so much damage that we must start anew?"

From the reports from each of the scouts it became clear that, while the city had sustained much damage, the wall could be repaired and the buildings built mostly of stone had survived. Of the warehouses only the foundations remained. The same held for the stables and various sheds attached to them. All houses made of wood had burnt to the ground. The charred bodies of many rats littered the streets, especially close to the outer wall of the city, but it seemed that few had made it out. That there had been few complaints from the tent city bore this out, though the guards on "rat watch" around the supply wagons still remained at their posts.

The mood that had started so light darkened with each new piece of information. Lieth had become a hollow shell. And the duty of firing the interior of the castle still remained. No doubt the human rats would not be the only ones to deal with if the tales of gluttony and greed proved even partly true.

Gaelen looked at the four spies. "Has a way been found into the castle? Did anyone manage to get inside and bring back news of what we may expect there?"

One man spoke up, the thinnest of the lot and the most experienced. "Yes, my lord, I found one hole on the east side but it is narrow and only I managed to squeeze through. But with a few hours work we can make it big enough for larger men. My concern is that we may be seen as we work and lose the advantage of secrecy. If seen we may be killed before we emerge on the other side."

"Where is this hole, exactly?"

"In the wall under the tower there. It leads into the interrogation rooms inside the walls. From there we will have access to the rest of the castle, just as in Bargia. I scouted many of the corridors that form the wall and saw no one the entire time. I finally ventured into the main area of the castle and saw only one guard posted. He stood well inside the great hall at the doors to what I expect were the lord's apartments. I believe Garneth must be holed up there. Time grew short so I did not remain to see what activity might be going on there or how many men remained inside."

The others nodded agreement. No other entry existed.

The spy, Karst, cleared his throat and Gaelen's attention went immediately to him. "Have you something more to say Karst?"

"My lord, I also saw a woman in the castle who was big with child."

Gaelen sighed and pinched the bridge of his nose. "I had hoped we could avoid this problem but it does not come as a surprise." He looked about at each one in the tent in turn, making sure he had everyone's attention. "Any ideas are welcome."

"My lord," Dugal spoke up, "is this woman not a traitor? We ought to wait until the babe is born and then execute her as we do all traitors."

Some nodded others looked uncomfortable and stared at their hands.

"That might indeed be the case, but another possibility also comes to mind." One of the older men spoke up. "This woman may have had no choice, or may already have been joined to a man inside the castle and stayed with him."

Dugal blushed, embarrassed that he had been so quick to judge. I was pleased when he nodded. "Indeed, it seems I spoke too soon. Forgive my lack of thought." Dugal managed a wry grimace. "I hope you will attribute it to my youth, though I promise I will be slower to judge in the future."

Gaelen smiled. "I, too, have made my share of such errors, Lord Dugal ... and been embarrassed by them." His smile broadened. "Those lessons are the ones we least forget."

While they discussed the problem I took the opportunity to send my senses into the castle to scan for the aura of the woman and see if I could detect any others.

"My lord."

All eyes turned to me.

"What is it, Liannis?" Gaelen seemed to welcome the interruption.

"My lord, there is another. She, too, is with child. Both auras show they are in fear."

"Do you have a suggestion as to how we may deal with them or any others you may not have seen?"

I had been thinking about this and so did not have to wait to respond. "I think that they must be taken without harming them. Then, before we decide on their fate, I should truth-read them. If they have been forced into slavery by Garneth or his men they must be protected. If they are inside because they are joined with any man there, we must ascertain what their sentiments are and whether they have directly committed any treason. If they stayed in the castle willingly, either as wives or as concubines, they will need some punishment to appease the people they betrayed. But the babes they bear are innocent and must not come to harm."

Gaelen gave me a cautious look. "Agreed...but what shall their sentence be, then, if we do not try them as true traitors?"

Murmurs of agreement came from several present and I saw a few heads nod.

I sighed, not liking what I knew I had to say. "Their sentence must be public and must cause them shame in a way that the people of Lieth will accept. After all, the rest of them starved while these few ate all they wished. The people will wish to see them suffer." I took a deep breath for strength. "I propose that they will have their hair shaved off and that they must not leave Lieth until after the birth of their babes."

After a brief silence one guard voiced what I sensed a number of them felt. "That will not be a true sentence! How will that appease the people?"

"Besides," another spoke up, "they can cover their heads with bonnets or scarves and no one will see!"

Gaelen held up his hand for silence. "Liannis have you anything to add?"

"My lord, I sense that these women have known fear for some time. Their auras are shot with red, the colour of fear. No doubt they worry for their babes as well as themselves. I am sure they know that Garneth cannot protect them much longer. I think that the public shame will be enough. More will serve no purpose other than revenge on those who have no power."

Amid the rumble from the men, some in agreement and others not, Gaelen responded. "Friends, before we pass judgement we must first know what crimes these women are guilty of. If, after Liannis has truth-read them, we find they have been only followers, I agree that her punishment will both show the people that we see the need to deal with these women and mercy for the babes they carry." When the man who had said they could cover their heads began to sputter Gaelen held up his hand for silence. "I agree that to cover up would almost make this no punishment at all, so I propose to forbid them any head covering until the snow lies on the ground. That will not be for several moons." He gave the dissenter a hard look. "Will that satisfy all of you?"

The man gave a grudging nod which I saw mirrored by others.

"Good. I want the others to be taken alive and harmed as little as possible. They will be tried as traitors unless Liannis senses that they had no choice when she truth-reads them." He looked around. "Now does anyone see any other problems with our plan to take the castle?" When no one answered, he said, "Then we are done for this night. You all know what you must do." He rose to signify the end of the meeting.

When all but Merrist and I had left I said softly, "My lord, you know that the castle must be fired just as the rest of Lieth has been. It cannot be spared."

Gaelen nodded with a heavy sigh. "I know. That is where the rats and vermin will have gone."

I made to rise but stumbled and fell back again. Merrist was at my side even before Gaelen. Noting my white face he said with alarm, "Liannis are you all right?"

Each took an arm and helped me to my feet.

"Help me to my tent. I need rest." Seeing that this satisfied neither man, I added, "I have needed to keep all my barriers in place in order to endure the pain and chaos here. I cannot escape it by finding some solitude. Searching for the women's auras has used up the last of my resistance. The pain has become unbearable."

Their looks of alarm increased. Gaelen was the first to speak. "How can we help?"

"I need to get away from all of this for a time...farther than this tent."
My legs crumpled and they found they needed to carry me by the arms to
my tent.

"My lord, I must take Liannis away for a time. How long can you
wait to start the trials, how long can we stay away?" Merrist appealed to
Gaelen.

I moaned as they lay me down on my blankets. Merrist found some
water and held the cup to my lips as Gaelen supported me.

Gaelen thought before answering. "Liannis, do you think that you
can recover enough to take part an eightday from now?"

All I could manage was a small nod.

"Wait here with her Merrist. I will have the horses and supplies
brought. Can you manage alone if I help you get Liannis onto your horse
with you?"

"Yes, my lord. I must."

Gaelen nodded and strode off.

72

HIATUS

That was the last thing I remembered until I woke outside our tent beside a small campfire. Above my head I saw the branches of tall trees. The only sounds that met my ears were the trill of birds and the crackle of the flames. No battering noise. No senses of fear and distress.

"Water." The demand came out as a hoarse croak.

Merrist was beside me in an instant, kneeling awkwardly as he placed one supporting arm under my shoulders and held a mug to my mouth.

I downed it in one draught. "Thank you." I whispered and fell back into a dreamless sleep as soon as he lowered me back down. The next time I woke to a canopy of stars, keeping company with a full moon, in a cloudless sky. Merrist snored softly beside me, rolled in his blankets. Between us sat a mug of cool water and a bowl covered with a cloth. I reached for it and pulled off the cloth to find the hind legs of a newly roasted rabbit and a chunk of black bread from the supplies Gaelen must have sent with us.

Merrist did not move when he woke at the sounds of my eating, so I did not immediately notice his study of me until he spoke. "So, you have returned from the dead."

I started at his voice and turned to find him grinning at me, pleased to have, for once, caught me unaware.

"I have, and feel as if I have not eaten for an eightday."

Merrist made an ironic face as he sat up. "Not so far from the truth. You have eaten almost nothing since we left Bargia and have slept almost two days." He jerked his head toward the rabbit bones in the bowl beside me. "I see you are enjoying the efforts of my hunt."

"Yes," I quipped back, "but I would rather it were a whole boar. What else is there to eat?"

He had already headed for the tree from which our stores hung. When he returned he lay a cloth beside me with a courtly flourish. "Your feast, my lady."

I found myself sharing a laugh with him, the first in many eightdays, and realized how much I had missed that quiet camaraderie which needed no barriers to hold the battering noise at bay. We sat in companionable silence while I ate my way through bread and cheese and washed it down with more water.

Merrist offered to make tea but I declined, enjoying Earth's offering in its pure form. Then, replete, I once more let sleep overtake me.

I woke to the sounds of Merrist poking our small fire back to life in preparation for making porridge and tea. He had no idea that I watched him covertly as he worked. He moved with the efficiency of long practice which made his work almost like a slow dance, each movement with purpose and a certain grace in spite of his wooden leg.

"Any white pine tea?" I had the satisfaction of watching him jump.

"Ah, you are awake. Yes, I know white pine is your favourite so that is what I am making." He sent me an appraising look. "How are you feeling? Have you slept enough? Any important dreams?"

I grinned at him. "Well, yes, and no."

"Good." He returned my grin as he handed me a steaming bowl and a spoon.

"Oh how lovely! Honey and butter in the porridge. How was Gaelen able to spare it?"

"Like me, he spoils his favourite seer...but don't expect any more special treatment from me. You look well enough to get up and contribute a little work."

I stretched and rose. "First things first. Earth calls!"

"Always trying to avoid work...bring back some greens," he called after me. "I have another rabbit to make a stew."

"All right!" The gaiety in my own voice sounded foreign to me. How long has it been since I was able to laugh, I wondered? Too long, I decided.

Just beyond our camp I discovered a small brook, no doubt the source of the water for our tea. I stripped off my gown and sandals and stepped into its cooling flow. A few strokes with my hands over its bed to remove the biggest stones made a depression just big enough to sit in up to my haunches. Soon, I shivered on the bank, shaking the excess water out of my streaming hair before putting my gown back on. I had gone halfway back before I remembered to look for the greens. Merrist spotted me through the trees, still empty handed, and called out.

"Nothing for the pot? Too good for honest work?"

"Forgot!" I waved gaily at him before turning back to the welcome respite of gathering greens in Earth's forest. It was a task that brought back pleasant memories of my childhood when Papa had taken me into the woods to learn how to find and survive on what nature provided. Those were memories I cherished. The next time Merrist spotted me my skirt held a large bulge filled with wild leeks, carrots, garlic and cress,

261

already washed in the stream. Merrist took them from me and added them to the bubbling pot.

While Merrist went out to check his snares I sat in quiet, listening to the sounds of the forest, Earth at her best. I had almost forgotten the wound on my arm. Now I looked at it and saw that it still had not healed. Seeing it reminded me that Earth still needed more from us, before she could heal. Without warning a new searing pain felled me.

* * *

Lieth castle. Fire filled the corridors. In the middle of the Great Hall huge flames engulfed a tall pile that could only be the draperies and linens from all the chambers in the castle. The smoke that funnelled up from it rose black and oily. Rats ran in every direction, often over each other as panic seized them in their chaotic flight. But all the exits had been blocked and they had nowhere to run. I could see that the walls bore no tapestries. These had also been consigned to the flames. My eyes followed a plume of smoke from chamber to chamber, into the kitchens, the storerooms and the dungeons. Wherever they touched flames rose up and consumed anything that burned.

When nothing remained that would burn, I heard a great wail and turned to see a bent old crone, watching. Her lank hair hung covered in ashes. She stood with her head thrown back, arms outstretched so that the sleeves of her ragged gown, grey with smoke and soot, fell back, baring her arms. There, on her forearm, just where my wound burned, I saw its mirror shoot out blue flames. Then she fell in a swoon and all sounds and movement ceased.

"Mother!" I cried out as I ran to her side, fearful that she had ceased to breathe, my own wound forgotten.

Earth stirred and I lifted her head. "Water!" she whispered and her head rolled back limp in my arm.

Water! Where would I find water? I looked about in near panic. Then, from the blackened earth at my feet, just where her hand had fallen to touch it, a small trickle bubbled up. I cupped as much as I could in my hand and held it to her cracked mouth. As soon as the life- restoring drops touched her lips, colour appeared there and spread until her robes regained their whiteness. Her lips once again looked rosy and her skin regained its healthy pinkness. Only her hair remained grey and the wound on her arm still showed an ugly rope of scarring. Her breathing steadied and after some moments she opened her eyes and smiled gently at me.

"Thank you, Daughter. You have done well."

I looked at my own arm and discovered that my wound had not scarred over yet like hers.

"Your work is not yet done. You will not heal until your task is complete. There are yet serpents in the city." The sadness in her eyes matched the emptiness in my heart.

"Mother, I do not know if I can finish this. There is so much pain."

"Go back. I am with you, even when you cannot see me for the darkness."

I hung my head, ashamed. "Yes, Mother." When I looked up she had gone. Only a small patch of green grass marked where she had lain. "Yes, Mother," I whispered again to myself.

73

RETURN

"Merrist, we must go back," I told him when I had recovered enough to speak coherently.

"But we have only been here three days! You have only begun to rest."

I nodded. "I do not know how I will find the strength, but Earth has promised to be with me. I have no choice. I must do my duty." I hauled myself upright with effort and began to break camp. Merrist immediately demanded I allow him to do the work, to which I gratefully agreed. Within a span we were mounted and on our way back to Lieth City.

Our return took almost two more days, time I spent mostly in silence. I used it to gather my defences around myself in preparation for the ordeal that awaited me...the trials of those captured from the castle.

Merrist rode beside me and I occasionally found it difficult to block the waves of concern that emanated from him. That made me wonder how I would manage the onslaught I would encounter on my return.

A scout spotted us as soon as we exited the cover of trees and, by the time we had crossed the open area half way, we were met with an escort who took us directly to the tent set aside for our meetings. Gaelen strode up just as we approached, followed by Lionn and his other advisors. A maid hurried behind with food and ale.

Gaelen wasted no time. "Liannis, you have returned sooner than we expected. We are about to begin the trials of the prisoners from the castle. We have Garneth, two of his men and three women. One is heavy with child, as you expected, and I suspect a second has quickened as well, as you said. I am glad you are here to assist. The women, at least, will need to be truth-read."

I nodded. "Earth has sent me. She told me I am needed. I am at your service, my lord." I glanced at Merrist as an unusually strong wave of concern washed over me. I tried to give him a reassuring smile and turned back to Gaelen. "What information have we?"

"It seems that, over time, those that supported Garneth and entered the castle with him gradually abandoned him and fled. When we took the castle only a handful remained. All but those few I mentioned were killed." He jerked his head in the direction of the castle. "As you see, the fires still burn. We had some difficulty managing the rats that fled but believe we killed most of them. I think that those few that escaped will not pose a hazard as they are intelligent enough to avoid the fires in the camp for a time."

I nodded again.

I knew rats to be very clever creatures. Their recent experience fleeing the fire that killed so many of them would make them wary. They would return, of course, but I knew that would take some time and by then the threat of contagion would be over. "And what do we know of the prisoners, my lord?"

"The guilt of the three men is clear. My concern is for the women. If they are to be spared execution the people must become convinced that they are victims, at least in part. I will rely on your public truth-reading to help convince them. Two claim they entered the castle as servants long before rebellion began and were prevented from leaving. Once the castle came under virtual siege they feared that even if they could make good their escape, the people would take out their revenge on them. I do not know how much to believe."

"And the third?"

"Hers is the saddest tale. It is she who bears the child. She claims that she was caught by a guard trying to leave the castle. As a punishment for her 'treason' she was held in a chamber and made to service the remaining guards there. She tells us she cannot tell us who fathered her child. She claims even Garneth raped her most cruelly, as well as five others. This one's tale has the ring of truth."

Indeed, as Gaelen explained, I could clearly see scenes of some of the trials she endured. Poor woman. And what would this bode for the child she bore? Would she overcome her loathing enough to love this reminder of her ordeal?

"It is as you say. She speaks truth. I regret that her shame must be made public."

"As do I, but if it is not, I fear for her future. Do you sense anything from the other two?"

"No, I must truth-read them. Earth has shown me nothing regarding these two." Already the press from so many around my fragile defences threatened to overtake me. "My lord, I must beg your indulgence. Please allow me to retreat some distance further until I am needed. I fear I have not been long enough away."

I must have gone suddenly pale, as Gaelen began to rise as though to catch me before I fell. Before he could, however, Merrist had already reached my side.

"Of course, Liannis. Have Merrist set your tent as far as necessary. I will send food and drink and will not call for you until all is set up and the prisoners are present for their trial. That will be tomorrow mid-morning. Will you be able to manage it then?"

It took no special gift to discern Gaelen's worry.

"I will, my lord. Earth will lend me her strength." My effort to appear confident seemed to have no effect on either Gaelen or Merrist as the tent flap was lifted to allow my exit.

74

ENDINGS AND BEGINNINGS

Those few traitors remaining after the capture of the castle met their deaths swiftly, after quick and decisive trials, at the ends of a rope. The survivors of Lieth watched the public trials and the sentences carried out. Those with any energy left often took an avid glee in the demise of the men who had held their entire city hostage for so long.

I remained as far away in my tent as I could, but even there the pain of their fear and rage, and the morbid delight the citizens took, assaulted me like a thousand cuts inside my head and body. I could barely breathe, let alone eat. I drank only a little watered wine at Merrist's urging.

Though it was necessary for me to be present during the questioning of both the men and women, I removed myself as far as I could from the rest of the proceedings. Even so, I spent most of my time curled on my side in my small tent, with my knees hugged to my chest, to prevent losing even the small amounts of water I managed to swallow. I slept only in brief snatches, and those were troubled by wild disjointed dreams of death, fire and pain.

I do take some solace from having used my gift of truth-reading to save the three women. The two who had already been employed in the castle, I found to have been victims, too, insofar as they started as loyal servants and had been unable to escape. They were sentenced to have their heads publicly shorn, and had been forbidden to leave Lieth, or cover their heads, until snow covered the ground for three days without melting. After this they could resume their lives as they pleased. My presence, and truth-reading, helped the people of Lieth see this as enough. While I did not think they would ever find true acceptance here I had no sense that they would be troubled by further violence. It was an empty victory for me.

The third young woman, the one who had been so ill-used, was given the option to relocate to Bargia where she could begin a new life, and where her shame need not be made known.

As soon as the trials ended I was once more granted a short reprieve. I desperately wanted to be alone. Gaelen requested that I spend the time with my parents instead, as he would have need of my gift during the meetings that would take place on his return to Bargia. But he would not arrive home for at least two eightdays, and so Merrist and I were able to make our journey a long and quiet one. I spent most of that journey only half conscious and Merrist often had to tie me onto Cloud so I would not fall off. The solitude did not serve to revive me more than just enough to cope until I returned to my mother's healing care. I became a skeleton, my hair began to fall out in patches, and the wound on my arm refused to heal. But Earth had not yet done with me. And I knew that more would be needed before our true healing could resume.

* * *

"Daughter." With great effort I raised my head from my arms, where I had laid down on the grass, to see her standing in front of me. My shocked gaze took in the wound on her arm that still showed red scarring, then the lank hair, her thin bent form. But her eyes shone with clear purpose.

"Yes, Mother." I pulled myself up to stand face to face with her and saw my weariness also in her eyes.

She managed a tired smile. "Daughter, your work is not yet finished. Your rest must wait yet a while. I have need of you."

"Mother, my strength fails."

"Yet, it will be enough. I, too, am weary, but the purging is done and now the healing must begin. Else all is for nought."

Words failed me and I looked for the understanding I hoped I would find in her face.

"You must go back to Bargia as Gaelen has requested. Go to your parents and await his return there."

I swallowed and managed a low whisper. "What must I do?"

"You must be present during negotiations for the future of Lieth. They may be difficult and I need you to speak with my voice so that they proceed as they must."

"And if my strength fails you...?"

She reached for my hand and sent warmth into my cold bones. "I will be with you. It will be enough. It must."

I could hear that even she hesitated and her voice trembled.

"And then may I rest?"

"Yes, daughter, then we may both rest."

75

BARGIA

My weakened state made it necessary that we travel slowly. I could manage only a few spans on Cloud each day. Kira flew overhead chirruping her worry, knowing that her perch on my shoulder would not hold her weight. Cloud kept her gait smooth and slow, and when she sensed I could go no further, sank down so that all I had to do was slide off her back into Merrist's waiting support. We spoke not at all. I was not capable of speech.

Every day, once he had laid me upon my blankets in the tent, Merrist set out snares and cooked the rabbits he caught. He tried to insist that I eat a few bites, but when I could not keep them down he boiled the meat in our one pot and fed me the broth in small sips, holding the cup to my lips as he raised my head. Our tiny store of tea became rationed and weak. It was our only luxury. Though he tried to tell me he needed none, I insisted we share a cup every night.

As I had not the strength beyond what kept me alive, I even cut myself off from mind-speak with Cloud and Kira.

Thus passed the days until we reached Bargia and he delivered me into my mother's care. I remember little of the period that followed. Later, I would learn from Mama that my father had sent Merrist away in a rage fuelled by fear for my life, and that Merrist had taken himself to our own cabin to await my wishes there. I would not see him again until much later, when Gaelen requested his presence at the meetings that would take place, and after Gaelen had explained to my father the care Merrist had given me.

Mama, it seemed, always understood. I sensed from her a memory of where she had found the strength to get up and walk down the ravine with my father. It followed her ordeal in the cave, when she would rather have lain down and died. She understood where we women found our fortitude. As she let me see her strength it became my source. Mama's face became the one I saw when I sought the face of Earth. Her small gift of healing, poured into me with all she had to give, began my slow ascent back into awareness. She tried to mollify my father, but with no success. I remained too weakened to care until I woke an eightday or so after arriving home and took a long look at my mother. She had lost weight, her hair had much more grey and her skin had become sallow and dry. All her efforts had gone into sharing her own life-force with me. She looked ten years older. The shock of seeing her thus gave me the push I needed to come to full consciousness.

"Enough, Mama. No more."

When she shook her head, my father, who had remained with us the entire time and had looked after Mama while she tried to heal me, intervened. "Brensa, she has taken all you have to give. You must stop. Liannis has returned to us and will heal on her own now." He took her gently by the arms and led her to the old rocking chair, which she sank into.

"Oh, Mama, what have you done? Will you recover?"

She nodded wearily. "Liannis, I would do it all and more again, to save you. Yes, my strength will return."

"Your hair, Mama. It is almost all white."

"It is only hair." She reached to touch me again.

"No, Mama. I will take no more from you." I realized I actually felt hungry. I looked at the hearth and saw that both tea and porridge stood there keeping warm. And I smelled stew bubbling over the fire. I made myself sit up.

Papa had seen my look and handed me a mug of tea almost before I had reached a seated position. He helped hold it as I drank greedily.

"Can you eat a little? Not too much, mind. You have not eaten for so long you need to begin slowly."

At my nod Papa returned to the hearth, ladled out a small amount of porridge, and poured some milk over it. He added a liberal dose of honey and quirked an eyebrow in question at me, the spoon for the honey still in is hand.

I managed a smile as I shook my head. "That is enough honey, Papa." It was the best meal I had ever eaten but when I asked for more my father shook his head.

"In a while perhaps, if this stays down."

At his urging I obediently lay back down and soon fell back into a deep sleep, though not a dreamless one. Once again, I found myself in Liethis' small cabin with Merrist, the small child at our feet. The smile Merrist sent me in this dream was different from what I had grown accustomed to in my waking life. It was filled with understanding, warmth, contentment...and a familiarity that comes with...? I could not put name to it. The dream filled me with such longing that when I woke my first words were, "Where is Merrist? I miss him."

My father's look darkened. "I sent him away. He brought you back half dead. I told him he is not welcome here."

Tears welled in my eyes, partly from longing, but also with sympathy for my father. His love for me had clouded is usually acute perception of human behaviour. It was the first time I had known him to misjudge someone, and his love for me had caused this blindness.

"Papa, I would be dead if not for him," I chided gently.

I saw my mother nod. "That is what I tried to tell him, Liannis, but he will not hear it."

A strange play of emotions crossed my father's usually inscrutable face, emotions that warred with his habitual logic; stubborn pride, chagrin, shame, pain, love, and back. Finally honesty won, along with the pain that had caused his lapse. "I wanted to hurt someone for your condition. He was the only one close enough. Forgive me."

"Oh, Papa." I took his hand, the only part of him I could reach, as Mama came and wrapped him in her short arms. He wept tears...long and weary tears, healing tears, the only ones I had ever seen him shed.

"We all forgive you, Papa, even Merrist. I am certain he understood."

When his tears subsided, and we all held mugs of calming camomile tea, I sought Merrist with my inner sight. I found his clear blue aura almost immediately. Usually so clean, now it was shot with the orange of worry. I wanted to hug him and tell him all was well, but that would have to wait until we met at the meeting of the council on Gaelen's return. That would take place only three days hence, I knew. A scout had arrived while I slept to request our presence there. Gaelen had sent the scout ahead the night before to let us know that he would be back. Gaelen wasted no time.

"I will go to Merrist and tell him to come to the meeting." My father would not meet my eyes as he made the offer. "I will tell him you are recovering...and ask him to forgive me."

"Thank you, Papa." I said no more, knowing what this cost him. Three days, then. Three long days.

76

HOMECOMING

Papa returned the evening before we were to meet Gaelen at the council. I did my best to hide my disappointment when he told me Merrist had agreed to meet us there, though I understood that both men felt awkward about his coming here until after we had all had time to find out where we stood together.

"But how fares Merrist, Papa? Is he well? Did you explain that you are no longer angry? What did he do when you told him?" In my eagerness for news of Merrist my questions took on a life of their own.

Mama gave me a curious look, worry behind the unspoken questions I could sense. Was my concern more than proper for a seer? What did it bode for me...and for Merrist? Though she said nothing, it made me wonder the same things for myself. I squirmed inside as I tried not to think what it meant. Or how it might connect with the dream that would not leave me alone?

Sleep eluded me that night and dawn found me dressed and ready to depart.

Mama would hear nothing of it until I had downed a huge breakfast of porridge, eggs, bread with honey, and tea. Strangely, it stayed down with only slight protest from my stomach.

"You may not be able to eat once there. At least this will sustain you until you return home." I caught a thought question, Will Merrist return with you? But as she had not asked it aloud, I let it lie. I did not know the answer, did not even know what I wanted the answer to be. So I did my best to leave it in Earth's hands.

Cloud and Kira both expressed their pleasure at our excursion into the city. Kira, especially, had missed me and came to sit on her perch on my shoulder, chirruping into my ear, never taking off in flight as was her usual wont. I stroked her and did my best to reassure her that I was well again and that I had not abandoned her. By the time we reached the city gates and she had to fly off to await my return she seemed mollified.

Cloud simply took the outing as her due and grumbled that she had not had enough exercise. I promised her some extra carrots tonight. These simple friendships helped me to feel connected to life once more, and assisted me in gathering my barriers around me, to gird me for the upcoming meeting. I could almost feel my strength gathering within me. Until now I had wondered if I would be able to manage the press in the city. Now I knew I could.

Papa appeared deep in thought as we rode. I had no wish to intrude, and so aside from mind-speaking Kira and Cloud, I contented myself with enjoying the late summer sun on my back and the familiar scenes of my home. For that short time all felt well. The council and the city seemed far off.

My heart leapt with a surge of wild joy when I spied a wonderfully familiar figure waiting at the city gates. "Merrist!" I urged Cloud forward. Merrist met my ebullience with a wide grin of his own as he reached up in his familiar way to help me dismount. I hugged him fiercely, with no thought of how this must appear to the astonished guards at the gate, or, indeed, to Merrist himself.

He, after returning my hug with an uncharacteristic strength of his own, recovered more quickly than I and disengaged, though his delighted grin did not disappear. "I am glad to see you, too, Liannis," he quipped. He turned to my father, standing silently to one side, a small frown between his brows. "Sir, it is good to see you again. Gaelen awaits us in the council chamber. He started early to bring those who had to remain in Bargia abreast of events in Lieth before we meet."

"Thank you. Let us proceed." Papa strode toward the castle leaving us to hurry to keep up.

The other members attending the meeting already sat around the great table. My eyes searched for Janest. He looked even frailer than the last time we had met here, but his eyes still met mine with the same eager twinkle that had endeared me to him so many years ago. I wondered how long it would be before this man would no longer be there to advise Gaelen.

I let my gaze roam the rest of the men around the table. All of Gaelen's advisors, the head of his elite guard and that of his army had seats on one side. Lionn sat to Gaelen's right. On the other side sat Dugal, Larn, Farsh, and Biel. Burrist had remained behind In Gharn during the campaign in Lieth, and so was not present. Those who had just returned from Lieth looked haggard. They had taken time only for quick baths and changes of clothing. Most wore beards several days, even eightdays old. The chamber held none of the buoyant optimism that normally accompanied a successful campaign.

Gaelen had donned his torque of office and it lent an air of authority and solemnity. Food, ale and wine sat on the table, and on platters, in front of everyone. Gaelen had not even allowed time for a meal before convening.

As soon as we entered, in spite of the fatigue that still plagued him from his illness, my father took his customary position behind Gaelen.

273

Had he been offered a chair he would have refused. His place remained behind his lord, guarding him with his life.

I took the last chair at the end opposite Gaelen. Merrist had already taken the one beside it.

My attention wandered during the debriefing. My presence, it seemed, was not necessary, a formality, or perhaps as a caution to keep everyone honest. At one point I found Merrist staring at me, his feelings momentarily unguarded. In his eyes I recognized the look he gave me in my dream. It caused me, once more, to wonder what it meant. At the same time it made me squirm with the sense that I ought to know. Again, I pushed it aside and forced my attention back to the meeting.

When those who had not gone to Lieth had been apprised of all events, a sober group filed out of the chamber to prepare for the banquet that would take place in the Great Hall. While not quite a victory celebration, it was at least a welcoming home.

Citing my recent illness, I asked to be excused to rest. My head pounded and I knew I would not be able to eat. My barriers remained weak, and I needed to isolate myself in the stone chamber set aside for me. I told my father he should remain with Gaelen and that Merrist would see to my needs. "And please find a chair and sit, Papa. You look about to fall over from fatigue. Mama will not thank me if I return home with you unable to walk." I smiled to take the sting out of my chiding. He took it with a sad smile and nod then walked away, leaving me in Merrist's care.

No sooner had we entered my chamber than my stomach chose that instant to rebel and empty itself of the last vestiges of my breakfast.

Merrist took control with his customary skill, as if he had never been banished from caring for me. I soon found myself tucked firmly into bed, and left alone to sleep, no trace of my mishap apparent in the chamber. Before he left, Merrist assured me he would check on my father's condition, and report back after the banquet once I had slept. I knew no more until a quiet knock woke me and I admitted Merrist.

"Lord Gaelen wishes to meet with us in his private chambers to break our fast this morning. Can you manage it, Liannis?"

"It is morning already?" I rubbed the sleep out of my eyes as he nodded. "Then I had better dress at once! Yes, Merrist, please tell Lord Gaelen I will join him...and how is my father?"

"After seeing to it that he ate something, Lord Gaelen insisted that he leave and get some rest. I trust he will be well this morning."

"Thank Earth. Can you imagine what my mother would say if he came home weakened from exhaustion?"

Merrist flashed me a quick grin of understanding. "I will leave you to join us then." He closed the door and left me alone to dress.

77

MAY THEY JOIN?

Gaelen, Marja, my father and I met, together with Mama, next afternoon over a cold supper at my parent's cabin. The location had been in deference to my fragile condition and my need to be away from the city. Lionn and Dugal had not been invited, something I thought a bit odd, but sensed nothing to be concerned about.

Gaelen cleared his throat to get our attention. "Friends, I have a proposal that I wish to get your thoughts on. As you know, the joining between Dugal and Sennia has been planned for the spring because we were of the opinion that Sennia, and possibly Dugal as well, needed some time to mature and to see if their attraction remained strong over that period."

We all nodded. I had an idea where this was going.

Gaelen continued. "I have discussed this with Marja but we decided that we might not be the best judges in this, especially where our view of Sennia is concerned. It is hard to see that our children have become adults." He smiled at Marja and received a warm smile in return. "So, we put it to you. This has been a difficult time for all of us. And since the harvest will be a meagre one, bringing the prospect of another hungry winter, the people need something to raise their spirits."

Another round of nods. While the Harvest Festival would occur even with poor crops, the celebration would not be as carefree as other years when the harvest was plentiful. The people knew they would face another harsh winter.

Marja broke in. "So what we are asking is whether you think it would be a good idea if we allowed Sennia and Dugal to join at the Harvest Festival."

Mama, still not having lost her romantic nature, clapped her hands in delight. "Of course, it is just the thing to lift our spirits." This brought wide smiles all round, and a fond look from my father.

Papa's thinking proved characteristically apt. "My lord, I do see benefits for both Bargia and Gharn in this. Bargia will have an added celebration to bring joy to the Harvest Festival, Gharn will have a new Lady and the prospects of successors for the ruling house. But I know you already have thought of this. So your real question is whether you think the young couple is ready to make such a commitment." He looked at each of us. "In view of the events of these last moons, I think we can all agree that Dugal has shown exceptional maturity, especially since the retaking of Gharn. He has kept his promise of alliance and has listened to good counsel. I have no concerns that he does not take his commitment seriously and I believe he will meet his responsibilities to Sennia with equal resolve."

"I agree," said Gaelen, "but can the same be said of Sennia?"

"I believe it can," Marja broke in. "She has shown no inclination to question her decision, and has not encouraged any of the young men who fancy themselves her suitors. In actuality she has ignored them. And she has learned during these hard times to curb her tongue and think before she speaks. She has not asked us to move the joining ahead but has accepted our decision to wait until spring without complaint, a big change for the girl who is used to pushing for what she wants. And she has become very dedicated to her studies and her work. She is still headstrong, though."

At that last we all laughed, and after a moment she caught the joke and laughed with us. Marja, herself, had never lost that quality. "I suppose she does have that from me."

"Indeed, my love." Gaelen answered with a twinkle. He turned to my father. "Klast, my friend, what do you think about Sennia? Is she ready? Will waiting until spring make any difference?"

Papa grew more serious. "My lord, I do not know if she is ready. As you know, Liannis has always shown unusual maturity and I have no experience with normal young women of that age. But I do not think that waiting until spring will serve any useful purpose." He turned to me. "Liannis, what do you think?"

As usual, the last word would be mine. But in this, Earth had given me no sign. I had only my own judgement to rely on. "My lord, Lady Marja, Earth has shown me nothing in this. But it is my opinion that the benefits, especially to Gharn, outweigh the risks. Sennia is young but she is strong minded and has a firm sense of duty. I have no doubt that she is in love with Lord Dugal and he with her." I smiled to soften my next words. "Yet I have no doubt that they will have their disagreements and that these may result in strong words between them. But I also believe they have the understanding and strength to overcome these hurdles."

Gaelen gave a great sigh. Marja still looked worried.

I decided to break the silence. "It seems we are in agreement that the joining should go ahead, then. Whether it be now or in the spring, the couple will face the same problems."

Papa nodded. "I agree that the benefits outweigh the risks."

Gaelen looked at Marja, and she nodded. "Then we have a celebration to prepare for."

Papa thought of something. "Since it appears the two in question have not been asked their opinion, perhaps it would be wise to do so before you go ahead."

Gaelen looked startled. "You do not think they will disagree?"

"No, but in such matters it is best to be certain...and it shows respect for their status as adults."

"Since we are in agreement that they are adults, I agree it is best to act accordingly." I smiled. "But I do not see any reason they would hesitate."

The young couple proved predictably ecstatic over the news. But Dugal brought up something the rest of us had missed. "My Lord Gaelen," he said formally, "I am lord of Gharn and so must think of my people first. They, too, have seen hardship and need something to celebrate. I feel it my duty to keep Harvest Festival with my own people."

I could see Sennia biting her lip in an effort to be patient. She looked to be almost jumping up and down in her eagerness to speak, though she managed to hold her tongue. I caught her eye and gave her a small shake of my head to admonish her to wait. She shot me a dark look but settled down.

Both Gaelen and my father nodded. Gaelen spoke first. "Do you have a proposal?"

Dugal looked to Sennia. "My love, how important is it to you that we be joined in Bargia, as tradition dictates? Would you consider celebrating the occasion in Gharn?"

I watched a momentary look of dismay cross Sennia's face, then disappear as she schooled herself to control. Her answer confirmed that she had learned much in the last moons.

"Of course I had looked forward to celebrating my joining before my own people, but I know Gharn has suffered more than Bargia in the last year. Perhaps Gharn is more in need of a happy occasion. I am willing to join with you before your people...who will then also be my people."

I had been thinking about how both peoples might enjoy the celebrations. "Perhaps a better way could be found, one which allows both Bargia and Gharn to enjoy their own Harvest Festival and then celebrate the joining in a way that makes both peoples happy...a compromise of sorts."

All eyes turned to me. Sennia, no longer able to contain herself, blurted out, "What do you mean?"

Marja caught on right away. "I wonder if Lord Dugal could return to Gharn until after the Harvest Festival and then come back here to fetch his bride. A delegation could accompany him, in state, with all pomp and colour. Then, the joining could take place here, according to custom. When the newly joined couple returns to Gharn, we could send our own delegation, perhaps even including Lord Gaelen and myself, to rededicate the joining in Gharn and celebrate with them."

It felt as though the air grew suddenly lighter.

"An excellent suggestion." Gaelen looked at Dugal. "What do you think, Lord Dugal?"

He looked at Sennia and they both nodded. "I think that may work very well. And it allows my people to see, once more, the strength of our alliance. My only concern is that we must all be home before the snows make travel difficult."

For the next span I watched the people I loved engaged in happy planning and relaxed. Here I was not needed and could bathe in the restorative waves of optimism.

78

HARVEST FESTIVAL

The day of Harvest Festival, always held at the autumn equinox, dawned crisp and bright. Most citizens had arisen early, busy with last minute preparations, and had witnessed a world bristling with white hoar frost. Every blade of grass, every tree and bush, and every rooftop sparkled until the warming sun uncovered the browns and greens of early fall underneath.

By the time I ventured out into the square with Mama, Sennia and Lady Marja, the smells of baking and roasting, along with the calls of the hawkers, invited all comers to sample their wares. Crowds of revellers jostled to reach the stall of their choice, amid cheerful exclamations over finds, and good natured competition between the vendors for the attention of potential customers.

At this annual celebration artisans and vendors vied for standing as the best of their kind. The results, to some degree, determined their reputations, and so, their success for the coming year.

Bakers, butchers and sellers of other foodstuffs had the prime locations lining the perimeter of the square. Small booths and shops selling dry goods, fabrics, trinkets and other items made by artisans and crafts-persons led out from the central square. Goods could be bought from all of the demesnes in the One Isle. Among these, finding space where they might, fortune tellers and sellers of amulets and love tokens beckoned the gullible, or those just pretending to believe. Further off, in the traders fields, poles hoisting colourful banners told of freak shows, contortionists, mummers and illusionists, all vying for a coin or two.

I looked into the centre of the square and noted musicians and players setting up on the large platform which had been erected there, preparing for the entertainment that would begin by late afternoon.

This was one of two celebrations in all the demesnes of the One Isle when all foods could be eaten without payment, in hopes that customers would return at other times to buy what they had tasted. The other was Summer Festival. One and all could eat their fill. Poor and rich mingled with no care for status or wealth. After the privations of the past year the throngs were larger than usual, though this did nothing to dampen the mood.

In spite of the press of the crowds I enjoyed the day. I sensed no danger, and the mood remained optimistic, so that I could keep my barriers firmly in place and only felt a mild headache by the end of the day. I did not allow myself to think of the sore that still festered on my arm and refused to heal, a sign that all was not yet well with Earth. She, in her turn, allowed me this one day of rest without visions or presentiments.

When I had watched Gaelen and Marja make their processional as the sun lengthened the shadows, filling their platters with samples from each stand around the square, I excused myself and went back to my chamber, tired but satisfied.

Today I could believe that all would be well again.

My sleep that night, too, remained dreamless.

79

A JOINING

Dugal arrived in Bargia an eightday after the festival to celebrate his joining with Sennia. The chill fall rains and frosty, wet nights had done nothing to dim his mood or those of his entourage. The entire company rode through the gates in high spirits, even the horses, though all were covered in mud and looked wet and bedraggled.

Tomorrow he and Sennia would be joined before all who could find space inside the great hall of the castle. As tradition dictated, Sennia remained in her chambers with her two attending maids, fretting over ribbons and hairstyles. She would not be permitted to see Dugal until the beginning of the ceremony.

As I helped Lady Marja and Mama with the last minute preparations I let my gaze wander about the hall. Bright banners of all colours, predominated by the blue and yellow of Bargia and the red and gold of Gharn, hung in profusion from the rafters and from the three huge candelabra. Along the walls, arrangements of stalks of maize entwined with the last fall black-eyed-susans poked between the tapestries and shields that hung there. They also lined the two grand stairs on either side of the hall, the one leading to the lord's chambers, the other to guest rooms. Smaller wreaths of the same flowers could be seen on every trestle table, with larger ones on the table set aside for the guests of honour and Lord Gaelen and Lady Marja. Bowls of apples, late plums and grapes had been placed beside them. Platters and goblets lined the tables, wood and clay below and pewter on the dais.

We had already toured the kitchen where the aromas of all manner of meats, fall vegetables and baking competed for our appetites.

Gaelen had convinced Sennia and Marja that, while the feast would be plentiful, restraint should be shown. He felt it important that the people see that, even now, for such an important occasion, he had not forgotten food would be scarce this winter. So the richest recipes, using the rarest ingredients, would not be seen on the tables today. Still, we would have honey cakes and sweet buns in plenty, and the wine and ale would come from Gaelen's personal stores, the best he could offer.

A last look, as the sun set, and Marja nodded, satisfied. Tonight Gaelen would dine in a separate chamber with Dugal and his men, while Sennia entertained the ladies in the lord's chambers, helped by Marja, Mama and myself. No candles would light the hall tonight, only the least number of necessary torches along the walls and at the entrances.

I watched Sennia do her best to hide her anxiety behind gaiety and false bravado. No one else seemed to notice, or at least did not let on.

I noticed that Sennia ate almost nothing the next morning. Marja, almost as nervous as her daughter, ate little more. Our fast broken, Sennia returned to her chamber, maids in tow, to have her hair arranged and don the gown she had sewn and embroidered for the occasion. Even her mother had not been allowed to see it, so carefully had she kept its design a secret.

As the time approached I took my place at the end of the long table on the dais. The four chairs behind the centre waited for Gaelen, Marja, Dugal and Sennia. Members of Gaelen's Council sat on one side and Dugal's party on the other.

When they came in Gaelen and Dugal remained standing behind their chairs, with my father in his usual place, unnoticed in the shadows.

At the sound of horns the heavy drapes at the top of the stair, that blocked our view, were swept back. Sennia stood revealed at the top, her two attendants a step behind. At the first note from the horns people had seemed to hold their breath. Now a collective gasp filled the hall. A quick glance at Dugal showed his mouth dropped open in surprise, as the reason for the secrecy around Sennia's gown became apparent. Tradition would have seen the bride wear the official colours of her home demesne. But Sennia had devised hers to combine the blue of Bargia with the gold of Gharn in such a way that the threads of embroidery shone out in golden contrast on the blue on one side, and the blue mirrored it on the gold on the other. The result set off her tresses, which wreathed her head in a copper halo woven in place by blue and gold ribbons and her pale skin appeared to glow from within.

Her complete poise belied the nervousness I had seen last night. Here stood a woman, the girl banished, at least for tonight.

Though guests customarily applaud the bride as she descends to meet her groom, the roar of approval that met Sennia as she glided down the stair filled the hall to its rafters. It did not die down until Gaelen had taken her hand at the bottom and brought her to stand beside an awed Dugal. Under usual circumstances, quiet would have resumed the moment Gaelen took her hand. Tonight he had to face the crowd and hold up his free hand before silence slowly returned to the hall.

With quiet formality, Gaelen turned to Dugal and placed Sennia's hand in his. It took a nudge from Gaelen before Dugal gathered his wits, took the proffered hand, held out his free hand to her to take with her other, and placed a chaste kiss on Sennia's lips.

Another roar of approval, this time much longer, as Gaelen did not interrupt it, completed the joining ceremony.

After the ceremony and feasting had finished, servants hastily stacked the tables along the wall and set the benches in front of them. This cleared the floor for the music and dancing that went on well into the night, the hall as bright as day under the light of hundreds of candles.

Though I had kept my awareness open to any hint of danger I sensed none. We could enjoy the celebration in joy and peace. I watched Dugal and Sennia dance until only those with the energy and abandon of youth still plied the floor.

As the candles began to gutter in the small sconces along the walls, and the older men and women began to leave the hall, I took my leave and went to my chamber to sleep. On the way out, I stopped by my father to suggest he do the same. He looked grey with fatigue but shook his head in refusal, in spite of my assurance that I sensed no danger, as I had known he would.

~ 80 ~

TO GHARN

Two days later the party, consisting of Dugal and Sennia, those that had accompanied him to Bargia, Lord Gaelen, Lady Marja, Lionn, and six elite guards gathered at the gate, ready to leave for Gharn.

I declined to go. While I would have enjoyed it at another time, I knew I needed solitude to regain my strength. I yearned for rest and the quiet of our own small cabin. But I felt that Merrist ought to go along, as he and Dugal had been such good friends. It would give him a chance to catch up and realize that he had not lost the good will of his old pals.

"But who will look after you and the animals while I am away?" Merrist's query came from a sense of duty. I could tell, both with my inner and outer senses that he wanted badly to be part of this.

"Stay with us," Mama suggested. "Will you not have the quiet you need at home with us? You know we will not intrude."

I looked from Merrist to my mother and then to Papa who stood behind her. He gave me a tiny shrug, as if to say he understood and would back whatever I decided.

Merrist gave another half-hearted try. "I have sworn to serve you, Liannis. I will honour my duty."

That decided me. The attempt was so transparently lame. "No Merrist. You must go with our friends to Gharn. I will stay with my parents until you return. I will be fine there. Go, and enjoy your freedom."

His guilty grin showed me I had been right. "As you wish then. I will not tarry on our return."

Sennia also did her best to insist I come along. She is a hard woman to deny anything she sets her mind to, but Lionn came to my rescue. "Leave off Sennia, you know Liannis would come if she could."

She acquiesced with a mock pout, making us laugh.

The people lined the street to watch the party leave, and crowded outside the gate, their mood buoyant and festive. Those that held them waved colourful scarves or pennants as they passed. As promised, the procession rode with all pomp and formality, Gaelen, Marja and Lionn, as well as the six guards, wore formal blue and yellow mantles over their warm cloaks. These also covered the horses' rumps. Dugal and his companions wore the same in the green and gold of Gharn. Sennia had had a special mantle made in blue and gold, to match her joining gown.

Its significance was not lost on those who lined their route, judging by the enthusiastic response.

I waved enthusiastically along with the others as they passed through the gate. Once they rode out of sight Mama, Papa and I made our way home. By the time we reached our small clearing the pain in my head cleared and I began to enjoy the warmth of the early winter sun on my back, and the glow it lent the brown earth.

Six nights later I watched the banquet in Gharn in a dream, almost the same as it had looked in Bargia. Gharn's people clearly took to Sennia, by the number of men I saw her dance with and the expressions on the faces of all those Earth showed me. The dream was to let me know that this was the beginning of the healing that needed to take place to restore the Balance.

My strength improved in the peace of my childhood home, under the watchful eye of my mother. I rode Cloud daily, which she took as only her due. Kira hunted by day and slept by my side at night, ignoring the enclosed space of my small loft, pleased that I had not made her remain outdoors. I found her pleasure amusing, as I knew that kestrels liked wide open spaces and shunned buildings. I welcomed her simple company.

Nine nights later Earth showed me that Gaelen and our party had left Gharn to return home to Bargia. Gaelen and Marja looked subdued, though they put on brave smiles. I understood that this came from the sadness of leaving Sennia behind. Sennia, too, looked wistful, though less so. She held Dugal's arm tight and he patted her hand as her parents rode out the gate.

81

PAPA

I told Papa that morning that I had dreamed Gaelen was on his way home. Papa decided he ought to go into the city to let the council know, so that they could send out a welcome party once the scouts had spotted them. Mama and I decided to make use of our time alone to bake bread together, an activity I had always enjoyed, one that calmed me.

"Liannis, pass me those raisins," Mama asked. Then she laughed, "And do not eat them all," as she watched me pop another handful into my mouth.

The morning passed in companionable quiet. After our midday meal we took out the dough to knead it for the last time. Then it would go into the oven outdoors that my father had built for Mama there. Papa had already started the fire in it before he left, so that the oven would be hot to receive the bread when we needed it.

I had my hands deep into the dough, covered with flour, enjoying the spongy feel of it under my palms, when a sharp pain lanced me just below the waist and I doubled over in agony.

"Papa!!! No!!!"

* * *

Papa stood beside his horse, a stunned look on his face, a bloody knife in one hand, the other holding his abdomen. Blood seeped through his fingers there. In front of him, writhing in the grip of the guard who held her by the arms, stood the woman from Lieth who had come to Bargia, to bear the child she had conceived by rape.

Though Earth spared me the sound, I could see the woman screaming and knew that her sanity had left her. A second guard had to come and help restrain her, so fiercely did she fight to get free. She wore the look of a wild animal in a trap.

Two more guards rushed over to see what the commotion was, and paled when they realized who had been stabbed. I saw my father shake his head, refusing help, climb painfully onto his horse and head for the gate that led out of the city and to home.

* * *

"What is it? What has happened to Papa? Wake up! Liannis, please..."

I woke to my mother shaking me frantically, a look of terror on her ashen face.

"Liannis, what has happened to Papa!?" She continued to shake me.

Awareness of what I had seen cleared my head in an instant. I shook her off. "He has been hurt. We must go to him!" I did not wait for her to respond, but ran out calling to Cloud. I leapt onto her bare back, having no time to saddle her, and fled, leaving my mother to catch up as best she could on Kenna. I sensed that she, too, had left her saddle behind.

My urgency must have reached Cloud even without mind-speak, as she put wind into her gait and almost flew underneath me. Kira fluttered overhead with frightened *klees,* trying to get reassurance. I could not answer her, my only thought, to reach Papa.

Mother, save him! No response.

I met him just as he had exited the city gate. He rode slowly, his one hand pressed hard against his side, his face pale as death. When he raised his head and met my eyes, I saw there the knowledge of what this injury meant.

No!! Earth, save him! But Earth remained silent.

I jumped off Cloud and ran to his side.

"Liannis, help me home," he rasped, his voice no more than a hoarse whisper of pain.

I had no time to answer as he raised his head to see Mama race up, Kenna's flanks heaving with the unaccustomed effort, Mama, too breathless and ghostly white with terror.

"Klast!?"

He shook his head, and in his eyes I saw a sad resignation and such tenderness as I had never witnessed before.

She understood immediately. "Nooo...Klast, no." She clasped his hand, fierce denial replacing her fear. "I will heal you."

His look did not change. "Take me home, Brensa."

She shook her head and reached for the hand that covered his wound, pulling it away so she could replace it with her own. I watched her pour out all the strength she could into staunching the flow there. When it slowed to a seeping trickle Papa gently took it away.

"Please, I want to go home."

"Mama, Papa needs his own bed. Come."

She gave me a blank look, nodded as though far away, and climbed back onto her horse. When our cabin came into sight she seemed to rally and rode ahead.

By the time Papa and I reached our door she had opened it wide and ran out to help me get him off his horse and inside.

288

82

DENIAL

Once we had helped Papa onto the bed, Mama knelt beside him, again insisting that she would heal him. I, numb with disbelief, made no attempt to dissuade her, but Papa, still the stoic soldier, kept his head.

"Brensa, dear one, this is a gut wound. You could not heal it even were you the most gifted healer ever known. I cannot take you to this death with me, though I know you would go, and gladly. But you have yet many years to live. Liannis needs you, Marja, too."

When Mama began to shake her head in violent protest, he reached out his free hand to touch her cheek. "Brensa, there is one thing I will ask of you, and it will take much from you. I wish to live long enough to bid Gaelen goodbye. He should not be more than a few days. I saw the messenger leave to tell him of my injury. He will not tarry. This much I will allow, but please, know that you cannot save me." The effort sapped his remaining strength and he sagged back against the pillow with a grimace of pain, still somehow retaining his grip on Mama's hand.

I watched the play of emotions over my mother's face and knew they reflected my own...denial, then a slow dawning of despair as we both understood that my father spoke the truth. He would die. Only the span and the day remained unknown. I sank down beside my mother and placed my hand over theirs. One question echoed in my mind. Why? Why? A part of my mind continued to plead, no, to bargain with Earth to save him. But even as I did, I knew that she could not. Papa would die. I needed him. He was my rock, my protector, the root of my tree. What would I do without the knowledge that I could always return to him? Where would I turn when I wanted guidance?

At my touch Papa opened his eyes and looked at me. "Daughter, I have taught you all I can. You are grown now. You have learned all you need from me." A tear leaked from one eye and rolled into his hair. "You have been Earth's greatest gift to me. I am proud of the woman you have become." Before I could respond, his eyes sank shut again and his head lolled to the side, awareness beyond reach.

I had been so wrapped in my own anguish that I did not notice Mama. She had let go Papa's hand and sunk back onto the floor, keening and rocking herself, overcome with grief. Papa was her rock, too, her strength, her joy, her reason for living. Only their love for each other had enabled her to heal from the savage rape she had endured before their joining. And only her belief in him had made it possible for my father to allow himself to love again, after the brutalities he had suffered as a boy. They had healed each other and built their lives around each other. Now their world lay shattered.

I rallied just enough to wrap my arms around my mother. We rocked wordlessly, finding some comfort together, until my mother's keening ebbed to a low moaning. From some deep recess, I found the strength to pull away. "Mama, I will make tea."

Mama's moaning ceased as, she too, gathered her remaining strength. A mute nod was her only reply. Then she turned once more to my father, uncovered his wound and examined it with both her eyes and her healer's sense. She closed her eyes, placed both hands over it and grew still.

I searched my mind for the right tea to make. Yes, the knowledge still lay there, raspberry leaf for strength and chamomile for calm. I went through the motions as one in a trance. When I tapped my mother's shoulder to give her the mug she let her hands fall away and lifted bleak eyes to me. "He sleeps. The bleeding is stilled." I read in her mind the words she dared not speak. That the wound had already begun to fester, and nothing she could do would stop it.

The next three days and nights became a round of my insisting Mama drink and eat what I managed to prepare, her efforts to slow the festering and control the fever that it brought on, and urging sips of broth and tea into Papa whenever he woke. Though I could see the toll her efforts took, something prevented me from trying to convince her to hold back.

In spite of his deteriorating condition my father never lost control of his reason due to delirium. His mind remained clear, and whenever he woke he would share brief words of love and encouragement with us. This much Earth had allowed him...and us.

83

GAELEN

Gaelen, Marja, Lionn and Merrist galloped into our clearing mid-morning on the fourth day. Their horses had been driven hard, as shown by their lathered flanks and hard breathing. Before we even had the door open wide to greet them, all four had dismounted and hurried in. They left the horses to graze what little they could find, not bothering to hobble them.

Gaelen went immediately to Papa's side, not taking the time to even acknowledge me or Mama. Marja took care of that for Mama with a hard embrace. Lionn did the same for me. Merrist stood by, watching me with an anguished expression.

Papa seemed to sense that Gaelen had come, as he roused himself from his semi-consciousness to reach out his hand. Gaelen grasped it in both of his and bent over Papa. "Klast." That was all, his voice a hoarse whisper.

Papa had never allowed himself the honour of naming Gaelen his friend, in spite of Gaelen's repeated avowal that he considered Papa his most trusted one. To Papa, Gaelen had remained his 'lord'. He did not deserve the honour of claiming friendship. Today, he looked at Gaelen with clear eyes. "Forgive me. I was careless, my lord. I am no longer able to fulfill my duty."

"No Klast. You have exceeded your duty to me. You have been my friend, my brother." The last words broke on a choked sob.

Papa's eyes glazed with unshed tears, and he reached his free arm over to cover Gaelen's hands with his. "Thank you, friend. I have had none better." His strength spent, Papa's free arm slid back to his side, though his focus remained clear. "My lady." Marja hurried to take Gaelen's place. "My lady, Brensa will need you."

Marja and Papa had never become close, always maintaining a cordial distance. That evaporated now. "Klast, you have loved her true. Forgive my block-headedness. I will do my best for Brensa. You know I love her as a sister. She will not be alone."

Papa gave a weak nod. "Thank-you. Lionn."

Lionn knelt beside his mother. "I am here, Klast."

"You must take my place now. Beware, be true."

"You know that I will." Lionn's broken rasp matched his father's.

Both Mama and I could see that Papa's energy was almost spent. She nudged Gaelen and Marja aside and took his hand in one of hers, placed her other on the wound and closed her eyes to pour her healing energy into him once more. I could not see where she found the strength, but when she had finished Papa opened his eyes once more to look for Merrist.

"Merrist."

Merrist hurried to kneel beside the bed so that Papa could see him clearly. "I am here."

"I charge you to care for Liannis. She will need you even more."

"I will. I swear it, on my life."

"She is sworn to Earth. You must follow her lead. Can you do so?"

"I can and I will. I am sworn to her as she is to Earth."

"Liannis."

As Merrist rose to make room for me I fell by his side in silent anguish, empty of words.

"Daughter."

I managed a choked whisper. "Papa."

"You are strong enough, now. Do your duty. It is not finished for you." He pulled in a deep breath with effort. "And Merrist will be there."

Papa looked at each one of us in turn, as if to burn our images into his memory. Letting his eyes linger at last on my mother he lifted one hand to her. She rushed to him, draping herself over his chest, head raised to hold his face in her eyes, one small hand cradling his cheek, tears streaming down her ashen face.

"Brensa, my love. Forgive me. You may do no more for me. Earth calls me."

"No, not yet. I can hold you yet some time. Klast, no."

"Brensa, my heart, you must not. It is time. Liannis needs you. You must live. I cannot take you where I go. Let me rest. My fight is done."

He looked at all of us again, and drew another ragged breath. "I have been honoured with true love and friendship, though I have not deserved it. You all honour me..." His eyes closed and his hand went lax in my mother's grasp.

We all watched his chest rise once, twice, three times, four...each more shallow than the last...eight, then one great shuddering breath and he lay still.

Silence. We each held our own breath waiting for the one that would not come. Then, "Noooooooo!" as my mother threw herself again across his chest and wrapped her arms around his head, drawing it to her breast.

I still sat on the floor, numb, unaware, empty.

Marja grasped Gaelen and they clung to each other.

After a long moment I heard Merrist, as if from far away. "Liannis...?"

292

My head, a great weight, swivelled slowly on my neck.
"Liannis, what may I do?"
No one had moved.

84

MOTHER

Some detached part of my mind watched as Mama and Marja washed Papa's body and wrapped it in a clean, linen shroud.

Lionn, Gaelen and Merrist dug a grave at the edge of the forest Papa loved so well.

Through it all, the horses remained in the clearing, making no attempt to wander away.

Mama stayed by Papa's body, unwilling or unable to pry herself away, as if to hold these last moments of nearness. No one spoke, except as necessary, each going about their duty as if by some unspoken understanding. We buried him at dawn the next morning. Marja held Mama tight to prevent her from throwing herself onto the grave, as the men filled it with damp earth, Mama weeping with great gasps as she attempted to join him in that cold rest.

That ought to have been my role, I knew, but my own grief prevented me from allowing such closeness. I had no barriers now and the emotions of those I loved melded with my own. I could not sort mine from theirs. I felt as though I walked through water, a great weight of it making every effort ponderous and lethargic.

When we had finished great snowflakes fell, and soon covered the grave in a pristine blanket of white, as though to warm him. Earth had taken back her son.

I spoke not at all, ignoring all attempts to comfort me. I was beyond comfort.

Gaelen and Marja left at midday. Lionn stayed behind, declaring that he would sleep in the shed with Merrist that night.

We drank tea, tried to eat stew and bread and avoided each other's eyes, each locked in their own private grief.

Mama rallied to insist Lionn and Merrist could share the loft in the cabin. "Liannis will sleep with me...the bed is empty now." So they would be warm tonight.

When we had all gone to bed, and Mama finally slept, Earth spoke to me.

* * *

"Daughter."
"Mother, where are you?"
"I am with you, Daughter. Come. It is time for us to rest."

"I cannot see you."
"You hear me. It must be enough."
"How will I rest?"
"I have prepared a place. Come."
"Yes, Mother, What must I do."
"I will guide you. You must come alone."
"Yes, Mother, I come."

* * *

I rose from my parents' bed and mind-spoke Cloud and Kira. Cloud came and stood outside the cabin door, while Kira alit on the edge of the roof, waiting.

No one woke as I made my preparations. Earth saw to their sleep and held them there. I saddled Cloud and filled her panniers to their brims with oats for porridge, all the white pine tea in Mama's sac, beans, herbs and some roots from Mama's garden. I rolled two blankets behind the saddle along with an extra cloak and my only winter change of clothing.

As dawn lit the morning sky I filled a small bucket with oats and set it before Cloud. *Eat it now There will be no more until we reach our destination. And there may be little grazing where we go."*

"Apple? Carrot?"

Even that could not draw a smile from my mind. I went back into the shed, found two shrivelled apples, and pulled a carrot from the bin of sand where Mama stored them for the winter. Cloud took them as her due, without thanks and polished off the oats after.

Before I could depart, there remained only one thing to do. Say goodbye to Mama. She would take it hard, I knew, another loss on top of losing Papa. But I had no choice. Earth called and we both desperately needed rest. The still unhealed wound on my arm reminded me with a throb of pain.

It seemed that the whole world burst into life at once, as Mama, Merrist and Lionn all rushed outside.

"Liannis, what are you doing?" my mother shrieked wildly, as she ran out in just her slippers and nightdress.

"Where are you going?" Lionn followed, still muzzy with sleep, wearing only his nightshirt and boots.

"Liannis, why did you not wake me to help you?" Merrist looked bewildered and hurt, as he ran a hand roughly through his hair.

I held up one hand. "Earth calls. I must leave." My voice sounded distant even to myself.

Mama stopped, stunned.

Merrist gathered his wits. "Then I will dress and go with you. What do you need? And you must eat first." He began to limp toward the shed. "I will saddle Warrior."

"No, Merrist, I go alone."

Mama found her voice. "No, Liannis, I need you. You cannot leave, too." Her panic roused me, just a little.

"Mama, I must. Earth calls. I must obey. Forgive me."

I watched her face crumple and her body sag with helpless understanding.

I managed to whisper again. "Forgive me, Mama." She gave a mute nod as I wrapped my arms around her.

Merrist had come to face me. "Liannis, my place is with you. You heard your father. He placed you in my care. I am sworn."

I shook my head. The only words I could manage were, "Take care of Mama. She will need you." I turned away from them and climbed Cloud's back.

In the corner of my eye I could see Lionn hold Mama back from me. "Liannis..." her wail already sounded far away as Earth closed off my senses.

85

WINTER

I have only dim memories of the days that followed. Cloud followed a call only she understood, and I did not attempt to ask her where she took us. Nor did I mind-speak Kira. I have a dim memory of many trees, of shelter at night under their branches, of long spans in the saddle with Kira above us. At night she came to sit by my side as I huddled against Cloud for warmth. Whether, or what, I ate or drank, I know not.

Snow hid our tracks behind us and added a stillness to our journey. I knew no one would follow us. Earth would see to it.

How long we travelled I have no idea, but we came at last to a small cabin, deep in the forest.

Daughter, we have arrived.

I blinked myself into awareness and recognized our destination. The safe-house, the same one where all this had begun, just inside the border of Gharn...how long ago? Was it truly two years? Dugal had not returned to it once since we had departed for Bargia. It appeared no one else had used it either. The same three stools, and the upended log I had perched on, still stood around the crude plank table. The mugs, bowls, a pot for porridge, and spoons sat in their places, clean save for two years of dust.

Dugal had trained his men well. They had cleaned up before leaving. Even the stew-pot, hanging on its hook over the hearth, had been scrubbed clean. All the hard bed needed was fresh straw and to give the blankets a good shake to relieve them of dust.

The shed in back still held straw, hay and oats (albeit somewhat stale) for the horses. Cloud would not starve. I opened the door and she found her own way to a manger that still held some hay. Need water. Her grumble shocked me into awareness. I hurried out with a bucket and filled it with snow. She would manage with that until it melted.

Kira fluttered about my head and followed me back into the cabin. *Make fire?*

Fire, yes, I needed fire. I looked for the corner where Dugal had kept a small pile of kindling and wood. Yes, there it was. Now where had he kept the flint box? A picture came into my mind of a tinderbox on the shelf behind me, above the table. There! My father's rigorous training kept me moving, tugged me into action, only half aware of what I did. Once I got a blazing fire started in the hearth I took out the dishes and pots to clean them with snow. I put more snow in the pot to boil porridge and tea. When had I done that last? When had I eaten? The memory eluded me.

These routine tasks, performed from memory, requiring a minimum of attention, gradually woke my senses. I began to feel hunger for the first time since leaving home. I opened the door to return to the shed and relieve Cloud of the panniers when I found her already waiting outside. She eyed a fox that sat waiting just within the light shed by the open door, guarding a dead rabbit. The fox tilted her head to one side and gave me an expectant look.

I opened my inner sense and heard her clear mind-speak. *Meat for you.* She cocked her head to the other side as if waiting to see if I understood.

I recovered my astonishment just as she made to turn and leave. *Thank you.*

She turned her head to look over her shoulder and melted into trees, her tail the last to disappear.

When I picked up the rabbit it was still warm, its neck broken but otherwise unblemished.

Cloud intruded on my musings as to how this had happened. *Take things off my back. Heavy. I not like. Want grass under snow. Things too wide for between trees.*

That startled me into action. "I am sorry, Cloud," I said aloud, my voice a hoarse croak after the long period of disuse. I still had not drunk my tea and my mouth felt like linen. But I set about lifting the heavy panniers from Cloud's back first and let her go, trusting that she would be there when I needed her. They fell to the ground as I untied them. Apparently I had lost strength in my arms on the journey here. Had I eaten or drunk at all? If not, how was it that I survived so long without food or drink? This remained another of Earth's mysteries. And the fox. Earth must have sent her.

I dragged the heavy panniers inside one by one. After downing two mugs of tea I began to unpack. My puzzlement deepened as I realized that none of the contents had been used either. It seemed that, just as I had found the strength to ride when I had not thought it possible, Earth had insured that I would not starve this winter.

I spent most of the remaining moons of winter in sleep. For the first eightday or so I found gifts of fresh rabbit outside the cabin door, always still warm, though I never again glimpsed the beautiful fox that must have brought them there.

The spans of wakefulness after that first eightday were spent setting and emptying snares, seeing to Cloud's stall in the shed, and mourning.

The gnawing, empty ache inside lifted imperceptibly as the days lengthened

Kira hunted most days and came to sit beside me nights while I slept. Cloud spent much of her time foraging, her diet supplemented with the oats and hay in the shed.

With the gradual return of my strength I spent more time awake, and interest in the forest and its inhabitants reawakened. I spent many spans exploring its secrets. One day, it may have been winter solstice, I discovered, to my delight, a white pine and spent the afternoon harvesting the needles at the tips of its branches for my favourite tea. My stores had only just run out. I took it as another gift from Earth.

Then, just as the first patches of green grass began to show through the snow, harbinger of spring, I looked at my arm and saw that the wound there had healed, leaving only a deep pink scar where it had been. I took that to mean that Earth's wound must also have healed. This began to awaken my curiosity. What would happen now? What did Earth have in store for us all? And what part would she ask me to play?

But the days kept getting longer with no message, no vision or sending from Earth that she required ought of me.

Cloud and Kira remained my only company, and while I began to miss my friends and family, I felt no urge to depart from here. This was where I belonged, at least for now.

Then the dreams returned; of family, friends, events in Bargia, Gharn and Lieth. And the recurring one of Merrist and me sitting in our cabin by our own hearth, doting on the child that played on the mat between us. That dream always left me both comforted and lonely, an odd combination that nagged at me, though I stubbornly pushed it away each time. Perhaps I feared its portent.

86

SPRING

Kira flew in excited circles overhead to get my attention, emitting such a series of anxious klees and chirrups as I had ever heard from her. I opened my inner senses.

Man comes! Wooden leg! Wooden leg comes on horse!

I had gone deeper into the forest in search of early greens and stood, bent over a patch of cress at the edge of the stream, where I had been getting my water. The snows had almost all melted, leaving only a few dirty patches under the evergreens where the sun could not penetrate. Merrist! It had to be. Wooden leg was the name Kira had given him. She did with all people. She could not understand names and referred to everyone by some identifying feature.

My head came up in alarm, resulting in a painful crack as it met with an overhanging tree limb. I fell into the water with a splash and watched my precious harvest float downstream. I pulled myself out by the same offending branch that had caused this mishap and wrung out my cloak and the hem of my gown as best as I could, silently cursing myself for my clumsiness.

I looked up at Kira. *Are you certain, little one? Where is he now?*

Wooden leg comes! On big horse. Come! Come see!

Part of me wanted to hide. I had grown accustomed to the rhythm of life alone in the forest, with only Cloud and Kira for company. It demanded little of me, only the day to day practicalities of getting food and caring for Cloud. Kira hunted her own food. I had found a measure of contentment here, away from the reminders of the death of my father or the demands of my family and friends … or Earth.

Perhaps my fall in the water was Earth's way of making sure I returned to the cabin quickly. Answering some call I had not sensed, Cloud appeared between the trees. *Go back now? Need ride?*

I gave up on the idea of running. The cold from the still icy water had reached my skin and I began to shiver. I needed a change of clothes, and soon. *Thank you Cloud. Yes, I need to get back to the cabin.*

Why are you wet?

Because I fell in the stream.

Hmph.

The disdain in her tone pricked me. Yes, I had been careless to let myself be caught unprepared. But she was a horse. I did not need to be chided by a horse. *Just get down so I can climb on. And hurry, I am freezing.*

Chagrined by my rebuke, Cloud hurried to obey, and I climbed on her back. Since we had been isolated here I had not bridled her or used a saddle. There was no one here to question how I controlled a horse.

Kira had flown off when Cloud appeared and now returned. *Wooden leg close to cabin. Come!*

Thank you, little one. You may show yourself to him. It will let him know that I am coming.

I go. The little kestrel hurried away,

I had no time to sort out how I felt about being found, or about seeing Merrist again. I knew it meant that my respite had ended. Was I ready? Just as I approached the last trees that sheltered me from view I heard his voice.

"Kira?" Is that you?" Kira's answering klees left no doubt. "It is you. I have found you. Where is Liannis? She must be near. There is a fire in the hearth. I see smoke. Is she coming?"

The eagerness in his voice warmed something in me that had lain unacknowledged all winter. I no longer wondered if I ought to flee. "Merrist! How did you find me?"

Cloud moved forward into his sight and Merrist turned to meet my eyes.

"Liannis! At last!." He limped in my direction.

I slid off Cloud's back and we stood looking at each other, each at a loss for words.

"How did you find me?" I asked again when I had found my voice.

A puzzled look came over his face. He opened his hands wide, "I do not know. I left as soon as the snows had melted enough to pass. I had to, though I could not tell you how I knew. I had no idea where to begin. And every time I chose another direction, Warrior refused to go, so I finally gave him his head and here I am."

The last words brought the familiar grin that made him so dear to me as he threw his arms wide in triumph. He had accomplished his mission.

At my answering grin our shyness fell away and he enveloped me in a great hug. Just as quickly he drew back, taking in my wet attire.

"Liannis, you are soaked! You need dry clothes!" He took my hand and pulled me, laughing, into the cabin.

AUTHOR BIOGRAPHY

Yvonne Hertzberger is a native of the Netherlands who immigrated to Canada in 1950. She is married with two grown children, (one married) and resides quietly in Stratford, Ontario with her spouse, Mark in a 130 year old, tiny, brick cottage, where she plans to live out her retirement. She calls herself a jill-of-all-trades and a late bloomer. Her many past paid jobs included banking, day care, residential care for challenged children, hairdressing (her favourite) retail, and customer service. She enjoys gardening, singing, the theatre, decorating and socializing with friends and family

Hertzberger is an alumna of The University of Waterloo, first with a B.A. in psychology, then and Hon. B.A. Sociology and stopped half a thesis short of an M.A. in Sociology. She has always been an avid student of human behaviour. This is what gives her the insights she uses to develop the characters in her writing.

Hertzberger came to writing late in life, hence the label 'late bloomer'. Her first Fantasy novel "Back From Chaos: Book One of Earth's Pendulum" was published in 2009. The third volume in the planned trilogy "The Dreamt Child" which will complete the trilogy, is pending.

LINKS

Website ~ www.yvonnehertzberger.com

Twitter ~ YHERTZBE

Facebook ~
http://www.facebook.com/EarthsPendulum.YvonneHertzberger.
author

Email ~ yvonne.hertzberger@gmail.com